Joy
of
Man's
Desiring

The Song of the World

Blue Boy

The Horseman on the Roof

The Straw Man

Joy
of
Man's
Desiring

~

JEAN
GIONO

Translated by
Katherine Allen Clark

COUNTERPOINT
WASHINGTON, D.C.

Library of Congress Cataloging-in-Publication Data
Giono, Jean, 1895–1970.
    [Que ma joie demeure. English]
    Joy of man's desiring / Jean Giono : translated by Katherine Allen Clarke.
        p.   cm.
    Originally published: France : Editions Bernard Grasset, 1935.
    ISBN 1-58243-044-6
    I. Clarke, Katherine Allen. II. Title.
PQ2613.I57Q413   1999
843'.912—dc21   99-16084
                                                          CIP

FIRST PRINTING

Cover and text design by Amy Evans McClure

C O U N T E R P O I N T
P.O. Box 65793
Washington, D.C. 20035–5793

Counterpoint is a member of the Perseus Books Group

10   9   8   7   6   5   4   3   2   1

JOY OF MAN'S DESIRING

I

It was an extraordinary night.

The wind had been blowing; it had ceased, and the stars had sprouted like weeds. They were in tufts with roots of gold, full-blown, sunk into the darkness and raising shining masses of night.

Jourdan could not sleep. He turned and tossed.

"The night is wonderfully bright," he said to himself.

He had never seen the like before.

The sky was vibrating like a sheet of metal. You could not tell what made it do so because all was still, even the tiniest willow twig. It was not the wind. It was simply that the sky came down and touched the earth, raked the plains, struck the mountains, and made the corridors of the forests ring. Then it rose once more to the far heights.

Jourdan tried to awaken his wife.

"Are you asleep?"

"Yes."

"But you answer."

"No."

"Have you seen the night?"

"No."

"It is marvellously bright."

She did not answer but heaved a deep sigh, smacked her lips, and shrugged her shoulders as if to rid herself of a load.

"Do you know what I am thinking?"

"No."

"I feel like going out to plough among the almond trees."

"Yes."

"The piece out there beyond the gate."

"Yes."

"Over toward Fra-Josépine."

"Oh, yes!" she said.

Again she made that movement of her shoulders and finally lay flat on her stomach, her face buried in the pillow.

"But I mean now," said Jourdan.

He got up. The floor was cold, his corduroy trousers glacial. There were flashes of this night everywhere in the room. Outside could be seen, as plainly almost as in the daytime, the whole plateau and Grémone Forest. The stars were everywhere.

Jourdan went downstairs to the stable. The horse was asleep on his feet.

"Ah," he said, "you know anyway. You didn't even dare to lie down."

He opened the wide stable door. It gave directly onto the fields. When the light of the night was seen like that, without a pane of glass between, one suddenly realized its purity, one perceived that the light of the lantern, with its kerosene, was dirty, and that its blood was choked with soot.

No moon, oh, no moon! But it was as though one were beneath glowing embers, in spite of the onset of winter and the cold. The sky smelt of ashes. It had the odour of almond bark and of the dry forest.

Jourdan thought that this was the moment to use the new metal plough. Its limbs still wore the bright blue of the last fair; it smelt of the store but it had a willing look. This was the time to use it if ever there was one. The horse was awake. She had come to the door to look out.

There are on the earth moments of great beauty and peace.

"If he really is to come," said Jourdan to himself, "he will arrive on a night like this."

He had sunk the point of the ploughshare into the edge of the field, turning his back upon the farm called Fra-Josépine and facing Grémone Forest. He preferred to plough in this direction because the odour of the trees came straight toward him. It was the horse who, of her own accord, stood facing that way.

There was so much light that the world was seen as it really is: no longer bare as in the daylight, but rounded out with shadow and a colour of rare quality. It delighted the eye. The aspect of things was no longer cruel, but everything told a story, all spoke softly to the senses. The forest lay yonder in the warmth of the hollows like a great pheasant with shining plumage.

"And," said Jourdan to himself, "I'd like to have him find me ploughing."

For a long time he had been expecting the appearance of a man. Who, he did not know. He did not know whence he would come. He did not know whether he would come. He only desired it. That is how things happen sometimes, and human hope is such a miracle that it is not surprising if at times it glows within one for no earthly reason. The main thing is that afterwards it continues to lift one's life on its great velvet wings.

"I believe he will come," said Jourdan to himself.

And moreover, it is true, the night was extraordinary. Anything might happen on such a night. It was the moment for the man to come.

Life on the plateaux is very hard. Little oats, little wheat, soil lumpy, sometimes red, sometimes yellow, sometimes light, but never black. It slips loosely through the fingers, and fosters an inhuman growth, weeds that are good for heaven knows what. No, truly, life on the plateaux is a trial.

He had come here with Marthe. He had expected to have to work hard. The first day he had gone over the whole place, and he had seen and then felt the wind and all, the soil, the leaf, the straw, and the splashes of sunshine that at the moment were dancing in the foliage of the orchard. And he had said: "This shall be called 'La Jourdane.'" He did that to renew his courage. One must always be helping one's self.

At the time he was no longer a young man. Since then, eleven years had passed.

He turned his beast; he lifted the plough. He sank the share anew.

"Ah! Coquet," he said, "giddap, we're going downhill."

He turned his back on the forest.

And then life, life, life. Not unhappy, not happy, life, sometimes he would say to himself....But immediately, at that moment, he saw the plateaux, and the sky lying over all, and far off, yonder through the trees, the blue breathing of deep valleys, and beyond, all around, he imagined the world wheeling like a peacock, with its seas, its streams, its rivers, and its mountains. And then he came to his consoling thought which said to him: Health, peace, La Jourdane, nothing to harm, nor to the right nor to the left any desire. He stopped, for he could no longer say: No desire. Desire is a fire; and peace, health, and all were consumed in this fire, and only the fire remained. Men, in truth, were not made to fatten at the trough, but to grow lean on the highways, to pass among trees and more trees, without ever seeing the same ones twice; to go forward through curiosity, to know.

That's it, to know.

Sometimes he would look at himself in the glass. He saw himself with his reddish beard, his freckled forehead, his hair grown nearly white, his big, thick nose, and he would say to himself, "At your age!"

But desire is desire.

He had come to the end of the row. The horse turned by himself and began to walk toward the forest. They were both deep in their thoughts.

And then, this is how it is: this lasts awhile and then comes old age and then death.

One day he had gone to the fair at Roume, on the other side of Grémone Forest. That was five years ago. Whew! How cold it had been! He had met old Silve of La Fauconnière and two others, one who was a horse dealer, and an edge-tool maker who had a booth on the fair grounds. They went to have a drink. More from necessity than from pleasure. It was bitter cold. They all four sat down at a table: Jourdan and Silve, who were from the plateau, the horse dealer and the tool maker from beyond the hills. They ordered hot wine; they filled their pipes, they talked. As long as they were waiting for the wine and were stiff with the cold, they talked in an ordinary way because they desired something simple that they would soon have. Once this desire was satisfied along came other desires.

Now they were sitting, all four of them, without a word to say, smoking their pipes and looking about them; a bad remedy. Then Jourdan noticed Silve's eyes, and then the eyes of the horse dealer and then those of the tool maker. He said to himself: "If my eyes look like that, we four must be a pretty sight." But in the café there were four or five more groups, and they appeared gay.

Jourdan sought the eyes of these men who seemed more normal. And then he percieved that the moment they stopped laughing they had the same look of care. More than care, fear. More than fear, nothing. A place where there is no longer care or fear; oxen beneath the yoke.

"Oh," he said to himself, "it is a disease of the country, like that of plasterers whose fingers drop off; like that of tanners who spew out their lungs; like that of miners who go blind; like that of printers whose intestines twist into knots; like that of shoemakers, of butchers, of carters, of labourers, of masons, of blacksmiths, of cabinet makers, of sailors, of cowherds, of woodsmen. One of those diseases peculiar to each trade." His heart sank.

The tool maker looked out of the café window. You could see into the street.

"There's Marion," he said.

It was she who kept the drygoods store on the Place aux Œufs. An old woman in a black apron, a black cape, a black fichu. As she walked, she gesticulated as if she were explaining something to the air in front of her. She was drunk.

"She has been drinking a long while."

"She drank before her man's death."

"And before the death of her girl."

"I believe you, and while she was bringing up the little boy."

"What has become of him?"

"Ah!" said the tool maker. "He has gone away."

"Beyond the seas?"

"I should say so, and beyond the rest, too."

"He was a dear little fellow."

"Beyond many things," said the tool maker. "They tell me . . ." He leaned forward and the other three moved close to listen. "He takes care of lepers."

"Lepers?"

"Yes."

"Where?"

"Wherever they are."

"Can you beat that!" said the horse dealer.

Old Silve looked at Jourdan.

"And," said the horse dealer, "has he learned medicine?"

"It's more for other troubles," said the tool maker. "Do you know what leprosy is?"

"Not exactly," said the horse dealer.

"Medicine isn't any good where it's a question of leprosy. It is a disease that rots you. Rots you to dust, it seems. The wind tears you apart. You lose your fingers, you lose your arms. Little by little, I mean. You feel yourself dropping away to nothing. And it's catching."

Old Silve was still looking at Jourdan.

"Yes," said Jourdan.

He was not answering the tool maker. For some moments it seemed to him that he heard the sound of a flute.

He returned to the farm as dusk fell, and in spite of the cold he took the long way that skirts the edge of the forest. He felt the need of walking. He felt himself advancing as in a dance, and the air of the flute was always there with ever-increasing precision; sometimes it rose shrilly to meet the thunder of heaven, and at other times it descended again to the earth and spread in music like a broad country with undulating hills and winding streams.

"Joy *can* be lasting," said Jourdan to himself.

"Only," he said to himself, "*that one* must come."

He was not thinking of Marion's grandson beyond the seas. No. He was thinking of another, no matter whom, he did not even know, but someone. It was enough for him to know that there existed men with healing hands, who were not afraid of terrible diseases that were catching.

One of those. That is what was needed. A man with a heart always aglow.

Just to know that such a person exists makes you hear the song of the flute, and hope sustains you even on the long roads that encircle the forests.

They had been standing still for some moments, Jourdan and the horse, without being aware of it. There was no hurry. Perhaps hope helps you to live.

Now the stars were shining in all their violence. Some of them seemed so crushed that they dripped long drops of gold. One could see the immense distances of the sky.

It might have been then about three o'clock in the morning.

He finished his row. It was the fourth. Once more he turned his back upon the forest and began to go down the fifth in the direction of Fra-Josépine. Nothing was changed. The horse walked along as usual. Jourdan kept the same stride; the grass crackled as before. The sounds, the scents, the golden night, all were the same.

Yet, there was something. Jourdan felt it at his back. He dared not look around. The longer he forced himself to resist his desire to turn his head, the more he felt that he must turn his head. No. He urged the horse on.

Already there was a change: the quickening swish of the soil split by the share and the clicking of the horse's shoe against the chain of the beam.

At the end of the row he said to himself: "Now, look!"

The field sloped upward toward the forest, but there it stopped short against the night. Just on that line appeared the form of a man. It was a man, because he was standing with his legs spread apart and between his legs could be seen the night and one star shining.

"Get along, horse," said Jourdan; then to himself: "And he will find me ploughing."

The man was waiting for him.

"Hallo," he said.

"Hallo," said Jourdan.

"What's the hurry?"

"There's no hurry," said Jourdan. "Things are just going along."

"And each in its own time," said the man.

"That's what I think," said Jourdan.

Then he dropped the handles of the plough and let his hands hang at his sides.

"Have you some tobacco?"

Jourdan felt in his pocket and handed him his pouch.

"I haven't had a smoke since I left Roume," said the man, "but in the forest it is better not. The oaks are dry."

"It hasn't rained since Hallowe'en," said Jourdan.

"The country smells good," said the man.

"Is this the first time you've been here?"

"This is the first time I've laid eyes on it. One season I did the valley of the Ouvèze." With his finger he traced a line in the night toward the east. "And another season, the wilderness in the blue hills." He pointed toward the north.

"I was near this region, so today I came on in."

He turned his back to the wind to light his pipe, and Jourdan could not see his face. He could take in only the shoulders of the man, huge ones that made a good barrier against the wind.

"I saw you ploughing," he said. "I said to myself: Why, he's ploughing! So I came to see."

"Yes," said Jourdan, "it isn't because I have to. This night made me want to."

"What kind of tobacco is this?" said the man, taking a puff.

"Grey."

"But you have added some red sandstone."

"That's so," said Jourdan.

"I know the taste of it," said the man. "And I like it. It is like a spring."

"What's that you say?" said Jourdan.

"Strong tobacco," said the man, "is already heavy in itself. If you add the red sandstone, it sweats. That makes a sort of friendly combination, if you like, of tobacco and stone, and gives the smoke a taste of good clean mud. Haven't you ever picked up a handful of mud out of a spring?"

"No."

"Do it and you'll see what I mean. It tastes like this smoke. Smell."

He puffed a cloud of smoke in his face.

"Do you smell it?"

"Not very well."

"Taste."

He held out his pipe.

Jourdan sucked the stem of the pipe. It was still moist from the man.

"Do you get it?"

"Yes, now I do."

He returned the pipe.

"In blue sandstone," said the man, "tobacco has the taste of iron. It's like that. I call it blacksmith's tobacco. It isn't exactly the taste of iron. It's the taste of iron scale. You know when they wet the white iron and then strike. Scales fly off. There, it smells like that, and yet not precisely the scales that fall, but the scales that remain clinging to the horn of the anvil. That is exactly what that smells like."

"You have a keen sense of taste," said Jourdan.

"Yes," said the man, "it's important.... The horse is shivering," he said after a moment's silence. "We must not let her stand there."

"Where are you going?" said Jourdan.

"I'm going to stay with you a little; long enough to smoke this pipeful of good tobacco. Keep on walking, I'll follow you."

Again Jourdan turned his horse Coquet, and in a straight line with the farm Fra-Josépine the sixth furrow began.

The man walked beside the plough. He was not talking now. He was whistling. He whistled a tune that was in harmony with everything: the new furrow, the fiery night, the vast expanse of plateau. He whistled it softly, between his lips. As though it were for himself and for Jourdan. Like a secret. And all at once Jourdan recognized the sound of that flute that had been ringing in his head until now. Then the song spread and became a living thing on the plateau and the horse could hear it.

"Well," said the man, "what is this place called?"

"Grémone Plateau."

"Are there many of you living here?"

"About twenty."

"Village?"

"No, farms. That one is mine. Over there, Fra-Josépine. The others: La Fauconnière with its boxwood, Maurice's, Mouille-Jacques. The other one is right on the shore of the little lake, near a maple."

"Are there many fields?"

"Big ones. Land is cheap."

"Yes, I see, you are pretty far apart."

They began the seventh furrow.

"Are you alone?" asked the man.

"I have my wife."

"How old?"

"About like me."

"No children?"

"No."

The man whistled again for a moment. But they were ascending the slope.

"You're fond of your horse?"

"Very."

"Is she old?"

"Fairly.

"And you keep her?"

"Yes."

"What do you think of this night?"

"I have never seen the like."

"Nor have I," said the man. "Orion looks like Queen Anne's lace."

"What did you say?" asked Jourdan.

"Orion is twice as big as usual. There he is, up there. Stop. Up there. There. Do you see?"

"No."

"I have never been able to show people things," said the man. "It's curious. I have always been reproached for it. They say: 'No one sees what you mean.'"

"Who said that?"

"Oh, someone."

"A fool," said Jourdan.

"But," said the man, "you haven't seen Orion, either."

"No," said Jourdan, "but I see the Queen Anne's lace."

"That's a pure heart," said the man, "and a good will."

At that moment the seventh furrow was finished. It was necessary to begin the eighth.

In spite of everything it was hard to get it out.

"Have you ever taken care of lepers?"

"Never," said the man.

But he seemed to think that perfectly natural. And that was a good sign.

Then he began to whistle. Truly, there are proverbs that have been made by men of the country, men who have seen a hundred forests, a hundred lakes, a hundred mountains, and a hundred times the revolutions of the heavens. You can't help believing that they know something about it. One of these proverbs says that out of an evil thing a lovely one cannot come.

The whistling was beautiful beyond telling.

It was flawlessly round. It went calmly. It went exactly into the right places. You felt that it was born of a healthy head. It made you aware of the gaze of two placid eyes, slow gestures, a man standing on Grémone Plateau with the stature and the deliberateness of a tree. Perhaps he was not a healer of lepers. But there are men who are predestined. It was sufficient perhaps to show him the suffering for the desire to ease it to be awakened in him.

And now they were to begin the ninth furrow and the land sloped upward and the horse was weary with this night work. It is curious how clumsy one is with supernatural things, or what one thinks supernatural. There was already the taste of tobacco, the red sandstone, the spring, the blue sandstone, and those iron scales. Now all the stars really looked like the flowers of Queen Anne's lace. He had said: "Orion"; that is a word that few people know. If ever I bought a young horse, I would call him Orion.

But they must begin the ninth furrow. That was too important.

"You have come to settle here?"

"No, I am just passing through."

"Where are you going?"

"Straight ahead."

"It is not out of curiosity," said Jourdan apologetically.

"I know," said the man.

But Jourdan was aware immediately that he was going to get things wrong. He wanted to let go of the handles of the plough, stop the horse, and then explain.

You must never explain. People are much better pleased when they discover things by themselves.

Instead of stopping, he pushed forward on the handles. He arched his back, gave all his strength, the beam struck against the horse's legs. The horse took three big strides, Jourdan also, and there they were, plough and all, ahead of the man as if to say: If you're going, good wind to you; *we* are staying here. We don't need anybody. Who risks nothing has nothing.

"You might stay over a day," said Jourdan turning his head.

"Why not?"

"As a matter of fact," said Jourdan, "I am alone and the place is big. Would you know of anybody who might help me?"

"No."

In order that the furrow be well made, it was still necessary to ask: What is your trade?

But there was too much magic already.

The grains of the stars could now scarcely be distinguished. They had grown branches. The sky was all greenish with them. Day was about to break. It was cold. The wind lengthened. Over at Fra-Josépine a door creaked. About the edge of the field the plateau began to grow larger. The green light began to spread over it to the far-away mountains still in darkness. From time to time, up in the sky, there passed a vibration like that of a great guitar string; then it died away, and each time the light grew brighter.

"If I could only see him," said Jourdan to himself.

He had reached the top of the field. He stopped the plough. But he examined the horse's shoes. All four. Then he said to himself: Let's see. And he straightened up.

He was a man with longish hair, a forehead three fingers broad, tanned complexion, well-shaven skin with the lights of mother-of-pearl. Lips simple and lacking complications, rather thinnish. Eyes so clear that they looked like holes. He might be about thirty-five years old. As for the rest of his body: good back and shoulders and arms. Delicate hands, almost the hands of a girl. An air of one who knows his own mind— unchangeable. His whole appearance was rather royal.

"Suppose," said Jourdan, "that you stay here a day or two? Your boss won't say anything."

The man smiled. He had pointed teeth.

"What is your name?"

"For convenience, let's say 'Bobi.'"

"Do you drink coffee?"

"Every morning."

"Come and drink some at the house. Day is breaking."

Then the stranger stood there and all alone he ploughed the tenth furrow, and the eleventh, and the twelfth, up to the twentieth, and the whole field, and he passed the harrow over it, and he sowed, and perhaps he even harvested immediately after, for all we know.

His eyes dwelt on the landscape under the wintry though cloudless sky.

"It is dreary here," he said.

Marthe was awakened before her usual time. She had suddenly felt cold from the empty side of the bed. It was just daybreak, the hour when couples, half asleep, always snuggle together to warm each other and are a little tender, even those unconscious of it, because day is dawning.

She had thought: Where is he? Then she had heard the metal of the horse's harness clanking in the ploughing.

"He ought to have told me," she said to herself. That sufficed to awaken her. It is very frightening to fall asleep, to feel about, not to find Jourdan, and then, outside, to hear the horse ploughing. It was still dark.

The window was flooded with a greenish light. A gust of wind split on the ridge pole of the house. The sparkling night was still quivering before the dawn.

"The stars must have been beautiful last night," said Marthe to herself. "And no doubt that is what made him want to get up."

She arose at once. She combed her long grey hair. Loose, it fell below her hips. She was fifty-seven years old.

"It has got him again," she said to herself, thinking of Jourdan.

There is a time, in spite of everything, when we feel that men are getting away from us. Oh, they do not go far! And it is not so much going away as growing apart. It seems that they had sought in us something which satisfied them for a long time, but which satisfies them no longer. We have taken care of them, petted them, made their nights warm with love; in short, we have been women, all that youth implies. And then there comes a time when it seems that the main object in their lives is to be seeking something.

She was walking about the room in her bare feet in spite of the cold. She was tall, heavy, as if sculptured in marble. She walked as if carved in one piece, but on supple, pliant feet.

We know very well that we are not everything, but when a man all his life has got his pleasure of a woman, it would be so easy to say to her: Marthe! No more. The way of saying it would do all the rest.

Outside, dawn was murmuring.

There is no woman's tenderness that is like the tenderness of a man. That is certain. But why ask of emptiness? Ah, how unhappy we are, when all is told!

She looked into the mirror to tie her fichu. She said to herself:

"I must make him some coffee. He is out there ploughing."

She looked out of the window.

She could not see the field from where she was, but she heard the clinking of the hames and also another sound that caught her ear.

"He is whistling," she said to herself. "Ah! If he could only be a little as he used to be!"

The bedroom window looked toward the east. Already, in that direction, a bit of the plateau was visible. It stretched into the distance with a broad marsh of low evergreen oaks and shadow. Far away, at the edge of it, floated the dawn. Another gust of wind struck the house. It was a little stronger than the first. The loft door struggled with its latch.

"East wind," said Marthe, raising her finger.

She stood still a moment listening.

Yes, the wind had just struck the other farm building. A tree began to cry. Silence returned.

"Yes," she said, "east wind. Already."

You always think that the dark days will not come back. And then there they are.

Above that little white hearth that the dawn had lighted on the rim of the world, a grey haze hid the day.

Downstairs, Marthe kindled the fire with the wood already prepared. The water in the kettle began to sing. The coffee was ground, the pot ready on the table. Marthe poured the dry coffee into the filter. It smelt strong. The fire, the song of the water, the odour of the coffee, were a construction much more solid than the house. Within them, one could find shelter much more surely than within any structure of stone. It was proof against the east wind. Marthe slowly poured the boiling water. The coffee began to filter through, drop by drop. It gave one the desire to sit near the fire, the hot cup in one's hand, and to drink in little sips.

One has the feeling that at heart men do not know exactly what they are doing. They build with stones and they do not perceive that each of their gestures in placing the stone in the mortar is accompanied by a shadow gesture that places a shadow stone into shadow mortar. And it is the shadow building that counts.

Voices were coming from the field.

"Who is with him?" wondered Marthe.

She thought of Carle of Mouille-Jacques, who for a week had been looking for his goat.

She looked out. She could see nothing. It was not light enough. Jourdan was with someone. They were all four returning: the two men, the horse, and the plough, but she could not tell who the other was. It was not a man of the plateau. He was walking with an elastic step.

They went into the stable. Then, after a moment, they could be heard coming along the side of the house, and that man was talking, but from the inside could be caught only a single word: dreary. They came to the door and scraped their shoes.

"And in the springtime it is just the same," said Jourdan.

"But," said the man, as Jourdan opened the door, "you have plenty of almond trees, they must bloom."

"They have white blossoms," said Jourdan. "The plateau is all planted with white almond trees. They fill you with despair."

"Good day, Madame," said the man.

There are builders of invisible things who do not bother with houses, but who construct vast countries better than those of this world.

"Good day, Monsieur," said Marthe, and she said to herself: "He thought of the almond trees."

The whole landscape was already a little changed.

"Plant red ones," said the man.

But he put his hand on Jourdan's arm.

"I see something," he said.

Marthe stopped in her movement toward the coffee pot.

"There aren't any hedges," he said.

"What's that you say?" asked Jourdan.

"You should plant some hawthorns," said the man. "Some hawthorn hedges around the buildings and hawthorn thickets at the corners of the fields. It is very useful."

Jourdan had not understood and Marthe did not stir. The man slowly looked from one to the other, then he passed his tongue over his lips to moisten them, as one who wishes to whistle and to give the exact note.

"Perhaps you have used the land too much from boundary to boundary. Man does well, I do not deny that, but Nature does not do badly, either."

He raised his finger in the air.

"You need hawthorn hedges to bound the fields, not as fences, but you take too much land in your ploughing. Leave a little for the others. It is rather difficult to make you understand, isn't it?"

Jourdan rubbed his cheeks.

"I'm listening," he said.

"Look," said the man, "supposing that the hawthorn is useless and besides, with its shade, you will tell me, it eats on one side the good seeds and on the other side, the sunny side, it also eats the seeds with its shade. For the shade of the hawthorn is dry and supple and it is much loved by a lot of thieving beasts, I know. One thing only, to make you understand. If you understand that, you understand all. With the hawthorn there are birds. Ah!"

He seemed to have marked in his thoughts a very important point.

Jourdan had covered his mouth with his big hand. And he was looking at Marthe out of the corner of his eye. Marthe turned and faced the two men. In one hand she held the little spoon and in the other hand the lid of the coffee pot. But that was not hindering her. She had just seen something.

"Jourdan," she said, "do you remember?"

The man raised his finger as before and again he wet his lips but he did not whistle.

"La Belline," she said, "the farm we used to have at Patis des Vergnes, in Bellossay. Do you remember? That hedge that ran from the sties to the pond: those were hawthorns. We were never lonely."

"We were young," said Jourdan.

He talked into his hand. He was struggling against his happiness. He was saying to himself: Not too fast, not too fast! He wanted to sit down and to say: There! like one who has finally reached his chair. He understood everything, nearly.

"What is young?" said the man.

"What's that you say?" asked Jourdan.

"Yes, I said 'young,' what is it?"

"Well, we were strong, limber; well, *young!*"

"Less money?"

"Yes."

"Less wisdom?"

"Yes."

"Less desire to plough to the very limit?"

"Perhaps," said Jourdan.

"Yes," said Marthe.

"Less hard?"

"Yes," said Jourdan.

"Yes," said Marthe.

"Let's drink our coffee," said the man.

There was scarcely anything more to be said. In his heart, Jourdan was thinking: It is he, it is surely he! Every time that this man spoke there was need for silence afterward. Marthe put three bowls on the table. The sound of the bowl against the wood, nothing more than that, hurt a little. There was need for everything to be still, as if a beautiful bird were about to fly away and they were waiting, breathless.

Outside, a noise was heard and Jourdan listened with pleasure. It was the east wind. Day had come but the light was no stronger in the window. The wind was sweeping away all that mist that had hid the dawn. They were low clouds. They trailed over the plateau. They caught in the trees. Pieces of them were torn off and went whirling away like sheep. Then the wind brought them back to the flock.

"Give us some bread," said Jourdan. "And sit down here with us."

Marthe drew up the stool. She had her back turned to the hearth. Jourdan opened his knife. Slowly, he cut a great slice the whole width of the loaf.

"For you," he said, and he handed it to the man.

"For you," he said to Marthe, "how big?"

"The whole slice; I am hungry this morning."

He cut another the same size for himself.

At that moment there arose outside such long howlings of the wind that all three sat expectantly, their huge slices of bread in their hands.

The man was lighted on one side and that elongated his slender nose.

Jourdan's greying beard was illumined.

Marthe had her back to the fire and her face was only a reflection.

Grémone Forest was moaning behind the wind.

A flash of lightning passed before the window. The wind, twisted with rain, was galloping over the fields. The loft door began to shake the house with great thumps. It was like a wild door too loosely fastened. A gust of wind whistled the length of the wall. Two tiles were blown along the roof. The thunder crashed over by the pond. Another flash illumined the forest. It made no sound.

"Black weather," said Jourdan.

"If you like," said the man.

"The night foretold it," said Jourdan. "You will be obliged to stay."

"Yes," said Marthe.

"Possibly," said the man. "At any rate," he added, "at least today."

The storm gave a great sigh, was rent asunder, and a splash of milky and shining day lighted the wet branches of the trees. But the light died out beneath an advancing shadow. Hail clattered on the tiles. A soft flash of lightning ran along the ground to the edge of the plateau. It rolled down into the valley like an avalanche of rocks.

"A while ago," said Jourdan, "up there in the field, I said something that you did not notice."

"That would surprise me," said the man.

"I asked you if you had ever taken care of lepers."

"Listen," said the man, "we've known each other only a few hours, but do I seem to you like a man who does not notice tobacco, or stars, or things that organize, spring for example—do I seem to be that kind of person?"

"No."

"Well, then?"

"You didn't answer me."

"Yes, I did, I answered No."

"I thought that you answered without knowing."

"I always know," said the man, "or nearly always."

He sat munching his bread for some time. He looked at Jourdan, then at Marthe. His gaze was clear but arresting. Arresting in the true sense. It was like the pull of a rope tied around you, holding your arms and body, and then, at the other end of the rope, someone pulling with little jerks: "Come, come, approach me."

He looked at the house. First that part of the kitchen where they were sitting. The hearth with its steady blaze, the walls, all that was hanging on them: a man's cloak, a woman's cape, a whip, a gun, the row of sauce pans. And then the shadow masonry that Jourdan and Marthe had cast all about.

"Look here," said the man.

And he turned his chair and he moved away from the bowl of coffee and the bread as if earth's nourishment could no longer serve in this case. And he placed his hands on his knees.

"The plateau," he said, "that we saw just now at dawn, how far does it go?"

Now, a heavy rain, lying on the earth like the waters of a river, was flowing over the countryside. The panes were dull, like pewter.

"As far as the Ouvèze River, just as you said."

"If I can judge," said the man, "by what one can see from below, it is a steep slope covered with dark evergreen oaks and then above runs a line of red earth."

"Yes."

"On clear days then you see, away off in that direction, the snow-covered Aiguines peaks and a whole fleet of other mountains."

"What's that you say?" asked Jourdan.

"Well, I think that mountains, with their snows, look like ships. Haven't you ever seen a seaport?"

"No."

"So much the better. When you see, you no longer imagine. So, way over there. Good. I must see clearly. *This* country cannot be imagined. I ought to tell you that I am not here by chance. Yesterday it was chance. But not today. Things are always decided without our understanding why. Do you understand?"

"No."

"But do you see?"

"Yes."

"Excellent. What was it like here before you came? What was it planted in?"

"As it is now."

"No, before. Before the last ones, and before them, and still earlier, at the beginning of time."

"I don't understand," said Jourdan.

"Why, there was certainly a time when this was not settled, either here or farther on. What was it used for?"

"Nothing, I imagine."

"Wonderful! It was a forest, no doubt, like the one over there?"

"I think so."

"When you arrived, were there oaks in your fields? I mean big oaks, very large ones?"

"No."

"Any maples?"

"No."

"Any ash trees, beeches, alders, poplars, whitebeams, ferns, heather, broom?"

"No, it was all bare."

"You didn't even find the suggestion of a tree?"

"The what?"

"You didn't find any roots, any old roots?"

"Yes, I did!"

"Where?"

"Out there, where I was ploughing last night. There was a hump that always jarred my plough out of the ground. So I took a pick and went to see what it was. It was an ancient oak root. Deep! Alive!"

Jourdan stopped, his mouth full of that last word.

"Alive!" he repeated.

"Does that astonish you?"

"Yes," said Jourdan, "yes, that does astonish me. It was at least six feet in the ground, without air, without anything, the upper part all scraped."

"Oh," said the man, "you mustn't be surprised at that! Roots are eternal. Then, here it was all bare. And what did *you* plant?"

"Peach trees, apricots, almonds."

"What did you sow?"

"Wheat, lentils, oats."

"You didn't plant any oaks?"

"No."

"You didn't sow any . . . any"—the man was groping for a word—"any daisies?"

"What for?" asked Jourdan.

"You asked me if I had taken care of lepers. I told you No. That is the truth. But I know how to take care of them. And perhaps I'd like to do it. Animals," continued the man, "what did you bring here in the way of animals?"

There was really no longer any daylight in the kitchen because of the rain and the clouds, and all about the farm the world was creaking like a great, revolving wheel. But there was one place where there was calm and clarity and light; that place was in the eyes of the man.

"Animals?" said Jourdan. "I brought a horse."

"Bridled?"

"Certainly; harnessed to the cart."

"You didn't bring a wild horse?"

"Bring a what?" asked Jourdan.

"You must not forget," said the man, "that I am called Bobi and that I can do this, for example."

He began a huge grimace. His face was no longer human. Yes, it was still human, but it was the masque of laughter. There was in his grimace neither sorrow nor bitterness. The mouth enlarged, the eye winking, the nose flattened, he made you burst out laughing. Deep down in your breast, he awakened laughter and there was nothing to do but give in to it.

Already Jourdan and Marthe . . .

But suddenly the face resumed its composure.

"Yes," said the man, "I am capable of this and of other things besides. That will find its use. I am called Bobi. Never forget that. And so you did not bring a wild horse?"

"No," said Jourdan.

"And for your mares, what do you do?"

"We take them to the stallion."

"You have one here?"

"Yes, at Mouille-Jacques."

"What do you do then? That interests me."

"We take the mare in; it takes place in the stable."

"And," said the man, "you stay there while *it takes place,* as you say?"

"Yes, and sometimes I help."

"With your hands?" said the man, nodding his head.

"With my hands, yes," said Jourdan.

The man began to whistle a few bars of music. He looked at Marthe. She was listening in silence.

"Listen," he said, "when it is necessary to remember that I am called Bobi, I'll say: 'Bobi!' So now I say: 'Bobi!' Just tell me: you knew that horses once were wild? Once upon a time. And that since"—with his hand he made the gesture of a wheel turning—"since mares have gone on bearing colts up to now, that proves that stallions do not need your help."

"That one needed it," said Jourdan.

"Now then," said the man, "I say a double 'Bobi' and at the same time I wish that Madame would stop her ears a moment."

"I think," said Marthe, "that I can listen. I see where this is leading."

"Can *you* make love that way? Don't let's say even before people, but let's say before a dog?"

There was a long moment of silence, and Jourdan and Marthe looked at each other. Ah! The great hedge of hawthorn and the gradual crumbling of the wide world!

"Good," said Jourdan; "I understand."

"That proves," said the man, "that we are already far ahead in the lesson and have not followed the order. Let's go back. Besides the horse—and I speak of you and the others up here—I see just about what you brought here: goats, a cow, chickens, pigeons. Not one of you thought of bringing stags or does or nightingales or kingfishers?"

"No," said Jourdan, "all those creatures are useless."

"Wait a minute," said the man.

He went to get the pack that he had carried on his back. Out of it he took a long rope at the ends of which were iron rings. He took out a woollen table cover with the king of clubs on it. He also got out of it a sort of garment, half red and half green, like a blouse with legs. And this garment he laid on the chair in the place where he had been a moment ago. It was a little as though he were unfolding and revealing a part of himself hidden until now.

He spread the table mat before the hearth. He took off his coat. Beneath his coat he wore a dark blue sweater. He took off his trousers. Underneath were tight, dark blue drawers.

He whistled.

He raised his hand in the air and laughed softly.

It was like a salute.

"The devil!" thought Jourdan, stroking his beard, and Marthe turned her chair to have a better view. "Where is all this leading? Where are we since the horse? And since the Queen Anne's lace?"

For Jourdan still had in his head that vegetal Orion swept by the wind.

The man lay down on the mat. He had taken a deep breath and was expelling the air. It was no longer the respiration of a human being. He raised his leg. He passed his leg over his head. It was his right leg. He raised his left leg and passed it over his head. He walked on his hands. He untwisted himself, but this time only to wind his right leg around his neck. Then the other one. He was legless. He continued to walk on his hands. He lay down on one side. He wound his right arm around his legs, then his left arm. He was a ball. He rolled on the mat like a ball. His chin was underneath and you could see a face on this ball, then his forehead was underneath and again it was a face, if you like, but a horrible one, a face where all rests on the forehead, where the eyes eat, where the nose breathes upside down, where the mouth sees with its one great eye and the whole will is in the chin. Then he turned, unwound himself, stood up.

He was a man, standing there, arms and legs, eyes and mouth, all as usual.

"Bobi," he said.

There was boundless admiration in Jourdan's eyes, and in the eyes of Marthe also. No fear. They had often seen this at the fair. Today, it is true, the long rain had settled outside and there were great marching shadows and, from time to time, long flashes of lightning with tiny cracklings as if someone were striking big sulphur matches. But they had seen that before, too. No fear. Only, suddenly, all this fitted in with the lepers, the tobacco, Orion-Queen Anne's lace, the hawthorn, the daisies, the mating of the horse, and suddenly everything revolved about this man who a moment ago saw with his mouth and ate with his eyes.

"I understand," said Jourdan slowly.

"No," said the man.

And it was true, he did not understand.

"Youth," said the man, "is joy. And youth is neither strength nor nimbleness, nor even youth as you described it; it is the passion for the useless.

"The useless," he added, raising his finger, "as people say."

3

It had snowed and then frozen during the night. The whole landscape was crystalline like fine glass. The faint warmth of the sun could be heard approaching. The branches would crack, the weeds bend down, rid themselves of their icy coat, and rise again, green.

The moment he opened his eyes, Jourdan jumped out of bed. Marthe was already wide awake.

"What are you going to do?" she asked.

"What he said: go see the others."

Jourdan dressed, then he opened the wardrobe.

"What are you looking for?"

"My cloak."

"It is hanging downstairs."

"The new one," he said, "it is for him. He hasn't anything to cover himself with. It will be cold in the buggy."

He approached the bed. Marthe was lying on her back. She still had fine old breasts with life in them. Jourdan put his hand on them.

"What a night!" said Marthe. "And then, what do we think we are, you and I, at our age!"

"We are alive," said Jourdan.

"Yes, indeed," said Marthe. "Only, it is too beautiful to last."

"And what are we going to have to eat?" said Jourdan.

"There is bacon."

"We should be at old Silve's about noon. But who can tell?"

"Your horse is well rested," she said.

"I'm not thinking so much of the distance," said Jourdan, "as of that confounded Queen Anne's lace. If he starts talking about that, it's going to be long."

"It will take time," said Marthe.

Jourdan could feel the tip of Marthe's breast harden beneath his hand.

"He has cared for lepers," he said.

"What are you always talking about lepers for?"

"It's just an idea."

And he began to laugh.

The new cloak smelt of camphor.

Jourdan shook it out. At arm's length it weighed like a bull's hide.

"He has gotten up," he said.

A noise was heard downstairs.

"He would easily grow accustomed to it all," said Marthe.

"So would we," said Jourdan.

"While you are gone today," said Marthe, "I'll bake you some fresh bread."

The man downstairs had lit the fire and the water was boiling. Jourdan could see now how he was dressed. Yesterday there had not been time to examine him. There were always too many things between. He wore a knitted jacket that was partly sailor and partly shepherd, because of the coarse wool and the blue and white stripes, and also because of the cut, high around the neck and tight at the wrists.

"Here's a cloak for you," said Jourdan.

After having drunk their coffee, they harnessed the horse to the buggy. Jourdan put into the wagon box a sack containing bacon and bread. He looked to make sure that he had his tobacco and his pipe.

"We've enough for the whole day," he said.

"We've enough for longer than that," said the man. "Let's be off!"

At first the light cart rolled across fields. Its leather hood creaked with the joltings. The frozen snow crunched beneath the wheels. There were only the sounds of the snow and the cold. The rest was silence. On one side could be seen the black border of Grémone Forest. Above it the sky was blue. Between the forest and the sky the snow on the branches lay like a bar. In the direction in which they were going the plain quivered with haze. Solitude.

"So," said Jourdan, "that is your real trade?"

"Yes," said the man, "and I don't know whether you noticed that long rope with rings. I stretch it like this from one post to another and then I walk on the rope."

"I have seen that sometimes," said Jourdan.

"I walk the tight rope," said the man, "and I walk the slack rope. It is my specialty. More than what I did yesterday morning, those human transformations.

"Of course," he said after lighting his pipe, "when one knows the trade, one realizes that it is all one, and that you will walk the rope all the better if you learn to do the transformations. Man, you see—I learned from myself—if you leave him to his own inclinations, prefers standing on his legs to standing on his hands. But you can force him to do anything. Even good. And notice that most of the time, *good* is exactly what I was doing on the card mat in front of your fire."

"I've always liked that," said Jourdan.

He stopped at this word and remained silent. They had just crossed the road. On the other side, they entered a softer field into which the wheels sank a little.

The horse ambled along.

"We shall begin," said Jourdan, "with the Maple Tree Farm near the pond. When it thaws, even here where we are now, it is a little swampy."

The pond, although hidden, announced its presence. It was beneath a thick fog. The snow, weighing down the rushes, lay out over the water. Jourdan touched Coquet with the whip and the horse broke into a trot. After a little, the cold smelt of the smoke of oak wood.

"Oh! Randoulet!" cried Jourdan.

A shadow emerged from the fog.

"Is that you, Jourdan?"

"It's me."

"I recognized the buggy."

He was a short, stocky man with several chins. He had little pig eyes and a red mouth beneath his moustache.

"We did not know what to do in this weather," said Jourdan. "We said: We'll go and see the country. I am with my cousin."

"Come inside," said Randoulet.

And he walked ahead of the horse.

The house looked small in front. Inside, one imagined a room running the whole length of it, but it was short and encumbered at the rear by a huge bed all unmade, covers thrown back, grey sheets, hollow mattress.

"Honorine, here's Jourdan!" said Randoulet.

Honorine was bending over a steaming kettle full of potatoes. She straightened up and wiped her hands.

"We weren't expecting anyone," she said.

"It's this weather," said Jourdan. "You don't know what to do."

"Come and get warm," said Randoulet. "Come closer. Move over," he said to a man who was sitting on the edge of the hearth.

"Is that you, Le Noir?" said Jourdan to him.

"Since the sheep have been sold," said Randoulet, "he doesn't know what to do with himself. He just warms himself."

"It's the season," said Le Noir.

"You've sold the sheep?" asked Jourdan.

Honorine had opened the cupboard.

"Don't go to any trouble," said Jourdan.

"I won't," said Honorine, "but you will surely take a little drink."

"They are all sold," said Randoulet. "Happily."

"Why happily?" said Le Noir. "*You* are always happy, *you* are."

"No, I am not always happy," said Randoulet, "but what would we do now?"

"Just as usual."

"You would tend them out of doors, in this weather?"

"No," said Le Noir, "I would leave them in the fold."

"What would you feed them with?"

"With the fodder."

"That fellow," said Randoulet turning around, "is terrible. He gets attached to his beasts. He'd like to keep them all their lives. Give him a glass just the same, Honorine."

"Well, here's how," said Randoulet.

"Ah, yes," said Jourdan.

"He's your cousin?"

"Yes, a cousin," said Jourdan. "We've always been like brothers."

"That's often much better," said Honorine. "Drink."

"What is this?" asked Jourdan.

"Ah, that," said Honorine, "is my special liqueur. A secret. It's a clever one who can guess."

Bobi tasted slowly.

"There is fennel in it," he said.

"That's easy," said Honorine.

Bobi took another sip.

"Wild thyme, a little juniper, and, wait a moment." At this, he smiled his smile. Jourdan said to himself: "It's beginning." Bobi licked his lips. He said: "You opened an oak gall. Inside is a little kernel of black paste. You took that on the tip of a knife, perhaps two of them, not more than three."

"Two and a half," said Honorine, breathlessly. "What do you know about that!"

"What a cousin!" said Randoulet.

Jourdan had assumed a happy little air as if to say: Ah, yes, we are like that.

"Mind," said Bobi, "that is not difficult. It is enough to have tasted oak gall once to recognize it all the rest of your life. But your great discovery, Madame Honorine, is marrying it with the wild thyme, the fennel, and the juniper. Those are cheerful plants full of the sun and the clouds and the joy of May. The oak gall, especially the heart of it, is black like the earth's sleep."

There was a silence, and then Randoulet asked:

"What did you say?"

"Yes," said Bobi, "I say that there are some things which, by their taste or by their colour, when one has them on one's tongue or in one's eye, give joy, and others that give grief. Three things of joy, one of grief, that makes a living thing."

They looked at each other.

Randoulet was about to speak.

"If you think that *he'll* understand," said Le Noir.

"In the first place," said Randoulet, "I am no stupider than you. I understood."

"No," said Bobi.

The shadow moved. Someone who had been crouching beside the hearth stood up. It was a girl about twenty years old. Her lip, whitened with a little saliva, was hanging loosely, but her eyes were beautiful.

"Here, Monsieur," she said.

Bobi held out his hands. She gave him a puppy. It was only a few weeks old. The girl had opened her blouse. There, in the shadow, she had been holding the puppy to her dry breast.

"Here, Monsieur," she repeated.

She made a gesture with her hands as if to say: Keep it.

"Well, Zulma," said Randoulet.

"Besides," said Bobi, "we'll have to be going. We've stayed long enough. And the horse must be cold."

He tried to put the puppy on the floor.

"Here, Monsieur," said Zulma again, "here."

She made Bobi keep the little creature in his arms.

"Pretend to do it," said Honorine.

"Thank you, Madame, for everything," said Bobi.

They went out with Randoulet.

"She is simple," he said; "you must excuse her."

"Yes," said Bobi, "here's the dog; take good care of it, it will be a fine animal."

"Good-bye," said Randoulet as they got into the cart.

"Yes," said Bobi, "we'll see each other again."

After trotting awhile along the edge of the pond, "The girl, Zulma," said Jourdan, "it was she, you might say, who gave the farm its name."

"That interests me," said Bobi.

"Look," said Jourdan.

At that moment they were at a little distance from the pond which lay spread out below them, and the ground, in spite of the snow, indicated pasture land. In the wake of the cart, the tracks of the wheels were green.

Bobi looked.

There was a tree, all alone in the midst of the barrenness. It hissed with all its black branches in spite of the great silence, or rather because of the great silence. It was a tiny sound.

"It is a maple," said Jourdan. "They wanted to uproot it; they would have had a battle with her."

Now, before them, on either side, and behind, lay a vast plain encircled with fog. Beneath the snow the soil rang hard. One could vaguely perceive through the fog, at the right, a sombre, sprawling shape which continued all along the horizon.

"Are we going back to the forest?" asked Bobi.

"No," said Jourdan, "this is Deffends Wood. One edge only. It is from there that the Ubacs plunge toward the Ouvèze River."

They continued at a walk; then at times the horse trotted. They went straight toward the dark form of the woods. It drew no nearer, but it was always visible, vague and black in the mist.

"The snow is deceptive," said Jourdan; "the wood seems near and it is a great distance away on the level land. The image of it comes to us by reflection."

"We don't see any birds," said Bobi again.

"They are in the wood."

"To whom does the wood belong?"

"It is communal."

"But you are not a commune?"

"No," said Jourdan, "but the fact is that we have all the ways of one. We agree once a year about it at Fra-Josépine."

They were now on a level stretch with very little snow. The freezing cold, which continued in spite of the daylight, gave free passage. The horse trotted for some time.

At noon they gave him a breathing spell.

Jourdan and Bobi got down from the cart. They covered the horse with the cloaks and gave him the feed bag.

Jourdan got out the bread and bacon. They ate in silence. From time to time they danced from one foot to the other. They seemed to be chewing smoking food. At each mouthful, their breath made a mist.

"We'll reach Mouille-Jacques at the stroke of one," said Jourdan.

"We don't see any birds," repeated Bobi.

In fact there was only the silent and lonely wilderness.

The horse champed his bit as he ate.

Mouille-Jacques was a house that stood all alone in the fields. Larger than Maple Tree Farm, with a portal, a window on either side of the door, three windows above, and before the middle one an iron balcony. A little path, carefully cleared of snow, led to the threshold. The yard was clean. On one side the silent and empty sties. On the other side a shed that sheltered ploughs, harnesses, a woodpile still surrounded by logs freshly split and a heap of dry forage which warmed one just to look at it.

The buggy entered the path and approached the house. The door opened and a man appeared in the framework. Behind him could be seen the flaming hearth. The man was smoking a pipe. He was dressed in russet corduroy. His bare head, which was quite bald, glistened. He had big ears. No beard or moustache, his mouth thin and twisted. His eyes were scarcely visible beneath enormous grey brows.

"What's the news?" he said.

With a familiar gesture he passed his hand over his head.

"Nothing serious," said Jourdan; "we're not even going to stop."

The man came out to the cart.

"Yes," he said, "come in a minute."

"This is my cousin," said Jourdan.

The kitchen was spacious and clean. Nothing was visible but a large walnut table scrubbed to the bare wood, and before the hearth a good square of shining tiles, clean, without a trace of ashes. The rest of the room was in shadow. Near the fire, Madame Carle was mending a knitted garment. The son Carle was examining his hands. With his finger he was feeling the palm at the base of the thumb to see if the callous spot was very hard; he ran his finger over the callouses and little warts.

"...just a bit of warmth," Carle was saying. "Sit down."

"It's a long time since we've seen Marthe," said Madame Carle. "You should have brought her along."

"And our evening soup?" said Jourdan. "We'll be hungry when we get home. This is how it is: we've come to see your stallion, Carle."

Carle led them through the little inside door. As they went along the corridor, they felt the gradual approach of the animal heat of the stable and smelt the odour of trampled straw.

"There are two steps," said Carle. "Be careful."

After the steps, the foot touched a soft floor made of the dampish straw. Eyes had to grow accustomed to the darkness.

The stallion was like a light. The day shone through the oval window on his coat. Gradually one could distinguish the animal's contours. He was in a strongly braced stall, narrow at the sides and closed behind by two great tree trunks. He was a noble horse. His whole neck rose above the boards. He was sniffing at the hay rack. The soft part of his muzzle was extremely mobile. He was not eating. From time to time he would draw back his lip and with a corner of his tooth pull down two or three wisps of hay. He chewed. He whinnied with the sound of a woman weeping. He spat out the little green ball of grass. He stamped with his forefoot. He arched his neck two or three times. He shook his mane as if he were running in the open prairies. He quivered all over, and his strength flowed through his skin and muscles. He was stirred like the bed of a torrent that suddenly holds too much water. He kicked out with a great thrust of his hind hoofs. He struck with his shoes against the tree trunks. Very softly he whinnied again just for himself.

Carle approached.

"I was obliged to turn this piece of wood around," he said.

"When it was cut, the ax broke off in it. It is still there. Each time he kicked it, it made the sparks fly."

When they returned to the kitchen, Carle insisted that they sit down a moment. Bobi winked.

"Just a little, then," said Jourdan.

Bobi sat down beside Madame Carle. He warmed his hands. He stretched like a cat.

"The heat feels good," he said.

"This weather freezes a body," said Madame Carle.

She laid her work on her knees.

"It isn't so much," she said, "the cold itself that freezes you, as being obliged to stay still."

"You have a fine horse," said Bobi.

"Yes," said Carle. "He is full of vigour. He succeeds in every mating."

"I mean," said Bobi, "that he is very fine in the sense of beauty."

Jourdan was about to say: "What's that you say?"

He refrained. He preferred to have Carle say it.

Carle rubbed his bald head with the palm of his hand.

"Yes," he said, "he is beautiful, as you say. And you haven't seen him yet in the full light of day. He has a nose long and pointed like an iris leaf."

"An iris leaf?" said Bobi, astonished.

"Yes, Monsieur," said Carle.

"If I understand correctly," said Bobi, "the front of his face is long, flat, shining, and pointed, with the point placed just between the nostrils."

"Exactly," said Carle, a little breathless. "You know horses?"

"No," said Bobi.

And he let the silence settle.

"Listen," said Carle, and he was panting; he was always panting and excited when he talked about his stallion, and he rubbed his head hard.

"It is a sign of breeding, that is; and then the withers trouble. I call it the withers trouble when the muscles are not lengthened but make a knot under the point of the shoulder blades. I'm not talking about what your heavy horses have here"—and he touched his own breast—"which is only a padding in front, as they say, and which appears because they pull with their collars; that is a reinforcement but a false one. No, what I mean is nerves"—he repeated the word making it tremble in his mouth—"nerves. It is a natural force, a horse force."

"Yes," said Bobi. "Then you know exactly what it is?"

"No," said Carle.

Bobi began to smile, and openly he winked his eye at Madame Carle, then at the son, and at Jourdan, and he turned facing Carle with a silent laughter.

"It is…" said Bobi. "Have you noticed poppy heads?"

"Yes."

"The bud is as big as your thumb and then it opens and gradually a flower as big as your fist unfolds."

"Yes."

"What your horse has," and he said the rest very softly, "is the seeds of wings.

"Yes," continued Bobi in the deep silence, still speaking softly. "There will grow out of them great white wings. And he will be a wingèd horse, and he will take one stride from here to Maple Tree Farm, and he will gallop ten metres above the earth, and he will never again permit himself to be harnessed, nor his sons, nor his sons' sons."

"That," said Jourdan, long after they were on the way to Maurice's in the early winter twilight, "that was anything but what I expected."

"It will often be like that," said Bobi.

"What struck me most," said Jourdan, "was Carle, that he should have come clear out to the cart, talking all the while, for, you know, he is not a talker, and that he should have said: 'I hope to see you again.' And then he added: 'And that means that I'd really like to see you again.' He doesn't care much for company. That is what astonishes me."

They went on for some time. It was cold. The sun was setting. Night was already trembling in the fog.

As they approached Maurice's place they heard shouts. They were the shouts of a man. There was a lighted lantern in the yard. Jourdan stopped at the portal before going in. The lantern was over near the shed. It lighted the framework of an arrangement for shoeing oxen, and three men bent over, almost motionless. In the wooden framework a man was crouched and crying aloud. At the edge of the shadow stood a woman, holding a child in her arms.

Bobi jumped from the cart and ran up.

"What's the matter?" he said.

"He has broken his back," they said.

"Move aside," said Bobi.

Jourdan came up.

"This is my cousin," he said; "let him manage this."

"If he touches me, I'll kill him!" cried the man.

They had tied his arms to the lower bar of the apparatus. He was old and hairy. He was breathing heavily. His eyes were wild. Then he became docile and tender with the eyes of a child and he wept.

"You *look* as though you would kill me; here, let me see."

Bobi went inside the framework.

"Untie him. Don't touch him any more. Let me manage him."

"Let him do it," said the man.

He was lying on the ground.

"There?" asked Bobi.

He touched him on the hip.

"No."

"There?"

He touched the tip of his shoulder blade. The man roared.

"Ah," said Bobi, "you got hurt where your wings sprout, too, did you?"

He stood up.

"Give me a fichu, a scarf, something long and soft, no matter what."

"This?" said one of the men.

He gave him a neck scarf.

"Yes. Come in here, Jourdan."

Bobi had passed the scarf under the man's arm. He gave the ends of it to Jourdan.

"Hold that," he said, "and stand still."

"A man," asked Bobi, turning toward the others.

A man stepped forward.

"You hold his legs, just hold them still."

"Are you going to hurt me?" asked the injured man softly.

"I am going to cure you," said Bobi.

He looked at Jourdan.

"When I say 'Hop,' you pull upward."

He took the man's hand. He grasped the wrist tightly.

"Hold his legs firmly."

He cried "Hop." He pulled the arm toward him; Jourdan pulled the scarf upward. The man yelled and threw himself backward.

"He hasn't broken his back," said Bobi; "his shoulder was out of joint. That happens sometimes."

"He doesn't budge."

"Go get some brandy."

"Let's carry him into the house."

"Be careful," said Bobi, "take him by his feet, and I'll take him by the shoulders. All right!"

As they entered, the old woman put her hands to her head. She was going to cry out. Her mouth was already open.

"He is cured," said Bobi.

Nobody knew him but he said nice things and he was laughing.

"In front of the fire," said Bobi, "and now some brandy for him and perhaps for us, too."

"It's dreadful to hear the old man cry."

"Oh, old man," said the old woman, "that's what he is."

The young woman looked on in silence. A little boy had come to seek her protecting shadow.

The men were wiping their brows.

The injured man, in front of the fire, seemed dead.

"Jacquou," moaned the old woman, while her hands faltered in the cupboard, clattering the bottles.

"He's coming around," said Bobi.

The prostrate man opened his eyes.

"You son of a bitch," he said.

"That's me," said Bobi.

And he leaned over him. He offered him a glass of brandy.

"Drink this. Move your fingers."

The man wiggled his fingers.

"Move your wrist."

The man moved his wrist.

"Your elbow."

The man bent his arm.

"Now," said Bobi, "for your shoulder you must wait until the day after tomorrow. Do you feel any pain?"

"Just a trace of it," said the man.

"Then get up and sit in a chair."

He helped him to rise. One of the men had pushed forward a chair.

"Well, Jacquou?" said Jourdan.

"Is that you, Jourdan? Well, you see."

"You're feeling better."

"Yes, but," said Jacquou, "I'd like to know. Who are *you*, you?"

"The son of a bitch," said Bobi.

"Are you the doctor?"

"Yes, I am the doctor, but don't tell anyone," said Bobi, laughing; "they'd put me in jail because I haven't any papers."

"The idea!" said Jacquou.

"Well," said Bobi, "what do *you* think? Bitches' children aren't so bad, eh?"

The old woman laughed and so did the men, and Jacquou drank, then he said: "This is warming." Then: "Don't laugh at that." Then: "The pain makes me forget my manners."

"Don't mention it," said Bobi.

"You'll eat with us," said Jacquou.

"Yes," said the old woman.

"Yes," said the two men.

"Certainly," said the young woman.

"No," said Bobi, "we must go home. Marthe is all alone."

"He is Marthe's cousin?" said the young woman.

"No," said Jourdan, "he is my cousin."

"Really not?" said the old woman. (She meant: Won't you stay?)

"Really not," they said.

"All he needs," said Bobi, "is to keep his arm in the scarf until day after tomorrow, and then for a little while not to do anything strenuous."

About two hundred yards from Maurice's place, Jourdan was obliged to stop and light the lantern. The night was pitch-black. Before hanging it on the side board, Jourdan raised the lantern at arm's length. One could not see farther than ten metres. Beyond, mingled with the night, seethed the silent hosts of the fog. Their forms could be seen rolling confusedly by, and the trembling of their frozen tresses.

"The horse is tired," he said. "We are half a day late. I had counted on being at La Fauconnière at noon, and now it is dark."

They started on again slowly. The fog opened before them but then closed in, brushing against the buggy, and it could be heard behind them touching the leather hood with its cracking fingers.

They were in the land of night. The horse felt the world with her long ears. She tried to see in spite of her blinkers. She turned her head. She walked uncertainly. Her foot slipped. Her breathing grew heavy. She started forward again, stretching her neck with a snort that made her belly shiver. All around them in the darkness there were moving forms in long robes of silver. The horse's fear flowed in waves the length of the reins.

Suddenly, there was a noise high in the sky. The form of a tree advanced upon them with its immense leafless branches. It seemed cut out of cardboard. Behind it could be seen the shapes of other trees. The fog dripped in their branches.

"The plane trees of the spring," said Jourdan.

"Ho, you in the buggy!" hailed a voice.

The horse stopped.

"Is that you, Silve?"

"Yes."

The steps of a man on the frozen ground.

The weight of a man leaning on the side rail pulled the cart down on Jourdan's side.

"What are you doing in a cart at this time of night?"

"I'm going home."

"Everything all right?"

"Everything all right."

"What are *you* doing here?" said Jourdan.

"Nothing."

"It's cold," said Jourdan.

"It's a change."

"The days are long," said Jourdan.

"And they are the shortest ones," said the voice.

"What are you doing at your place?"

"Nothing."

"Don't you want to get in?"

"No, I'll walk; it's a change."

"Then," said Jourdan, "everything's the same?"

"Do you have any hope of its changing?" asked the voice.

"Yes," said Jourdan.

"So much the better for you."

"Don't you think so, too?"

"No."

"Then what?"

"Why, this."

The cart shook slightly. The man of the night had doubtless just made some gesture that designated the night.

"However," said Jourdan, "men…"

"Yes."

"Yes, what?"

"Men."

"Haven't you any faith?" asked Jourdan.

"No," said the voice.

A moment's silence, then the cart was eased of that weight pressing on it. It swayed a little. It regained its equilibrium.

"Good-bye," said the voice.

"Good-bye," said Jourdan.

The horse once more started on his way.

A long time afterward, far off in the darkness, gleamed two tiny lamps.

"Fra-Josépine," said Jourdan. "It is late, they will be in bed," he continued. "We'll go home."

As they drew near, the lamps separated.

Now they shone far apart.

"The farm house and the château," said Jourdan.

"That is what they call it," he continued. "It is only the owner's house, but people say 'the château.' Are you asleep?"

"No," said Bobi.

The two lights were now square. They were two windows.

"It will be three years, the seventh of February, since I was here last," said Jourdan, "just about here. Behind the bank of the irrigation canal. It must be in this direction."

He pulled on the left rein.

"Get around, Coquet," he said to the horse.

They left the lights on their right. They rode along in a line with them.

"We were watching," said Jourdan. "The light was just about the same as this evening, but there wasn't any fog. At ten o'clock he shot off his gun. Into himself this time. It put out the light. A dirty job. That had been going on for two days.

"The fifth of February," Jourdan went on, "I was sharpening my scythe. My wife came to me. She said: 'Listen!' I listened. Someone over at Fra-Josépine was shooting. I heard someone running. It was the wife and the little girl. 'He is shooting at us.' 'No,' I said. 'Yes.' I dropped everything. I straightened up. Yes, a bullet had even grazed the little girl's forehead. Thirteen years old she was. He had gone crazy!

"Yes, he was crazy. He had pushed everything in front of the door: bed, dresser, chairs, sofa. They were people of property. He must have laid in a supply of cartridges. He fired more than a hundred shots. First on his wife and on his little girl. They immediately thought of coming to our house. He shot at them again as they were running across the vegetable patch. What saved them was that they fell. He thought that they were dead. Then he went to the other window to shoot at the farmer and his family.

"He was a thin man, gentle-eyed, full of big words and fine phrases. An educated man. He had not come here, he said, to be a peasant all at once, since he was not a peasant by training, but to live at last as he liked, in peace and simplicity. He had hired the best farmer in the region: Adolphe. He was known far and wide. He had never had any trouble. He had a room full of books, a sort of loft. He had a wife: gentleness itself. If she was wanted, she came. If she wasn't wanted, she stayed away. He had plenty…! From Fra-Josépine, you can see Grémone Forest, the end of the plateau, the pond and all the fields. You can see the work of all. You have only to sit on the stone bench in the lane of plane trees and you have the whole world before your eyes. He had a beautiful little girl. And she was called Aurore. He had everything!

"Yes, he had everything. That is what *we* said. When *he* had cast up his accounts, he found he had nothing. You have everything. Yes, according to others, it seems that since everything is there, before you, you have only to take it. But the appetite? Ah, that's the important thing! Offer pheasant to someone who wants to vomit. That's the way. It is a question of constitution. The essential thing is that your body must have the desire. Otherwise, you have everything in vain, you have all, but you have nothing.

"Well, I'm not an educated man, I don't know much about things. But I have to think about that, because I also, because everybody . . . Well, sometimes, when I am alone, or when I think about that, I say to myself that it is queer, it's like something that isn't made right. There is one thing that I do not believe; that is that anyone deliberately wants us to be unhappy. I think that things were made so that everybody can be happy. I think that our unhappiness is a sort of disease that we create ourselves with big chills-and-fever, with bad water, and with the evil that we catch from each other in breathing the same air. I think that if we knew how to live, perhaps we wouldn't be ill. With the habits we've gotten into now, all our life is a struggle, we strike out in the water, we fight, to keep from going under. Our whole life long. Whether it be your animals, whether it be your seeds, your plants, your trees, you've got to police against them all. What we want, it seems that the entire world does not want. They seem to do it on purpose. That must have given us a distaste for everything, in the end. That must have forced our bodies to produce any old way, how can we tell? . . . The world forces us to shed blood. Perhaps we are unconsciously creating a special kind of blood, a blood of distaste, and instead of there flowing through our bodies, everywhere—in our arms, in our thighs, in our hearts, in our stomachs, in our lungs—a blood of desire, our great pipe system washes us with a blood of disgust."

The lights had disappeared. They had been slowly turning away from them. The ground rose gently. The cold solidified the night like cement in the bottom of the mortar box.

"Look at the signs," said Bobi.

Before them, in the distance, golden signs had just blazed forth. They looked like letters. One was a capital L. And after this letter was a sort of apostrophe. They were level with the ground. There was a sign that made a capital E, but the E from time to time became an F. They were really signs and they were indeed of gold. But they could not be read.

Jourdan tried. He squinted his eyes. He said: "L-apostrophe-e-f, l-apostrophe-e-f. What does that mean?" As they drew nearer, the letters changed shape. The one that was an L had almost become an O, a little square, and the apostrophe had melted into it. The other letter became an M laying on its side. "We ought to mark them down on paper," said Jourdan to himself. To know. Prescriptions are sometimes written out like that in strange letters, and he who does not know them looks at them and does not understand.

"L-apostrophe-e-f-o, l-apostrophe-e-f-o-m," he said to himself, like one of those great, formless words that must have signified the sun, the moon, and the stars in the mouths of the first men.

"It is the house," said Bobi.

Jourdan pulled in the reins. The horse stopped.

"What?" asked Jourdan.

"The signs," said Bobi; "it is the house. Marthe has lit the fire. She has closed the door and the window shutters, and there in front of us is the light flowing through the joints around the door and the shutters."

Jourdan remained silent for a moment.

"One who knows is worth ten who seek," he said.

But he did not shake the reins to make the horse start and he laid his hand on Bobi's knee.

"Stay with us," he said. "We are like the lepers, without help or remedy. Among the best of us, you see, there are few who still have hope."

"It is difficult," said Bobi.

"You have done it so simply," said Jourdan, "since the other night."

"I have only given little remedies."

"But they have affected my whole being," said Jourdan.

"The great remedies," said Bobi, "are more discouraging."

"One must command one's self in order to cure others," said Jourdan, "and besides, now you are responsible for a great deal. You have already made us see what can comfort us. But we scarcely know how to go about it, amongst all those flowers of Queen Anne's lace, and all those golden signs. One time we think we are only seeing the old stars, and then again we imagine worlds and it is only the light shining around our door."

"Everything can be cured, but we do not know how to choose, and one who knows is worth ten who seek."

The house, as they drew near, smelt of bread freshly baked.

4

It was early when Bobi rapped on the door.

"Hello!" replied Jourdan.

He had just awakened at the knock.

"The sooner we begin…" said Bobi. "And this will be the day, I think."

"Fair dawn when the meadows bloom," sang Jourdan, as he made the bed creak.

Marthe called.

"Don't get up," said Bobi through the door. "I know where everything is. But soon, if I am not mistaken, it will be good to be up."

Jourdan looked out of the window.

"This is the great frost," he said.

It was the great frost. During the night the north wind had come. It had blown quite softly, without violence, scarcely more than a man's breathing. But its strength was in its coldness. It had swept the sky clean. It had glazed the snow. It had dried up the last sap in the cracks of the bark. It had turned the forest into a solid block. It had locked the earth. All night long it had worn down the sky with cold, cold, cold, ever new, more and more biting, like one who polishes the bottom of a kettle with steel wool, and now the sky was so pure and so smooth that the sun scarcely dared to move.

"Brrr!" said Jourdan, shivering as he got into his trousers. "As soon as the air touches you the blood rushes back to your heart. I am frozen like an almond blossom."

At the window joints the north wind, light but tenacious, was whistling softly like a cricket.

"If you notice," said Jourdan, "not a thing is stirring. It is absolute death. Except for the people inside the houses, there are not three living creatures in the world."

"And what do you want to do?" he asked after having breathed on the pane and cleared off a good-sized piece of frost. "The sky is as stiff as iron."

Bobi had lit the fire downstairs. He was standing in front of it. He warmed his hands one after the other. Then his feet, one at a time; then again his hands. He was like a wheel that the cold had set in motion.

Jourdan entered the room and approached the fire. And he, too, began to imitate a wheel. Quietly, without a sound, as when the power is just turned on and the wheels revolve before setting the belts in motion.

"You still have some wheat?" said Bobi.

"Yes."

"Much?"

"Two loads."

"You still have it all, then?"

"No. I sold two loads. Half."

"Are you keeping this for sowing?"

"Mostly that. But I could have sold at least another load. Only the price went down."

"What good is the wheat to you?" asked Bobi.

"Sometimes," said Jourdan, "I have trouble in understanding what you ask me."

"It is always that way when it is simple," said Bobi. "The wheat, what do you use it for?"

"For bread."

"For Marthe and you?"

"Yes."

"How much do you need a year?"

"One load."

"Then, the rest?"

"I sell it."

"And so," said Bobi after a moment, "with some of the wheat you make bread for you and Marthe. That is as it should be. With some more of your wheat you sow the new wheat; that is right. With what is left, you make money. You give your wheat to someone. He makes out the account. He takes out his pocketbook. He gives you a banknote, two, three bills. You put them in your pocketbook. You come back to La Jourdane. You take out your pocketbook. Out of it you take the bills. You show them to Marthe. You open the wardrobe. You put the bills underneath Marthe's chemises, or she does it herself. You shut the door of the wardrobe. Good. At that moment you realize that you are a leper. Of your work you have made three parts: one which gives you your food, you and Marthe, that's one. When I say 'you,' I mean both of you. Good. Another part which gives you the certainty of living next year. A third part which is in paper under the folded chemises. What have you done for the leper in all that? Nothing. When one has done nothing for the leper, he becomes more and more leprous. There is a part of your work that is lost. It is that part that is changed into paper and lying thin and flat under Marthe's chemises. Lost, I say."

"How lost?" said Jourdan. "It is money."

"I say more than that," continued Bobi. "It is that which gives you leprosy. Let us understand each other. I exaggerate a little to make you understand. The germ of this leprosy, you have at birth. It has come down to us from mother to mother. It is a little black spot in a woman's womb, just at the place where the head of the child presses."

"And so," said Jourdan, "we've all been promised the catastrophe."

"No," said Bobi, "on the contrary."

"If one is born with it," said Jourdan.

"That germ of leprosy," said Bobi, "is more necessary than the heart."

The fire roared. The water boiled. The shutter creaked. The pane cracked in its putty with the cold. Then Jourdan said: "Explain."

There was a beautiful morning over the earth. The sun was daring to venture into the sky.

"What you call leprosy," said Bobi, "is love without use. Yes. What do you think you are?"

"You look at me," said Jourdan, "as if you wished me harm."

"No," said Bobi, "and you know it. I am looking at you because I am reproving you."

"What am I?" said Jourdan.

"Yes, you are a man, a speck, that's all."

"I am a man," Jourdan repeated to himself. And he looked at himself.

"Nothing more," said Bobi.

"Nothing more," repeated Jourdan.

"The mistake," said Bobi, "is to think one's self more."

And Jourdan was silent because he was trying to understand what that meant.

"You have to love the world," said Bobi.

There was still something not quite clear. And the explanation had almost ceased to come from Bobi, from his voice or from his words. The enlightenment was coming from the warmth, the fire, the frost, the wall, the windowpane, the table, the door rattling in the north wind, from the tiles of the floor, whose clay, in spite of its age, was sweating slightly. The enlightenment was coming from all these things, but it was still clumsy and awkward. Bobi's sole advantage was that he used words in contrast to the mute message of fire, of clay, of wood, and of the pure sky. He tried to explain it with words. But it was not quite the same thing. If only there were fire words and sky words, then it would be easy.

"You must," said Bobi. "Here you are, in the act of creation. That began, Jourdan, when you were still attached to your mother. Yes, before you were cut free; at the first leap. And they were there waiting for you. All of them. That makes a great many. They said: Ah! Here's another. We'll teach him. And they have taught you."

"What?"

The house was gently creaking like a sleeping faggot.

"Cure yourself of leprosy," said Bobi, "since they have taught you. The wiseacres!"

He stopped to calm himself. Upstairs, Marthe could be heard humming as she moved about in the bedroom.

"Before you were born," said Bobi, "you knew more. And you knew the exact truth. And what taught you was the place where your head rested against your mother's womb. A spot as big as that."

He showed the nail of his little finger.

"But its voice is, as one might say, electric."

He left Jourdan a moment with the memory of the words about him. Not alone. Not just with that alone. There was the fire that kept him company, the sound of the fire, the colour of the fire, the smell of the fire. There was the great sky, so pure, so closely pressed against the windowpane that it could not be ignored. There was the cracking of the frost, the ice under the roof tiles that was stirring softly like a rat. There was the sun, whose real face could not be seen, for blinding the eyes, except through the window that was clouded with mist; and it was all crushed, soft, and sticky like a ripe apricot fallen in the grass. And all that is maternal. And Bobi knew it, and Jourdan was beginning to know it.

"And today," said Bobi, "with your money, what can you buy with your money to cure your leprosy today?"

"Nothing," said Jourdan. "And who do you think I could buy anything from?"

"From the world."

"What world?"

"How many are there?" asked Bobi.

"That one," he said, pointing to what lay outside the window. "The forest, the plateau, the earth, the sky, the cold. Today, well, you, too."

They heard Marthe coming downstairs.

"You have wheat," asked Bobi, "enough for your bread, enough for your sowing?"

"Yes."

"Then you are rich. Then," said Bobi, "we shall buy something that your mother told you about, long ago, while you were ripening."

Marthe entered.

"I looked out of the window," she said smiling. "This is the great frost. There is not a thing in the sky or on the earth. We are alone for a hundred kilometres around."

She saw the two of them, Jourdan and Bobi also, like cornered rats. They wore that deep wrinkle like a rush blade in the middle of their foreheads. They had a look of reflecting and being trapped in the midst of their reflections. And again came the thought that men are very unfortunate to be wishing, wishing, always wishing.

She smiled again, at both of them, her fine white teeth showing between her old lips, that still made one desire to eat with her, to be beside her, and to bring her things to eat.

"Where is your wheat?" asked Bobi.

"In the storehouse," said Jourdan; "it is drier there."

"Come on," said Bobi.

"Well!" said Marthe. "This morning they haven't even thought of their coffee."

Bobi had found a besom of Scotch broom. He carried it in one hand. In the other he held the corner of the sack of wheat, and the two of them, he and Jourdan, went out by the little back door.

Bobi swept the threshing floor. He cleared it of its lumps of frost and its clots of earth. Now the ground was as hard and as clean as a plate.

He emptied the sack of wheat in the middle of it. There were about fifty kilos. Jourdan was a little ashamed. He said nothing. He was not ashamed of emptying the sack on the ground, but it hurt him to see that his wheat, of which he had been so proud, wheat with a grain like rice, he used to say, fine and hard like powdered stone, had lost all its colour and it appeared pale and muddy compared to the surrounding brilliance of the frost.

"There," said Bobi dusting his hands, "we must go inside. We'll watch from the kitchen."

They stood at the kitchen window. They looked. Nothing happened outside. But here inside there was the smell of coffee and of bread that gave them patience.

"It seems to me…" said Jourdan.

But he shut his mouth tightly.

A bird had just flown by. They could not yet tell to what breed he belonged. He had just made a little flash with his wings. He was flying toward Fra-Josépine. He seemed to crush himself against the sky, his wings and tail wide spread and showing a touch of red colour. He was slowing down with all his might. He stopped, breast to the wind; he was already falling when he gave a great push with his feathers. He was coming back. He curved his flight as when the wind bows the curved willow branch at the end of which is the flower. He struck the pile of wheat like a whip. He shook himself. He was astonished. It was a green finch. He did not even think of singing a tiny song. He began to eat.

Jourdan pulled out his pouch, filled his pipe, passed his pouch to Bobi, without looking. He was watching the bird. Bobi took the pouch, got out his pipe, filled it, returned the pouch. Then he struck the match and gave a rapid glance at the light in his fingers, and Jourdan lit his pipe, but kept watching the bird out of the corner of his eye.

He was all fluffed out with the cold, three times as big as usual. The golden quill feathers, widely separated, showed the down beneath. His breast was spotted with white like clematis cotton on the grass. He was eating.

Their eyes were on the bird, but the glance is like a ray and above there is a zone where things can be seen without definitely looking at them, because it is the halo of the eye's ray. What one sees in this halo is always deformed like what one sees in the fog.

It seemed that the sky was like the lid of a cave where drops of water form, swell, and drop. The illusion was perfect, even the spread of the light of the drops of water pierced by the sun as they fell. But as soon as one was conscious of all that, the eye still fixed on the little ruffled green finch, so spry, eating so hungrily, and already chirping, they were no longer drops of water; they were birds. Other birds. The mind was full of the two pictures; the blue cave, the great drops, the tiny sound of running water, and then, no, they were birds, and the cave was the sky, and the noise, that of the birds singing, and the warm golden brown was not the fleeting ray of sunshine but multi-coloured plumage that opened and swished and slowed down so that the bird could alight gently in the wheat.

There were at least thirty. There was one enormous missel thrush, a turquoise-blue *turquin,* a seven-hued tanager, red, blue, and black bullfinches, a yellow bunting all of gold, a lark waving his red crest and striking to right and left with his black wings, reed larks, siskins, *agripennes,* goldfinches, tropical sparrows, linnets, yellow thrushes, redpolls, winter warblers, sparrows.

And still others were coming.

"We must go out," said Bobi.

Jourdan looked at him without replying at first.

"They will fly away," he said.

"We can go out by the back way," said Bobi.

"What are you looking at?" asked Marthe.

"Come and see."

"I love bullfinches," she said. "The big blue ones. At home we used to say to them: 'Binery!' That is how we used to call them. I remember, when I was a girl, I had a friend who set traps for them. Ah!" she said. "He caught more birds than girls! There was . . . "

She had, so to speak, greased her lips two or three times with saliva, like a person who is getting ready to talk a long time, and she stood there with her lips shining. She thought that she wanted to talk. It was only the desire to think of new things.

"Softly," said Jourdan, pushing open the stable door.

It opened behind the house and they could not even hear the sound of the birds, but they could see Grémone Forest.

They could see the sky.

This is what they saw: the land sloping upward toward the forest. It hid the trunks of the trees. Rising above the earth were the black branches. They appeared the blacker as they were laden with snow. Then the sky, bright, clear, pure; and as they were sheltered from the sun, a terrible sky, whose immeasurable emptiness, infinite solitude, frightful and boundless cruelty lay revealed. And that sky came to an abrupt stop at the farm-house roof. This is what I mean: that sky was made to go on, so to speak, to the end of time, of space, and of duration. And he who could have peopled it with an alga as big as a flea or a lichen round as a fingernail, that person would have been powerful, believe me. But, from the stable door it appeared to stop short at the tiles, to be cut by the jagged edge of the roof. Below that, was not much, if you will, but it was joy and love. Here was no longer an insensible world. Here were tiles of baked clay, the lace of the ridge, the fresh cheek of the roof. They say that man is made of cells and blood. But in fact he is like foliage: not pressed together in a mass, but composed of separate images like the leaves on the branches of the trees and through which the wind must pass in order to sing. How can the world be expected to use it if it is like a stone?

Look at a stone that falls into the water. It makes a hole. The water is not harmed and it goes right on doing its work of rolling and wearing away. It must win in the end, and there at the end of its course, with little pats of the waves, it levels the docile mud of its alluvium. Look at a branch of a tree that falls into the water. Held up by its leaves, it floats, it moves along, it never ceases to gaze at the sun. At the end of its transformation it is the germ, and trees and bushes spring up anew in the sands. I do not mean that the mud is dead. I do not say that the stone is dead. Nothing is dead. Death does not exist. But, when a thing is hard and impermeable, when it has to be rolled and broken to enter into a transformation, the turn of the wheel is longer. It takes millions of years to raise the level of the seas with millimetres of mud, to remake the granite mountains. It requires only a hundred years to develop a chestnut tree from the chestnut, and anyone who, on a spring day on the wild plateaux, has smelled the intoxicating fragrance of chestnut blossoms will understand how much it means to have it flower often.

Yes, the house was joy and love. Jourdan was not thinking of the prints of human hands on the clay of the tiles and that the mason's thumb had marked the mortar in building the wall. But he was thinking of that wheat out there full of famished birds. The grains had been colourless when he had heaped them in the middle of the dazzling threshing floor. Now, brilliant as rice, the wheat flew in the beating of the golden wings. He remembered that a moment ago he had seen the green finch take a grain in his bill, tilt his head, swallow it. He thought no farther along that line. In reality, it was not a thought but a secret leaven in his body. He was obliged to swallow often. He was drunk. He had just lost the poorly human sense of the useful. No longer could he lean to that side. He could not yet lean toward the useless, but he heard the swelling song of the flute that sings for the lepers.

"Come," said Bobi, and he took his hand.

"They will fly away," repeated Jourdan.

They both spoke in whispers. They turned the corner of the house. They came to the other angle of the wall. They could hear the birds chirping.

Marthe had remained by the window.

"There are some reed warblers now," she said.

They came in jerky little flights. They were river birds, from the Ouvèze, to the west. There were turtle doves, warblers. It was no longer possible to distinguish all the different birds.

It was evident now that all the bushes had been told. There must be some strange message in the sky, something syrupy and dancing like heat waves in summer. The flamingos that inhabit the marshes at the edge of the plateau and that garnish their floating nests with the wool of the sheep of Maple Tree Farm flew by in the sky. They were a family apart. They were not looking for wheat. However, they circled round and round. One could see their long legs. They seemed to be dazzled by the multicoloured ball that was dancing down there beneath them, and that burst, sending in all directions the fluttering wings of black, white, red, gold, green, and blue.

From time to time a frenzied bird came and beat its head against the windowpane. Marthe drew back, then returned to her position.

She was thinking of the great empty sky of a while ago, and now this host! She had one regret: she wished that she had thought of the grain all by herself. She said to herself: "And tomorrow, will they have any?"

She would have liked each bird to store some away. If she had known the location of the nests she would have gone and put some grain near each one. She was afraid they would hurt themselves jumping upon one another.

"Thrush," she said from time to time.

Because the thrush, larger and greedier than the others, was fighting with his big beak.

Marthe wondered: "Where have those two gone?"

But she was content to be alone. She felt within her a force whose limits she could not foresee. It was a woman-force and in such cases one did not need men about.

She had been pregnant just after her marriage with Jourdan, but had not been able to go to the end. She remembered how at first she felt her breasts grow firm and painful, then the gradual filling of all the voids of her body and that plenitude was organized within her. It was now as though she were once more filled, but this time there were two joys mingled: first the beatific joy of the fertile body, and then a cheerful, wild joy; for she knew very well that she was now too old to produce from the seed of man, and yet she was amply nourished in her most feminine and secret being. She felt the coming of contentment of all her needs of mother and woman. Even her age no longer prevented anything; it gave on the contrary a softness, a nobility, to all her movements, which she could not name, but of which she understood the importance. As when she walked barefoot in the summertime in the fields, dressed in black; her large body well balanced, her bust erect, her steps long and solid, with her slow movement, her peaceful smile.

Ah, how things speak to a woman! And it is not true that the time comes when one no longer loves. One always loves. And it is the only good thing in the body. Then, why should it end before the body? What would one do while awaiting death? One would await death: that is all that would be left to do. What they had been doing, in fact, before that man came to the plateau.

For her, indeed, that had recommenced with that little affair of the stallion, the day of the north wind. The day? Did it not seem like an age ago? It was the day before yesterday.

How many mysteries there are in the world!

She saw some golden orioles. She thought of the west wind. Because golden orioles always appear with the squalls. She saw some reed warblers. She thought of the Ouvèze River lying at the bottom of its wild valley where the nests of these birds dance among the reeds.

She saw some larks with their rust-coloured spots. She thought of the summer's end, of the tufts of stubble, of the moaning of the earth, of the sound of the carts, the desire to drink, the moors buttered with sunshine.

She saw some kinglets, green, grey, black wings and golden crests, and instead of continuing to see the kinglets, she saw and smelt the heather, the mountain plants, she heard the descent of the flock and the voices of the shepherds.

She saw jays and rollers, partridges, quails, for now all the birds of the plateau had been named: hedge sparrows, grey tomtits, blue-crested larks, thistle birds, and a kind of bird that she knew well and whose name was the "silent bird." It never sang, even in mating season.

Each time that the whole band scattered around the pile of grain, inside Marthe a feather flower burst into bloom, but it had wings of wind, of plains, and of mountains, eyes of sunshine, a blue breast of evening in the country, and the rustle of all the meadow insects.

She could scarcely hear the birds' chirping through the window. She wondered again: "What can they be doing?" thinking of the men. She said to herself: "What are they going to bring me next?"

At that moment she saw Jourdan, or rather the body of Jourdan, without his face. He was coming around the corner of the house.

"It is he," she said to herself. "What is he going to do? He looks as though he is spying."

Jourdan was motionless. No, he was moving, but so slowly that his movements were no longer those of a man. It was a great disappointment to see those corduroy trousers and that cloth coat out there.

She did not think for a minute that Jourdan could harm the birds. But she felt all at once that there was no longer any confidence. She trembled at the approach of the man. She was already less fertile. Hardly at all. She was on the side of the birds.

Jourdan's face appeared around the corner of the house. Marthe made a gesture to say to him: "Go away!" But here, in the darkness of the kitchen, she could not be seen. And Jourdan had no desire to budge. His face was ecstatic and hard like one who is walking in his sleep.

"Go away!" said Marthe.

He advanced a little farther.

"Go away!" said Marthe.

He scarcely moved his feet. His progress was inperceptible. He had taken his place in space like a tree. No one paid any more attention to him. And he advanced.

"Go away!" said Marthe in a whisper.

The birds had hopped backward. All together. The thrush turned his head two or three times. One could see the gleam of his right eye, then of the left one. He returned to the grain. From time to time the thrush stopped eating and looked at Jourdan. The other birds also stopped eating, sometimes with the grain in their bills. They looked. They had their wings ready. Then the wings fluttered and grew still and the birds swallowed the grain and they pecked in front of them without looking up.

Then Jourdan moved forward.

And so he reached the heap of grain. His feet touched the heap of grain. And the birds stayed there without fear and one even hopped on Jourdan's shoe and another, flying from the thrush's beak, struck his head against Jourdan's trousers.

Jourdan held his breath, and to see the birds he slid his glance along without moving his head.

"That is well, my husband," said Marthe in a whisper.

"No," said Bobi, "I don't know anything about birds and I don't know anything about anything. You must not make me out greater than I am."

Evening had come. They were all three gathered around the table for supper.

"What made you think of it?" asked Jourdan.

"I saw the great cold," said Bobi, "and then I thought of the birds."

"You thought of the birds?" said Jourdan, scratching his head.

"Does that astonish you?"

"No; from you that does not astonish me. But I don't think that it is simple."

"Yes," said Bobi, "it is the simplest thing of all. Here is what I thought: Everything must eat."

It was cabbage soup with bacon and potatoes.

"We'll take out the vegetables later," said Marthe, "and we'll divide the bacon in three parts. I didn't do any cooking, you can easily understand."

"Yes, Marthe," said Jourdan.

"Aren't you hungry?"

"Yes, I am," he said, "but I feel as though a little will satisfy me."

"There is a great joy that comes to us from the wild creatures," said Bobi.

"Yes," said Marthe.

"And there are many wild creatures," said Bobi.

"Many," said Jourdan.

"Have you ever seen hares running?" said Bobi.

"Certainly," said Jourdan.

"And roebucks?"

"No," said Jourdan, "but I am told that there used to be some here in times gone by."

"Around the farms?" asked Marthe.

"There weren't any farms," said Jourdan.

"But," said Marthe, "did they come up close to people like that?"

"Yes," said Bobi, "they came up close, but that was a long, long time ago."

5

"The truth is, my good Jourdan," said Madame Hélène, "that after lunch I do not feel I have the courage to spend my whole afternoon alone at Fra-Josépine. I said to Aurore: 'Go hitch up the carriage.' You can't imagine how that little one loves to be around horses, to fool around with all that sort of thing."

"Yes, Madame Hélène," said Jourdan, "with the springtime full upon us. . . ."

"The truth is, my good Jourdan that if I am not disturbing you, I am going to sit down on the bank and watch you work, because for me, I'll tell you frankly, all this"— and with her little mittened hands she designated all the springtime of the fields—"all this is black, black, black."

She hid her face in her hands.

"It was that service yesterday," said Jourdan. "You ought not to have come."

"What else could I have done?" she said. "He was our nearest neighbour; you on one side, he on the other."

"Sit down," said Jourdan, "I have the time."

She was a lady. Even after the death of her husband and when she had to oversee Fra-Josépine with the farmer, she was never dressed otherwise than in her Sunday clothes and well groomed. She was beautiful in body and face, rather delicate-looking, her contours regular though a trifle soft. She had violet eyes. She smelt good without perfume. She wore a skirt of a soft woollen stuff, a black blouse trimmed with lace, a white gimp at her throat, thread mittens, and a béret. A grey mouth.

"And Mademoiselle Aurore?"

"I told her to let me down near the bush. I wanted to see you, my good Jourdan. Aurore has gone in the direction of the forest with the carriage. She is probably galloping over there. The little one's blood is getting hot, Jourdan. It is going to end in giving us some worry, you will see."

"You are looking on the dark side of things today, Madame Hélène."

"Oh, no, my good Jourdan, no more today than other days. What do you think? I often think about everything. I think," she said, "that one can never get things straightened out."

Spring had now come on the plateau. The forest at the far edge of the fields was already gleaming like a green cloud. The air was warm with occasional stirrings that opened cold crevasses where could be heard the murmuring sound of the earth at work.

"Who found him?" asked Madame Hélène. "They told me that it was Maurice's farm hand."

"No," said Jourdan, "it was Vignier, his own man."

"Had he suspected anything before?"

"Yes. He told me that for some time he had felt it coming. So much so," said Jourdan, "that he had already taken the trouble to look for another place."

"What is that you are telling me?" said Madame Hélène.

"It is like this," said Jourdan. "Vignier and Silve had been together since, let me see, I think this makes almost fifteen years."

"And didn't he try to stop him?"

"What could he stop, as he said? They were both alone there at La Fauconnière. They knew each other pretty well. Vignier said to me: 'Remember, I knew very well that he would end up by hanging himself. I had already found work on Aiguines Mountain. I had told them: "I cannot tell you the exact day"' He said that when he saw him hanging there it didn't surprise him very much. He had said: 'Well, it's come!'"

"My good Jourdan," said Madame Hélène, "you say things that are more terrible than all the curses of the prophets!"

"Yes," said Jourdan.

"That doesn't seem to affect you," said Madame Hélène.

Jourdan was filling his pipe. He looked out over the plateau toward the Ouvèze Valley. Above the mist of the valley, the high frozen mountains rose into the clear sky. They were not rooted in the springtime, emerging from the blue breathings of the earth; and it seemed that the slightest wind might set them adrift.

"Yes," said Jourdan, "it does affect me. Yesterday, when I saw you two coming, I thought of your husband. Silve's mother, when she died, was carried to Roume. Silve's wife, too. Carle's father was taken to Saint-Vincent-des-Eaux. They are all buried far from here. But your husband was buried up there by the forest, and they've put Silve up there by the forest, beside your husband, who was the first to die of our disease. That's what I was thinking."

"Yes," said Madame Hélène, "that struck me too. My husband asked to be buried up there, but Silve?"

"No," said Jourdan. "Silve left nothing in writing. What he left, Madame Hélène, was the 'god damn its' that he said from time to time. But there was no need to discuss it. They said: 'We'll bury him up there beside the other.' Excuse me," said Jourdan, "but that's the way they said it."

"There's no harm done," said Madame Hélène.

The afternoon was slowly coming to a close. The wind was full of odours and it went to one's head a little. The early afternoon had made one want to sleep. Now the desire was gone all at once and one awoke in a warm world.

"I have been thinking," said Jourdan, "that up there we ought to surround them both with a hedge of hawthorns. What do you think of that?"

"Oh!" said Madame Hélène. "Why, the hawthorn is a good idea."

And she looked at him with her violet eyes.

"It would be a little like the stars," said Jourdan.

He felt that Madame Hélène drew back a little from him as when you want to look full at the person who touches you.

"Stars," he said, "are white and in clusters, if you have ever noticed, and so is the hawthorn. That is what I mean."

At that moment Madame Hélène resumed her position. She strummed on her knees with the tips of her fingers. They remained some time without speaking. The air was so still that they could hear the fire crackling on the hearth yonder at La Jourdane. The almond trees were about to burst into bloom. On the horizon, the high mountains receded in the haze. Jourdan puffed on his pipe. Madame Hélène rested her arms on her knees. She sat leaning forward, her hands clasped. Her fair hair was twisted in a knot well above the nape of her neck. She had the pink, satiny skin of little new-born creatures.

"And what are you going to sow in that field?" she said.

"If I told you, you wouldn't believe me."

"Why," she said, "what has happened to you? I don't recognize you any more!"

"Do you think that I have changed?"

"A great deal. You have a young look."

"Well, here is what I am going to sow," said Jourdan.

He arose and went to pick up a package made of a big piece of grocer's paper. He opened it. They were seeds. He poured some of them into his hand.

"Let's see if you can guess."

They looked like seeds made of brown steel, of a winged shape like maple leaves.

"That," said Madame Hélène, "is English forage."

"As big as that?"

"It does seem to me a little large."

"Then guess."

He shook the seeds in his hand to show all their sides. They were all ready to fly from his fingers.

"I know," said Madame Hélène. "Spanish lentils."

"No," said Jourdan.

He stood a moment, silently tossing the seeds in his hand.

"Periwinkles," he said at last.

"Do you mean…?"

"I mean periwinkles, like those in the waste land toward Chayes," he said.

"What is happening?" said Madame Hélène.

"And over there, below the house, in the hollow, I found it damp. I have sown it with narcissi. That's all done and they're coming up. There will be flowers in two weeks."

"Are you going to grow flowers, Jourdan?"

"Yes, Madame Hélène."

"Do they sell well?"

"They are not for sale," he said. "They are for me. You may take as many as you like."

"Jourdan!" she said.

She was speechless. She looked at the field. It was capable of yielding five loads of oats. And over there in the hollow there were already little green narcissus shoots piercing the ground.

"Say something," he said.

"I don't know what to say."

"What do you think of it?"

"At first I was afraid that you were making fun of me, Jourdan. But now I wonder, perhaps…Why, yes, I can see them plainly. Unless those are summer leeks."

She raised her eyes to Jourdan, who remained standing, holding the seeds in his hand. It was not quite clear by those violet eyes and that twitching and trembling mouth whether Madame Hélène was upset or what. But she was waiting for Jourdan to say: "Yes, they are summer leeks." Then the eyes and mouth would resume their usual expression.

"No," said Jourdan, "look closely. There aren't any rows, they are growing as they like, and if you stood up you could see down there."

He raised his arm.

Madame Hélène got up at once.

"Yes," she said.

"There are three in bloom already," he said.

"Could we go and see?" she asked.

"Yes, indeed," he said. "On the contrary, that is what it is for."

The two advanced. She had taken a long step, like Jourdan's.

"There," he said.

It was the beginning of the field. Here it was rather toward the north and in the shade nearly all day long because of a dip in the ground. The narcissi were just peeping through: two green leaves up a little way and a sucker as white as snow digging down into the soil.

Madame Hélène leaned over, then she got down on her knees.

"Sure enough," she said, "it is true."

The field, now that they were close to it, extended farther than the one up there destined for the periwinkles.

"In short," said Madame Hélène, "my good Jourdan, you must tell me, I do not understand. You seem to have led me to a mystery!"

"Look," he said, "at the beautiful leaves! It is already thick-looking, but come and see."

She was walking along the edge of the field. She was doing as one does with garden plants. One must not walk on them.

"Oh! Come right in," said Jourdan. "It is solid. This is a wild plant. It is made this way on purpose. We'll walk straight ahead. The flowers are over there."

She entered the field. She was a little afraid and a little ashamed to walk on the plants. It was something indefinable. New. She looked back at her footsteps. The crumpled leaves were uncrumpling. The flattened plants were lifting themselves with their own nerves.

There were more than three blossoms. There were perhaps ten or twenty, one could not be sure; but they were already like chips of white sapwood with a golden spot on each. And the fragrance was beginning.

"You see," said Jourdan.

"I see," said Madame Hélène.

"Isn't it beautiful?" he asked.

"Yes," she said. "And what are you going to do with it, Jourdan?"

"Nothing," he said. "It's just as it is, for pleasure. I have had enough of dreary work."

He stooped over to gather the flowers.

"Don't pick them," said Madame Hélène.

"Yes," he said. "Don't worry. I shall have more than a thousand, maybe, later on. These shall be for you. They are the first, Madame Hélène."

"And the first on the plateau," she said.

He made a little bouquet.

"You have no idea," said Madame Hélène, "of the joy that you are giving me."

She breathed in the fragrance. She closed her eyes the better to see inside herself. She held the bouquet out at arm's length. She turned it about in her hand. She examined it on all sides.

"It's strange."

"What?"

"Oh, nothing," she said.

Jourdan thought of Orion-Queen Anne's lace. He had wanted to speak his thought a while ago about the veins of the leaves. The thing welled up in him, then, upon reaching his lips, turned to smoke.

"One would say," he said, "that they are…"

"Oh," she said, "these are narcissi! Narcissi."

Someone was calling them from a distance. They had not heard the carriage galloping through the soft fields. The young girl pulled on the reins. The horse stopped short, planting its feet in the grass. They came out of the field toward the carriage.

"Look at my daughter," said Madame Hélène. "Just see what she looks like!"

Aurore was holding the horse with taut reins. With one foot pressed hard against the dashboard, she was leaning backwards, her body stiff and straight. She wore a muslin dress, pink near her body, white and rippling around it. Her head was bare but her hair was smoothly held in place by a ribbon that banded her forehead. A forehead that was hard, as were her eyes, but her mouth was tender like a cherry, and below her little chin, soft as a lamb's knee, her light chestnut hair billowed about her shoulders.

The horse grew quiet. Black rivulets of sweat steamed the length of his neck and shoulders and around his crupper.

"It seems," whispered Madame Hélène, "that she has no peace save when she runs or is carried away."

They came up to her.

"Where have you come from, my child?" she said.

"From the forest."

"From over there?" asked Madame Hélène, pointing with her finger.

"No, from all along there," said Aurore, designating the whole front of trees. "I unharnessed the horse," she said, seeing her mother looking at the wheels.

"You rode horseback?"

"Yes."

"My child," said Madame Hélène, "horseback without a saddle! And like a boy?"

"Yes."

"With all the fresh linen that you put on just now?"

"I took it off, Mamma," she said.

"You aren't a little girl any longer," said Madame Hélène.

She looked at the horse's back that her daughter had clasped with her bare legs.

"No, Aurore, you aren't any longer."

"Ah, Mademoiselle Aurore is full of energy," said Jourdan. "Let her alone."

"But you understand…" said Madame Hélène.

"I understand."

And he looked at the bouquet of narcissi. All three looked at the bouquet of narcissi.

"I have never seen those flowers before," said Aurore, dropping the reins. "Give them to me quick, Mamma."

"There have never been any on the plateau," said Madame Hélène.

"I planted a whole field of them," said Jourdan. "You can come here with your horse. It is to be for everyone."

He watched them as they went away. The child turned the carriage sharply on the two front wheels. She was driving with less fire. From time to time she leaned toward her mother, over the hand that held the bouquet.

It was now too late to sow. All the sounds of spring were awake, and earth and sky were filled with echoes like the valley of a mountain stream. Green grasshoppers were already shrilling, crickets chirped, and the great bumble bees buzzed inside the earth. The grass made a supple and form-less sound.

Jourdan cast a handful of periwinkle seeds. He was not accustomed to them. They slipped less easily than grains of wheat. To tell the truth, they were poorly made to be sown by hand, for they clung to the skin.

Bobi had said that they need be sown only once and that after that they would renew themselves.

Jourdan looked toward the forest. Over there the evening was still bright. Above the trees smoked the mist from the plains. The slanting sun lit up in it false rainbows coloured only red and blue, but of a lovely curve that arched like the reed at the edge of baskets. Below, beneath the haze and the rainbows, beyond the forest, below in the lush fields, passed the road to Roume, the town. Then, after that, the world, with other roads, railroads, canals, rivers, cities, and men. No sound could be heard from all that.

Bobi had been gone a month now. Not quite. A month the day after tomorrow, at exactly six o'clock in the evening. He had said it would take a long time. He had not specified a date. He had only said that they needed larger seeds.

"Seeds for us," he had said. "We must also change the sow-ing within ourselves."

Once again he had spoken of money. It had really been necessary, since it had been decided once for all to cure that leprosy of unhappiness. And to establish all that on the plateau. Yes, on all the land stretching from Grémone Forest to the Ouvèze Valley. On us, up here in the sky; on us who hear nothing of all the noise of the world. . . .

Jourdan listened.

No sounds other than those of the earth, the grasshoppers and the crickets and an early bee and a heron that was pecking with its beak in a ditch near Maple Tree Farm. Yes, us.

"It would be too much work," Bobi had said, "to do it for the whole world."

He had smiled.

"For everyone is in need of it, everyone suffering from your disease, the whole world is rotting with earthly flesh. It doesn't smell bad yet but it is the pasture of the wind. Leprosy, indeed," he had said.

He had smiled still more broadly.

"What can you expect?" he said. "We cannot do it for everybody, but we are going to do it for us. Perhaps it will serve as an example."

Then there had arisen the question of money. But he had solved that like the Bobi he was. There was in what he said a justice that touched you.

"Then it *is* good for something?" Jourdan had said.

"Yes," Bobi had said, "since all about us men only accept that in exchange. Since it is necessary to exchange in order to get what we have not yet got; since we have become so poor that we can no longer do everything by ourselves. We still need money. But, the less one thinks of it the better it will be."

Jourdan had shown him his savings. They were not folded under Marthe's chemises. They were in a corner of the stable. He had to dig to pull out the iron box.

Bobi had grown very grave. He had touched Jourdan's arm. He had said to him: "Wait!" Then: "Have you really made up your mind?"

"What do you want me to do?" Jourdan had said. "I already know myself that this remedy cures. I know how well I have felt since I tried it."

"You have a lot of money!"

"But I am very sick," Jourdan had said. He was beginning to learn to speak a little like Bobi.

"Very well, then," Bobi had said, "give it to me."

And Jourdan had given him some of the money. Willingly.

"This is the first time that I have given money so willingly," he had said to Marthe some time later.

And then Bobi had departed to buy the large seeds to sow in our hearts, in ours and in those of others. I mean the others on the plateau. Us up here. And perhaps—who knows?—for the others down there beneath the smoke of the plains. Those who live in the jostling of the roads and the railroads and in towns full of cinders. Yes, he had gone. That was almost a month ago. It was exactly the sixteenth of last month, at six o'clock in the evening. It was already dark and the weather was mild.

Jourdan went into the house. He called: "Marthe!"

"Here I am."

She answered from the storehouse. In there, from the round window, the road could be seen.

"In my opinion," said Jourdan, "he will come in the daytime, and it is getting on toward night now."

"To my thinking," said Marthe coming in, "he will come in the night. He came in the night. He left in the night. He will come back in the night."

"Here," said Jourdan, "put the seeds away."

"You didn't sow?"

"No," said Jourdan; "Madame Hélène interrupted me."

"Did she come to the field?"

"Yes, it was four o'clock. I was just about to begin. She sat down. Then I sat down. Silve's death has touched her very much."

"Me, too," said Marthe. "Especially now that perhaps we are going to end by being happy."

"Why 'perhaps'? It is when a person doubts that it makes everything go wrong. It is not 'perhaps,' it is 'surely.'"

"I do not doubt," said Marthe, "no, ah, no indeed! Because if I doubted…"

"What?"

"Ah, I don't know," she said.

Then she looked out of the window.

"Here is the night. Come and look."

He approached.

"Look," she said, "the narcissi shine. Just the leaves, already."

The narcissus plants, glazed with rich sap, were gleaming on the ground.

"There were already some flowers," he said, "I gave them to Madame Hélène."

"Did you explain to her?"

"Not everything. I told her that I was going to sow periwinkles."

"Here comes someone," she said.

Someone could be heard walking along the road and a shadow moved but was still too blurred and not at all the shape of a man.

"It isn't he," he said; "this one has a stick."

There was a rap at the door. Jourdan went and opened it.

"Is this La Jourdane?"

"Come in," said Jourdan.

"It surely is far," said the man. "I have never come this far before."

He was a dried-up man, of uncertain age, rather oldish, with a white moustache.

"Come in, mister," said Jourdan. "Are you from Roume?"

He remembered having seen him in town.

"Yes," said the man.

"Sit down," said Marthe.

She went and closed the door. She drew a chair near the hearth, where a little spring fire was burning.

"I'll sit down," said the man, "because it is far. I don't advise you ever to subscribe to a daily newspaper."

"Because?" said Jourdan.

"Because I am the postman," said the man. "I came on my bicycle to the foot of the rise. I put my machine in the bushes and I took the shortcut through the forest. Once is all very well, but if I had to do it every day…"

"You'll drink a glass of wine?" said Marthe.

"I won't say no," said the man. "This weather makes you thirsty. Ah," he said, "I mustn't forget…"

He was carrying on his back a big leather satchel. He opened it. He fumbled a moment because he was seeking something very small inside.

"Here."

It was a green telegram.

"Open it," he said. "It's not bad news, but it is rather urgent."

Jourdan bent forward to be lighted by the fire.

"Come to meet me Wednesday evening by road. Wait for me at the Croix-Chauve. Bobi."

"And this is Wednesday evening," said the man before drinking. "That is why I came."

"You see," said Marthe.

"What?" said Jourdan.

"I was right. He will come by night."

"About what time is it?"

"Oh, wait," said the man, "I'll tell you exactly."

He pulled out his watch. He shook it.

"About seven o'clock."

"Then," said Jourdan, "it would be a good idea for me to put on my jacket."

"I'm going with you," said Marthe.

The bearer of the telegram went off toward the left. Jourdan had told him that there he would find a shortcut that was not so steep as the one he came up and easier to find at night. And it was true, but especially since he had read the name "Bobi," Jourdan wanted to be alone with Marthe, alone with the night, alone with his joy.

The night was velvety and liquid. It lapped gently against the cheeks like cloth, then it receded with a sigh and could be heard swaying in the trees. Stars filled the sky. They were no longer the stars of winter, separate, brilliant. They were like fish spawn. There was no longer any form in the world, not even of adolescent things. Nothing but milk: milky buds, milky seeds in the earth, the sowing of creatures, and star milk in the sky. The trees had the strong odour of the time when they are in love.

"How far is it to Croix-Chauve?" said Marthe.

"Five kilometres by the road."

Once, far off in the night, they heard the sound of the pond. It was the murmur of reeds and lapping on the stones. The sound grew fainter and was lost. There was nothing around them but the flat moor. There came the far-away odour of the marshes. The stars were blurred in the east and in the south. At other places they had disappeared behind clouds. The rain walked on the moor. It stirred up the odour of earth, the odour of stone, the odour of bark. It was a fine rain, suspended from the sky like a serpent dancing on its tail. It touched three plants here, three plants there, here a tree, there the corner of a field, there Marthe without touching Jourdan. Then the serpent tumbled down from the sky; the weight of its body crushed the earth, the trees, the dry leaves that carpeted the woods, and it could be heard running before them in the rustling humus of the forest.

The wind was speaking. It was a milky wind like all the rest. It was full of shapes, full of images, of gleams, of lights, of flames that did not illumine a centimetre of the earth but lit up the whole interior of one's being. It swept along with it words, like stones in a mountain torrent, making them ring. It said: "Mountain, ice, resin of the pine trees, valley of the Ouvèze River with water, reeds, the haunts of birds ready for mating; the almond trees at the edge of the plateau are in bloom, the claybanks of Chayes have been set in motion and the clay is slowly flowing toward the valley; I have passed over new clay; there will be young foxes; there were eight foxes, they will at least double in number; the vixen has been calling, calling for three nights but most of all tonight; listen; wait, I'll go look up there"—it climbed up into the night—"up in the sky it is like the vault of a cave, listen, I can strike my head against it, and I turn and roll about in it, and here I am"—it came down again—"a great broad vault, with vast regions below, full of echoes and stirrings, and trees and live beasts, and men walking on the roads and hearkening to me as they go, and that carries them along and reassures them, so that they no longer think of steps added to steps, but, thanks to me, they see the vault of heaven that contains all, and everything is alive and undulating gently in this night like a litter of innumerable piglets beneath the warm belly of the sow."

Then silence.

They were nearing the forest. The leaves had not yet unfolded. The forest did not speak. At its edge, the pale buds of beeches and alders growing in profusion made a phosphorescent barrier across the road.

"The night is soft," said Marthe.

Waves of silence ran over the heath. They came with a drumming of the wind, a pattering of the rain. The water was warm. Two or three drops remained on their faces.

The Croix-Chauve was a cross in the heart of the woods at the intersection of the road and a forest trench. A clearing had been made around it by cutting down the trees. The night was lighted by the milky stars and by the glow of the buds. The forest was a vast structure of pillars and beams. The clouds swept by with the fine rain that hissed like a snake as it wriggled through the branches. One moment they brought opaque shadow. But everywhere, except beneath the cloud, could be seen the scaffolding of the trees, the transparency of the branches that lay, like rafters, from pillar to pillar, although supporting no roof. Between the interlacing foliage persisted the shimmering incandescence of the sky. Then the cloud passed on. The gleaming trunk of a beech could be seen rising close by, then the smooth body of a birch bearing, like a marble column, a frieze of moss at the place where the branches rose from it. Here and there, wherever the whipping rain glazed the alder bushes bright with dazzling buds then went off leaving them glistening, corridors could be seen opening in the edifice of the forest. The breath of distant clearings murmured through them. Deep in the heart of the resounding chambers, a little white willow crowned with leaves was dancing.

"Listen," said Jourdan.

He thought he heard the sound of steps on the road. It was a weasel that was purring in the back of its throat. Then it made a leap among the dead leaves. For a moment not a sound. Then the call of the little female could be heard and the male's smothered purring grew louder and louder.

"It must be after eight o'clock," said Jourdan.

At one time there was no longer either rain or wind, and the warm tranquillity of spring spread over all. The forest glistened. It was everywhere motionless like a block of black stone with glints of quartz. The lights shone down the avenues where only dreams could pass and they disappeared beneath the trees or rose toward the sky.

The whiteness of the broadened road lighted the cross all around.

"Come," said Jourdan.

He was ill at ease, here in the middle of the clearing, listening to the thousand sounds of the night.

He gave Marthe his hand. He helped her to sit down beside him on the bank.

"Sleep if you like," he said.

"I am not sleepy," she said.

But she moved closer to him and put her head on his shoulder.

The wind spoke a long word that was incomprehensible to Jourdan. The beech above the heads of Marthe and Jourdan split the whole length of its bark from the bottom to the tip of a big branch. It scraped against the trunk of a birch beside it. It was a young birch. It bent over more than was necessary. It was swollen with adolescent sap and full of enthusiasm. It passed the word on to some myrtle bushes, to a whitebeam, to a maple, to a little grey oak. And then from there the word flew, making the beams and rafters of the forest ring.

Jourdan felt that the warning was for him also, but he could not understand. He made a great effort. He considered. He thought of the golden signs of that winter night, the third evening when they were returning to La Jourdane in the thick fog. He had tried to read the letters and it was only the door and window of the farm with the fire inside. He thought of the Queen Anne's lace, of the mysterious plants of the heavens about which Bobi was a better countryman than he. He said to himself: "Poor, poor! Here I do not understand." Here were the two of them, he and Marthe, like wretched outcasts. Everything around them understood, from the tiniest plant to the tallest ash, and the animals, and no doubt even the stars, and the earth here under his feet with its clods and its mat of undergrowth and its slender water courses. Everything understood and responded. They alone remained hard and impervious in spite of their good will. They must have lost the fine heritage of man to be so poor, to feel so despoiled and weak and incapable of understanding the world.

Long after the forest, they felt that something had just happened. The forest was already lost in a magic joy. It had begun its nocturnal fête of spring.

"Marthe!"

"Jourdan!"

"Look over there!"

"I see."

"What is it?"

"I don't know."

A beech had suddenly burst its buds and unfolded its leaves, and from black it had become snowy and shimmering.

"It floats!"

"Yes, but look! It stays in one place."

"It is a little tree."

"It wasn't there a minute ago."

"Smell that odour!"

"It is almost a taste," said Marthe.

"It smells like sugar."

"It comes from there," she said, turning her head; then quickly: "Oh, look!"

A maple had just split open its flower buds. It was illumined with a dull glow like a tree of flour. Each time that a bud opened, a little shining spark flew off and the odour of sugar flowed after.

"Look," said Marthe, "that is happening all around us."

Maples were lighting up in all the chambers of the forest. In the luminescence of the opening buds, new halls, new pillars, new corridors, new rafters of branches, became visible.

"The forest is deep," said Jourdan.

"It smells like linden!"

"Look up there," said Jourdan.

"Those are maples," said Marthe.

"No," said Jourdan, "look, that is swelling, it is growing bigger. Look, it goes from one branch to another."

"Look," said Marthe, "it lights up underneath and over there it looks like a cave."

"Lamps!" she cried, pointing with her finger.

The willows were unfolding their leaves, bud by bud, the length of their straight branches. There was only the light of the stars and the light of the buds. But more than all the others, new willow leaves are luminous and each bud cast a light around it on the golden bark of the branch. Thus about the willows there gradually spread a copper-coloured halo.

"Stand up," said Jourdan; "we must look all around."

Everywhere the buds were opening; all the trees were gradually lighting new leaves. It was like the brightness of several moons. A white light for the willow leaves, the maple petals, the leaves of the beech, the poplar fuzz; a golden-brown glow for the birches whose delicate foliage reflected the trunks and was in turn reflected in the bark; a copper gleam for the willows; a pink light for the white-beam and an immense green effulgence that dominated all, the lustre of the dark foliage of the pines, the firs, the cedars.

The odours flowed fresh. It smelt like sugar, the meadow, resin, the mountain, water, sap, birch syrup, bilberry jam, raspberry jelly in which the leaves have been left, linden tea, new woodwork, shoemaker's wax, new cloth. There were odours that walked and they were so strong that the leaves bent with their passage. And thus they left behind them long furrows of shadows. All the rooms of the forest, all the corridors, the pillars, and the vaults, were silently alight and waiting.

On all sides could be seen the magic depths of the house of the world.

They were waiting for the wind.

Then it came. And the forest began to sing for the first time that year.

"Marthe!"

She was already close beside him. She sought shelter against his shoulder.

At that moment he heard his name called by a man's voice that came from the opposite side of the clearing.

"It is the arrival of spring," said the voice.

"Is that you?" cried Jourdan.

"Yes."

He saw Bobi's silhouette standing out darkly against the phosphorescence of the trees.

"Here I am. Wait for us."

A huge shape that was lying in the bilberry bushes and which seemed a part of the ground rose slowly like a piece loosened from the soft spring earth. It was an animal, bigger than a donkey. It walked behind Bobi. It was impossible to tell what it was that was making lights dance about its head. They could hear the movement of its knees and the trotting of its little feet. They guessed that it had horns, but they did not know, for it also seemed to be a gleaming mane.

"What has he brought us?" said Marthe.

"I have found what I wanted," said Bobi, with his loud voice. "I stayed a long time, but now everything can be sown and all will grow fine and strong. As well for us…"

Jourdan thought of the narcissi and then of this forest that was murmuring beneath its heavy constellation of leaves.

"…for us as for the others!" cried Bobi. "You will see how we are all going to be like the springtime. In the whole wide world only men are sad."

He had come up to them. He said: "Good evening, Marthe. Good evening, Jourdan." His breathing was audible, he smelt of corduroy and perspiration. But in replying: "Good evening, my lad," they could not take their eyes from that great form that was following him and that was there now.

It was a creature, half beast, half tree. They could see the gleam of large eyes, gentle but male.

"What is it?" asked Jourdan.

"A stag," said Bobi.

He had broad antlers.

"Only," said Bobi, "I was obliged to look for one that was almost human in order to make a proper mixture, you understand."

"No," said Jourdan.

"What is he doing with his eyes?" said Marthe.

"He is looking," said Bobi. "And look, both of you, see how a thing that is pure and unfettered lights up the darkness. You see his eyes are the same colour as the buds, and see how our sight doesn't help us at all when we are in the pitch-dark amongst the wild things, as if our lids were weighted down with dead stones, because we have lost the joy of the seasons and innocent gentleness. See how his eyes shine!"

The stag did not stir. They could see his broad antlers and beyond, the bright forest.

"He stays with us nicely," said Jourdan astonished.

"That was the difficult part," said Bobi, "for he had no way of knowing that we deserved it. And we have deserved it for too short a time for animals to be aware of it."

"How difficult it is!" sighed Marthe.

"Yes," said Bobi, "but I held all the trumps. Let's sit down a moment; I'll tell you about it."

Seated on the grass, they saw the stag standing before them. He had thin legs, a stout body, waves of hair beneath his belly; his neck was erect, his head motionless, his wide antlers filled with black sky and springtime stars.

"His name is Antoine," said Bobi.

He patted him gently on his rump with his hand.

"Lie down."

The deer lay down beside them. He stretched his head between their feet. His hot breathing warmed Marthe's legs and rose higher beneath her skirts, living, like the rhythmical throbbing of blood.

"Yes," said Bobi, "the difficulty was in finding an animal that would accept."

"I beg your pardon?" said Jourdan.

"Our odour," said Bobi, "it is our odour that disturbs them. We no longer smell like a man or a woman. We smell like a sort of mixture and they have keen noses. I wanted to find an animal that was already used to it but that still had enough of the old freedom. How can I explain? Indulgent," he said, "that's it! Not a slave like a gelding, nor ready for battle like a stallion, but an animal that says to itself: 'You smell bad but I forgive you.' And then one who will be able to appreciate our good odour when we have it."

"Do you think," said Marthe, "that he can recognize it?"

"Like a fist blow on the nose," said Bobi, "that's certain."

Marthe was pleased because the deer was sniffing her. And he was not moving away. And he did not seem disgusted. He was breathing gently and rhythmically.

"Moreover," said Bobi, "the three of us must have an odour this evening that is almost our true one. Spring is in the forest."

"And," said Jourdan, "how did you do it?"

"He was in the National Circus."

"Where?"

"Oh! At Sermoise there is a tiny little circus."

"Did you go by train?"

"No," said Bobi, "on foot. That is what made it so long, but I had to. The tracks I followed were on the road."

The forest was singing. A creature called from the depths of the woods. The voice rolled along its echoes. The deer raised his head. They could hear the scraping sound of his tongue on his lips.

"His name is Antoine," said Bobi. "I have known him for a long time. We have worked together. He used to love to watch me. I used to love to look at his eyes. We have often talked to each other about our mutual desires. I went to get him and he will help us. And now we are all three of us in the forest with him. And already we have lost the hearts of the inhabitants of the valleys. It is night, it is springtime in the trees. The forest is singing."

"Let's listen," said Jourdan.

And all four were silent for a long time. The forest was singing its most solemn song.

~

6

The news had spread.

The deer was at liberty and Friday evening he had trotted as far as Mouille-Jacques. He came to Carle's lucerne field. The son was finishing the irrigating. He had cut off the flow. He was listening to the singing of the last waters among the roots of the lush field. He heard the sound of hoofs. He raised his head. The deer was there within three metres of him and was watching him.

"Good God, I saw his eyes!" he said.

"And what are they like?" said Carle.

"Agreeable," said the son.

"That is…?" said Carle.

"I had been in the lucerne field since noon," said the son.

This piece of Carle's land was a little flat-topped mound, not very high, barely noticeable, but high enough to enable one to see far in all directions.

"The water," said the son, "was flowing all alone. It takes twenty minutes to go from one end to the other, you know. I have timed it, and it has to be done sixteen times, and each time with a wait of twenty minutes. All you have to do is open the sluice gate, stand up and wait. That's all there is to it."

"Then what?" said Carle.

"Then," said the son, "those eyes, that breaks the monotony."

"I have seen the animal, too," said Madame Carle. "I saw it when all at once it began to gallop. It must have been doing it just for the fun of it. It would go away and then come back. It leaped in one spot. I stood watching it for a long time. It is wonderful," she said as she went over to the pot in which the potato soup was boiling.

Carle rubbed his head with the palm of his hand.

"I'm going to see," he said.

"And," said Madame Carle, "I saw the lady of Fra-Josépine."

"Ah," said Carle. "And what then?"

"Well, you know how she talks. I can hardly understand her. She uses extraordinary words, she talks fast, she looks at you in that odd way of hers. I don't know exactly what she did say, but from what I understood, it is just what he told us, Maurice's Jacques. Jourdan has sown flowers. Blue ones and yellow ones; narcissi, she calls them."

Carle rubbed his head. But this time vigorously, as though he were not aware that it was his own head he was rubbing.

"I'm going to see," he said.

Saturday the wind began to boil. It was a very young wind. It carried along clouds, dust, sunshine, shadow, cold, and heat, all together, as in a sack. Then all at once it emptied all that on the earth, and, as soon as all that was liberated, each gently regained its place. It was enchanting to see that stirring of the youth and the vigour of spring.

The stag came out of the shed and sniffed the air. Then he darted straight away, rather fast but not with too great haste. Not as fast as the wind that surrounded him, pushed him, ran ahead of him, and whistled in his antlers as in the rigging of a ship. The stag's path was toward Fra-Josépine this time because the wind was pushing him that way. He saw no one. He went around the house, mounted the wide steps, clicked his hoofs on the terrace, nibbled a little grass that was growing between the tiles, and then went off at a walk toward La Fauconnière, against the wind, tossing his head up and down as if opening a passage through cold bushes that he alone could see.

At La Fauconnière everything was closed since Silve's death and Vignier's departure for Aiguine Mountain. The stag lay down beside a spring in the black grass. He stretched his neck out toward the stream, he began to drink, then tore up mouthfuls of cress and ate and drank all at the same time, dribbling a terribly abundant green saliva. Finally this bothered him and he made a bound toward the sunshine. He had seen a clean place carpeted with warm grass. Here he stretched out like a dead horse, lying on his side, his legs straight out. He slept, then he awoke, but even then he remained still. The gliding of the clouds was reflected in his eyes, the wind gently pricked him beneath his hair. The barbed pistil of a plantain flower settled on his nose and he dared not budge to chase it away. He only twitched his lips.

At noon it was suddenly very hot for the first time. The stag listened. Shouts of a man could be heard toward Maurice's. It was far away. It was like the song of a great bird, modulated and in short spurts. The stag got to his feet. Far off, in the bright daylight, he saw black dots in a field. They must be three men and a horse. He went toward them at his light little trot.

When he came near the field, he saw that they were three men that he had not seen before. One who was old but still very dangerous as to gestures, and with a voice that was obeyed, and then two young ones about the same age. The horse was one of those horses without an odour such as one usually meets on the roads or in the fields. The stag sniffed between his own legs to make sure, then he sniffed toward the horse. Yes, the horse only smelt of hair, sweat, and dung. The three men were making him work. The stag stopped to watch. In the distance was the odour of the farm. The old man smelt of leather and corduroy. He was standing on the grating of the harrow. He held the reins in his hands. He was being pulled along by the horse. He also smelt of an old tooth because he kept shouting with his mouth wide open. The other two men smelt of sweat and earth. They were running along on either side of the harrow. The stag sniffed toward the odour of the farm that came from afar. There were women and children there. But all was dominated by the strong odour of the old man. He was the chief. He was standing on the harrow. The horse was dragging him along. The two men were running alongside. One of the two slept with a woman over yonder. He must be the father of the little children. The other man slept in the loft. But the old man's odour was everywhere. He was standing on the harrow. He held the reins in a firm hand. The field flattened out beneath him. He was shouting.

At the top of the field, they turned the horse and the harrow. The stag stretched his neck and called toward them a friendly little scolding sound. Then he galloped through the sunlight, describing a wide curve around the group of men and the horse. The old man, standing on his harrow, was taller than the others.

After a time, the stag found himself once more at the edge of the lucerne field where he had come the night before. The young man was no longer there. The field smelt strong because it had been watered the day before. The stag again found the print of his hoofs at the spot where he had stopped to watch the young man irrigating. But he also found the tracks of a hedgehog. Then he found the hedgehog, who immediately rolled himself up into a ball. After a moment the hedgehog stuck out his head, opened his little eye, saw the stag, and then unrolled without fear. For he had rolled up without knowing, merely at the noise. And away he went in the grass.

A little farther along the stag found an otter trail. The otters had passed along there two by two. They were going north in the direction from which came the odours of reeds, mud, and sheep. He also found a spot trampled by a heron and a bit of frog's entrails. He heard the kingfisher singing. He heard the lapping of a body of water. He turned his head to look at the lucerne field. He remembered the young man and the eyes he had. Man's eyes, but gentle, and in which he, the stag, had seen his reflection, with his antlers like bare branches on his fore-head. The young man was no longer there. He must be in the farm house. The stag could not be sure, for the odour of that house was the odour of a male horse, a prisoner; the accumu-lated and terrible odour of a horse that has been deprived of its mate for a long time.

Then the stag danced for himself. He was on the barren heath. He felt sad as he thought of the horse. He lifted his feet one after another. He lowered his head, he raised it again. He sneezed. He was sad. The naked land, the spring-time, the absence of females, the horse, the old man, the young man who was irrigating.

He danced the dance of the old man, he danced the dance of the young man with gentle eyes. He danced the unhappy horse and the sad deer. He danced the moor. He danced his springtime desire. He danced the mist and the sky. He danced all the odours and all that he saw, and all that touched his eyes, his ears, his nostrils, and his skin. He danced the world that had thus entered his being. He danced what he would have danced if he had been happy. And he became happy.

He galloped to the pond. He went into the water. He drank. He looked at himself in the water.

He walked in the meadow. He passed beneath a solitary maple tree. Slowly, at a walk, and noiselessly, he approached the fold. He smelt the odour of a ram. With his forehead he tried to push open the door. It was fastened.

He asked the ram through the door: "What news? The mist is warm. The frogs are singing. Who is the horse at the farm? The old man was standing upon the harrow. Spring is here."

The ram got up from back inside the stable and approached the door. No, things were not well. He did not know. He was from the mountains. Here since yesterday. He had come on foot; he was weary. Two days' journey from here the hills are abloom with thyme. Here the grass is rather bitter.

They sniffed at the lock joining.

The deer felt someone looking at him. He drew off. It was a young girl. She had her finger in her mouth. She was twisting her hand in her apron. She did not smile. She did not look surprised. She did not move except for her hand.

He approached her and she did not recoil; she did not cry out. She was not surprised. The stag watched his reflection grow larger in the motionless eyes of the young girl. He stopped one step away from her. She held out her hand. He stretched his neck. He sniffed her hand. At that moment he felt the desire to dance the old wild dance of the stag who has found his mate. However, this was a man's mate, but they all have the same odour.

He drew back his lips. He licked her hand. He licked her wrist, then her arm. He looked at her. She did not move. Again he saw his reflection in her eyes. He was seized with the desire to stand erect and clasp her in his forefeet and bend her to the earth.

She said: "Zulma!"

Then he leaped backward and fled at a gallop across the swampy fields.

At evening he drew near La Jourdane. He saw that the man and Bobi were by the field of narcissi that was all in bloom. He approached at a gentle trot. He stayed beside them. He followed them step by step. The two men had peaceful odours.

Bobi was saying: "It is a beginning. Let's not be in a hurry, everything will come."

The other man said: "Yes, that is sure."

They all three walked toward the house. The door opened. The woman appeared.

"Here he is back again," she said.

"There is no danger of his going away," said Bobi. And he patted the stag on his forehead.

The stag uttered a plaintive sound under the caress. He turned his head away from the field of narcissi that smelt strong.

"He seems to be asking something," said Marthe.

At Fra-Josépine the lights were lit. Madame Hélène had lighted the lamps in the drawing room.

"Why do you want to open the blinds?" she said. "I don't like to stay on this ground floor in the evening, just the two of us alone, if the shutters are open. The French windows open right onto the terrace."

"I should like to open them," said Aurore, "so that we can see the creature if it comes back again."

Madame Hélène looked at her daughter.

"Come here," she said, "come under the lamp. Stoop down so I can see you."

Aurore knelt in front of her mother.

"Look at me. What eyes you have!"

"What's the matter with my eyes, Mother?"

"And what have you done to your hair?"

"I washed it, Mother, and dried it in the sun. It was such a fine day!"

"You have combed your hair in an odd fashion," said Madame Hélène.

Madame Hélène's hair was arranged in flat, regular bands, very smooth, and, with her lovely face, she was immobility personified. The eye of love, but motionless and waiting.

Aurore had brushed all her hair back. The sun had fluffed it, and with her sharp, smooth face, polished by the winds, she personified the speed of a darting bird.

She raised her face. Thus, she was even more rapidly borne among the stars.

"You have taken great pains with yourself today," said Madame Hélène, "and you have not run in the fields, but you have been sitting on the terrace."

Aurore patted her mother's hand to try to make her understand these difficult things: youth, the facts of her being, like dry wood, flames. Sometimes one succeeds in making them understand by patting their hands like that.

"Yes," said Madame Hélène, "today you have taken great pains with yourself. You have put on your silk blouse, your woollen skirt, your shoes that creak. My child, I do not understand," she said, clasping her hands as she saw more clearly the magnitude of her care.

"Mother," said Aurore, "you always are astonished."

There was a sound on the stones of the terrace. It sounded like tiny horny hoofs stepping along lightly, and with it the breathing of an animal.

"No," said Aurore, "that is only the branch of the elm rubbing against the balustrade."

"How quickly you recognize things!" said Madame Hélène.

"Oh," said Aurore, "at first I thought as you did, then I realized. I have been listening to that branch since morning and I soon saw that that was it."

"I thought," said Madame Hélène, "that it was the deer again."

Aurore smiled.

"So did I," she said, "but all day long I thought so. So now I know."

"Stand up, my child."

Aurore stood up and went and got the armchair to sit beside her mother under the lamp and begin the wool work that was the usual task on spring evenings.

"You walk like a boy," said Madame Hélène.

Aurore stopped.

"You walk like a boy and you dance at the same time. And," she said, "you do not realize it. Before your mother that doesn't matter, but before other people it might."

"I do not understand, Mother," said Aurore. "I walk as my legs let me."

She dragged the armchair over. She came and sat down under the tall lamp. She drew up the basket in which lay the wool of three sheep. She began to clean it with the tips of her fingers. She worked with great delicacy, which was natural to her, for she had tapering fingers and a light touch.

The drawing room was peaceful and rustic. It had great solid chairs of wood polished with use and shining as though it were wet. The clock ticked out the slow seconds. A red beet, cut for the soup, was lying on the table.

"Have you been waiting for the deer all day?" asked Madame Hélène.

"Yes."

"Did you watch him a long time this morning?"

"He did not stay long. He danced on the terrace, then he galloped toward the fields."

"It was after that," said Madame Hélène, "that I found you on the stairs in your chemise?"

"Yes," said Aurore.

"You had gone downstairs to see him?"

"Yes," said Aurore.

"Was it you who opened the door onto the terrace?"

"Yes."

"Afterward," said Madame Hélène, "you washed your hair, you put on your silk blouse, your creaky shoes, and you went and sat under the plane trees, and you waited all day long?"

"Yes," said Aurore.

Gently she pulled a little dry straw from a big wad of white wool. She held in her hands the animal's hair, light, warm, and now without blemish.

"He was so beautiful!" said Aurore. "And this spring weather makes you long to be dressed in flowers and to sit and wait."

Over all the plateau trails a reddish fog the colour of the moon. It was very thick toward Maurice's. The son-in-law, who came in first, said: "If this keeps up it is going to freeze."

The old woman said:

"The soup is ready. Where is the master?"

"He is unharnessing," said the son-in-law. "Where is the wife?"

"She is putting the little ones to bed."

The farm hand entered, approached the fire, warmed his hands, drew up the stool, sat down. He tried to look into the pot under the steam to find out if it was potatoes that were boiling, or turnips, or cabbage, or bacon soup.

The old man walked down the hall. He entered. He said:

"Where are my boots?"

"What do you want with them?" said the old woman.

"I want them," he said.

The son-in-law rolled a cigarette.

"They are on the shelf."

The old master went to get his boots.

"And some bacon fat," he said.

"And then what?" said the old woman.

"I'm not asking you anything," he said.

"You asked me where your boots were."

"Yes," he said, "but after that, nothing."

"You asked for some bacon fat," she said.

"I know where it is," he said.

He opened the table drawer, took out the bacon that served to grease the knives. He sat down near the hearth and began to grease his boots.

The young woman came down from the bedrooms. She had just put the children to bed.

"I thought you were eating," she said.

"We were going to eat," said the old woman, "but he is greasing his boots."

"You go along to the table," said the master. "I'll come later."

The two women set the table. The farm hand got up and came and sat in front of his plate. The son-in-law puffed on his cigarette.

"You've time for that tomorrow," said the old woman.

"I want them tomorrow," said the master.

With care he greased the seams of the soles, the uppers, the leg, the straps, the nails, then he threw the rest of the bacon into the fire. It burst into a long, bright blue flame.

He came and sat down at the table.

"Soup," he said, holding out his plate.

He ate his soup.

"Have you seen the animal?" he said.

"What animal?" said the women.

"A deer," he said.

"Jourdan has bought a deer," said the son-in-law.

"No!" they exclaimed.

"Listen," said the master. "Tomorrow morning I am going to see him. Will you come?" he said, turning toward the son-in-law.

"And I?" said the young woman.

"Come along," said the master.

"And the children?" said the old woman.

"We'll take them," said the master. "And you, too. We have only to get out the market cart. Take some ham and some eggs so all six of us won't take them by surprise. Charles will look after the farm."

"Yes," said the hired man, "go along. I'll go next Sunday."

In the region of the pond the haze was lighter. The moon was reflected in the water and there were thus two sources of light.

The otters had discovered a hole where young pikes slept. It was under the black roots of an old willow tree.

They both came together, gliding through the night as through the water, and the brightness of the moon made them shine. The willow was near the sheepfold. The otters stopped before the trampling of the deer. A little farther on they found the odour of the young girl. They recognized it. They were accustomed to finding frequent traces of her across their path, beside it, and around the pond. But here something unusual was inscribed. Nevertheless, they went as far as the water to look. The pike were not asleep yet. They were undulating in the black water. At times, even, there was the flash of an eye or a jaw. It was too early. It was better to find out at once what was marked in the tracks. The otters returned to the sheep-fold. There was a ram inside the door. He called. He spoke loudly. The otters had their night voices for talking among themselves that could be heard by no one except an otter. Besides, the ram talked only the language of the hills and the otters did not even talk the language of the brook or of the mountain stream, where there is an analogy. They were pure Grémone otters and they talked the language of Grémone pond.

But the ram seemed to have been there behind the door for a long time. That proved that there was something new, and they must find out everything. The deer tracks were still warm with scent. The curious thing was that those of the young girl were too. Here they were three metres apart. Here the deer had approached. The girl had not moved. She had only had an impulse to do so. She had bourne down heavily on the tip of her foot with her heel raised, like one who bears the weight of his body forward because his spirit draws him forward and he is about to advance. But she had remained in that spot.

The door of the house opened. There was a light, and a man appeared on the doorsill. The otters glided toward the willow. The pike were sleeping but one could not dive yet.

"It is very light," said the man.

"The important thing," said a woman's voice, "is for the pond to be light. She knew the land roads well enough not to risk anything. What I am afraid of is when the pond is dark. Then she might not see the difference and put her foot in the water."

"Not tonight," said the man. "You can see as plain as at noon, even better."

The man went in and closed the door once more.

The otters plunged. There was hardly a sound. Then they emerged from the water dripping like bunches of grass. Each bore in his mouth a shining pike that struggled and lashed with head and tail.

"No," said Randoulet, "this evening there is no danger."

"Oh," said Honorine, "this is not the first time this has happened, but every time she goes out at night I always wonder if, some evening, she will not do something with all that water, with her dreamy head. That's what worries me."

In the back of the room, which was long and narrow like a corridor, the bed was unmade. There was dry mud on the blanket because Randoulet had lain down fully dressed during the afternoon. He was tired after the long journey behind the flock the day before. He had not even taken off his shoes.

Honorine had prepared the evening meal. She was laying the cloth on a semi-circular table pushed against the wall. She went to the cupboard to get the plates, and each time she disturbed the shepherd, Le Noir, who was seated on a pile of empty sacks in front of the hearth repairing the thongs of a shepherd's whip.

"What are you thinking about?" said Randoulet.

There was a moment's silence, then Honorine said: "Who? I?"

"No," said Randoulet, "Le Noir."

"I?" said Le Noir.

"Yes."

He stopped plaiting the thongs.

"Thinking what, about what?"

"The sheep?"

"They are sheep just like any others."

"The ram?"

"It's a ram."

"Now that spring is here," said Randoulet, "do you think that he will fill the ewes?"

"He will fill them," said Le Noir.

He set to work again plaiting his thongs.

"And the lambs?" said Randoulet.

"There will be lambs," said Le Noir.

"Come," said Honorine, "here is the soup."

Le Noir put his whip in the corner of the hearth, pushed aside the sacks, took the chair, and sat down.

"What do you mean?" he said.

"Nothing," said Randoulet.

He cut some bread into his soup. He opened his knife, wiped it on his trousers.

"If I only knew," he said, "whether we ought to keep the creatures instead of selling them again immediately; if we should keep them a little longer?"

"Just as you like," said Le Noir.

"And what do *you* think?"

"How will you keep them?" asked Honorine.

"What I think," said Le Noir, "is difficult. I must know what you really wish to do."

"Really? What do you want me to say? What I'd like to do is to keep them, have the ewes mated, have lambs, wait. Maybe have another ram, buy him or get him somehow. Maybe wait until a young one is old enough. Mate them again and wait. Well, just keep them!"

"What for?" said Honorine.

"We'd see later."

"Sure," said Le Noir.

"What would we wait for?" said Honorine.

"Shut up," said Randoulet.

"What I want," he went on, "is easy to understand. If you look around here at all that belongs to us, that reaches from the road clear over to the ledge of Chayes; it is all meadow land, the richest on the plateau. Isn't that the truth?"

"Yes," said Le Noir, "except beyond the pond where the grass is chocked with rushes."

"Good," said Randoulet. "But on this side?"

"On this side?" said Le Noir. "I have always told you it was magnificent."

"And how many sheep could that keep?"

"As far as eye could see," said Le Noir.

"Let's not talk about as far as eye can see. You see pretty far. But keeping things human, a hundred and fifty? Two hundred?"

"Five hundred, easily," said Le Noir.

"Well," said Randoulet.

He looked for the salt cellar. He peppered his soup. He tasted it. It was lukewarm. He ate two or three spoonfuls.

"Free sheep," he said; "I'd like to have beautiful animals."

"And," said Le Noir, "have you seen Jourdan's deer?"

"Yes."

Randoulet sat a moment looking into the shadow. There was scarcely a sound in the house, save the sound of the fire. Honorine listened to the men's dreams.

Outside, not a sound. The moon was gliding along the mountains in the west. The otters had gone. An owl was silently watching on the loft pulley. From time to time he would open his red eyes. The pond softly sucked the sands on its little shores. The fields were black. Ploughed land does not let itself be lighted by the moon. Only the grassy banks glistened. The fog had melted. Beneath a flowering almond the fox was licking his paws. Green grasshoppers were singing. They were all motionless on the shaggy thistles that kept the warmth of the day. The grass stretched. A moonbeam was reflected in a long oat blade. The reflection lighted the stony eyes of a grasshopper. The fox stopped licking his paws. He looked at those two tiny golden specks. He crouched, sprang; the grasshopper spoke to him between his paws. The fox saw it light up, then go out. He leaped in the air as if to try to bite the night, then lay down and howled softly.

Far away toward the forest, beyond the road, a partridge heard, woke up, and flew a short distance. He fell back into the grass, slept, re-discovered his fear, flew, fell, slept, and finally remained in the grass, trembling but heavy with night.

Badgers walked in the furrows, dragging their bellies. Beneath the flowering tree the fox had recommenced his leapings after the grasshoppers. The moon was setting in a far-off pass in the mountain.

Some doves that nested in the almond trees near La Jourdane heard a noise. The first to wake up was a dove four years old, with a blue throat, that was already brooding. She laid her head on the edge of the nest and, without opening her eyes, listened. There was a step in the soft earth. She cooed to warn the other nests, two in the same almond tree with hers. Then she opened her eyes, slowly, as if she were afraid of the noise that her little greenish eyelids might make. She saw someone pass along the edge of the field. It was a woman. She could see her plainly. She was between the moon and the dove. In the other nests there were two solitary doves who were resting, heavy with eggs. They did not awake. The dove with the blue throat drew in her head, bent her neck toward the warmth, and fell asleep.

Suddenly the moon disappeared.

The woman was walking toward La Jourdane. She was quite a young girl. She approached the farm house. Everything was asleep. She glided along the shed with its wooden walls.

With her hands she fumbled for a slit. Having found it, she put her face close to it, not to see—it was now black as pitch—but to smell.

The odour that she found told her to go a little to the left. She had to examine in this way five or six split boards before reaching the right one. There, on the other side, slept an animal that woke up and, without getting up, stretched out his neck and sniffed at the crack from the inside. His breathing was audible. His breath was hot. Then the beast dropped his head as if to sleep and his great horns could be heard rubbing in the hay.

The young girl lay down beside the wooden wall of the shed. She laid her cheek against the crack. On the other side the animal had also laid his nostrils and he was breathing regularly hot and cold as he slept.

The girl looked at the stars that were lighting up one by one. And she fell asleep. The breathing of the animal stirred her long lashes.

It was Sunday. Bobi rose at dawn and went up to the loft. The green sky was sparkling with larks. A beautiful day in prospect.

From the great hay window opening onto the wide plateau, one could see the whole green expanse. The meadows and the wheat fields were shining with dew but barred with long black strips of flattened grass; some wide, others narrow; some curved, others straight and darting toward distant goals like the flight of an arrow. They were the paths and tracks of the nocturnal creatures. They crossed, ran side by side, parted, drew together, mingled, separated, branched off toward banks, trees, burrows, nests, dens, or toward the dry bed of the heath where the earth was warm. In some of the tracks the grass was already beginning to stand up again. All these paths were empty.

The day was now steadily growing lighter.

Bobi had been there for some time when he heard the sound of a horn. There were seven or eight notes, long, husky, and sad.

He tried to see through the mist over the grass. Nothing was visible but pink splotches of flowering almonds.

Again the horn sounded. The last note was a melancholy note that evoked the vision of the broad plateau lying helpless beneath the sky.

"The bugle of the beginning," said Bobi to himself.

Once he had taken a trip in the mountains to the east. A comrade had accompanied him who did not know how to do anything but play the bugle. But it was very important. He would stand in the village square and he would begin to blow in all directions. He always repeated the same tune, like this sad horn of the plateau. He would make four quarter-turns on his heels to play to the four corners of the earth. And all the village would come out. Then Bobi would spread the card mat under the "liberty" elm, beside the fountain, and become the human wheel, the human toad, the human sun.

This morning it was impossible to see who was blowing the horn. The mist that was steaming from the grass laid its curtain over all the horizon around. It allowed only the rose of the flowering trees to penetrate. At last it let the distant roof of Mouille-Jacques shine through.

As far as eye could see, the earth was deserted. The grass that was drying from its dew rose slowly, gradually darkening the fields. The tracks of the animals were being effaced. After a moment only the roads of man with their wagon ruts were visible. But the plateau was still empty. No one. Nothing, save the sparkling of the larks.

Then once more came the horn.

This time Bobi saw the brass gleaming through the morning mist. Then, a little later, he distinguished the black form of a man walking across the fields. He was at the edge of the almond orchard. He reached the field of narcissi. The man put the horn under his arm and looked at the flowers. He leaned over to pick some. He put them to his nose. He breathed in their perfume. For a long time he stood motionless with the flowers against his face. Then he put his horn to his lips and he played his slow, sad tune, turning his mouthpiece to the four corners of the heavens as if to call. Then he walked toward the farm. Bobi hid behind the window frame to watch without being seen.

The man approached cautiously. He was distrustful of La Jourdane. He did not wish to be seen, either. He did not wish to wake anyone. However, upon reaching the other side of the narcissus field and a hundred metres from the shed, he once more lifted his horn to his lips and called with his song. But he seemed to be addressing some great living thing beyond the earth and the clouds.

Bobi retreated backward toward the stairs. He went down. Jourdan and Marthe could be heard below. Bobi opened the kitchen door.

"I think people are coming," he said.

"Who?" asked Marthe.

"First a man who plays a bugle."

"Who is it?" said Jourdan.

"Carle's son."

"Well," said Jourdan, "that's amazing!"

"That little one?" said Marthe. "He's a sly one. He never has anything to say."

"And now," said Bobi, "there he is trying to speak with the great tongue."

"I beg your pardon?" said Jourdan.

"Oh! He's found it," said Bobi. "He is talking from afar. He blows into his bugle. He says very clearly exactly what he wants."

"And what does he want?" said Jourdan.

"Like the rest of us," said Bobi. "He's had enough. That's what he said."

He winked.

"Marthe," he said, "this is a beautiful morning."

"Yes," she said.

"Give us—for once—the little glass of brandy."

She went to the cupboard to get the bottle.

"For this morning," said Bobi, putting his arm around Jourdan's shoulder, "we are going to drink for the last time we three."

"What do you mean, for the last time?" said Marthe arresting her gesture. "Are you going away?"

"No," said Bobi, "but we shall scarcely be together any more after this. Even though we are still side by side."

"A body never knows what you mean," she said, and she stood silent and motionless beside the cupboard.

"You are thinking, too," said Bobi to Jourdan, hugging him. "You don't say anything. You don't ask me as usual 'I beg your pardon?'"

"Yes," said Jourdan, "I am trying to think what you mean. And if this is the last time that we drink together I'd rather smash the bottle and the glass at once."

"That wouldn't stop anything now," said Bobi. "Listen, both of you. Once upon a time..." he said, raising his hand in the air.

Something was scratching at the hall door.

"Come in," said Marthe.

A push shook the door.

Bobi went and opened it. It was the stag. The animal's lips were white with saliva. He was whinnying. He tried to get his wide antlers through the door. He stamped on the sill with his hoofs.

Bobi put his hand on his forehead. He pushed him backward and went out with him.

"What do you see?" he said. "What is it that you smell?"

The deer rubbed his nose against Bobi's sleeve.

"There's nothing to get excited about. What are you trying to tell me? Yes, the sky, certainly it is a beautiful sky. Yes, the trees, I've already seen the trees. They are in bloom. Yes, I saw them this morning through the spring mist. Yes, the earth, what do you smell in the earth?"

The deer uttered a long, deep word that made his throat and lips tremble. He uncovered his teeth, breathed a few drops from his nose, opened his blue nostrils, sneezed, and began to walk toward the shed. He looked to see if Bobi was following.

"I'm coming," said Bobi.

He followed.

All at once he noticed that the great April sky also was abloom with thick clouds, dappled and dancing like an orchard in the wind. He had felt the warmth in his flesh, and the sun, risen and already hot, was no longer simply sunshine but a nutriment which was filtering through his skin into his heart, more nourishing than flour and saliva mixed.

He felt almost deer, almost beast. He knew in advance through animal knowledge that where the deer was leading him was deer interest and interest for his, Bobi's, heart, nourished suddenly by the golden flour of the sun.

He had thought of calling Jourdan and Marthe, then he said to himself:

"I'll tell them later. After all, I do not know where he is leading me. What I do know is only that we are beneath the flowering branches of the sky."

"I'm coming," he said.

The deer had turned around, looking at him with his beautiful round eyes, and softly uttered a loving little phrase.

They turned the corner of the shed.

Suddenly Bobi saw the field of narcissi, entirely covered with flowers, and across the field a young girl was fleeing.

He darted forward in pursuit. He heard the four hoofs of the deer dancing behind him, then the rushing of the beast as he gained on him, then the easy little gallop by his side. The deer had thrown back his head, turned up his lips; he was laughing and the wind whistled between his green teeth.

The girl wore wide skirts. She was running fast with strong bare legs. She ran up the bank of the irrigation canal, down the other side, and disappeared.

Bobi reached the summit, running straight ahead. But there was nothing but the deserted plateau with two or three plumes of mist. The deer, rearing on his hind feet, shook his antlers and darted toward the left. Bobi followed. The girl was running over there ahead of them toward the edge of the forest.

Now they could not lose sight of her. They must catch up with her before she reached the trees.

She held her skirts high. She ran as fast as her legs would carry her. Her bare thighs made her white underclothes billow. She turned toward the right. There, was an orchard in bloom. She crossed it. She was running toward that part of the sky where the clouds of a morning storm were piling up. On the bare heath she was alone, white against the deep blue clouds.

She stopped, turned around, put her hand to her heart, and waited.

The deer approached her at a walk with a little ambling gait, nodding his antlered head with its gentle eyes.

As Bobi came up, "You have caught me," she said, "because of my heart."

She pressed her left breast beneath her hand. She was breathing open-mouthed and heavily. Each time that she breathed in, her eyes closed with peace and pleasure.

"Why were you running?"

"I didn't want anyone to see me."

"But people see you just as plainly when you run and then they want to run after you and catch you."

"If it had not been for my heart," she said, "I should be far away."

She was in fact the very image of speed, with smooth flesh and all her hair thrown back and foaming like dust that is raised in the path of a powerful storm.

"One can go very far even with one's heart," said Bobi.

He had his fine man's eyes. He felt that their light increased and sprang from him, brilliant and pure.

"Do you want to come back?" he said.

"Now that I am calmer, yes," she said.

He held out his hand. She took it. They turned back toward the farm.

For a moment the stag remained motionless. He took several steps forward, straight ahead, in the direction of their flight, toward the stretch of plateau, the woods, the horizon where, beneath the storm, the distant landscape trembled. Then he turned, pawed the ground, and followed the man and woman. He walked with his head down, his antlers tearing at the pale tips of the weeds.

"My name is Aurore," said the girl.

"And mine, Bobi," he said.

"Was it you who brought the deer?"

"Yes, he belongs to me. You make me express myself badly," he added. "He is not mine, he is ours. Yours, too. Everybody's."

They were holding each other's hand. They were walking with the same step. They were swinging their joined hands.

"I got up early to come and see him again," she said. "I thought of him all night long."

"You have seen him before?"

"Yes, yesterday. In the morning. He came, he put his head beneath the branches of the willow that are already in leaf, he looked all about him. He leapt on the terrace. I was watching him from my bedroom window. This morning I got up early to wait for him."

"Were you already up when someone played the bugle?"

"Yes. I had already been waiting some time. And under the willow the shadow was still very black, and I imagined that the deer was there in that shadow waiting for the first ray of sunlight to pass through the branches, when I heard the bugle."

"Ah," said Bobi, stopping for an instant the swinging of his arm, "tell me more; that interests me."

"I thought: The deer will not come."

"Why?"

"What that one was playing was sad...."

"Yes, but it was sad and broad," said Bobi. "That is to say, it was exactly like this plateau and it had as many wide open roads that penetrate the sadness and the breadth. And, in fact, all of a sudden that made me think that on one of those roads or perhaps on all, one could find joy. And then it made me feel as though I'd like to set out; that perhaps joy was above the earthly roads like a rainbow, and that it strides over them all and that when one does not see it, it is only because one is badly placed. It is enough then to walk to the spot where one will be in the rain, beneath the shining rain, don't you think so?"

"I don't know," she said, "I just had time to get a scarf—and I lost it just now among the narcissi when I began to run—I crept softly downstairs and I came here."

"You are the young lady of Fra-Josépine?"

"Yes."

"I know all the others on the plateau, but I didn't know you. By sight," he added, "because, in fact, Jourdan has spoken to me of you."

"And you didn't know me as I am?"

"No," he said.

At this moment he felt the little hand in his. It was warm and smooth. The skin rather soft. The fingers pliant and tender like little alder branches. He examined the hand, the wrist, the arm, the shoulder, then the face. Her eyes were violet and misty and the border of the eyelids was of a sand-like purity.

"Usually people do not like me," she said.

"Why say *usually*? For," he continued, beginning to swing her little hand again, "if one person doesn't like you, if two, three, fifty do not like you, the one who comes after the fifty will perhaps find reason to like you, and when you go away with him into the wide world you will no longer think of the fifty, but only of him, and you will say: Usually people like me."

"I don't know," she said. "The more you talk, the less one understands."

"I always thought they understood me better," he said angrily.

"No," she said, "but it is pleasant to hear you talk. It isn't necessary to understand. One just listens. Do you know me better now?"

"Yes, and what about me?"

"I do not know you at all," she said.

"I am the man with the deer."

"That's so," she said, "the deer, I had forgotten him."

They were nearing the farm house. The young bugler was making signs to them. At the same time he was motioning them to approach without making any noise. He was near the shed. He was looking at something on the ground.

"This is the morning for the young girls," said Bobi in a whisper.

It was another girl. She was lying near the wooden side of the shed, her cheek against a crack in the planks.

"It is Zulma," said Aurore. "I know her. She is beautiful."

"Yes," said Bobi, "she is asleep. God bless her!"

"I got this far," said the young bugler. "I saw her. I've been watching her sleep."

"You are Carle's son?" said Bobi.

"Yes."

"I remember having seen you, the day your father showed me his stallion."

"So do I," said the boy. "I remember."

"We mustn't wake her," said Aurore. "Look, she has a lovely smile on her lips."

"She is Randoulet's girl," said the boy. "It doesn't often happen that she laughs."

"Then come," said Bobi. "But how is it that you are here, you three?" He had taken the boy's arm. He still held Aurore's hand. "One who plays the bugle at dawn, one who runs and holds her heart, one who sleeps on the hard ground with a smile?"

"I have come to see the deer," said the boy. "Where is he?"

"He was following us," said Bobi. "He must have gone to see Marthe. This is the time when she gives him bread. Come."

As they approached the house they heard gay voices. Old Jacquou from Maurice's had just arrived with the whole family: the old woman, the young one, the son-in-law, and the two little ones.

"The hired man stayed behind to look after things," he was saying as he descended with dignity from the wagon, "but he will come next Sunday."

"That was a good idea of yours," said Jourdan. "It's the kind of idea you had the time we went together to buy cows at Aiguines."

"Time has passed," said Jacquou. "We are getting old."

"No matter," said Jourdan, "since, you see!…And then, you others, you must get down from the wagon and come into the house, Barbe, Joséphine, Honoré, and the little ones. I think that this is where you were bound? Yes? Then what are you doing up there?"

Old Jacquou wore his Sunday and holiday manners. He was more ponderous than usual on those days. He had the appearance of weighing down very heavily on the earth. Old Barbe took a thousand precautions in descending from the market cart.

"I'll help you," said Bobi. "Wait."

He dropped Aurore's hand and the boy's arm.

"He still held me by the hand," said Aurore to herself. "Here, in front of everyone."

She rubbed her hand on her skirt.

"His arms are like iron," said old Barbe.

He had just lifted her gently to the ground.

"You weigh as much as a grasshopper," he said.

"What a crowd!" cried Marthe from the doorway and the came forward.

"Give me your hand," said Bobi to Joséphine.

"Oh! Young lady," said old Barbe, "you are already here! And Madame Hélène?"

"She's coming," said Aurore.

She thought: "When she sees that I have left the house, she'll come."

"She's here," said Marthe.

"Who?"

"Your mother. She's been here for a full hour. She is drinking coffee. Come, Barbe. How long it's been since the last time! Come, Mademoiselle Aurore. Jourdan, you look after the men."

"Joséphine," said Barbe, "bring me my hood. It is on the seat."

"Well?" said Jourdan to Jacquou.

"Well!" said Jacquou to Jourdan.

And their glances ran slowly over the flat country. Joséphine leaned her shoulder heavily against Bobi. Bobi had clasped her around the waist, lifted her from the wagon, and placed her on the ground.

"There," he said.

"Thank you," she said.

She shook out her skirt and drew her blouse down tight over her bosom.

"Are you coming?" cried Barbe to her as she was about to enter the house. Aurore followed them. She was saying to herself:

"My mother is here already. She's been here an hour. She came without telling me."

She examined Joséphine. She thought her very womanly, at a great advantage physically.

"She is as tall as Bobi," she said to herself. "She is plumper than I. Her cheeks are more tanned than mine."

She felt the warmth of Bobi's hand in hers.

"To think," she said to herself, "that we walked in step with each other, swinging our hands."

"Come in, Mademoiselle Aurore," said Marthe.

She looked at Bobi before going in. He was laughing with the children. Joséphine was watching him. She was standing erect beside him, with her well-rounded woman's bosom and her curved hips.

"Joséphine," cried Marthe, "come and get some hot coffee."

Joséphine approached with a long step that was like a peaceful dance.

Honoré was rummaging in the wagon box.

"We've invited ourselves," said Jacquou.

"You did well," said Jourdan.

"We brought a hare," said Jacquou.

"That was wrong," said Jourdan. "We would have made out."

"It is better not to have to make out," said Jacquou, "but to find everything arranged. We couldn't drop in on you, all six of us like that, without warning and without bringing anything."

"Help me, Jules," said Honoré to Carle's son. "Take this."

He held out a hare. It was not bloody but clean and neat, and all solid like animals caught in nets.

"If I had known," said Carle's son.

"What?" said Honoré.

"I think that my father is coming."

"Well, then," said Honoré, "he shall eat with us; so much the better. Wait, there's still the ham. And the wine, Father? Where did you put it?" he called to Jacquou.

"In the wagon box," said Jacquou.

"It isn't in there."

"Why wine?" said Jourdan.

"To drink," said Jacquou. "Look in the bottom; the bottles are under the straw."

"Well," said Bobi to the children. "Soon I'll show you the big animal. He has a sort of tree planted in his head and he is so gentle that you'll want him to lick your faces. And the best thing," he said, "is that he does it."

The children looked at him without saying a word. Then they ran toward the house.

"Look," Jourdan said to him, "see all they've brought."

They had laid the hare on the grass, stood the bottles in a row, placed the ham and the three big fat sausages beside them. Honoré was still searching in the box, pulling the straw about.

"There's enough here for a week," said Bobi.

"Nothing would suit us better," said Jacquou with a wink.

He passed his hand over his moustache.

"And why not?" said Bobi. "One only has the time one takes for one's self."

Jacquou became serious.

"What is all this they've been telling me?" he said.

"What can they have been telling?" said Jourdan.

"You have sown flowers?"

"I'll explain to you," said Jourdan.

Honoré straightened up.

"I can't find it," he said.

"What?"

"The big round bottle."

"It must be there," said Jacquou.

"It isn't there."

Jacquou climbed up on the edge of the wagon with the movements of an old man slightly stiff but still commanding.

"Let me see."

"Where is the deer?" asked Bobi.

"He was here," said Jourdan, "and he ate his bread. But when he heard the noise, he went out by the back door."

"Barbe!" cried Jacquou.

He was standing on the wagon rail and was very angry.

"What?" replied Barbe from inside the house.

"Did you forget the big round bottle?"

"No," replied Barbe. "There wasn't any more room. I poured it off into quart bottles. They are there."

Jacquou and Honoré jumped onto the grass.

"That's right," said Honoré, "there's the wine and here is the brandy. If we had looked we'd have found it."

"Honoré," said Jourdan, "unhitch, put the mare in the shed. The oats are in the box at the left."

"Yes," said Honoré, "and in the meantime get me a pointed knife. I'll skin the hare when I get back."

He took the mare by the bridle and turned her around.

"Are you going to roast it?" he said.

"Of course," said Jacquou.

"The best thing," said Bobi, "would be to set that up outside."

"Yes," said Jourdan, "I think Marthe must have her idea about the indoors. She is not going to let you do everything, and we also have Madame Hélène, and you, Carle, you are staying."

"If you like," said the boy with the horn. "And my father will be here soon. He said so."

"We'll make him stay," said Jourdan. "Listen, go around back there…"

"I'm coming back," cried Honoré as he was leading away the mare and the cart. "Get the knife ready."

"You go around back there by the old stable and bring some stones; we'll make a fireplace."

"Leave your bugle," said Bobi.

"I'd forgotten about it."

"Oh," said Bobi, "you mustn't forget it. Put it beside the bottles."

"Which direction is the wind coming from?" said Jacquou.

"From the forest."

"Here's where we'll make the fire," he said, tracing a square with his foot.

"I'll go get the knife," said Bobi, "and see if Marthe wants me to help her."

"Well," said Jourdan, slapping Jacquou on the shoulder, "you can't think how happy I am!"

"Yes," said Jacquou, "and that is just what I want to talk to you about."

"Marthe," said Bobi, "I need a pointed knife."

"Ah, here he is," said Madame Hélène. "I have not yet seen this young man. You have spoken to me about him, but it is better to see him. He isn't old at all."

"He gave me his hand a little while ago," said Aurore to herself, "and we walked in the fields. His arm is firm and light."

It seemed to her that that hand was now very far away, that never again would he look at her with his clear, gentle eyes, and that he would never again fall into step with her to walk far from everyone, she and he alone.

"Look in the drawer," said Marthe; "there must be one there."

"I'm going to put on an apron," said Joséphine.

"I'll pluck the chickens," said Barbe, "but to do it quicker, I must scald them. Have you some hot water?"

"What are you going to do about the fire?" said Marthe, looking at the fireplace.

"You use this one," said Bobi. "We are going to build a fire outside for the hare and the sausages. The knife is not here."

"You can't find anything."

"Men never can find anything," said Joséphine.

She was laughing; she had a large, healthy mouth and wide teeth; the swelling of her lovely throat rounded out the soft column of her neck.

"They find," said Bobi, "but at the right moment."

"They find," thought Aurore.

She was sitting in the shadow and was gently smoothing her thighs through her skirt.

"…he found my hand, he caught up with me and found me in the fields. They find at the right moment."

She thought he had said that for her. For her alone and he had looked at her as he said it.

"But we are not going to stay," said Madame Hélène, standing up. "You have quite enough to do."

"Yes, you are," said Marthe approaching her. "Yes, do us this pleasure and do yourself this pleasure, too," she said laughing.

"It is true that it would be a pleasure for me," said Madame Hélène, "but nothing had been decided about it."

"Nothing is ever decided in advance," said Bobi, "and then it happens. Stay, Madame. Carle is coming. We shall be almost all here together."

"Carle is coming?" asked the women.

"His son said he was coming."

"This *is* a celebration!" said Barbe.

"And my knife?"

"Here it is," said Marthe. "It was under the spinach. I cut some this morning by chance."

"Then set me to work, too," said Madame Hélène.

"There are enough of us," said Joséphine. "You can look on."

She made one feel that she could do everything alone, and do it well. She had tied a large napkin around her waist and had hidden her hair beneath a cap made of two twists of a scarf. Her face was well formed, round, gay, and firm, of generous proportions and very human.

"No," said Madame Hélène, "I want to work. Give me the spinach; I'll clean it; and give me the vegetables, too."

Bobi went over to Aurore.

"Get your feet warm," he said.

"I am not cold."

And she had to look up at him, for he was standing and she was sitting down.

"Yes," he said, "you walked in the wet grass."

"*We* walked," she said. "You did, too."

"Yes, but I am huskier," he said. "Stretch your legs out to the fire."

She did not want to do it. She wanted to go against his will. Not to do as he told her, since he no longer walked in step with her.

He stooped down. He took off her little socks. He touched her bare feet.

"You are cold and wet."

He placed her feet on the edge of the hearth.

"Stay there like that," he said.

She stayed there. She looked at him with eyes that thanked him for having come back and for having given to another part of her the warmth of his hands. But he had already turned away.

"This makes one want to sing," said Madame Hélène.

The fire purred. Marthe brought some large pieces of wood. Barbe looked to see if the water was boiling.

"Come here," Joséphine said to Bobi.

She constantly put herself directly in front of him with her plenitude of sun-browned woman, and she looked him straight in the eyes with a smile.

"Get me that basin up there, you who are so tall."

She was commanding him and he was obeying. It was scarcely worth while to warm one's feet at the fire. However, Aurore did not move. It was nice to obey him just the same.

The bugle sounded outside. The same phrase as in the morning, but this time livelier and as if the whole wide plateau had begun to undulate and ripple like the sea beneath the wind.

"What is it?" said Bobi going out.

The spring morning, bluish with the storm and all splashed with sunshine, was swaying the trees. The birds flew over in flocks. The wind, full of shadows, bent down the grass.

"Here come some others!" cried Honoré.

"It is Randoulet," said Jourdan.

"Well," said Jacquou, "he ought to have brought a kid. The pieces of hare are going to be small."

Randoulet's covered wagon had just emerged from the orchard of flowering almonds. It had hesitated a little in the fresh furrows but now that it had the hard stubble beneath its wheels, it came at a gallop. Randoulet's arm was swinging the whip.

"Blow," said Jourdan.

Carle's son put the horn to his lips. The women came to the door.

"Who is it?" asked Joséphine.

Marthe shaded her eyes with her hand.

"Randoulet," said Jourdan.

"We are arriving with the storm," shouted Randoulet.

"Not so fast," said Jourdan. "Stay over there to unharness. The spit is already being set up out here."

"Then come and get the bundles," said Randoulet.

"Have you brought a kid?" asked Jacquou.

"I've got one," said Randoulet. "Get busy, you, Le Noir," he said to his shepherd. "I am going to see the others. Unharness the horse. Are you coming, Carle?"

"Is Carle with you?"

"He is in the back of the wagon. Hey, Carle!"

"Here I am," said Carle. "I am all mixed up with the baskets and bottles. Wait till I get untwisted."

"I have a kid," said Randoulet; "it is all ready, all covered with strips of bacon, and rolled up in its hide. All you have to do is to put it on the spit."

Marthe hailed him from the door.

"Is Honorine there?"

Honorine was helping Le Noir unharness the horse.

"Come," Marthe called to her, "leave the men's work. There is women's work here. Bring her in."

"We have lost Zulma," Honorine said to Jourdan.

"What do you mean?"

"Since last night."

"She is here," said Bobi.

"Have you see her?"

"I have seen her. She was sleeping. Don't worry."

"To tell you the truth," said Randoulet, taking Bobi by the shoulder, "I have come to see your deer."

"Don't let's mix things," said Bobi. "Now is the time for cooking. The rest will come later."

"What *is* coming," said Le Noir, "is the storm."

A blue mountain was gliding slowly down the sky and the wind spurted beneath it. It had begun to put out the sun.

"It is only going to be a hail storm."

"The sun is behind it."

"What shall we do?"

"We'll put the kid here on the spit," said Jacquou, "here with the hare, all on the same one. We'll make a fire. And for the sky to put it out, it will have to be a big sky. I'll watch the spit. And for the sky to snatch it away from me, it will have to be a mighty sky. The young ones will have to step lively! We old fellows are still sturdy! Light the fire."

"We met Carle on the road," said Randoulet. "He owns the sire of the horses. He was walking."

"That was wrong," said Bobi.

"So we said to him: Get in, we're going, too."

"The son left early with his bugle."

"Get to work," said the boy. "Instead of talking, *I* am carrying wood. You go get some wood, too."

They had made a hearth with huge stones. Jourdan measured two paces.

"My spit is two paces long."

"That is too long," said Jacquou, who was putting on the wood a piece at a time, as he watched the draught. He had pushed back his hat off his forehead and his tie of silk twist was undone.

"No," said Randoulet, "we'll put the kid in the middle and the hare on one side and the sausages on the other."

The fire flamed and had just begun to leap to all sides of the stone hearth when a heavy rain was heard beating the drum in the flowering trees.

"Ah!" said Le Noir, and he pointed his finger toward the pale heart of the storm.

It grew visibly larger, round and heavy and white like a millstone. It was coming upon them at full speed.

"The spit," said Jacquou.

"Here," said Jourdan.

"The kid," said Jacquou.

"Here," said Randoulet.

"Put it on the spit."

Disturbed by the growing darkness, Marthe had come to the door.

"Come in, men!" she cried.

"No," they said all together.

"The hare," said Jacquou.

"Here it is," said Honoré.

He had just skinned it and emptied it with swift hands. His fingers were sticky with blood.

Jacquou struck the fire. It lay in blazing embers. Two little blue flames hissed on either side of the hearth. Jacquou killed them beneath his heel.

"Lay on the spit. Leave the wood in a dry place; we'll go get it as we need it. There," he said, "now if you want to get under shelter, go along. *I* am going to stay."

"We'll all stay," they said.

"All's well with the world," said Bobi.

"That depends on what you mean," said Le Noir.

And just at that moment he pointed to the granite heart of the storm that was falling straight down from the heights of the sky, and suddenly they were all lashed by stiff rain and the wind pushed against their backs, raised the dust, bore off the hot embers on its wings, made the larding pin sing as it trembled beneath the weight of the kid. The thick odour of damp earth.

Jacquou leaned back.

"Some dry wood," he said.

He had turned his back to the wind to protect the fire that the wind was trying to lift and carry away.

"The kid!" said Jourdan.

"Let it be," said Bobi; "the rain gives it a flavour."

He was dishevelled and smiling and his eyes were terribly clear.

The women cried: "Come inside, you fools!"

But a gust of wind slammed the door upon them. Through the window, only a face was visible; they did not know whose. The woman was beckoning.

"No," said the men, "what of it?"

Their faces were all oiled with the rain.

The two Carles, father and son, came running to bring the dry wood. They threw it on the fire and suddenly a flame shot up, thick, lush, red as blood, as if one of the earth's arteries had just been cut. But they needed a great deal of wood. The two Carles had set off again at a run; Jourdan, too, and Bobi, Le Noir, Randoulet.

Jacquou lifted off the spit. For the moment it was a question of conquering, of making the flame rise, of showing that nothing rules—neither storm, nor sky, nor women—when man wills.

Le Noir threw a great armful of wood on the fire. The flame leaped upon it. Honoré cast on his armful of wood. Then

Jourdan, then the Carles, then Bobi. The flame hissed like a serpent that is put into a cage. Then it howled. It darted out its tongue, opened its blue jaws, and crushed the wood in its wide, soft, bleeding lips. It began to sing in the rain the song of the fire.

The men drew back.

The storm turned and was carried toward the southern horizon. It began to roll in distant echoes, crushing the farm lands in the plain, from which suddenly arose the odour of vegetables. It rolled over the hills and through the pine woods. There came the odour of resin. At last it disappeared, boiling down through a gorge at the far end of the valley. Now it made only a faint echoing sound like the rumbling of an empty cart over a stony mountain road. The sun came out once more. The sky was washed and alive with little daisy-coloured clouds. The trees sighed. The tiles of the house roof moaned. A dove cooed. The wind took two or three more steps, then lay down in the grass. Its long silent limbs flattened the grass and it stayed there, exhausted and all golden, suddenly fallen asleep, with just the peaceful breathing of some fair labourer who smiles in his sleep.

The door opened. The women came out of the house. The sun made the wet faces of the men glisten. They had a sort of rainbow in their beards, in their moustaches, in their hair, and in the down of their cheeks.

"Well, you bull-headed fellows?"

"We won!"

"What good does that do you?"

"We won."

"You are soaking wet."

"We'll dry off."

"The idea! And stubborn as billy-goats! Just look at you!"

"This is the life!"

The women all had magnificent eyes, a little larger than usual and full of colours, for they reflected the faces of the men.

"And now," said Jacquou, "we're going to do the cooking."

Again he began to beat the fire to make slow embers. He laid on the spit with the help of the two Carles and Honoré.

The women looked at the sky.

Aurore came up to Bobi.

"You are wet," she said.

"And you," he said, "are your feet warm?"

"I am warm," she said, "I obeyed you. *You* obey *me* and come dry your head."

He looked at her with eyes grown sad. He said to her:

"Come with me. We'll see if the horses were frightened."

And they went toward the shed. He took her by the hand and began to walk as in the morning when they returned from their chase.

"He must be Italian," said Madame Hélène. "See how smooth and pure his forehead is and then that mouth with dimples on each side according to the words he pronounces, and those little, thin lips."

"He's a handsome man," said Joséphine. "He has broad shoulders."

She put her two hands around her waist. She felt naked in her clothes, naked and firm, with a softness in her inner-most being, from looking at that man. She was a handsome woman.

"Wait," said Bobi.

They had turned the corner. They were alone. The horses were quiet in the shed.

"You have told me to obey you and you have said to dry my hair."

"Yes," she said.

She was a trifle shorter than he; she stood with her back against the wall, he in front of her, their arms hanging, for he had let go of her hand. And he was stooping over a little from his shoulders.

"No one has ever looked after me," he said.

She looked at him without replying.

"I have always been alone," he continued, "and it has always been I who have looked out for others. You are scarcely more than a little girl and there are many things that you do not know. But you have just said some words and made a little gesture, the movement of your hands toward my hair, as if to dry it yourself. And that, no one has ever done. And here I am facing a new thing. I have always been alone, always. And it is always I who have tried to dry the hair of others, do you understand? When my head was wet, I knew that nobody cared, do you understand? And that was bitter, do you understand?"

She lowered her eyes.

"I have tried," he said, "to make companions of all the things that do not usually count. I may seem a little crazy to you and I must be a little crazy. I have gradually made a companion of everything that will accept friendship. I have never asked anything of anyone because I have always been afraid of being refused, and because I fear affronts. I am nothing, do you understand? But I have asked a great deal of the things about which one does not usually think; of which one thinks, Mademoiselle, when one is really alone. I mean the stars, for example, the trees, the little creatures, so tiny that they can walk for hours on the tip of my finger. You see? Flowers, countries, and all that is in them. In short, of everything except other men, because, in the long run, when one is used to talking to the rest of the world, one acquires a voice just a little difficult to understand."

She looked at him with her eyes gleaming with their violet lights.

"I understand," she said.

He took her hand.

"Do you understand, Mademoiselle, that if I have asked for nothing, it is not because I have not needed it? Do you understand, too, that if I have always given, it is precisely because I was so in need myself?"

"Yes," she said, "I understand, but only in part. And what I understand best is that you are talking to me and that your head is still wet from the storm, that you have not obeyed me, that you are not drying your hair, and that you are going to catch cold, especially here in this draught blowing between the barn and the shed."

"That is so," he said. "You are right; one should do things simply."

She untied her apron and he dried his hair on the wrong side of the linen garment. The cloth was warm.

Jacquou had succeeded in mastering the fire, in conquering the spit that was turning round and round, in dominating the women (they had returned to the kitchen), in bossing the men (he said to them: "Baste the bacon"; they spooned up the juice in the dripping pan and basted the bacon. He said to them: "Some wood"; they went and got some wood. If he said nothing to them, they stood there watching the revolutions of the kid and the hare that were already golden brown like suns). He must also have succeeded in mastering the weather. There was no longer a trace of the storm. There was now a great clear sky such as one sees in the late spring toward the end of the morning. The shining green fields, stretching far in all directions about the farm house and the men, were sparkling like water.

Jacquou, seated near the fire, was listening to the big iron spit that was gently creaking beneath the weight of the meat.

Jourdan, on his knees, was watching the cooking. The flesh of the kid had at that moment split at the shoulder. It was like a mouth with a whole lining of raw meat inside. This slit had opened with a click and immediately the two lips of thin skin had begun to sputter with the odour of burnt milk. Jourdan took the ladle and poured juice into the hole.

"That's right," said Jacquou.

"Have you stuffed it?" he asked Honoré, pointing to the hare.

"Yes."

"What with?"

"The liver, and the liver and heart of the kid, half a sausage, and some chopped meat," said Carle's son.

"Yes," said Honoré, "some chopped spinach, too."

Randoulet looked at the fire. Perspiration was running off his face. He wiped the sweat. He began to perspire all over again. He could not help following the slow revolutions of the spit which carried the viands toward the fire (and they could be heard sputtering and crackling), then turned them toward the fresh air of the fields (and the wind, perfumed with narcissus and the flowering trees, could be seen passing over them). Randoulet was a fat man with three chins and a paunch that discouraged belts.

Carle rolled a cigarette.

"Some wood," said Jacquou.

Carle went to get some wood. He moistened his cigarette with his tongue.

Le Noir looked at the sky. No, now there was no longer any bad weather in the offing.

A woman was singing in the kitchen. It must be Joséphine.

"On July twenty-ninth
At the cutting of the wheat,
There came a young girl to me
Bearing flowers in a sheaf.
She was not a city maid,

But her body, regally,
Like a jonquil gently swayed,
And all the goodness of her heart
Was breathed from her lips apart."

Bobi came up. He saw the men gathered around the fire. Carle was returning with his arms full of wood.

"Go and get some more, you," said Jacquou.

Carle's son went off toward the woodpile. Randoulet watched the spit turning. He was still perspiring and he wiped himself with the palm of his hand. Jourdan, ladle in hand, was watching the slits in the roast. Jacquou put the wood, piece by piece, into the little white valleys of the fire and he put several very dry fragments on the red summits that burst into flames. The meat began to sputter. Jourdan recoiled, covering his eyes with his hand.

The men had dried off in standing around the fire. They smelt of damp cloth and hair. They were still steaming a little at the edges of their trousers. Bobi thought of Aurore's apron with which he had dried his hair and neck. A warm apron because she had had it tied around her body.

"Gently put her mouth
Upon my brow…"

sang Joséphine. Then she could be heard pounding with the chopper on the pieces of chicken that had been dipped in boiling water (for the women had decided to make a fricassee), and only scattered words of the song came through:

"Made me a star…my heart…my sorrow…love."

At last the women sang the chorus together. Marthe sang the alto, Madame Hélène the soprano, Barbe the falsetto,

Honorine the monotone, and high above them all, because of its freshness, danced Aurore's voice.

"Ah; fair maid, tell me the truth,
Even if for all the world
It is a lie,
I will believe it."

"They are singing," said Jacquou.

It was a strange event.

"That's so," said Randoulet.

And Carle, who was returning with the wood, said, too: "Have you heard?"

Randoulet cleared his throat. His three chins trembled and he stood up on his short legs and turned toward the house as he opened his mouth. The others knew what that meant.

"No," said Jacquou, and he raised his hand. "Listen, we've already had the storm but it was all right; it was just before we began to cook. Nothing was in danger of being spoiled. Now, if you sing, the sky will grow dark, the earth will dance, the lightning strike, and we still need a good fifteen minutes of fair weather for the meat to be well done. You can sing after we eat."

"Oh," said Randoulet, "I just wanted to help them with the chorus of 'The Pretty Drummer Boy.'"

"Yes, all right," said Jacquou, "that would have been enough."

"Well," said Randoulet, "if a person hasn't the right to sing!"

"But you *do* have the right," said Jourdan. "Sure you do. Only just wait. Look. You opened your mouth. Look and see if we are lying. There are some plovers already."

Three plovers, fringed with red, passed across the sky.

"There, you see."

"No, but the fine thing about it," said Bobi, "is that one wants to sing. That's the great thing. What do you think?"

He looked from one to another, a glance for each. He saw in fact that they thought it was a fine thing. He also saw that all at once they were a little afraid and they looked at the plateau, the earth, the world. Everything was indeed still the same, but there was a fine thick field of narcissi all in blossom and another field with periwinkles; the air was thick with this perfume, the morning was all sweetened with it, and the usual aspect of the earth was completely changed by this sudden beauty. Far beyond lay the greyish fields and the enclosing line of the horizon.

Randoulet wiped his brow. He went up to Bobi.

"What about the deer?" he said.

"Yes," thought Bobi, "that's so."

"Ah," said Randoulet, "I must have a talk with you about that. The deer has given me some ideas. I have been thinking things about the sheep, about animals, about the earth, my pasturage, my grass, in short, you shall see."

"What you ought to do," said Jacquou, "is to set up a table. Outside there it is going to be shady, we'll be very well there. You'd think the weather had been made to order."

"How soon will it be ready?"

"It will be done in a quarter of an hour."

"And the women?"

"Ask them."

"Women!"

"We have names!" they cried.

Jourdan and Jacquou looked at each other and smiled.

"It's always the same," said Jourdan, "when they are together, they get independent."

"What do you want?" cried the women.

"When will you be ready?"

"We'll be ready right away."

"Then," said Jacquou, "that means that we have time to set up a table. Get about it, young ones."

Marthe approached.

"Come here," she said to Bobi.

And she scolded him.

"For," she said, "I do not say that you knew about it this morning, but now, you should have thought about it, you and Jourdan. First you and then he. Go change your shirt. Go put on a shirt that is a little cleaner. Go put on your light blue shirt. And then afterwards I'll make him go too. I do not like it. We are all going to eat together, I want you to be clean, both of you. Get along!"

The women were eager for all to look well and they went into little details. It was clear now how the day was being organized, as when one begins to build a house: at first there is just a pile of stones, a heap of sand, then a square ditch dug out of the ground, then a wall that is on the level with the soil and that is the foundation. Then the walls rise, then they are covered with a roof, the windows open, the partitions cross, and henceforth it is a place where one can live, with rooms to the north, rooms to the south, corridors in which the east wind sings, and of the four master walls, when midday comes, two are in the shade, two are in the sunshine, and the median line which divides the day from the night passes diagonally across the roof.

Bobi went up to his room. Suddenly he drew back from the window and he hid to watch. He had just seen the stag. The animal was not alone. Beside him walked a girl. The one who, at the beginning of the morning, had been sleeping so soundly in the hollow of the furrow and whose smile Bobi remembered. The deer and Zulma were there at the edge of the orchard. They were both walking in a sort of halo.

"Oh, yes," said Bobi to himself.

Behind them was the orchard, with its flowers and the black serpents of branches, the shade of the orchard, a soft and floating shade, not black but green like the light at the bottom of a brook. The trees did not blot out the sky. The hills, with their heath of juniper, the little ploughed fields, the groves, and the forests of evergreen oak resembled the rough, reddish-brown woollen rugs such as are made during the winter evenings with the tag-ends of the spinning. The mountains were still solid ice at this time of the year. A tiny village could be seen away up in the highest hills, in a lonely spot. It was round, notched, and russet like crowns one sees on the heads of kings in pictures. At another place, smoke filtered through the lumpy covering of the oak woods. That must be the encampment of some woodsmen. Toward the east, the trees, fields, even the rocks, were tinged with green through the stream of light which, springing from the low-lying sun, flowed directly over the earth. But, as one turned toward the west, all the details of the distant world were separated from one another by the shadows, a play of colour, and one no longer saw the smooth greenish mass of hill, but one could distinguish a tree and its shape; one could almost see it sway; one could see the shadow of the oaks on the meadows, the little carpets of deep grass beside solitary farms, the colour of the walls, the angular form of the houses and the twinkling of the dovecots whose plastered walls are starred with pieces of glass so that the sun, beating upon them, attracts the wild pigeons from the farthest woods. One could picture all the human life there; over there beneath the trees and through the tall grass, hear it walking in its thousand paths with the rustlings of an ant hill. Then, if one turned further toward the west, all melted again, this time beneath the haze. The humidity of the valleys and the green force of the forests streamed in mists beneath which terrestrial life, men, trees, tilled fields, leas, and woods were all uniformly of the colour of the sky.

Before the orchard walked the deer and Zulma. They were coming in step. The two bodies glided along side by side with the same swing.

"What has she around her hair?" said Bobi to himself. "One would say a crown of wheat spikes."

He withdrew to the corner near the bed. He changed his shirt. He heard the step of the deer and the step of Zulma pass beneath the window. He ran toward the door. He descended the stairs. There were cries everywhere in the house and all around it.

8

Bobi crossed the empty kitchen. The women had abandoned the fricassee. He reached the doorsill. They were all outside with the men, looking. There were no cries now. Everyone was silent. Only the step of the deer could be heard.

He was advancing at Zulma's side with great assurance and gravity. His shoulders and back were like moving mountains and the antlers on his head were a tree. He fascinated one like a star by the brilliance of his coat, his free eyes, and the radiance of his peaceful movements.

As for Zulma, her bare foot could be seen as it stepped in the grass; all the toes separated, then the toes closed, then the foot was hidden under the long skirt; the other foot advanced. And thus she walked, slowly, slowly, very heavily, resting on some great solid thing. She was carrying an armful of grasses. Her head was tilted to one side, her eyes cast down, her mouth sad. She reminded one of the bitterness of the harvest.

"It is her hair," said Bobi, "it is her hair that is gold like wheat."

And, moreover, she had plaited it in little strands like wheat ears; she had some behind her ears, she had a cluster at the back of her neck, she had two or three lying on either side of her forehead.

It was indeed like the ripe ear of the wheat with everything: the hard shining grains and the barbs and the stem of the spike; and all was made of blond hair reddened by the sun. Only to see this head dress brought to one's nose the stifling heat of July with its odours of sweat and dust.

Zulma's face was sad and still, bending to one side as in a great weariness. The mouth bitter. She reminded one of the abandon of the sheaves in the empty fields.

"Where have you been?" asked Honorine.

"I went to get some cress," she said.

She was carrying a bunch of cress that she must have torn by handfuls from the streams.

"But you went away last night?"

"Yes," she said without raising her eyes, scarcely moving her bitter mouth.

"Let her alone," said Jacquou.

"No," said Randoulet, "for, you see, this is what she does." He pointed to the cress. "She is always roaming about places where there is water." (With the tips of her fingers, Zulma touched her hair, then her cheek, then she carefully put a little plait over her ear.) "And some day she's going to drown herself, that is what will happen."

"Let her alone," said the women. "Let us tend to this. Come, Zulma."

Marthe put her arm about her waist.

"Give me," said Madame Hélène, and she took the big bundle of cress. "Come."

"Her belly is all wet," said Joséphine. "Look."

"Yes," said Honorine, "that's the way it is. She lies down flat on her belly, she leans over the water" (with the tips of her fingers Zulma touched her hair), "and this is how she comes home."

"That might do her harm," said Joséphine. "Come, Zulma. Let us take her inside; we'll dry her."

Old Barbe looked on, shaking her head.

Aurore called softly: "Zulma! Zulma!"

She put all her tenderness into her voice. She remembered having leaned over Zulma as she slept in the early morning. At that moment this girl slept and smiled and she looked at peace and happy. Her body was not wet, she had not been leaning over the dangerous water. That is how grief comes. Aurore called softly:

"Zulma! Zulma!"

All the women were returning to the house, leading the girl with her downcast eyes. She allowed herself to be coaxed. She did not walk any faster than before. This house must naturally be on the mysterious road that she was following, which she alone knew. The women fell into step with her. That made a great rustling of skirts and from time to time a few gentle little words: "Come, my pretty," and then Aurore, who called: "Zulma! Zulma!"

Honorine followed, talking to herself. She was trying to make great gestures with her short arms. She seemed to be saying: "What is to be done with all this? What are we going to do?"

Bobi stepped aside from the doorway to let them pass. He wanted to see the girl's eyes. She did not raise her lids. They were large, bluish, and weighed down with long curling lashes, thick as the blade of a feather.

"Get out," said Joséphine, "and go along with the men, you. We are going to undress her and get her dry."

And she gave a woman's laugh. Her lips shone. She had strong teeth. She looked at him squarely with eyes that were most likely never hidden and that said frankly what they meant. She sighed. Then she shut the door.

The deer had come up to it. He sniffed the stone on which the girl had just put her feet. Then he raised his head, shook his antlers, stretched his neck, opened his mouth, and uttered a long complaint, looking all around over the fields. A long thread of froth trembled under his chin.

"I don't know what to say to you," said Bobi.

"Oh," cried Jacquou, "such music!"

He stopped his ears.

And Jourdan, also, and Carle and Honoré, one after the other, put their hands over their ears like shells. Le Noir looked at the sky.

The two children, who had been forgotten outside, began to run toward the house, and they beat with their little fists on the door, because it had been shut and bolted. Joséphine opened to them and took them inside. Through the half-open door a tall red flame was visible, and in front of it a white form and the harvest hair.

"Quick," said Joséphine, "make the animal keep quiet, you."

She shut the door.

"What do you want?" Bobi said to the deer. "I don't know any more about it than you. They are not going to hurt her. They are drying her; a woman's body is delicate."

"Blow on your horn," cried Jacquou.

Carle's son put the bugle to his lips and began to play as he had done at dawn, as he had done a while ago, always his seven or eight peaceful notes, flat but sad, that seemed to lift the horizons, to make their echoes ring and reveal the roads that led out into the world.

The deer stopped roaring and looked at Bobi.

"Yes," said Bobi, "you see. Maybe. There is still hope. I'll speak to them about it presently."

He patted his shoulder.

"Listen," Bobi said to him, "listen to what he is saying with the bugle. The moment they stop talking with their words, one would say they understand. It is deep down in their hearts. There is still hope. They have already felt the need of a little music. It is a good sign."

The deer rubbed his nose against Bobi's breast.

"Yes," said Bobi, "they seem to be answering you. What they are saying isn't bad, you know."

And he began to smile.

"Ah," said Jourdan, uncovering his ears, "that's better. What got into the beast?"

"Nothing," said Bobi. "He wanted to tell you something about the young girl, something about all of us in general."

"Does he often get that way?" said Jacquou.

"Whenever it is necessary."

The deer was now moving off toward the hay.

"Animals have strong voices," said Bobi.

"It is mostly," said Randoulet, "because it hits you here."

He put his hand on his chest.

"That comes from the fact that they have not lost the habit of speaking as one ought to speak," said Bobi.

"Why?" said Jacquou.

"Because they have not lost the habit of doing what one ought to do."

"Naturally," said Carle.

"Not so stupid as you'd think," said Bobi. "I'll speak to you about it after we've eaten."

"We'll remind you of it," said Jacquou.

Jourdan said nothing. He had just felt inside him the same joy he had felt that winter night when Bobi had spoken for the first time of Orion-Queen Anne's lace. He felt within himself the good and the pure. It was slightly painful.

"What about the meat?" said Bobi.

Fortunately, Jacquou had thought of drawing the spit back from the fire. Besides, it was still turning all by itself with its spring. Everything was done.

The great table was set up.

"If only the women were ready," said Randoulet.

The door opened and Joséphine called out: "Well, men?"

"It's ready," they said.

"So are we," she said.

She left the door open.

Le Noir went up to Bobi. He took hold of his coat.

"Listen," he whispered, "it's true."

He raised his finger in the air.

"…I understand," said Le Noir, "and I mean everything. It is all true."

"Leave off," said Joséphine, "she is getting warm. She is all right. You will see how fast the table is going to be set."

Marthe came out with a sheet. It was to serve as the table cloth. Barbe brought the plates, Honorine the basket of forks.

"A big platter," said Jacquou.

He drew the kid off the spit.

It was noon, the crickets were singing. The damp earth smelt strongly. The wind had fallen. The sun seemed to be taking a moment's rest. It seemed heavy and limp.

The kid was kept whole in spite of the ladles full of juice that Jourdan had made it take through all the openings of its skin. It slid from the end of the spit onto the huge platter. It settled of its own weight, with its roasted bones and its golden flesh. The juice began to trickle out and gradually to rise around it.

Honoré was thinking of his hare. He waited until his father-in-law had finished taking the kid from the spit. But it seemed that Jacquou would never have done scraping the spit very deliberately with the fork.

"A little more and you'll take off the iron."

"You are certainly from the land of thick-heads," said Jacquou. "When you can't see it you can hear it. You don't know that this is the best part, eh? Where the beast has lain on the spit is the best. Yes, but it is true that in your country they only eat beets. Here, take your spit."

"If you think that spit is so good, we'll keep it for your share. Don't worry, there. You'll see that, for a beet, this hare is rather not bad, if I do say it. Damn, that's hot!"

He slid the hare along the spit, pushing it with the fork. Slowly the odour of mountain herbs, cooked in the mixture of liver, blood, and basting lard, began to rise.

"How are we to sit?" said Joséphine.

"Wait," said Bobi, "you will see, here…"

"Where will you be?" she whispered, bending toward him.

"Opposite you."

"Next to me," she said.

"Opposite, we can see each other," he said.

"Beside each other, we can touch," she said.

Madame Hélène came up. After her work as cook, she had tidied herself up. She had washed her lovely arms. She had asked Marthe for some powder. She had powdered her hands, her wrists and arms, and her cheeks and neck. She wore a white silk blouse with short sleeves, a very open neck, just a little gathered with a wine-blue-coloured ruching. The upper part of her lovely breasts was visible, firm and ample, slightly plump. She was very desirable. Her eyes were rather saddened by her widowhood.

"It's a pity," said Carle.

"People wonder," said Jourdan, "why he killed himself."

He was thinking that until now things had hardly been seen clearly.

"We couldn't see clearly ahead of us," he repeated.

"Yes," said Carle, "I don't know why it is, but I have the feeling that now we can see."

"It smells good," said Madame Hélène.

"It's Honoré's stuffing," said Jourdan.

"Did he make it after the manner of his region?" she asked.

"Oh," said Carle, "his region, that's fat-head land."

"Yes," said Honoré, kneeling beside the platter where he was carefully carving the animal, "but big pots hold more than little ones."

From the belly of the animal began to steam the full odour of the stuffing. Carle bent over the dish.

"You brute," he said, "that's not bad."

Madame Hélène licked her lips. She looked at Jourdan.

"You have a nice odour, too, my good Jourdan; you smell like damp corduroy."

"I smell like old hair, yes," said Jourdan.

"Why old?" she said. "I love that odour."

"Take your seats," cried Marthe, "I am bringing the fricassee."

"Come," said Bobi, and he took Aurore's hand. Each time it was as though he were going to lead her away to the ends of the earth.

"You are to be beside me," he said.

"What is she doing?" asked Randoulet.

"She's being dressed in beautiful clothes that belong to Marthe," said Honorine. "She seems calm. She is humming. I'll go get her."

She went toward the house.

The others were finding places on the benches and chairs. They had brought out a huge peasant armchair covered with old flowered satin, but no one dared to take it and sit in it. It stood all alone on the grass. Aurore saw that Joséphine sat down on the other side, but directly opposite the chair that Bobi was to occupy.

"There," said Joséphine, "this will be nice. Opposite, we can see each other."

She smoothed her hair and then, almost unconsciously, she passed her tongue over her lips and her lips became shining and swollen, and they were like a great flower that had just opened. She was ashamed of it.

"How are you, Mademoiselle?" she said to Aurore.

"Very well, Madame," said Aurore.

But she was thinking in fact that, from across there, Joséphine would be able to look at Bobi all the time, that Bobi would see her all the time, and that she, Aurore, was very unlucky only to be beside him.

Honorine found Zulma in front of the fire. She no longer needed to dry herself. They had changed her underclothes and her dress. They had dressed her in some of Marthe's clothes of the time when she was a girl: soft things with lace, then a quilted petticoat with little rococo roses and a mulberry-coloured jacket.

"What are you doing?"

Zulma was examining herself. She still did not raise her eyelids, but she was looking at the pretty things on her. She was very much moved, for her long lashes were trembling.

"Come," said Honorine, "we are going to eat."

She took her by the arm to raise her. It was an arm all limp and soft. When you touched it it made you think of the water in brooks and ponds.

"Come," said Honorine, "tell me," and she knelt down beside her, "why did you go off last night? You know that every time I nearly die of fright."

The long lashes stopped flickering; they only fluttered occasionally like a motionless bird listening to the wind.

"And what made you come and sleep in the furrow near the deer's stable? And why? With all there is around you, my child, in the night, on this plateau! You who walk without looking where you are going. And this morning, why did you go off with that animal? He might have hurt you. You could surely hear us talking and laughing."

Through the lashes, the gleam of the eye could now be seen: it was green and very bright.

They had just served the fricassee and had said: "Where is Honorine?" when they saw her coming from the house with Zulma.

"Zulma is to sit beside me," said Bobi, "I have kept a chair expressly for her. Come."

"I have to help her," said Honorine, "I cut her food for her. It would be better for her to sit here at my end."

"I'll help her," said Bobi, "don't you worry."

He made her sit down.

The fricassee was well portioned out. Only a little remained; hidden in the gravy was a fine piece of liver.

"If only I had seen it!" said Randoulet.

But Bobi gave it to Zulma. He cut her a slice of bread. He said to her: "Eat." He bent his head. He was trying to see her eyes, but the lids were obstinately lowered. Only the long lashes were visible.

"You must eat, too," he said to Aurore.

("His voice is gentler when he speaks to me. His hand made a movement toward mine. He restrained himself.")

"How I like to look at Joséphine," thought Bobi, "She is so nice…"

He saw Aurore once more running through the field of narcissus, but he could not be unconscious of the fact that the breasts, the hips, the very moist laughter of Joséphine existed, and Zulma's hair, harvest sheaves! Something was going to come from these three women. He thought of dawn rising from behind three mountains.

"He looks like he's dreaming!"

"Are you talking to me?" he asked.

"Yes, to you."

"Yes, I was dreaming a little."

"Dreaming at table?"

"He's like that," said Jourdan.

"Oh," said Bobi, who had begun to eat, "this fricassee!…"

It was good. Jacquou was mopping his plate with huge pieces of bread, then he opened his mouth—it was impossible to imagine a bigger mouth—it was a toothless hole. He stuffed his bread in, closed his mouth. Then he looked at everybody with his little rat eyes. He looked as if he wanted to speak, but he could not with his mouth full. He said: "Oo, oo"; he pointed to the platter, to his plate, to his mouth, to his stomach.

"Oh, you!" said Barbe, "Just so you are eating!"

But she was eating too, and only when there were little bones would she empty her mouthful into her hand, pick out the bones, and put the rest back. But she was able to talk while she ate. She did so continually.

"How do you do it?" asked Carle.

"Do what?"

"Eat and talk at the same time?"

"I don't know."

Carle was gnawing a chicken carcass. He thrust his tongue into it as far as he could to lick the inside of the bones.

"You can't be tasting anything."

"I taste everything," she said.

They all made a great deal of noise with their elbows, with the knives and forks, with their feet under the table, with their mouths as they ate. They also called out to one another.

"Eh, Carle!"

"Eh, Randoulet!"

And Randoulet would drum on his paunch with the tips of his fingers as if to say: "I am eating." And he *was* eating!

Marthe had brought the fricassee, then she had remained standing beside her chair. She had looked from one to another to catch their first movements after the first taste. It was to hasten toward the plate, then toward the platter. So it was good! Jourdan was licking his fingers.

"Women," she said, "you see!"

Joséphine waved her hand as if to reply: "Yes, I see, they all love it, we have worked well."

"When I suggested it," said Marthe, "I knew that it was good in the spring of the year, a fricassee of chicken."

She sat down and began to eat.

"Marthe," called Madame Hélène from the other end of the table, "you are like a hotel chef."

"There's not enough gravy," replied Marthe.

"No," said Honorine, opposite, "there's just enough." Then she leaned toward her neighbour, who was Honoré.

"What did you say?" she asked.

"I was saying," said Honoré, "that your name is Honorine and mine Honoré and they've put us side by side. It's curious."

"That's so," she said. "Feed your little ones."

He had his two children beside him, at the end of the table. They had been rather overlooked.

"Wine!" cried Carle's son.

Then Jourdan rose and went to get the big demijohn.

"We'll begin with mine," he said.

"You are not going to drink all that?" said the women.

But they knew that they would. And they were afraid of it, and suddenly they were inwardly light with a great happiness as if from the distant woods and forests came the dull, monotonous thumping of a dance drum at whose rhythm they would soon be forced to turn and dance.

Jourdan poured all around. He went from place to place. He tipped the demijohn over the glass. It was so heavy that he had to bend over with it at the same time, and when he raised the neck he straightened himself up also. He looked as though he were filling the glass from himself. His wrists were red and trembling with the effort.

The wine seemed charged with tiny leaves of gold and flowers of light as it was being poured. But in the glass it was suddenly heavy as lead and it lay waiting.

Jacquou raised his glass and drank. At the other end of the table, Jourdan, who was about to serve Honoré, stopped. He looked at Jacquou.

"Yes," said Jacquou.

"Pour me some," said Honoré.

The men drank the whole glassful at a gulp, the women in little sips. Jourdan served Marthe.

"Here, darling," he said softly.

She looked at him out of the corner of her eye and breathed more quickly. And she drank and heard the rumbling of the drum that filtered louder from the woods, the forests, the trees, the grass, and one might even say from the earth itself. It seemed as though one could hear its throbs in the ground, here, beneath one's feet, here under the table, like the violent throbbing of blood in the arteries of men inflamed.

Jourdan went around the table once more pouring out wine. The demijohn was growing lighter.

Honoré put his arm around Honorine.

"Don't get upset," he said, laughing beneath his moustache, "this isn't for you."

It was to touch the shoulder of Carle's son.

"Come and help me."

Carle's son got up. They both went to the hearth of red embers where the roasts were simmering.

Honorine could still feel Honoré's warm arm about her.

"Look out," said Carle's son, "the platters are red-hot."

"You carry the hare," said Honoré. "I'll carry the kid."

"The wine is good," said Carle's son.

"Oh," said Honoré, "look at the sky!"

The sky was sprinkled all over with little round clouds with violet hearts that were sailing slowly over a fine smooth blue like the basin of a clear fountain.

They brought the platters.

"Let's drink!" cried Jacquou.

"By drinking…" said Madame Hélène.

She was conscious of Jourdan approaching her. He was there again with his demijohn. He poured wine out for her.

"By drinking…" she said.

"It's all right," he said, "drink."

"No," said Jacquou, "it's not strong. You must drink."

It could not be true that it was not strong. She felt the fire being rekindled in the depths of her flesh, in a place where she thought all was extinguished since the death of her husband. And now she had just felt the flame's sparkling and painful caress. She, also, heard the rumbling and the drum beats and the cadence and the wild rhythm of the dance drum.

"My blood is throbbing," she said to herself, "it is my blood that is pulsating. It is the sound of my blood."

The tips of her breasts grew hard merely from rubbing against the silk of her blouse.

"My good Jourdan," she said to herself under her breath.

And she perceived that the sound of the name in her undertone had a form and an odour, and gestures and weight, and that her body rejoiced in it.

The roasts were heavy and juicy, and at the first stab of the knife they broke open. The gravy was like bronze with golden reflections, and each time that it was stirred with the spoon, the lardings or the greenish sediment of the stuffing or bits of still pink young bacon would come to the surface. The meat of the kid broke open and appeared milky inside, smoking in its clear juices. The skin crackled and at first it was dry to the teeth, but as the morsel was bitten into, all the tender flesh melted and out trickled a salt and creamy animal oil that could not be swallowed at a gulp, it gave so much pleasure, and it oozed a little from the corners of one's lips. One had to wipe one's mouth.

"It's my turn!" cried Jacquou.

He got up and walked over to his bottles lined up in the grass.

"My wine," he said, holding the big bottle up to the sun.

"Now he's going to act the fool," said Barbe.

But Carle was beside her, between her and Jacquou, and everything was making his blood throb. He had become red and his neck was swollen. For a long time he had been hearing the *tum, tum,* of the savage drum. He had drunk deep three times of Jourdan's wine. Each time the thundering had increased and the cadence quickened. He felt his feet come loose from the earth, his body come loose from the earth, his head come loose from the earth. He thought of the galloping of his stallion, if he were to let him loose in the fields. The drum of his blood bent with the dull thumps of that gallop that he had never heard.

"Nobody's crazy," he said.

He did not know exactly what he meant or what he was saying. He was always like that, very soon after drinking wine. He meant that a stallion with a nose shaped like an iris leaf was made to gallop like the wind over the earth and to make men dance with the beating of his hoofs.

"Yes, but…" said Barbe.

"You are too old," he said.

He seemed to be winking, but as a matter of fact he was trying to open his eyes and only one would open.

"No disrespect," he said, "I mean"—he raised his finger in the air—"give me something to drink."

And he held his big glass out to Jacquou.

Jacquou's wine was like its owner: dry and strong. And it commanded.

They let it stand awhile in the glasses. The kid was fresh and tender, and their mouths relished it. They still retained the frank taste of Jourdan's wine.

The big hare was waiting on the earthenware platter. It was a spring hare, fat and strong. This was quite evident now that they had the leisure to look at it while eating the kid. It must weigh twelve pounds without the stuffing. And Honoré had packed it with a stuffing such as they made in his region: an almost magical cookery with fresh garden and mountain herbs that Honoré had brought mysteriously in his vest pocket. When he showed them, they looked like gillyflower cloves or bits of old iron. They were reddish and dry and hard. Touching them told nothing. Smelling them did not tell much, just a slight odour but wholly mountain, it is true. Only, Honoré had steeped them in vinegar and they could be seen to unfold and stir like living things and they were recognized as buds of terebinth blossoms, flowers of *solognette,* cress pods, and then leaves of plants whose names were unknown even to Honoré.

At least, so he said. But then, when he had chopped them up himself, and kneaded them and mixed them with the spinach, sorrel, tender teasel shoots, a quarter of a clove of garlic, a handful of pepper, a handful of coarse salt, three liberal pourings of oil, and a soupspoonful of country saffron made with the pollen of wild iris, then, oh, yes, then!…And all the perfumes already flowed from between his kneading fingers; nevertheless, it was still incomplete. He had not added the bacon, but quickly he clasped it all in his hands and stuffed it into the belly of the hare. He sewed up the skin and it was all that that had been turning on the spit. The juices had mingled. They were black and shining in the earthen platter.

"Well, what about that wine?" asked Jacquou.

"No one has drunk any."

"Let's drink."

"Wait," said Jourdan, "let's finish my jug first. Yours," he said, "is black as pitch. It is the same colour as the hare. It will go well with it. Look at mine." He held the jug up at arm's length. "It is the same colour as the kid. And it is a little like a goat."

He began to dance lightly from his hips and took a little leap to show how his wine resembled a goat. It was true, he was right, Jacquou's wine was the colour of the hare.

"He is right!"

"Look at him," said Marthe, "he acts like a boy with his wine. Look at him!"

"Yes," said Madame Hélène to herself, "he is young."

She, too, had a great youthfulness within her, dancing and goatlike, that made her breath come quickly. And the blood beat dully, boom, boom, boom, like the savage dance of all the earth, and the sound seemed to filter from the forests, the hills, the mountains, and even from the sky.

Again Jourdan made the rounds of the table, pouring wine.

They were about to remove the platter of kid. Only the bones were left on it.

"Wait," said Barbe, "I am an old woman. Your hare is very warming. I know Honoré. Give me some bones." She took four or five big ones which she put on her plate.

"Break them for me," she said to Jacquou.

Jacquou laid the bones over his knee and broke them like tree branches.

Barbe began to suck the marrow.

"I like this," she said, "it is good for the stomach."

"But," said Carle, "the rest of us would rather have something strong and solid. Wouldn't we, fellows?"

It was evident that his eyes were blinking like those of a person who is looking at the galloping of a foaming horse against the sun.

It was Honoré who served the hare. He insisted upon doing it. He said:

"You must have a little of this and a little of that."

They would say:

"I have enough."

He would say:

"No, if you haven't got this—you see this little thing?"—he took it on the tip of the fork and deposited it on the plate—"if you haven't that little thing, the hare isn't any good."

And so, for one, he added a bit of terebinth bud, for another a cress leaf, to Aurore he gave a whole cooked bunch of field parsley, thick and broad as hemlock and dripping with gravy.

"There," he said, "that will keep you busy, that makes your innards work."

He served Jourdan. He served Jacquou. He served Barbe in spite of her bones.

"To please your husband," he said, "eat heartily, not that marrow that makes you flabby."

"What a way to talk to his mother-in-law!"

"Drink," said Jacquou.

And this time they drank, for everything seemed to harmonize: the odour of this hot food, the hare's black flesh, and the black wine that was waiting with its lights of pitch.

Jacquou's black wine was a terrible master. It did not delay. It took command of everything at once.

There was also the perfume of the *solognette*. It is a very peculiar odour and bearable only when it is growing under a boundless sky, well swept by the winds on the mountain tops. It is the blood herb, it is the herb of great muscular love.

"By heavens!" said Jourdan, and he struck the table with his fist. His reddish beard was all spread out about his face. Usually, his beard was not remarkable, being only a man's beard. Now it stood out. He was looking off into space with ecstatic eyes. And he was chewing calmly and forcefully.

There were the love herbs. There was the black flesh of the hare made of the best things from the hills. There was the strength of the fire. There was the black wine. To all this was added the air they chewed at the same time as the meat, air scented with narcissus, for the light wind came from the field; the sky, the springtime, the sun that was insistently warming the supple corners of the body; one would think it knew what it was up to: it warmed the tender armpits, the hollows of the loins, those two parts between the body and the thighs that join, just in that spot! It warmed the nape of the neck sometimes with a nip such as big tomcats give to increase the desire of the females who call to them but who wear themselves out alone. The fact was that everything suddenly took on form and odour. The whole plateau exuded its plateau odour. It was as though one were on a wide ram skin.

Marthe looked at the forest. Her blood thumped. The beaters of the dance drums were no longer hidden beneath the trees. They had leaped beyond the borders. They were beating their drums in the open. The whole sky vibrated to them, all the echoes rang with them. This pulsating filled the head. One was seized with the desire to dance. Not to dance face to face and erect, with music, as one usually does, no. To dance as this incessant throbbing of the blood demanded. One did not know exactly how, but to dance and be free.

That's it, above all, to be free. Madame Hélène could no longer breathe. Her blouse confined her. She had just felt her abdomen. It was hard and alive. She felt a life rising from the earth the length of her limbs, flowing through her body to her breast, up into her head where this life swirled as the wind sometimes does in empty barns.

"All out of gear!" she said to herself.

She smiled. It was an expression of her farmer. He always said: "It's all out of gear, Madame!"

Jourdan saw the smile. He answered it by his own special smile, silent but very bright, with his full lips parted in his beard.

However, Madame Hélène, who was looking at him, did not see him. She was listening to the whirling of the new life in her head and this took all her strength, even that of her glance. But she felt something like the passing of a spider web along her bare arms, on her bare skin, and all the skin quivered the length of her, beneath her clothes to the most secret parts of her body. She then saw that Jourdan was laughing at her with a friendly laugh.

Marthe at the other end of the table was thinking:

"Jourdan is happy."

"More!" said Jacquou.

He got up. His knees were weak. He went around the table pouring wine. He leaned upon the people's shoulders.

"Hand me your glass."

They held up their glasses. He poured, and as he progressed, it became evident that Jacquou was having trouble in navigating. The company ate, drank, chewed silently with only the sound of teeth, tongue, plate, fork, knife, with sometimes a single word or phrase: "Bread" or: "Look out!"

"The sound of sheep grazing in fine hay," thought Randoulet.

There was scarcely a sound. So little that the singing of the mole-crickets could be heard in the fields and the movement of the awakening wind.

But, above all, there was that drumming of the blood, the rumbling of the blood. It thumped in both men and women upon a deep-sounding drum. At each blow, it struck as it were the hollow of the breast. Each felt bound to this cadence. It was like the blades of a threshing machine. It was like the flail that strikes the grain, flies back, strikes the grain, flies back. It was like the travail of the man leaping in the wine vat. It was like the steady gallop of a horse. If he gallops like that, constantly, with his heavy hoofs, he will go to the end of the world, and beyond the end of the world he will gallop through the sky, and the vault of the heavens will resound at his passage as the earth is resounding now. Always, always, without ceasing, because blood does not cease to beat, to explore, to gallop, and to demand with its black drum to join the dance.

It calls and one does not dare respond. And it calls and one does not know if one must . . . and one's body is filled with desire and one suffers. One does not know and one knows. Yes, vaguely, one realizes that it would be good, that the world would be beautiful, that it would be a paradise, happiness for everyone and joy. To be guided by one's blood, let one's self be beaten, explored, let one's self be carried away by the galloping of one's own blood to the infinite prairie of the heavens smooth as sand. And one would hear galloping, galloping, beating, beating, exploring, exploring, and the thundering drum beneath the great black palm of the pulsating blood.

But it would be the dance, the true dance, one would obey with true obedience. One would do what the body desires. All these calls of the blood would be calls of joy. Whereas here, one does not know, one is not sure if one ought. One knows that one ought, but one does not stir, one is bound. And from the hollow of the breast one is also bound, that dance music, and the calling blood, it is as though one were torn in two. Because the poor body no longer knows. Because the young blood that is just made knows.

That's the difficulty. One thinks one can take one's pleasure all together and suddenly one realizes that one is on the wrong track, since along this path on which one finds one's self, one cannot continue.

How can one be expected to talk? One says: "Yes, no, some bread, move over, look out. The wind is in the grass like a cat. We ought to sing. There's nothing else to do. A great song of sadness..." Or gestures. Now we've had enough! In short, the blood has won.

Joséphine unbuttoned the top button of her blouse, then the second, then the third, then the fourth. She was looking in front of her. She was watching Bobi. He was smooth and tanned. His face was as smooth as the stones rolled by the river, and tanned by the sun, by the wine and his blood. He had blue eyes. That could be seen now. But a very light blue, very, very light, scarcely blue at all.

She unbuttoned the fifth button. It was the last. She opened her blouse. Beneath, was only her summer slip. She had only to to shrug her shoulder and her firm breast leaped over the slip. It stayed there, beneath the shadow of the blouse, but visible. He must see it with his light blue eyes. She felt the wind on her breast.

"This feels comfortable," she said.

But nobody was paying any attention to her, save perhaps Bobi, and even then that was not certain. One could not tell where he was looking. Except perhaps that girl over there: Aurore. She had hung her head and blushed, and was fumbling at her blouse to unbutton it, too. But her blouse did not unbutton, it laced, and even if it were unlaced it would have revealed nothing. It would not have opened very far, and besides there was scarcely anything underneath. She was a young girl. Joséphine was a woman. A woman gains by her married life.

"He is looking at me with his bluish eyes."

Bobi was looking straight ahead of him. He was thinking of all of Joséphine's grimaces and tricks during the meal. He was thinking that she had supple hips, that she was soft from hip to shoulder. It would give him joy to clasp that form in his two hands. To feel the warmth and suppleness of it. It must be fruit and warmth, full of juice and life. To feel the weight and the heat of the breasts on the edge of the hand, the length of the index finger, then to seize them and caress them.

He lowered his eyes. He saw beside him Aurore's soft white hands. They came and went, fine as bread dough. The sensitive fingers, the slight wrist, the round arm, muscular and covered with youthful skin, pinkish, with blue veins and golden down.

"No," said Bobi, "that will not come from women. Nothing can come from women but the desire of women. All will come from me."

From where he was sitting, by looking past Joséphine, past Jourdan, Carle's son, Honorine, and Honoré, beyond those who were sitting opposite him, on the other side of the table, he could see La Jourdane, and on either side of the house the plateau that stretched flat with its fields into the distance.

He said to himself: "Here I am." He was thinking of all the regions he had traversed. He was thinking of those four or five places in the world where he had lived for a short space. "I do not know," he said to himself, "if it is seeing this land so flat…" He unconsciously made a gesture with his arm as if to depict to the secret parts of his body the broad expanse of the plateau—and he touched Aurore's breast.

"Excuse me, Mademoiselle," he said.

"That's all right," she said.

She no longer knew what she was saying. She only knew that he had just touched her gently for the first time, there in the very place where she was very sensitive, in the shadow of her firm little breasts.

"This flat land," he continued to himself, "makes me believe that this time it is for a long time. For good." He repeated: "For good."

And he looked past Joséphine at the fair plateau that spread out around them all.

"It's a question of contentment," thought Bobi.

He thought of that night last winter, with its extraordinary stars.

"To come," he thought, "from below on the plain, with very little hope, and suddenly to find a road just on the edge of the woods. And then the road ascends. I come to the top. I cut across the fields. I hear the clanking of a horse's collar. I find a man ploughing. I say to him: 'Have you some tobacco?' He says to me: 'Have you ever taken care of lepers?'"

"Monsieur," called Aurore softly.

"I am not a monsieur," he said.

He waited. She did not continue.

"What was it you wanted to say?" he said.

"I don't know now," she said.

Her face was redder. She was surely very hot. He saw that her face was without malice and that all the lines were pure. It was a face that gave gravity and purity to all.

This time he also saw Joséphine's breast.

"Monsieur!" he said to himself. "This is the first time that has happened to me. For this, too, it is the first time." He looked at the fair, pure face, so young, so confident, so well suited to him that he shuddered beneath its gaze like a flower beneath the wind.

"Yes," he cried to Jourdan, who was making signs to him, "everything is fine, don't worry. What are you saying?"

Jourdan was trying to make him understand something. Everyone was talking.

"What do you want?"

"He's trying to say," said Marthe, "Orion-Queen Anne's lace."

Now Jourdan was leaning toward Jacquou and he must have been explaining this, for he was pointing to the sky, and then he made a sign with his hand, a circle, touching his index finger to his thumb.

Jacquou listened gravely without looking at the hand. He was looking at Bobi, but with a puzzled look.

"No longer to be harassed by the desire for gain," said Bobi to himself. He was thinking of that constellation, Orion, so vast, so ablaze that winter night, that he had immediately had in his mouth the two names together, Orion-Queen Anne's lace. "He was sensitive to it," he thought, "and when I said it he stopped his horse and said: 'I beg your pardon?' To go aimlessly through life," said Bobi to himself.

He emptied his glass of the black wine.

"For…" he said to himself as he wiped his mouth. Then he realized that perhaps he was thinking aloud. He closed his mouth. "For I know more about it than the rest of them. I know better. They do not know and that is why they were sad." He remembered old Silve. That voice in the night when they were going the rounds of the plateau, he and Jourdan; the weight of the man leaning on the buggy. And afterward he had hanged himself.

"After all I've been through," he thought, "for, indeed, if there is any reason for being unhappy I ought to have been. Prudence? Never prudence. Economy, or this or that thought for the future? Never. The passion for the useless," he said. "Passion! Useless? Useless for their world, but the moment we know that our work in this world is to make riches for others, isn't that precisely useless? And if one argues, for I argue, I am arguing with myself, so, if one argues, isn't everything that has been my passion precisely useful?

"It's odd," said Bobi aloud, "but there are really people who are dead in the world."

It was perhaps his reflection, but he had just said it aloud. As for some time he was no longer eating, by his stillness he had seemed to wish to speak to everyone. They all stopped talking and eating. They looked at him in silence.

Honoré said: "Keep quiet, folks!"

There was only the sound of the wind.

"I didn't leave enough time between 'dead' and 'in the world,'" thought Bobi.

He repeated:

"People who are dead. In the world."

And he made gestures.

"Dead!"

He opened his hands, spread his fingers as if to say: "Nothing, they no longer have anything. Nothing, nothing, all has flowed away from them."

"And in the world!"

He made a motion with his arms to imitate the wide horizon and at the same time with his long, caressing hands he gently outlined forms of trees and imaginary hills.

Just then the horses began to neigh; then, in the silence, a light step was heard. And the stag was seen approaching.

9

"Don't be frightened," said Bobi. "His name is Antoine!"

The deer was approaching with tiny steps. He was chewing a bit of dry hay. He was not paying any attention to anyone. Everybody watched him. The horses and mules were neighing over in the shed.

"Look at him!"

"He is as proud as a rich man."

"He doesn't see us."

"He sees us but he doesn't give a rap."

"His eye reflects things."

"He is beautiful," said Aurore.

At this, Zulma turned her face toward her as if to look at her. But she did not raise her eyelids. It was rather with the intention of showing herself with her lovely, regular features. A simple idea.

"I was just about to speak to you about him," said Bobi. "Spring is here, you can smell it. And that deer, he's as strong as a Turk and he isn't used to doing without what his body desires. We ought to think a little about buying him a doe among us all, there!"

They looked at each other without a word. Jacquou belched loudly in the silence, but it was because he had just attempted to speak.

"One doe, or two," said Bobi.

"Why didn't you tell me?" asked Jourdan.

He was very serious. First because what Bobi had just said was serious and chiefly because he no longer had good control of all his facial muscles. Suddenly his beard was poor, his nose pinched, his eyes wide and still, and there was a great wrinkle in his forehead.

"I thought," said Bobi, "that we could all have a hand in it."

"No," said Jourdan.

"And why not?" cried Jacquou.

"Yes!" shouted Randoulet.

"Yes," said Carle, "why not?"

"For…" cried Jacquou.

"No," said Jourdan.

And he shook his head vigorously. "No, no, no."

"Now *I* am going to say something," said Bobi, "if only you'll listen to me awhile.…

"In the first place, Antoine, you're a nice fellow"—the stag had come up behind him and was nuzzling his nose into his shoulders—"but I'm tending to you. Get away. Lie down. There.

"Jourdan, I understand you and you are right, but wait! You don't have to shout. You, Jacquou, Carle, Randoulet, and even you who haven't said anything, I understand you and you are right. You see that I understand the whole affair. That is precisely why everything is going to come out all right. But, say, you aren't eating any more. Aren't you going to eat anything more?"

"Oh, you go on talking, you idiot!" cried Jacquou. "You can

see we're not eating. Eating's not the only thing in life!"

"I agree with Jourdan," said Bobi, "and I agree with the rest of you. You may think that it is because I want to be on both sides. Not at all. It is because in reality there are not two sides. You are all of the same mind.

"Now listen to me and don't make any noise. I am going to talk to Jourdan. We have a special language, we two. Listen to us, you'll see. You'd think it was play-acting but it is out of this that the whole thing will grow. But, before I start with Jourdan, are you all agreed? Are you really expecting something? Are you expecting something to happen?"

"Yes," said Jacquou.

"Good," said Bobi. "Then listen to the two of us, me and that rum fellow over there. Jourdan!"

"Yes."

"I understand what you mean."

"That's easy."

"Yes, it's easy. You mean that you bought the stag, that the stag belongs to you, and that you can buy the does, too, all by yourself."

"Yes."

"No," said Bobi, raising his hand, "don't talk, don't say anything. Leave me alone with Jourdan. It is just the same as when the midwife comes. She says to you: Get out and don't bother me. I say to you: Act as if you had gone out and let me do this. It's the same thing."

"Yes," said Jourdan, "I want to buy the does myself. I don't need anyone else."

"To buy them, you mean?"

"Yes."

"It's a question of money, you mean? I mean that you have enough money to buy the does, is that it?"

And with difficulty Bobi calmed down the audience with a gesture of patting a horse. For it was a question of money, and that often makes people take fire out of pride.

"Yes."

"In other words, you want to be the proprietor."

Jourdan sat a moment without replying.

"No."

"Then what?"

"The stag belongs to me, I want the does to belong to me."

"That's what I said. Only the word 'proprietor' doesn't seem to be the right word to you."

"No, it isn't the right word."

"Good. Then we're going to agree because it is precisely that 'proprietor' that might spoil everything. The moment you realize that for the does and the stag this is not the correct word, after I've explained a little further you'll see that it isn't correct either as a thing. One minute," he said to the others, "I'll just be a minute longer. Be good. Now we are going to talk the secret language. It's a little like animal talk. But you'll all understand," he said, "for it is enough to have a pure heart.

"Jourdan, do you remember Orion–Queen Anne's lace?"

"I remember."

"You asked me: 'Have you ever taken care of lepers?'"

"I remember as if it was yesterday. You answered: 'No, I have never taken care of lepers.'"

"You were dragging around a great sorrow."

"Yes."

"No more taste."

"No."

"No more love."

"No."

"Nothing."

"Old age," said Jourdan.

"Do you remember," said Bobi, "the vast night? It closed the earth in on all horizons."

"I remember."

"Then I said to you: 'Look up there, Orion-Queen Anne's lace, a little bunch of stars.'"

Jourdan did not reply. He looked at Jacquou and at Randoulet and at Carle. They were listening.

"And if I had said to you: 'Orion,' all alone," said Bobi, "you would have seen the stars, nothing more, and that would not have been the first time you had seen them, and yet that had not cured the lepers. And if I had said: 'Queen Anne's lace,' all alone, you would only have seen the flower as you have already seen it a thousand times with no effect. But I said to you 'Orion-Queen Anne's lace,' and at first you said: 'I beg your pardon?' to make me repeat it, and I did repeat it. Then you saw the Queen Anne's lace in the sky and the sky was all abloom."

"I remember," said Jourdan in a low voice.

"And you were already partly cured, tell the truth."

"Yes," said Jourdan.

Bobi let the silence lengthen. He wanted to see. Everybody was listening. No one wanted to talk.

"Of this Orion-Queen Anne's lace," said Bobi, "I am the proprietor. If I don't say it, nobody sees it. If I say it everybody sees it. If I don't say it, I keep it. If I say it, I give it away. Which is better?"

Jourdan looked straight ahead without answering.

"The world is wrong," said Bobi. "You think that it is what you keep that makes you rich. You've been told that. I tell you that what you give makes you rich. What do I have? Look at me."

He stood up. He exhibited himself. He had nothing but his shirt and under that his skin. He raised his long arms, waved his long empty hands. Nothing. Nothing but his arms and his hands.

"You have no other storehouse than this one here," he said, striking his breast. "Everything that you pile up outside your heart is lost. . . .

"Give me something to drink," he said softly to Aurore.

She stood up, took the bottle, poured some wine for him.

"Give him some fine black wine," said Joséphine.

"That's what it is," said Aurore.

"Don't drink it all at once," said Marthe, "you are hot."

"Let him wipe his mouth and sit down," said Barbe.

"Thank you, everybody," said Bobi. "Now the play is finished, we can all talk together."

"I agree with you," said Jourdan.

"Good," said Jacquou. "Well, then, what do you think, over there?"

"As far as I'm concerned," said Bobi, "now it is easy. I think we ought to buy two does, or three."

"How much will that cost?" said Randoulet.

"There are two ways," said Bobi. "Either buy them, or go get them ourselves where there are some. Who knows the Forest of Nans?"

"I do," said Honoré.

"Do you know it well?"

"I'm from Verrières, just below the Nans."

"I slept there three nights last summer," said Bobi. "Not at Verrières; in the forest. I saw some does."

"There are some there."

"But," said Bobi, "to take them alive, we need nets."

"We could ask old Richard for some. At Verrières, I can get anything I want."

"Then listen," said Bobi, "it's a question of knowing how. In your estimation, how many could we take?"

"Three," said Honoré, "four."

"Do you know the method?"

"Yes. You have to surround the glade at Lénore. I'll see to it."

"Good," said Bobi, "but how many men will we need? For I tell you, that is very important. I'd rather have us all there."

Honoré looked at the men seated around the table. He went the round like that with his eyes. He said:

"We'll need every one of us."

"I'd rather," said Bobi, "for a big reason. This is it. I don't want these does to belong to anyone. You understand? In the place where we are going to get them, they belong to no one. Here they will belong to everybody, that is to say, to no one, you understand? There will not be any proprietor. Do you understand me, Jourdan?"

"Yes," said Jourdan, "better than you explain it even. The stag belongs to everybody. That is what *I* say."

"Thanks," said Bobi; "shake on it."

He stood up and so did Jourdan and from their distance, above the table, each clasping his own left hand with his right, they gravely shook hands.

"How shall we go about it?" said Bobi.

"We choose a moonlight night," said Honoré. "We bar the glade at Lénore with the nets. We go to the openings that I know. We blow a horn. Lénore is the place where they have the habit of going, and then, once there, we have them. We may get another stag with them. Then we'll see when we get there. What do you say?"

"No," said Bobi, "one is enough. He'll be the stock; it will be better."

"Well, then," said Honoré, "we could free the other if we catch him?"

"Yes," said Jacquou.

He said this very loudly. And he struck the table as he said it. It seemed like a "yes" that came with great force after perhaps a hundred thousand words of reflections, of those mute words that sing, fly, die, are revived in a twinkling like the sparkling of the sun on the water.

They looked at him.

"I understand everything," he said; "I have understood it all." He was beaming with delight.

"We'll set the other free," said Bobi, "if we catch him. He'll go back into the forest. We only need two or three females for our male. That is all."

"But afterwards?" said Carle.

"Afterwards, we'll come home. We'll have the does in the nets. We'll have to be careful about their legs. They have slender little legs as brittle as glass. We'll talk gently to them all the way home and give them bread and sugar and pat them gently above their noses, where you yourself have those thick fox eyebrows. There they are very sensitive. As soon as we get here, we'll open the nets. Then, at first they will tremble on their little feet and perhaps they will weep. For they weep. And then, all of a sudden, when they see they are free, they will take a leap and a jump, then another, then another, dancing and leaping and turning their heads. And their little tails will clack. And from time to time they will stop and call, then start leaping again. And like that they will go clear to Grémone Forest. They will go into the forest. And that will be that. And some time later the love season will come along. No, Carle, that is not done for a profit or, at least, for a profit as you understand it. It is done for the great profit. It is done, old man, so that we can keep our joy with us."

"Yes," said Carle, "and how are we going to keep our joy with us?"

"Then," said Bobi, "the love season will come along and the male will burn with desire for the female. One fine morning, he'll make himself handsome; he'll lick his coat, he'll rub his head against the shed post to get the fuzz off his forehead. He'll look at the sun and the sun will light up his eyes. He will sniff the May wind and the May wind will be rolled in all the caverns of the bones in his head. And so he will advance to the edge of the field. He will be completely surrounded by freedom. He will stand motionless in this freedom, like the blade of oats that does not know on which side to bend and awaits the wind. And then he will hear a call that makes no sound, an odour or a part of that air in which the female has slept the night before and which has retained the form of the female in its hollow, just as when you walk along the edge of the pond and the mud retains the shape of your foot, and I see it and say: That's Carle's foot. The male will find the form of the female in the soft area of the air and then the wind will blow. He, too, will leap forward at a bound, turning his head, smacking his thighs, stopping, looking about him, calling all the way to Grémone Forest, where he will hear the flight of the females through the leaves."

"Yes," said Carle, "but how are we going to keep our joy with us?"

"You are asking too much," said Jourdan.

"Let him alone," said Jacquou; "he is right in asking."

"Then," said Bobi, "the rest will take place under the cover of the forest. This won't be the first time she has worked for us. It will be the first time that you will be aware of it."

"But our joy!" cried Jacquou.

"No," said Jourdan, "don't say what you are saying."

"Yes," he repeated. "All right, I'll keep quiet. That's all right, but here's the truth: can I say it?"

"Go ahead."

"What are we going to do? I told you that I understand everything. Yes, Barbe, I understand everything, keep quiet and stop wagging your head and muttering under your breath. Listen. Do you know why I came here? I don't know. Who knows, here among you who have all come? As if there had been a summons. Here is the truth. What must be said is that we needed something."

"I've been saying so for a long time," said Jourdan.

"Needed what?" asked Jacquou.

"Needed everything," said Joséphine.

"What are you complaining about?" said Honoré.

She turned toward him.

"I am complaining that nothing is right."

"Need," said Randoulet, "yes. I don't know, but nothing goes as I'd like it to even when it goes as I want it."

"Need to be friends, my friends," said Marthe.

"Need of freedom," said Carle's son. "This morning I was happy."

For some moments, Le Noir had been clearing his throat. He was not a talkative man, but he wanted to say something. Twice he leaned toward Marthe. He bent over a third time.

"The boss," he said, "is going to buy five hundred sheep."

He raised his index finger and shook his head to indicate that for him, that was the thing.

"Three weeks ago," said Jacquou, "we buried old Silve."

Then, there was a brief silence and while Jacquou was getting his breath to argue loudly and long, "The truth is," broke in Bobi, "that we need joy."

"That's it," said Jacquou.

"That's the whole thing," said Bobi. "We'll go after the does, and you'll see."

———

It was evening. The air had become strangely audible. Far off in the hills, trees could be heard creaking and stretching. Grémone Forest seemed quite near; its foliage murmured like water bubbling out of the earth in great sombre spurts. There could be heard the sound, not only of the Ouvèze River, but of its entire valley with the song of all its little secondary valleys, the rustling of the reeds, the trot of the current over the gravel, and the rumbling of the road that followed all the windings of the water and over which, at this hour, marched the long caravans of carts loaded with rock from the quarries. Beyond Grémone Forest— and that must be far away at the foot of the slope—could be heard the buzzing of the slender steel wheel of a mechanical saw. Down in the plain a train whistled. A bird flew over La Jourdane. It came from the mountains. It was going down toward a broad country that it must already have seen from above. It was moving with great flappings of its wings. They could be heard in spite of the height at which it was flying. It flew over the orchard. The beating of its wings clacked in the echoes of the flowering trees. The rapid rolling of carts awoke the echoes of the poplar groves in the plains, and in the short moments of deepest silence could be heard coming from beyond more than twenty hills the dull roar of the city where everyone had come out to enjoy the evening beneath the new foliage of the great elms.

Everything had grown clear. All about the plateau could be heard the expanding of the life of the world.

"Need of joy," said Bobi, for those who were beside him and opposite, Aurore, Zulma, Joséphine, and for those who were farther along the table talking softly among themselves. But they heard, mingled with the sounds of the earth, the voice of the man and his confidence.

"And in fact," said Bobi, "it is the only thing that people seek and that they work for. And if you look at the ants there in the ground, Mademoiselle...you *have* watched the ants?"

"Yes," said Aurore.

"You see them," said Bobi, "going hither and yon, and you wonder what they are doing. And we have already turned up the whole field with our spade and there they are running with bits of straw, grain, eggs. You have already seen that, Madame?"

"Yes," said Joséphine.

"One wonders what they are so busy doing. They are in need of joy, that's all."

He looked at Zulma. She did not stir beneath her wheatear head dress.

"Well, Zulma," said Joséphine, "aren't you going to talk? You haven't said a word all day."

The lids drooping over the hidden eyes were as still as death.

"Well, Zulma," said Joséphine, "don't you ever talk more that that? You don't say a thing. Don't you hear? What do you do when you are with your boy friend?"

The long lashes began to tremble and she raised her eyelids. She revealed her eyes.

"When I am with him," she said, "I don't talk. I listen."

It was time to go home. They lighted the lanterns. The horses were rested and willing. Over in the house, by the light of the hearth, the women were gathering up shawls and blankets. The men were hitching up the carts.

"Let's move closer," said Jacquou, "let's make room for Madame Hélène and the young lady. It's only a little out of the way to take them home."

"Well," said Bobi in the darkness, "is it agreed about the does?"

"Agreed."

"Carle, you get up here."

"And the son?"

"I'm walking home."

"Don't forget your bugle."

"Where is Le Noir?"

"He followed the deer."

"Le Noir!"

"I'm coming."

"Then it is understood about the does?"

"Yes. You name the day."

"Thursday," cried Honoré. "But I'll see you again."

It took time for all to find their places. The horses stamped their hoofs, backed against the shafts, grated their teeth on the bit, and nipped the bells.

At last, Randoulet's cart started slowly across the light soil that surrounded the farm house. The lantern swayed. The springs creaked. Randoulet clicked his tongue to arouse the horse. The beast strained his back and his hind legs to drag the wheels out of the soft places in the fields. On a little slope the cart tilted and Bobi saw once more in the red light of the lantern Zulma's wheatlike head dress. Immediately afterward, the cart and the horse ceased their marine dance and came upon level ground. At the same time arose a strong odour of crushed flowers. They were crossing the field of narcissi. Then Randoulet shouted: "Hoo-oo!" a sort of throaty howl like the cry of a dog. His horse could be heard breaking into a trot. Then the cart having turned and the right side now being hidden, the lantern was no longer visible and even the sound died away.

"That's that," said Jourdan.

Jacquou's cart went off toward Fra-Josépine.

"A single star," said Bobi.

"Where?"

A tiny red dot, twinkling on the horizon, toward the north.

"No," said Jourdan, "that must be a lamp in the mountains."

"One could be guided by it."

"What good would that do?" said Jourdan.

Bobi looked at him. The light that came from the house lighted only the upper part of this face: the curve of the forehead, the bridge of the nose, the cheek bone, the shining corner of the mouth. The rest was in shadow or hidden under the beard.

"It would be worth something to go toward a star that is a lamp in the mountains," said Bobi, "that's all."

They went back toward the house.

"Well," asked Marthe, "what do you think of it all?"

"*He* can hardly say, but as for me, it doesn't seem real," said Jourdan. "This is the first time that we have ever all been together on this accursed land.

"I spoke to Jacquou," he added.

"I had thought of him as perhaps not being very impressionable," said Bobi. "Is he the one who has the most land?"

"He has the best fields."

"They are three men and two women?"

"For the harvest, they generally send for two lads from Verrières, kind of brothers-in-law of Honoré, I believe."

"And," said Bobi, "I found him, on the contrary, hidden under a rough exterior, his heart concealed, perhaps sick."

"No physique."

"No."

"Besides…"

"How did you get that out of him?" gently inquired Marthe.

"I talked to him nearly all the time," said Jourdan. "He has the same idea as the rest of us."

Marthe sat still. She was looking neither at Bobi nor at Jourdan. Outside could be heard the strident song of the prairie night.

"I don't know what is the matter with you men," she said, "what you are looking for, what you want. One would say you are like Zulma, with your eyes fixed on something out there on the water, that you are walking toward it without knowing whether it is the ground that is bearing you or whether you have already entered the pond. And then all at once the water drowns you."

"Women don't understand," said Jourdan.

"They know what they want," said Marthe. "And what they want is on the earth; they can walk all around it and take it without getting drowned."

Bobi went to give the stag some hay. The night was pitch-black. As he approached the shed he heard a rustling in the hay.

"So," he said, "you are here, woodland child?"

"I am here," she said.

"Who are you?"

She came toward him. By her step and her odour, he recognized Joséphine.

"Haven't you gone home?" he said.

"I gave my place to Madame Hélène and the young lady," she said. "They are going to take them to Fra-Josépine. I'll catch up with the cart at the Bornans willow."

"Is that far?" he said.

"I have time," she said. "I am strong. I walk fast. I thought that you would come."

"Where is the stag?"

"I don't know. When I came here he got up and went off toward the forest. I took his place. He left a great nest and lots of warmth in the hay. Come and see."

She took him by the hand. They entered the shed.

"Stoop down," she said.

He stooped down. She crouched beside him. She had a strong woman's odour.

"Yes," he said, "he has made a great deal of heat."

But he rose at once and said to her:

"Come."

They walked side by side toward the road. They swung their arms gently and from time to time the backs of their hands touched.

"You know," he said, "I shall be very glad if we go for the does in the Forest of Nans."

"It will be easy for me to make Honoré do it," she said, "if by any chance he forgets."

"Make him do it," he said, "I'll appreciate that, Joséphine."

But he did not stop walking and as she had hesitated a little in order to stop and face him, she had to take a big stride to catch up with him.

"He is known up there," she said, "and I think they'll lend him everything that is necessary."

"I'm going a little way with you," he said to explain his regular pace, and as she continually had the desire to stop and wait . . .

"We might sit down," she said.

"I am sure that it is better to keep on walking," he said. "They must have the desire for the does," he said.

"The desire, they have," she said. "And what desire one has, one holds onto."

She had advanced with two or three quick steps. She found herself in front of Bobi. She had, so to speak, cut him off and they had suddenly found themselves one against the other, she standing still, he moving on her until he touched her from hips to shoulders. To keep from falling he caught her in his arms. Then gently she leaned her head forward and kissed him full on the mouth, on his lips, just as he was about to speak.

He made a slight movement of recoil. She slipped from his arms. She must have leaped backwards, her skirt had swished. She had run away. Now, she was there no longer and there was no sound in the enveloping darkness. She must have run toward the road.

For a long time he had the scent of narcissus in his mouth.

"I couldn't have had it explained more clearly," he said.

The night stirred. It had soft and supple movements, the cosmic freedom of the movement of blood in a sleeping man or animal; the dance which oceans must obey, and the moon and the stars, and that causes the gentle flow of blood while the creature is sleeping. The night raised the earth's odours; the scent of the field of narcissi no longer signified flowers, but, at the end of its syrupy unfolding in the black sky, it descended again to touch the earth and Bobi standing alone in the field.

Bobi tasted the odour that had remained in his mouth. He still felt on his lips the weight and the warmth of Joséphine's lips.

"It is difficult," he said to himself.

He thought of his plan: the stag, the does, the flowers, the search for joy. To sow joy, to have it take root and be like a lush meadow with millions of roots in the earth and millions of blades in the air. To have it the participant, like the dancing sea, the dancing river, the dancing blood, the dancing grass, the whole revolving world.

"I know very well what she wanted," he thought; "I am not a fool."

He called out: "Joséphine! Joséphine!"

He had a peculiar voice, springlike, that came from down in his throat. It was made for the call. With that voice one could not say: "Orion-Queen Anne's lace." One could only call.

"Perhaps we each have our own joy," thought Bobi.

His springtime voice choked in his throat. He called no more.

"Perhaps there isn't any world joy," he said to himself.

It was at this moment that he heard the bugle. It was playing far off in the night. It had winding, liquid tones. Its notes were like the soft hands of God. They opened and in the damp of their palms could be seen living seeds, split wide open, overflowing with forests and beasts. The forests poured from between the moist fingers, they flowed over the earth, they sprang from the earth with their mounds of foliage, their long echoing corridors, their rafters glistening with leaves and sunlight. All the paths were open and the horizons no longer hidden but raised above the paths like tents.

On the slopes of Mouille-Jacques, before he went to bed, young Carle was playing the bugle as he turned to the four corners of the night.

For the first time, Bobi heard the lyricism of man's hope. The beginning was completed.

CHAPTER

∽

IO

Nothing would have happened had it not been for the blue wind. After one has drunk, one makes up one's mind; one does not do so on an empty stomach. But the blue wind came up from the sea.

The sea is not far away. It is far, if you like, if you measure the distance that separates us by a man's pace or even with the trot of your horse. You have to go up and down hill after hill, and over plains, and through valleys, and climb more hills like the back of a cow with a ridge sharper and barer than a saw blade, and as blue, almost steel-blue, treeless, grassless, made of rocks that reflect like mirrors and are so noisy with the wind that sometimes, when they surge suddenly from the milky morning sky, you think you have come upon the sea and are surprised by an immense schooner in full sail. But it is even farther away. It is at the end of the red lands. And there it looms so wide, so terribly wide, so flat, so deeply sunk in the sky, that you realize, in thinking of Grémone Plateau, that it is very near. For, without that need it has of being fastened to the curve of the earth, it would rise so high, though still remaining flat, that we would see it appearing above the Aiguines Mountains, swept by ships, and with its great black fishes that sleep while the sun and the waves play over them.

The blue wind came up from the sea.

It was laden with clouds. It blows only in the springtime. Beneath it, it trails the rain and the heat. It spreads great shadows over the meadows, over the land where the wheat grows, over the groves of trees. These shadows, thickened by the reflection of new sap, are the bluest of all shadows. The sky from one end to the other is completely inhabited by immense clouds in the shapes of monstrous men, or wild beasts or horses. The wind carries them along, drags them, and pushes them, and above all animates them with a great life that is not confined within each cloud, man, beast, horse, but which passes from one to the other without a barrier; so that at any moment the form of a man flows gradually into the spine of a beast, the horse has made a gigantic leap, then he lets his thickened legs trail away; his thighs, his hoofs, join, and he has become like a mountain. His name is a forest of trees. Then, again, it flows and slips into all the shapes in the world. The sky is in a great passion.

The rain was falling unceasingly upon the plateau. It had assumed the slant of the wind and its caprice. It was not falling from the sky; it leaped out of the south in great spurts as if it were thrown up from the sea. The earth of the plateau, crushed by the falling weight of these waves, wounded by the cutting of these blades of water that struck it on a bias, streaming with mist, skinned, its tender places uncovered, flowed in thick streams of mud down every slope. The seedlings, caught unawares in their subterranean life, were struggling, clinging with all their roots to little clods of earth, but the rain was exhausting them, and the sudden flood of waters tore them from their holes and carried them away, their roots outspread like little medusas.

The wheat fields were buried beneath the silt of the new streams. The trees, whose heavy foliage made the branches groan, resisted the wind and the waters; then the weary main branches split almost noiselessly, clear to the sapwood, and great weights of leaves fell, tearing long strips of bark.

Suddenly, in a parting of the clouds, the calm and the sun fell like a spray of fire. The puddles, the grooves in the tall grasses, the veins in the leaves, the tips of the thistles, the wet earth, everything that kept a thread of water or an oozing, blazed with reflections. Banks of light carried the dazzled eye from the ground to the grass, from the grass to the trees, from the trees to the caverns of the sky, where among the moving clouds flew sparkling sunbeams like flocks of doves. Then everything began to glide from what was the colour and light of the earth like the dazzling motion of the scales of a moving serpent. The rose tint of the distant roof of Mouille-Jacques melted into the green of a meadow, the blue of a cloud passed into the azure of the sky, the green of the meadow gradually melted until it mingled with the dark fronds of the elms on the edge of old Silve's abandoned field; the sky grew white, the shadows ran over the plateau like footprints; the water rang along the grooves in the grasses, gathered in drops at the joining of the veins in the leaves, suddenly cast a thousand new reflections before going out beneath the swaying undulation of a new grey rain that the wind was bringing up from the sea.

"I have never felt more carefree," said Jourdan.

He was filling his pipe. He complacently heaped the tobacco with the tip of his finger.

"You don't think the narcissi will be hurt?"

"On the contrary," said Bobi, "they love water."

All around La Jourdane the earth was gorged with rain. Water welled up from every hole. At the edge of the field, in a moment of calm, a poor mole was seen passing, sleek as a rat that is pulled out of a jar of oil. It did not know where to go, and without the security of the earth, it must have hidden in a hollow in the wall near the empty sties.

"Bad for the wheat," said Jourdan.

Not only could they not work, but the old work melted under the rain. Gradually all was lost and, besides, there was no telling how much time it would take for the ground to dry after the end of the rain.

Moreover, it showed no signs of letting up.

"But, I should worry," said Jourdan; "I haven't planted any wheat. I have enough for three years."

"You'll sow this autumn," said Bobi.

"Whenever I find time," said Jourdan.

"Just to have a little in advance."

"Yes," said Jourdan, "only a little in advance, two or three years, and not in money, in wheat."

And he thought with a calm joy of those two or three years of which he was already assured. His work was no longer changed into bits of paper lying flat under Marthe's chemises. It was changed into three beautiful years with three winters, autumns, springs, and summers.

"The weather is bad," he said, "but it is not ugly."

They had left the door and window open, for it was very hot. The earth smelt strong. At each gust of wind, the sky revealed new depths.

On the afternoon of the third day, they heard the galloping of a horse. It was Honoré who appeared, riding bareback. His eyes were a trifle wild and he insisted upon rubbing down his horse before he would come in and change to dry clothes. He had just passed through the downpour. And this time the rain had been more violent than before, pierced by two long, sulphurous flashes of lightning.

"I saw the lightning leaping in the meadows like carp in the ponds," he said.

He said that Jacquou was like a devil. Their huge field that extended all the way to old Silve's land was all furrowed by streams and the topsoil with its wealth of green wheat had been stirred like a pudding.

"Our sowing," he said, "is gallivanting down the Ouvèze."

When the rain ceased, torrents could be heard pouring down the slopes of the plateau and echoing through the river valley.

There was nothing left, he said, but a tenth of what they had done. And he regretted his labour less than this sowing, already sprouted, and which had been carried off with its blades, its roots, and its promise.

Afterwards, he told a little of what Jacquou was doing. It was not in hot anger. It was as though one said: "The hell with it, anyway," and threw down one's tools and went and sat down and let the rest go hang. That man has had some hard knocks. He lost a son in '04, Joséphine's brother. She did not know him, she was born after. Their house burned down. That was in the valley of the Buëch River, near the mountains.

"I didn't know that," said Jourdan.

"Yes," said Honoré, "here they began all over again. This weather will never let up," he said.

Then he spoke of the does. He asked if that was still a go. The idea pleased him. The other evening, Joséphine had talked to him about it.

Yes, but Bobi said they needed nets, and that the people of Verrières ought to be notified.

Then Honoré said that the people of Verrières had been notified. And there was a moment's silence in which only the sound of the rain could be heard.

He said: "The truth is, that before coming here, I went somewhere else."

That was why he was so wet, a little wild, and why he was so profuse in his thanks about the horse. He was assured that the horse was now quiet and eating fine hay.

Then, here is what he had done. He had gone down off the plateau by the Ubacs road. He had crossed the Ouvèze on the wooden bridge and he was afraid of only one thing: that was not to find the bridge upon his return, for the river was rising visibly. He had gone as far as the road, hoping to meet some men from the quarry. It was there he got the worst of the storm. At last he saw, not a quarry worker, for anybody was crazy to expect to see any in that weather, but the pedlar of Chartreuse elixirs.

"He is blind," he said.

He, Honoré, had taken shelter in the roadmenders' shed; hardly a shelter, a roof of branches. He heard someone singing. That gave him a turn. He saw a queer specimen of a fellow coming toward him. Everyone had known him for a long time, but to see him walking in the rain without hurrying, his head up, his cane out in front of him, and to hear him singing, gave you a queer feeling. Especially as in spite of the time of day there was an odd light under the clouds and the rain.

"You understand," said Honoré, "in spite of all that, it wasn't that. I've seen other queer things. But when he heard me, he came and sat down beside me. And then, well, to see him like that—he is old, you just can't imagine how old!—with only his little pack (as long as people buy bottles from him it's all right, but when nobody buys, how does he get along?) and him alone on the road. Blind. In the rain. I tell you, to see him like that, and then, to look at him carefully, to listen to him, to realize that he is happy as can be, really happy, and that he sings because he is happy, well!…

"Anyway, that fellow," he went on after a moment, "you can really say that he has nothing."

The pedlar was, in fact, going to Verrières. And when you know the road that climbs up there, you wonder how he manages to get up, blind as he is, in bad weather and sometimes at night.

He had answered that, for him, it was always night.

"Just get that!" said Honoré.

"I know," said Bobi. "And there are things that are even more extraordinary. That is why people must have confidence."

"Well, then," said Honoré, "I said to him: 'Since you are going to Verrières, would you mind telling old Richard? You know him?'

"'Do I know him?' he said. 'His is the fourth house from the street beyond the fountain, at the corner where the grocery store is. There used to be an old mulberry tree in that place a long time ago. They've cut it down.'

"I said to him: 'I don't know anything about that.'"

"He answered: 'I do, don't you worry.'

"'Well,' I said to him, 'you tell Richard.'

"He said to me: 'Yes, I'll tell Richard. But I can't simply say to him: "I tell you." Tell him what?'

"'Tell him that we're coming.'

"'Who are "we"?'

"I was stumped to tell him. I said to myself: 'Will you tell him?' Anyway, what did I risk? I said to him: 'It is to trap some does in the Forest of Nans.'

"Then he said to me: 'Don't count on me.'

"I said to him: 'I am asking a favour of you.'

"He said to me: 'No, you are asking me to do a beastly thing. Beastly things,' he said, 'are things I don't do. I might be able to do them to skunks like you or to your kind, but what you've told me, no.'

"I looked at him. I took in his old face. I said: 'What do you mean, beastly thing?'

"He replied: 'It would be even worse to try to explain to you and, besides, I've got to be on my way.'

"He stood up.

"'You have eyes,' he said. 'You are fine creatures to have eyes! I've never had them since I was born. So I don't exactly know what you call "seeing with your eyes," but, judging by what you do, it doesn't seem like much. Or else you must be a fine lot. Because' (and as he spoke, he started away, and if I hadn't held onto him, he would have been gone) 'because you bear the consequences,' he said.

"I held him by the arm. I said to him: 'Sit down.'

"'No.' And he pulled away toward the road or the rain. 'That's all I have to say to you.'

"Finally I said to him: 'If I tell you, you'll understand. If I don't tell you, you will imagine the usual things and you are wrong. Sit down, I'm going to explain. You'll see if it isn't worth the trouble.'

"I was about to say: 'He looked at me.' No, for he is blind. But he turned his eyes toward me, and then I saw his eyes, empty; the road, empty, the rain, empty; the world, empty. And I thought (I swear to you) I thought, no, the world is not empty.

"'Sit down,' I said.

"'Are you going to kill them?' he said.

"'That's exactly what we're not going to do.'

"'Are you going to catch them alive and then sell them?'

"'Not that, either.'

"'What's even worse,' he said, 'are you going to put them in cages?'

"'Not that, either.'

"'Then I don't understand.'

"'I am glad to hear you say so. And now I am going to explain it to you.'

"Well, I'll tell you the truth," said Honoré to Bobi, "I'll tell you what I told him, but I've no idea, really, what you want to do."

"What did you tell him?" said Bobi.

"What seemed the most logical thing to me."

"Then that must be precisely what I want to do," said Bobi.

"Listen," said Honoré. "He was all this time staring at me with his empty eyes. I said to him: 'I am from Grémone Plateau.'

"'I know.'

"I said: 'Life isn't pretty.'

"And I swear that he answered: 'Life is very beautiful.'

"I said to him: 'We have bought a stag.' I said 'we.' It was Jourdan, but I said 'we.'"

"You did right," said Jourdan.

"'We have bought a stag.'

"He asked: 'What for?'

"I thought a moment. 'For nothing.'

"'What do you mean, for nothing?'

"'Just to have around us.'"

"And that is God's truth," said Bobi.

"But it took me a long time to make him understand."

"What didn't he understand?"

"That the stag was free. He said: 'You have shut him up somewhere?'

"'No.'

"'He goes where he likes?'

"'Yes.'

"'All the time?'

"'Yes.'

"'He runs all over the place?'

"'Yes. He comes to see us. He pays us visits. He looks at us, then he runs away and we watch him run.'

"'He must spoil your fields.'

"I thought to myself: If there are any left! The rain was coming down hard enough to split the earth, and I heard the torrents tearing down the Ubacs, carrying the sowing with them.

"I said to him: 'It doesn't make any difference to us.'

"He sat a moment, turning the idea over in his head. And afterwards I had the feeling that he wasn't talking to me any more, but maybe to the horse. The horse was there beside us under the branches, and from time to time he stirred when the cold water dripped onto his spine.

"'This is something new,' he said. 'You can never tell what they'll end up doing. They may end up by seeing truly.'

"He said to me: 'Well, and the does?'

"I said: 'Well, the does are for him.'

"'So that he can have them for himself?'

"'Yes.'

"'Free?'

"'Yes.'

"'You are going to catch them in the net, carry them to the plateau alive, then let them go, and he will find them if he likes?'

"'That's exactly our plan.'

"'And afterwards?'

"It was then that I invented. 'Afterwards,' I said, 'that's all. They will have little fawns, one, then two, then four, then ten, and we'd be glad if there were a hundred. And they'll all start running about.'

"'And what would you do with them?'

"'Nothing,' I said. 'That's all. It would make us glad.'"

"You have invented nothing," said Bobi.

"Is that really what we're going to do?"

"Just that," said Bobi. "Then what did he say?"

"He was still a moment. Then he said: 'You have a big chance of having eyes.'

"Afterwards the rain let up some. It was about ten o'clock this morning. I said: 'I can count on you?'

"'You can count on me, as many as there are of you. I will do your errand.'

"I said: 'Excuse me, I must go. I am going to tell them that all's well.'

"He said to me: 'Go.'

"I led the horse out. He called me back and he asked: 'Are you the one who thought of that?'

"'No, it was a man.'

"And I told him about you.

"'Tell him,' he said, 'that I would like to know him.'"

Honoré was afraid of the night in such weather. He went off in the twilight. There was a moment of brightness. The sun with fully a quarter of its rays had succeeded in forcing the seam of earth and sky. Another fourth of its rays pierced the clouds and, passing under three tunnels of mother-of-pearl, illuminated, in the darkest part of the storm, a mysterious cavern of gold, sulphur, and coal. Colours were suspended in the air in places where there was nothing to hold them save a delicate web of mist.

Honoré, with his head bowed, passed through them on his big horse. He carried the reflections with him, and with red thighs, green head, yellow arm, and black back, he was like a cavalier on parade.

~

They had agreed upon the first fair day. That was the following week. They set out with four light carts: Jourdan and Bobi in one, Honoré and Jacquou in another; in still another, Carle and his son (they had borrowed Madame Hélène's mare, and that very morning, while they were harnessing her, the stallion smelled the female and began to kick. This started Carle to thinking of something entirely new, but he said nothing about it). The other cart belonged to Randoulet and he was in it alone.

The four vehicles, coming from the four corners of the plateau, met at the crossroads by the fig tree, just above the steep slope opposite the mountains that descends into the deep Valley of the Ouvèze.

It was just at the verge of daybreak. The sky and the earth were still full of shadows but the cuckoo was singing. The weather was unsettled. Jourdan and Bobi, who had come the farthest, were the last to join them. They brought up the rear of the caravan.

At the head was Jacquou's cart driven by Honoré, who knew the way. Just before plunging down the great slope which, by twenty zigzags twisting among trees, rocks, and ravines, descends toward the Ouvèze just at the wooden bridge, they turned to look back at the plateau. They had left up there, besides the women, Le Noir and Jacquou's hired man. Those two men were charged, during the afternoon, to ride on horseback on a patrol through the territory to protect the women. Against what, they did not know, but, having thus decided, they were reassured. Especially in the neighbourhood of La Jourdane and of Mouille-Jacques, where Marthe and Madame Carle were alone.

Then, here is how they went: at the head, Jacquou and Honoré in a cart nearly new, with hubs shining with grease, a dappled horse with enormous rump who held back the whole weight on the slope just by swelling his haunches in the shafts. About five or six metres behind came Carle and his son, in a cart or rather a buggy, not very even on its axle and swung on two high oval springs. It bobbed from side to side. Carle was driving. He accustomed his wrist to the mare's gait. Madame Hélène had always had a decided leaning toward elegance, and the mare walked with a long stride, rather delicate but very pleasant. For a man's wrist it was enough just to get used to it; afterward it was no more disagreeable than anything else. So Carle thought. He was also thinking about his idea of that morning. Randoulet had left a little space between him and Carle. He clearly saw how things were going up ahead: that buggy that went squeak-squeak and that mare with her crazy little ways—it was all very well for ladies. But he had his solid market cart, his strong red horse, a mechanical contraption for putting on the brake, so strong it could stand any test. It was everything he could wish for. He had passed the reins over his right arm. His hands were free. He was rolling a cigarette. Behind him he could hear Jourdan's cart, ten metres away, and it stayed at ten metres, steady, as though held by a bar. That came from the fact that Randoulet, for balance and regularity, was the first man in the world, and that Jourdan followed well, accommodatingly, it must be said.

The four equipages thus descended the slope, one behind another, at a walk.

The trees were wet. Water flowed in narrow little flutelike ravines. Cuckoos sang on every side. The sky was pale with light and the earth still black with shadow. The long days of rain had made everything new. The odours were very heavy. The horses sniffed them. In the soft and tender air could be heard the rustle of great distant rains, far behind the mountains to the north.

As they emerged from the trail that wound downward, the men saw the straight road ahead of them. It crossed the Ouvèze by the wooden bridge, made straight for the mountains, dipped into a vale, climbed along the slope, and disappeared above in a forest of oaks. It wound over the landscape. It gave ease and escape to all. It fared forth amongst the shadows and the pools of sunlight, the meadows, woods, fields, hills, hillocks, and valleys.

For a moment the horses continued at their peaceful pace; the brakes still screeched against the wheels. They went swinging across the country. The men all realized that this was not simply a promenade together in a caravan—that in itself was fine—but that they had set out in the search for joy. Then, they loosened the brakes, they clicked their tongues, and the horses began to trot one after another—Jacquou's horse, the mare, Randoulet's, Jourdan's—and the four carts crossed the Ouvèze on the wooden bridge. Everything creaked and jumped—the planks, the cables, the piles, and the props—and this was not prudent. The river growled a moment beneath the horses' hoofs, beneath the cart wheels; then they were once more on the road; with the song of the trees, and this time the sun, for morning was coming. Then they entered a valley and gradually the light grew duller. A cuckoo began to sing in the willows by the river.

At noon, they had already crossed the first six hills.

Six pearl-coloured hills with their grey grass with russet feathery tops. The wind flattened the grass and it was grey. The wind ceased, the grass straightened up, the plumes spread, and over the whole hill swept those sparkling reflections that one sees in seashells. And with it the sound as of cat's fur being ruffled.

They had crossed the first six hills, ascended, then descended, climbed up again, and so on, and each time Jacquou's cart was the first to disappear on the far side of the slope, then Carle's, then Randoulet's, then Jourdan's, and after that, as there was no one else, each time a cuckoo began to sing on the lonely hill. But the cuckoos on the other side were quiet and hid under the leaves, for the four carts made a loud noise as they descended. No longer could be heard the rustling of the grass like cat's fur. The cuckoos that could see one another in the branches watched one another. What is happening? they said. If the one in the oak flies away, I'll fly, too. The one in the oak did not fly away. They all stayed hidden and waiting. Down in the valley the upgrade was beginning. The horses slowed to a walk. There was no more tinkling of collars. The cuckoos began to sing again. And it was like that for six hills. For they were wild hills where one does not often go, where at any rate a caravan like that of men and horses had never passed before.

At noon they were on the crest of a hill. They rode along the crest of a ridge that was higher than the others, really a mountain, less friendly, shaggy with holly and box, and where there were at intervals a few larches in their winter garb. The cuckoos were no longer heard. A crow flew over.

To the right unfolded an immense country with hills, that were like molehills, stuck one against the other, their heads all yellow with sunshine, their black bellies flat against the earth. Far away in the haze lay a sort of flat raft such as woodsmen sometimes make for floating the logs down to the plains. It was Grémone Plateau. On its edges the sun was boiling in the forests. To the left a bar of mountains rose very high, covered from head to foot with a thick cloak of black firs. Behind it, a still higher mountain with snow, and behind that one a whole cluster of mountains entirely covered with ice and making the distant wind whistle and steam.

The horses went at a walk. They were approaching the stopping place. The men looked reflectively to the right, then to the left.

They did not talk much during the halt. They could not help thinking of the vast landscape and contemplating the monstrous relief of the earth. The horses were near them, unhitched but hobbled, because they had stopped in a very rich pasture and the animals had suddenly become very greedy. The air was light, and over all was silence. A bird passed slowly over the encampment. It was a reddish bird, a metre wide, with enormous feathers. The transparent border of his wings flashed in the sun. He flew indolently in spite of the lightness of the air in these altitudes. He went a-voyaging above the immense abyss that contained tiny hills, tiny valleys, the little river, the little Grémone Plateau, the haze and the wide, unknown plains. He felt himself being borne along by the air. Then, ceasing the flapping of his wings, he began to sleep, motionless, wafted like a leaf upon the water.

In the course of the afternoon, the caravan entered a narrow defile that cleft the two schist mountains from top to bottom. There was just room for a sort of flimsy and threadlike road, beside a big torrent all in knots and rages that spat in the very faces of the horses. The road wound thus for a long time, at the bottom of this ravine, in almost nocturnal shadow. The men's heads were filled with the noise of the torrent. It was impossible to think. Only at times the views of the morning flashed in their memory: the pearly hills or the sight of sandy Grémone Plateau far away in the haze. But what was solid within them, in spite of the monstrous and brutal purring of the green waters, was the sense of journeying forward toward something. And all together; that, too, gave a stout heart.

From time to time Jacquou could be seen ahead turning around to see if his companions were following. As they could not make themselves heard in that noise, they did not call out, they only raised their arms in the air and that meant: we're all together. Then Jacquou would turn his face forward once more, the arms were lowered, the men began to watch their horses' step, the four carts turned in and out the bends, climbed the slopes, passed through the fords. All four crossed from one bank to the other, following the road, without ever becoming separated, and thus the procession moved forward.

At the first hours of an evening golden like honey, they arrived at the entrance of a broad mountain vale, full of forests and pastures. The massive palisade of Nans barred road, earth, sky, hope. At the edge of the wood rose the smoke from the village of Verrières. The road wound up to it through meadows covered with flowers that already smelt of milk.

They found old Richard.

"Ah, yes!" he said.

Suddenly they were afraid that the nets were not ready for some reason or other, or that the pedlar had not done the errand.

"Yes, he did," said Richard.

The house was on the edge of the village. The whole forest was spread out before it. Where was the clearing of Lénore?

"Up there," said Richard.

He showed them a tiny open space high up on the side of the mountain.

"We'll go this evening," said Jacquou. He looked at the others. "This evening."

"Just as you like," said Richard.

The horses were tired. The men had wanted to know immediately whether anything had happened to prevent the great dream that they had dreamed all day long in the swaying of the carts, and they had jumped to the ground without thinking of unharnessing. Now, it must be thought of.

"Come," said Richard.

The mountain stables were magic stables for the horses. There was a warmth that seized you all at once and a smell of hay hard to imagine. The horses entered timidly, thinking: No, it isn't true! No, this is not possible! Then, why, yes, it was both true and possible!

The nets were rolled up behind the feed bins. They smelt of hayseeds and were full of dust from the dry grass.

Three great bundles of nets were carried and spread out in the meadow beside the house. When they began to open them out, all the village children flocked around.

Gradually the valley filled with a soft night. It grew suddenly cool, and smelt of trees and damp meadows.

Jacquou felt the texture of the nets. The weave was heavy, of flat green cord. In short, it imitated a leaf. Honoré held one end of the net. Randoulet held the other end. This piece might be twenty metres long. It was unfolded. Jourdan, Bobi, Carle, his son, Jacquou, and Richard stood looking at it.

"Strong," said Richard.

Bobi had visions of the does running into the net and remaining there, prisoners, not for long, but *ours* (that thought came in spite of everything).

A great star had already opened the eastern sky where the night was heavy like velvet.

Richard told them calmly but kindly to come first and eat in the house. They said that they had brought food and would stay there in the field so as not to bother the mistress.

"Some hot soup," said Richard.

Those were sensible words. They could not resist. But they ate their soup out of doors. The grass had suddenly grown very cold with the evening, but the taste of boiled cabbage went piping hot down their throats.

"Do you remember?" asked Richard.

"I remember," said Honoré.

He saw again the whole familiar forest of his childhood: the paths, the tracks, the ravines, the lairs, the clearings. It seemed to him that the does of his boyhood were not dead and that it was these who were to be hunted.

Richard pointed out to them a few ruses of place and time. He told them to encircle Lénore, leaving the side between the north and west open. And as Honoré looked at the sky he saw that it was the direction opposite the moon. Already a spray of shining foam lighted the night.

"To dazzle them," said Richard.

He also said three or four names. They designated places almost impossible to find. Finally he went and got his trumpet. It was a cow horn, hollow and open at the small end. He blew into it. They saw that even though not a great talker, he knew how to speak to things under his command.

A dull roar came from the horn. It filled the whole valley, struck up the mountain echoes, and the forest awoke like a flock of sheep called by the shepherd.

They set out in the pitch-dark—Honoré at the head, then Bobi, then Jourdan, Jacquou, who carried the horn, Randoulet, Carle, and Carle's son, loaded with nets.

When Jacquou let his repeater strike softly in the hollow of his two hands, it was eleven o'clock and they had just reached Lénore clearing.

The moon had not yet come over the mountain. The sky was light but, in contrast, in the black of the trees and under the shadow of Nans the night was terribly closed in on all sides.

By their odour, Honoré recognized birches and beeches.

"Don't stick hooks in the birches," he said, "the bark does not hold."

He had said that without thinking. He remembered that his father used to say that long ago.

They had to feel the trees with their hands, the height of the trunk and its diameter, to know if the tree was tall and strong. Good. All the while, above their heads they could hear the leaves talking the tree language.

Carle's son had brought the hooks and the wooden mallet.

"This is a beech," he said.

"Let's see," said Honoré.

Honoré had assumed an air of great importance. He touched the tree. He had said "see," but that was misleading. He meant, "wait until I find it to be really a beech," and he discovered it by touching it and by sniffing its leaves.

"Yes, that's one."

"You know everything," said Jacquou.

"Here, yes," said Honoré. "This is my country."

Carle's son got up on Randoulet's shoulders. From there he hammered the hook into the tree at a height of two metres.

"Is it secure?"

"It would hold an ox."

They talked in low tones. They scarcely made a gesture. One could hardly hear them, like the sound of a boar turning over in his lair.

To the hook, they fastened the net and so on. It was two metres high and encircled the whole of Lénore clearing.

"We must fasten it at the bottom," said Bobi.

"Yes," said Honoré, "but without stretching it taut. It must be slack enough to make pockets."

He began to crawl on his hands and knees in the grass.

"Come here. You see," he said, "this is strong."

Bobi crouched beside him. It was a holly root. Honoré dug all around with his hands.

"Give me the rope."

He tied the bottom of the net to the root.

"Come softly," he said.

They crawled all around the clearing.

"Holly," said Honoré, "I can trust, it makes hooklike roots."

They went one behind the other, like bears. Honoré was looking for holly.

"Another one here."

Bobi heard Honoré scratching in the ground.

"Tie it. Do not pull it tight," said Honoré. "Leave some give to the net. That'll do. Come softly."

Carle's son could hardly be heard as he hammered muffled blows with his mallet. He was still on Randoulet's shoulders. He had taken off his shoes so as not to hurt him.

"You won't find them again," said Randoulet.

"I don't care, I'll go barefoot. This is ready," he said.

Carle handed him the end of the net.

"Unhook it," said the son. "It must be caught in a bush. There, it is coming."

"Stop dancing around like a grape treader," said Randoulet.

"I'm doing the best I can," said the son. "It is heavy, this net."

"Do the best you can," said Randoulet, "but don't mash my ears."

Carle's son leaped to the ground.

"Where is Honoré?"

"He's gone."

"Come along," said Carle. "I'm going to try."

"If it was a question of horses," said Randoulet, "I'd trust you. But for choosing trees…"

"Come along anyway."

At the next beech, all three of them stood feeling and sniffing. Then Carle's son smelt beneath him a slightly bitter odour. It was like the odour of the sap that had already run over his fingers.

"This is one."

Randoulet put his back against the tree, clasped his hands in a basket. Carle's son put his bare foot into Randoulet's hands. With two movements, of the calf of Carle's son and Randoulet's arms, the boy was lifted up the trunk. Carle handed him the hook and the mallet. He drew up the net in readiness.

Jourdan and Jacquou were watching the moon. From where they were they could scarcely hear the sounds of the others. However, they did not move, and they listened intently.

There was a sort of stirring beneath the leaves far down by the torrent. At first they thought of some great bird swimming in the branches, but beside them a curlew flew away. At the sound of its wings they could compare and judge. Those were ground animals who, going to drink, were rustling through the brush. Grass fleas were shrilling all around. From time to time, a long, sombre, and strangely sonorous note descended from the heights of Nans. The moonlight was warming the air in the crevasses of the mountain and the great plaques of granite boomed.

"I've often wondered…" said Jacquou.

Little steps were heard, then sounds of water. The leaves were caressing one another. The trees moaned.

"All this is living its life," he said. "It doesn't care a hang about anything else."

They were both lying under the foliage at the edge of the clearing. The earth smelt of mushrooms and the scent of anise that comes from the roots of all trees. From time to time a golden fly crossed the darkness and its light went out beneath the moon. Grass that nothing touched, neither foot nor wind, unfolded, in the coolness of the night, merely with the force of its sap. From the heights a wave of bitter cold swooped down at times, then melted in the trees. It could be heard flowing along the leaves and falling in great tepid drops smelling of stone, upon the two men.

"The fact is," said Jourdan, "if we aren't enjoying ourselves here, it is our own fault."

The moon was at its full and exactly in the spot that Richard had predicted.

All seven of the men went into the forest. They walked toward the moon. They went Indian file. According to the denseness of the foliage, there fell upon them the white light of the sky or shadow. Ten metres from the path that they were following, on either side, the forest maintained its indifference. The trees glistened. Understanding was about to be born between these men and life.

"What attracts them is the water," said Honoré. "Where we have to frighten them," he said, "is near the water. They have been running. They are thirsty. The night is cool. The water sings loud. It can be heard in the farthest places in the woods. The night is still…"

"Keep quiet," said Jacquou.

All seven walked with the same stride. As they crossed the torrent, Bobi said: "Stop!"

He went back a little way. He stooped down. He struck one flat stone against another, the sound was carried by the echoes.

"Something is moving away," said Jacquou.

"It is the sound," said Bobi. "I think that it is here that we ought to start blowing the trumpet. It will be heard everywhere."

Jourdan and Jacquou remained alone in the bed of the torrent. The other five returned toward Lénore.

"Lénore," said Honoré. "You see that beak of mountain up there? Well, Lénore is directly underneath. That is how you can be guided. Walk straight toward the beak of the mountain and you will reach Lénore without fail. Now, let's each go our way, meeting at the nets presently. Wait till the trumpet has blown good and loud and then off we go."

They scattered in the woods. They were scarcely alone, each separated from the other by forty or fifty metres of underbrush, when the trumpet began to sound. Bobi had chosen the spot well. From where Jacquou blew the first blast it was immediately like the snoring of some enormous beast in the throat of the horn, but after a moment, when it had been thrown back by a hundred rocky throats, it became like the cry at the end of the world, just a little before the earth shakes like a sheet. The animal knows the earth sounds, the cry of the rock, the murmur of the mud, the whistling of the dust. The does, lying highest up on the slope of loose shale, pricked up their ears. They looked toward the steep mountain. The wall of rock was all shimmering in the moonlight. While sleeping the doe always weeps, quietly; when she awakes, her eye is all brimming with tears. Through the tears and the moonlight, the does saw the mountain begin to crumble. They bounded over the slope to flee into the trees below. There were five of them. The stones showered beneath them, around them, behind, with the sound of a river aroused. The trumpet sounded again. When they reached the firs, two does trotted in one direction and three fled toward the summit of Trédon. The sound of the falling stones rang through all the echoes of the forest. The trumpet blared. The two sounds mingled struck the underbrush, the bushes, the leaves, the meadows, the rocks, the waters, and the whole country awoke in the night, from Verrières all the way to La Frasse Pass. The squirrels ran around the tree trunks, instinctively seeking shade in which to hide. But the darkness and the noise were everywhere. Marmots whistled from tribe to tribe. The male sentinels growled. The females gathered the little ones with their paws.

The three does, as they crossed the little valley of Verel, met the old herd. There were five ten-year-old does and a famous stag whose cracked left antler buzzed with the slightest wind. The stag was leading his band toward La Frasse, across the Peloux pastures. The three does joined them. The five females sniffed. The three stretched out their noses, stood motionless a moment, foot lifted. The stag looked at them. The five females, who had been full for more than a month, were not jealous. The three does entered the herd. The stag led them at a little trot through the grass. The trumpet sounded. The herd began to gallop faster and faster. The wind murmured in the stag's hollow antler. A solitary little doe that was drinking at the torrent saw them pass and at that moment the roaring of the trumpet and of the mountain reached her. She leaped the stream in a single bound. Her first instinct had been to speed away alone. She was in the season of love with a great desire for solitude, for solitary calling and waiting. She began to trot under the trees. She was all alone with her longing and her fear. The herd of the stag of Epelly went off toward the Saix meadows. The foxes of Serveray ran toward the old millstones of Salenton. The squirrels in the Auterne woods hid their heads in the forks of the high branches.

The trumpeting continued. The otters plunged into the torrent, came up, plunged again, sleek and tense. The birds ran in the trees like rain. All the hedgehogs rolled themselves into balls. Under the burdocks the skunks lighted and extinguished their golden eyes. Weasels turned in mad bounds around the bushes, where their little nests were hidden. A boar awoke, stood up, listened, growled, and lay down again, burying his muzzle in his paws.

The herd of the stag of Epelly stopped in the hollow of La Frasse Pass. He did not dare to go further. The does were pressing against him and whining in his coat. He felt against his rough skin the warm lips and the little cold clacking of trembling teeth. He saw, down in front of him, rising from the white grass, the shining roofs of the village of Frasse, where two dogs had been aroused.

Bobi heard some foxes pass close to him. He saw a pale creature breaking through the undergrowth in a flash of phosphorescent flight. He saw the mountain beak against the sky. Honoré stepped on some soft animal. Carle called. The trumpet blared.

"What lungs!" said Randoulet to himself. He did not know that below in the torrent Jacquou and Jourdan were changing places.

"Give it to me awhile," said Jourdan.

He blew. He aroused the whole forest. The countryside heard and trembled from Verrières clear to La Frasse Pass.

Up in the pass, the stag of Epelly lay down. The does huddled against him.

Carle's son said to himself: "I am going to get lost."

He looked at the mountain beak. The little solitary doe was pursued by the sound of the trumpet. At the same time her love desire was not assuaged. She was alone, she was afraid, but she could only be alone and afraid as long as this roaring filled the country and as long as she did not meet the solitary stag seething like her with desire.

Honoré's legs were wet. The doe stopped to lick her legs. Bobi was thinking of the clearing surrounded by nets. The two does on the high slope sought shelter in the trees. They called to know if the three others were following. The trumpet sounded. The two does began to trot once more in the woods. Randoulet thought: "What are the others up to?"

He heard sounds of animals everywhere, in the leaves, in the bushes. He would have been glad to hear Carle's step, or Honoré's, or Bobi's, or his son's—someone's. In the midst of the sounds, the two does became aware of an ancient odour that they remembered from the year before. It was the odour of hemlock in flower all around the Lénore clearing.

Carle's son said to himself: "Is this the mountain beak that marks the way, or that one?"

He was afraid of getting lost. He called.

The little solitary doe heard a man's voice. She smelt by the odour that the two does had passed not long since, very close. Two empty does. The kind that live without a stag. She followed them. The man continued to call.

"Here I am," said Randoulet.

He was not very far away.

"I was afraid of getting lost."

"Come along."

The foxes of Severay had just understood. The noise was too regular. It was simply a question of getting back to their holes and not budging. The three does came to the Lénore clearing. For them, the world continued to tremble and crumble, like a tree struck at its base. The trumpet sounded. The hemlock was in flower.

"Come along!" cried Honoré.

He had just heard the whining of the does. One was already struggling with her horns against the net. She was taken at once. Randoulet threw her and lay on top of her. It was the doe of the shale slope. At first she thought it was a stag. Then she smelt the odour of a man.

Finally Bobi came up. He saw that Randoulet held one.

"Get the other one, you!" cried Randoulet.

He saw Honoré, Carle, and the son lying in the grass. He looked around the clearing. He saw two great golden eyes motionless in the dark.

The little doe in love, motionless in the dark, had begun to weep as at the approach of a deep sleep. The trumpet sounded. From beyond the tears, beneath the moon, the whole world crumbled like mountains of water. A black shape leaped toward her. She recognized something living and male. Her female desire held her relentlessly fixed to the spot, welcoming anything, even death, provided that it be appeased. The male leaped upon her, overpowered her haunches. He did not smell like a stag but had a strange odour. The doe fell to the ground. She suffered a mingling of love and death. She closed her eyes.

After a moment a man's voice cried:

"Come here!"

The trumpet answered, then it was silent.

The men reached the outskirts of Verrières at the moment dawn touched the summits of the mountains. They were walking across the pastures in a thick, cold, rosy mist. They carried the three does on their shoulders.

Long before they reached the village, they met Richard waiting for them.

"Halt!" he said.

Then: "How many?"

"Three."

"Did you stay awake to get here so early?" they asked.

"No, you made too much noise. You woke everything."

Down in the village the tinkling of the harness and the sound of the horses' stamping could be heard.

"Do you want them alive?" asked Richard.

"Yes," they said.

"Then you'll have to leave at once. I have harnessed your carts. You have made too much noise," he said. "The village men have been to see me. They said: 'They can keep the meat, but they must leave us the hides.' If you want to keep the does alive, leave at once. I'll see about settling with the village."

Through the mist, they came to the threshing floor, where Richard had tied the four horses that were already harnessed. They loaded the does in Randoulet's cart. They drove the horses along the meadows so that there would not be any rolling of wheels or noise of steps. They made a detour around the village. They came once more to the road at the bottom of the valley where it enters the gorges.

When day broke, they were already far away, having left the bed of the torrent and climbed over the mountain. To their left, flat in the distance, lay the immense country where they were to descend, and to the right the heap of mountains with icy summits and red light.

The night still filled the valleys. At that moment they heard in the depths the roll of thunder.

Toward noon they were in the hills. Instead of seeing the day break, they saw it grow pale. The cuckoos were not singing. A swamplike calm had immobilized the grass, the trees, the air. The sky was stirred with rolling floods of clouds that pushed one another onward with a metallic sound.

At the head of the procession, Honoré whipped up his horse and put him to a trot. Carle awoke his son.

"I wonder," he said, "if this mare can trot as long as we'll have to?"

Randoulet tried to catch up with the others. But as soon as his horse began to trot, he heard the heavy heads of the does striking against the floor of the cart. He called out to stop and the whole caravan halted.

"They'll be killed," he said. "We can't trot. At least *I* can't. *I* can't trot."

"Then nobody shall," said Jacquou.

And they set out once more at a walk under the stormy sky. On all sides arose a perfume of crushed earth.

The little doe had opened her eyes. The other two does had their eyes closed but they were breathing hard and their noses were dry.

As they descended toward the Ouvèze Valley, the weather grew worse. The sky was not calm enough to allow the rain to fall and it was still sweeping violently from one boundary to the other, grumbling beneath the urging of the blue wind. But the darkness was increasing. Between two hills, they saw Grémone Plateau. It was smoking all over like a charcoal pit. With the fog caught in all the trees it seemed split and surrounded by the smoke of a covered fire. The earth was black. The torrents of the Ubacs roared. The Ouvèze River tore by with a terrific noise.

A woodsman heard the carts and came out of the woods. He raised his hand. The caravan halted.

"Where are you going?" he said.

"Grémone Plateau."

"You think you can go this way?"

"We came that way yesterday morning."

"Since then everything has changed."

"Since when?"

"There's been a storm. The hail was as big as hen's eggs. The wooden bridge has been carried off."

He pointed to some small oak branches which had been broken off clean, across the grain, as by an ax.

"What you are going to find up there will not be pretty," he said. "This morning your plateau spilled water and foam like a boiling pot. What you'll have to do," he said, "is to go down as far as the stone bridge while it still holds. You never can tell when it will start up again. I am going to the Quarries."

"We'll take you if you like," said Jacquou.

"No, I'll be there before you," said the man. "I've been watching you coming down the road over the hills for some time. You have been crawling along as if you were bearing the Holy Sacrament."

II

"They are eating," said Marthe.

"All three of them?"

"Yes, but the one that is eating the most is the littlest."

"And your men?"

"They are sleeping. When I saw you coming, I was afraid you were coming to get us for Jacquou."

"He is asleep," said Joséphine. "Honoré is asleep. The weather is sultry."

"I think," said Marthe, "that the bad weather is over."

"And the stag?"

"He came and sniffed at the crack in the door. He has already talked with them. He went off toward the woods. They heard him. It is since then that they have eaten."

Marthe sat down. It was hot. A huge motionless cloud was rotting away in the middle of a sun-filled sky.

"I am tired."

"You are very lucky," said Joséphine.

"What about?"

"I'd like to be tired," said Joséphine, "to be able to lie down any old place, to sleep and think of nothing."

"What's the matter with you?"

"I have no peace."

"We are going to have happiness, Joséphine."

"What happiness, Marthe?"

"What do you mean, what happiness? Good heavens!"

"Don't talk so loud. They are asleep."

"You want me to get mad," whispered Marthe.

She was smiling. She smoothed her grey hair with the palm of her hand.

"You'd have to have been pretty well off before not to know what we're talking about now when we say 'happiness.'"

"You know very well, Marthe, that I have never been happy."

"You are going to make me say some hard things to you."

"You have always been very gentle with me, Marthe. We've been a long time without seeing each other. Today, I wanted you to talk to me. That's why I've come."

"I've been worried about you, my little Joséphine. I must admit. Do you remember the day we met at the fair at Roume?"

"Ten years ago! I remember. That's why I came today."

"I have been worried ever since, until I knew that you were to be married. And since then, you have had children, and then you have calmed down."

"What do you know about it?"

"It's evident."

"Well, nothing is evident and everything is deceiving."

Marthe sat a moment in silence. She was gently smoothing her hands.

"I've had moments of pleasure, certainly," said Joséphine, "like everybody else."

"Then you've nothing to complain of."

"I am complaining of restlessness."

"Cure yourself of it."

"Cure yourself of your own blood, you who are so good at giving advice. Aren't you ever restless?"

Marthe smoothed her hands.

"Yes, I used to be restless all the time."

"If you aren't any longer, tell me what you did. I shan't have come all the way here in vain."

"I still am," said Marthe.

She pretended to be examining her hands. The two women spoke slowly and in an undertone. They were in the kitchen of La Jourdane, the wide door open to the afternoon.

"Everything makes you wish for something," said Joséphine.

"Are you talking about restlessness or about always wishing for something?" said Marthe.

"You have nothing," said Joséphine, "you get something, then it goes."

"The taste remains."

"Regret."

"That burns hotter and hotter within us. I am not arguing against you, Joséphine. I am saying the same thing as you."

"Time is passing. The present goes, everything goes. I am thirty-two years old."

"I am almost twice that."

"In ten years it will all be over."

"I am almost twice that, and when you say all is over, it isn't true."

"What is left?"

"Desire, Joséphine....I didn't expect you today," continued Marthe after a moment. "I was at peace. I had gone to see if they were asleep. Jourdan is asleep. Bobi is asleep. The horse is asleep. I was still a little uneasy about the does. They were not eating. Now they have begun to eat. I felt at peace, calm, without any care, empty. Then I heard your step. You came in. You said: 'Hello, Marthe.'"

"That happens to me ten times a day, Marthe; one minute of calm, one minute of peace, a minute of nothing, nothing hurts any more, and then something comes in and says: 'Hello, Joséphine.'"

"I wonder," said Marthe, "if that isn't necessary? I think it must be."

"Why, Marthe? Other things aren't necessary."

"Because, Joséphine, if you consider, if you realize that since my first long skirts, I…I remember, and when I say since my first long skirts, I am wrong. Since before that, always, to be correct, but at times when one is young one does not realize. Yes, it is necessary."

"What are you talking about?"

"Restlessness. Always waiting for something. Always wanting, being afraid of what one has, wanting what one has not. To have it, and then immediately being afraid of losing it. And then, knowing that it is going to slip through our hands. And then it does slip through our hands. I was going to say, like a bird escaping. No, like squeezing a handful of sand, that's what it's like. I think it is necessary, that we have it when we are born, like the frogs whose hearts at birth are three times as big as their heads."

"That isn't true."

"What?"

"When they are born, frogs have nothing but head, and scarcely any body, a thing like glass. Inside, the heart is a tiny speck like a red flea."

"Joséphine! If you think it is size that I mean!…The heart has three times as much will, and when the frog is big, his head is still the same head but the heart has grown so big that you can see it beating through the back and it is bigger than a hazel nut. I know what I'm saying, my girl."

"Talk lower."

"Don't be afraid. We aren't going to wake them. They are tired out. They are like the horse. They've all been a long way together."

"Listen, I think they are moving upstairs."

"I don't think so."

"Keep still, Marthe. Listen."

"It is Jourdan. He is lying on his back. He is snoring. He does that when he is tired and when he falls into a deep sleep. I went to look at them just now, all three of them. Bobi was lying on his side, his nose almost buried in his pillow, his mouth half open, like children when they have worms. If you could see him, he looks like a child. Don't be afraid. Let me talk. I know that they are asleep."

"Marthe, do you have faith?"

"In what?"

"In what they are going to do?"

"Yes."

"Do you believe all they say?"

"It has already been proved."

"Not everything."

"What have you to complain off?"

"I have nothing to complain of. I have nothing to blame anybody for. I haven't even seen him since the Sunday we ate here."

"You have something bothering you."

"No, I tell you."

"Yes, you have."

"Yes, I'd like to know what he wants to do."

"I am an old woman."

"What do you mean?"

"I'm just talking to myself. I understood at once what he wanted to do. And that is because I have lost what you have and because the desire is still there."

"You mean restlessness?"

"I mean that I'd like to lie flat like the water of a spring."

"What do you mean, Marthe? Tell me."

"I mean that the house is quiet and there is no longer any sound either in the fields or in the sky."

The wind passed very high, at least two kilometres above the earth. It was a mountain wind, but at a certain moment it descended a little. It met a big cloud. It began to thrash it with vigorous blows, but silently, and soon the sky was filled with down as if someone up there had begun to pluck a goose. A shower of shadows fell on the earth. The drops were as big as fields. Each one covered groves of trees or meadows, summits or hillsides. The shadows walked on the earth. What was covered the moment before, was uncovered. The shining poplars stopped blazing with their cold flame; the shadow was passing over them.

At the edge of Grémone Forest there was a field of vervain. It was a lonely spot. From there the pond could be seen. The kingfishers could reach it with one sweep of their wings. They came there to sleep in the coolness beneath the velvety leaves. Sometimes there were more than fifty of them, crouched under the grass. The sun gleamed on the hairs of the leaves and in the little rim of the eye that kingfishers keep open even when they sleep. When there was blue underneath the weeds, it was not shadow but the wing of a bird. This pearly vervain has a fine penetrating odour. The kingfisher detects the fish, chiefly through the little yellow pad at the hinge of his beak, and the length of the four long red feathers that border his wings. For it is with these hard feathers that he strikes the fish below the ventral fins to burst the air bladder.

The stag came upon some box that had remained a russet colour. He tried to eat some, but the hard little leaves stuck to his palate. He chewed a bit of a box branch. It was an old plant that had only its autumn sap. Terribly bitter. The stag tossed his head. It was to chase away images that had entered his head at the same time as the bitter odour of the old box. He remembered the lofty heights of the mountains at the place where the sloping pastures stop short against the sky. He pawed the little box bush. He heard a whir of birds passing, then nothing more.

In the stable at La Jourdane, the little doe had eaten some hay. It had a prison odour, and that made her sad. The other two does had been caught after their evening grazing and now they were chewing the cud of forest odours, odours of Nans, that made them drowsy, and for that reason they did not touch the hay. Their tear glands were full of tears ready to fall as soon as deep sleep came.

The little doe approached the door. She smelled free air on the other side of the door. There was a strange sensation in the soft part of her shoulder and between her thighs. The muscles of her legs grew taut. She tried to call. She had only her love voice. The two other does awoke. The big horse kept on sleeping. The little doe lay down beside the door. She spread her hind legs apart. She licked herself a long time between the legs. She was licking the odour of a female in heat. It was better than hay, better than the grass of Nans. It was salty as stone, hot as stone that has been in the sun. She shut her eyes. She felt the tear glands swelling and growing heavy on either side of her head. Then she spread her legs wide, lay on her belly on the cold floor. She stretched out her head and sniffed the air that came under the door from the outside.

I 2

During the very first days of autumn, Bobi went to Fra-Josépine. The herd of does and fawns had already been seen several times passing far away across the fields. The stag came only rarely to La Jourdane. Someone had said that they had their quarters on old Silve's deserted lands. That seemed quite possible because of the springs and the rich grass, but it was surprising in one way, for Grémone Forest was shadier, more mysterious, and Bobi had said that deer loved mystery more than grass.

After crossing two hummocks of land, you could see Fra-Josépine. At this time of year, it was a great human thing with high clumps of verdure, tall, wide, round, drooping, bowed down with thick leaves in which the cold night winds had cut only the slenderest openings. The house was surrounded by ancient sycamores which had always been allowed to grow naturally. They were in magnificent health and pride. The trunks, with their protruding reddish-brown muscles, rose toward the heavens with such force that they raised the earth about their roots. Under the shelter of the trees, the shade developed a thick grass beneath which seeped the overflow of a broad spring.

The house seemed dead. The wind could be heard whistling in the north attic window.

"It looks as though they are not at home."

It was, in fact, the hour when Aurore, mounted on the young red mare, rode in the forest. She had been doing that all summer. It had become a habit. She fled everyone's company. She spoke to no one. If someone called: "Aurore, come here!" she would prod her horse with her hard little heels and go on, pretending to be deaf. She seemed to have confidence only in this human speed that flowed in her body with her blood, and that bore her far from everything, even when she was standing still. She had become elusive and as hard as a brook stone.

Sometimes, when she passed by you, and if you did not call to her, if you looked at her as she went straight on, you could see, quickly extinguished beneath her eyelids, a long look as sad as July verdure.

Bobi went up the steps to the terrace. His foot made no sound on the moss-covered stones. The French doors were shut. He approached to look through the glass. All within seemed to be in order. It was a large drawing room inhabited by furniture.

Bobi went around the house. Silence everywhere. To the south, the attic window was stuffed with a sack filled with straw, but the window of the wide hall on the second floor was open, and inside the wind gently shook the bedroom doors.

It was four o'clock in the afternoon.

"I'll go and see the farmer," said Bobi to himself.

No one knew this farmer of Fra-Josépine. The one who had been there during the master's time had been gone a year. He had taken a farm in the valley to the west. The climate of the plateau did not suit his wife, who suffered with sciatica. And besides, his youngest daughter was beginning to get a goitre, although no one knew the cause.

"It seems to be the water that makes it," he had said.

"We drink it, Aurore and I, my good Adolphe."

"Well," he had replied, "what can I say?"

His wife was the daughter of a baker in Roume. Some people try to get rid of their ills by ordinary methods; others wait for the healer of lepers. It just depends upon the person.

This woman always said: "What are we doing here?"

"We're working," said Adolphe.

"We can work anywhere," she said. "Look at the valleys. That's easier. You bank up a hundred artichoke plants, you'll be sure to have them. You get peas in May, as many as you like; and you'd be in an easier country. Because . . . "

She told him this when he came back from work and she was waiting for him at the door. Because . . . Yes, you have only to look. Wherever they went could only be easier country.

"We're doing very well here," said Adolphe, "you can't deny it, even if it isn't gay. But we're getting along, mark that."

He said all that very slowly as he straightened himself up.

"And besides, I'd hate to leave Madame Hélène and the young lady alone."

"Who said to leave them alone?" she said. "Anyway, they are grown up, aren't they? You always put yourself out for people who don't do a thing for you."

"It depends upon who they'd get," he said.

"Well, then, find someone yourself; you'll be easy then. You'll know who they'll have. If you had half the care about us that you have for them."

Her poor little grey face was all drawn to one side by the grimace that the constant pain in her shoulder made her wear. She called: "Catherine!"

The little girl appeared. The goitre was certainly bigger every day. At any rate, it was not getting any smaller.

Adolphe went off to find his successor. The whole plateau had great regard for Adolphe. He had never wronged anyone, by a penny or by word or gesture. He never went anywhere at the wrong time. His liberty never trespassed upon the liberty of others. He was trusted. No one would have to speculate about the man he would bring. He would surely be a man.

They saw him only at a distance in the fields, sometimes in the meadow, sometimes among the potatoes, sometimes in the wheat or in the oats. They'd call out to him: "Hallo!" He would straighten up and reply: "Hallo!" Simply on the credit of Adolphe, who had been gone six months, they lent him fifteen hundred kilos of sesame; Jourdan six hundred, Jacquou nine hundred. They knew only that he was alone, that he did everything for himself besides the farming: his cooking, his housework, and all. Everything except his laundry, which was given, with that of the ladies, into the hands of old Cornute.

At first they had simply asked: "Are you satisfied, Madame Hélène?"

"I miss Adolphe," she said, "but I am very well satisfied."

So, good.

The farm house was two hundred metres from the manor, in a clearing in the fields. It was a long building, almost blind, with tiny windows and one low door. From the doorstep one could survey all the appurtenant land. At present it was stubble, the fallow of a field of potatoes, a meadow in second growth, and seven rows of vines from which the grapes had already been picked.

The door was open.

"May I come in?" asked Bobi.

"Yes."

"Hallo! You don't happen to know where the ladies are?"

"Hallo! I don't know."

The man was sitting at his dining table. He was playing with his open knife but he was reading a book.

The two men looked each other over for a moment.

"You are the one from La Jourdane," said the man.

"Yes. I was told that the deer are on Silve's land, so I came to have a look."

"I knew," said the man, "that we should meet some day."

He closed his book and faced him.

"I haven't tried to force it," he said; "sit down."

He was a man at the beginning of middle age, fair, thin, and hard. His muscles were long; he had no fat anywhere. His hair was bleached by the sun. His hands were finely shaped, but tanned; his wrists slender but strong; his shoulders broad but hollow, with a blue hole under his breast-bone that told of his perseverance in his work and of his courage.

"So," said the man, "you are the one who gives away happiness?"

"I don't make myself out to be any stronger than others," said Bobi; "I try to be reasonable."

"I have watched everything and listened to everything," said the man; "I know what you are doing. I saw your little animals go by here the day before yesterday. The little doe has three fawns, another has two. The third doe is dead. I buried her. She smelt bad in the grass."

"What did she die of?"

"Of death, as far as I could see."

"You are a country-bred man?"

"What a funny question!" said the man. "If I were not, the others would soon find out. The fields are there. Look at them."

"You were reading?"

"I am reading."

"You live alone?"

"Yes."

"When I came here," said Bobi, "they were at the end of their resources. Have you been here long?"

"Three years. Time has nothing to do with it."

"It makes one weary."

"It helps, too. I mean that it isn't a question of time or country. It is a social question."

"I am talking about sadness."

"So am I. I am a buyer of hope, like everybody else."

"I try to give them joy."

"So do I."

"Then, explain to me."

"No," said the man. "You have begun the experiment, not I yet. It's for you to talk."

"I have seen many unhappy men."

"That's easy, in this world."

"Since I've been on the road, in the villages, through the countryside, I've seen so many!"

"What are you?"

"An acrobat."

"I thought as much."

"What?"

"I didn't exactly say 'acrobat' when I spoke to Mademoiselle Aurore; I said 'poet.' A poet. All right, go on."

"I was comparing myself with them. I thought: *You* are happy. I said: *Yes.* I wondered why. I couldn't answer, or exactly figure it out."

"If you called yourself happy, you were so no longer; that isn't possible."

"I wasn't so any longer, that's exactly it," said Bobi. "The unhappiness of others prevented me."

"Too bad," said the man. Then, after a silence: "Too bad that men like you are misled."

"However, sometimes in the evening, alone by the roadside, sitting beside my little sack, watching night come, watching the little wind go off in the dust smelling of grass, listening to the forest sounds, sometimes I almost had the time to see my happiness. It was like a skipping flea: it was here, it was gone, but I was happy and free."

"Freedom does not exist."

"Free to go where I wished."

"Not free to keep from smelling the grass or hearing the sounds of the forest."

"I liked that."

"But that entered your body, you understand, your head. You were not you, but you plus the forest, plus the grass, plus all the rest. Therefore, not free. Flint is not free. Yet it is hard. But it is not as impermeable as it seems. That isn't the point. Go on. But don't talk about freedom."

"The world is a sustenance."

"That is possible. The certainty is that it is a place where you work."

"I think differently."

"Suit yourself, but the truth is the truth. It's as plain as the nose on your face. Have you the time? Then tell me what you think."

"Listen to what happened to me once," said Bobi.

"I don't like stories," said the man. "If you want to find the solution, you must work with the fewest words possible."

"This one is short and it helps save time. One time, in the mountains, I was near the house where I was born. I went into the home of one of my friends. He was an old man, paralysed, in his bed, fed on milk, unable to budge. Cared for by his daughter all alone. I go in. I see him. I stay a moment. I think: He'd be better dead."

"Yes."

"Is that a thought, or would you have killed him?"

"Only a thought," agreed the man.

"He would be better dead. His daughter was there. Once he looked at us. He was making an effort. He moved his eye. A sign. Then I saw her. She went and got the pipe. She filled it with tobacco. She lit it, putting it in her own mouth and drawing. Once well lighted, she gave it to him. He began to puff on it gently. He closed his eyes. His daughter said to me: 'Come, let's go out. He likes that.'"

"The end of the world!"

"One single joy and the world is still worth while. You have nothing to say?"

"You trouble me."

"A solitary joy and we have patience."

"You have touched me in a spot deep down inside me that I've forbidden anybody to touch."

"The joys of the world are our sole nourishment. The last little drop keeps us alive."

"Shut up! It seems to me that I am going to awake with a terrible hunger."

The man remained motionless a moment, looking straight ahead of him.

"I have always thought so," he said, as if talking to himself. "We need poets. A man like you can awaken the great hunger of all. You have touched me in a spot that each day I cover with earth. I have felt it alive down there, at your appeal, like water beneath the divining rod. You know that I need joy. You know that nobody can live without joy. Life is joy. The serious thing is that you are right. But what is also serious is that your joy is not a solid one."

"It is based on simplicity, on purity, on the common things of the world."

"It is animal."

"We are animals."

"Yes, tragic animals. We make tools."

"Let us become once more…"

"Become is forward. Never backward."

"Is it for that that water barks in all the valleys, that the wind sways the forests, that the grass ripples, and that, unceasingly, the white clouds cross the sky like ships?"

"I am for the power of men."

"The night wind has passed over the hills of vervain. That perfumed air this morning, it was your horse, your dog, your goat, and the crazy little snake that drank it and enjoyed it. *You* will remain for ever shut up within yourself with your miserable torturing and biting tools, your files, your saws, your planes, and your spades, your iron jaws, your iron teeth, your brush fires that you cannot put out now, like a person who thinks he will carry the lamp and sets fire to his beard, his moustache, his brows, his hair, and stands blind and drunk in his joy with no desire left but to flutter his flame-licked hands."

"Stop taking advantage of your being a poet. Don't keep covering me with visions. Stop showering me with all those images that lick me with their tongues. Don't talk to me any longer from up there where your voice echoes the stars. I told you only a few words are necessary. Don't say so many. Say just what is necessary."

"You yourself…"

"Yes, I let myself get caught, as you see. However, I am hardened to that idea. In a discussion, I want the fewest possible words. But poetry is an initiating force, and a great force; dynamite that lifts and tears out rock. Afterwards, they have to come with little mallets and strike patiently in the same place. And thus they make building stones."

"You are explaining great things to me."

"We are explaining to each other."

"You are learned."

"No, I'm in love."

"With what?"

"With what I don't have."

"What?"

"What one sometimes has that doesn't last."

"What?"

"What you are looking for. Joy. Don't keep asking. When I don't say, it is because I don't want to. Do I have to say it? Everybody is looking for it."

"The important thing is to keep it."

"To find it."

"I have found it."

"Where?"

"All about us. As inexhaustible as air. The essential thing is to become again the light vagabonds of the earth. I am against the power of men."

"At last we've got to the place where you are going to say something."

"Well, old man, we think we're the angels of the universe and we are just about like the aphids. I think that if, instead of struggling, we'd let ourselves go, everything would be all right."

"Let ourselves go? We, men? You're joking!"

"Yes, I'm turning the joke on you. You cry: Joy, joy joy! It comes. Then you say to it: So you think, Miss, that I am going to let myself go!"

"Let's talk like men who know the value of sadness."

"Not the value, but the reason for sadness. We don't do anything human."

"I see the thing from the social point of view," said the man. "I said that we needed poets, but I also say that, occasionally, we'll be obliged to give them a kick in the pants."

"I came here in the middle of the night. I saw a fellow ploughing. I thought to myself: Well, that's not so good. The fellow gave me some tobacco. We smoked. I began to talk. I was saying just anything, I merely wanted to cheer him. Finally, he asked me: 'Have you ever taken care of lepers?'"

"The very thing we want is for there not to be any more of those lepers."

"I assure you it does something to you when a man gives himself into your hands to be cured. They received me like God Himself."

"You are going to make their fields smaller?"

"Yes, and they aren't going to work any more except casually, for their pleasure."

"I understand. That's exactly what I think. Work has become beastly rot. It's as if someone had first spoiled it, to ruin us afterwards in order to restore its original virtue. However, *he* is the fine vagabond with hair the colour of a cow's tail. What you are doing is not stupid. You can no longer use work, it is rotten. It is no longer the ideal, you understand? I mean that it is no longer one of the beautiful things. So you lead your people away from it. That isn't a bad idea. To think that this work has been so abused that you are forced to reject it and go backwards!"

"I am one of those hundred million beggars running among the haymows."

"If there were not any suffering, you would be right. This will be the death of the weak, and suffering exists."

"We aren't saints."

"Yes, we are: saints of hewing, of ploughing, of forging. Saints of man's power."

"You are using the words of a poet."

"Because I'd like to bring you around to my way of thinking. You want to live on the ancient earth. I want to live in the new world."

"The earth is already made and it made you."

"I'll put it to my use."

"You think you are very wise."

"The earth has made everything save hybrids. I was thinking about that in my vineyards. If it weren't for hybrids, you'd be drinking water. You are drinking wine. Who made hybrids? Man."

"Behold the saintly cultivator!"

"Yes, and see how joy increases. Soon, there won't be any more weaklings."

"Have you found the secret of blood?"

"No, but I have found what you are looking for: I have found the secret of joy."

"Everything is silent. Tell it quickly, we are listening."

"I see immense fields that with a single sweep, from horizon to horizon, level plains and hills as oil on the sea smooths the waves. Furrows joined end to end, as if I had rolled the whole earth in my corduroy coat. People will no longer say 'my trees,' or 'my field,' or 'my wheat,' or 'my horse,' or 'my oats,' or 'my house.' They will say 'ours.' It will come about that the land will belong to man, and no longer to Jean, Pierre, Jacques, or Paul. No more fences, no more hedges, no more walls. He who sinks his plough in at dawn will go straight ahead through dawns and dusks before reaching the end of his furrow. This furrow will only be the beginning of another: Jean beside Pierre, Pierre beside Jacques, Jacques beside Paul, Paul beside Jean. All together. Horses, ploughs, legs, arms, shoulders, all forward together, for all. Work? Joy? Generosity that is joy? Generosity that puts to shame all your stupid morality? That is how it will be established on the earth.

"Listen, don't say a word: no, don't speak; no, I won't let you open your mouth. Listen to one little thing beside the big ones. One little thing that is like the sow of the big ones. The sow with ten teats like sugar loaves. Listen. Here. The flower. You see the flower. You see the flower of trees, of fruit trees. Do you see it? Do you see how light and fresh it is, and delicate and sensitive and frail, and easily killed by hail or frost? You see? Because of that frailty the earth, our world, the world where we are, has great wastes of deserts: either sand or snow or cold or storms, or whatever people like you call the curse of the world and that I call the ignorance of the world and of the plants, or maybe wastes of stones, of silex, and of alabaster dust. All that beneath the sun. Do you still follow? Good.

"I'm talking. Yes, I'm talking. I've got to talk. I've got to talk to you, to talk, as you say, with poetic words. Without practice, that gets nowhere. I am talking to you because I respect you. We'll not always be talking. Some day we'll be discussing all this with blows of fist on jaw, we against the others, we against those who are interfering with our joy, and paying us with cardboard sous. Then you'll be with us.

"Listen. The flower. The fruit blossom. You know how that works? It makes love to itself. It grows poor, small, weak, it bows down like everything, like the world, like the law of the world, like a stone that you throw: it rises high, then it falls. Now the flower is weak. Frost, storm, drought, and it is dead. From that come the waste places on the earth. Because of that, there are among mankind vast forgotten numbers who have never eaten peaches, pears, melons, watermelons, plums, apples. Understand me, I don't know whether what I am going to say is true: I'm thinking about hybrids. Someone comes to this flower,

~ 249 ~

someone intervenes. Get that word. You said 'become once more.' I say 'become'—someone intervenes. This flower, they don't let it make love to itself all alone. To a wild female flower they bring the male pollen of one of these weak but fruit-bearing flowers. I am making this up, but from there we go somewhere else. Anyway, just imagine. I have made hybrids. I am thinking of making others. If it isn't by this means it is by another. We'll find it. We'll produce flowers that will resist anything. We'll give to the flower our tenacity and our desire. You can imagine it: the new earth, all covered with orchards from north to south. Where there was alabaster dust, orchards. Where the sand was, orchards. Where there was snow, orchards. The mountain will be cleft with springs, orchards. The tree will be acclimated everywhere, guided, made according to our desire, orchards, orchards over all the earth, orchards for all."

He stood up.

"It's a question first of knowing," he said, "that we are opposed. We'll agree or"—he made a gesture of overthrowing something—"you will burst like a dying star. It is an astonishing thing. We must think of the great mass of workers. Just imagine! It's enough to drive you mad when you think that we are millions upon millions. And with terrible weapons. A force!"

He whistled between his teeth.

Surely he must have been seeing before him the world of his dream, for he stood there motionless, with his ascetic face and his muscular body.

Bobi stood up.

The man held out his hand.

"Glad to have met you."

He went with Bobi to the door.

Outside it was now night.

CHAPTER

~

13

At last, autumn began to filter into houses and stables. It was an odour like when the boxes of medicinal herbs have been opened. Jourdan looked up at the chimney shelf. The boxes were shut. Nevertheless, the odour was there. It made one think of beds of branches, of camps in the woods.

One, two, three, four, then all the maples were alight. They passed the flame from one to another. The evergreen oaks remained green, the oaks remained green, the birches remained green. Great assemblages of trees kept their calm and their colour but in amongst them the maples were ablaze.

There was also a little vine like a clematis but not so woody. Its summer boldness had carried it to the forest roof. It had led its whole life up there, lying over the leafy branches; from flowering to seed time, it had clung everywhere with its tendrils; it was wedded to more than a hundred kinds of trees. It began to turn yellow, then to dry up, and after two or three days it was dead. The weather continued hot. The sun passed a little lower. The sky was the same, but the little vine was dead. And yet all summer long it had borne the weight of the birds and the shadows of the clouds.

One evening, Jacquou was sitting in the kitchen. The soup was simmering. He was alone. Barbe had gone out to get some parsley. Honoré was finishing his ploughing. Joséphine and the children had gone to the well. The door was open. Every evening, the sky was magnificent. The sun went down after a great battle. Jacquou sat listening. He heard someone walking outside. There were scraping sounds as of dragging feet. It stopped and then began again. There was a little wind; the poplar was swaying. Jacquou said to himself: What can that be? He thought of one of the little children, then of Honoré perhaps stopping outside to look at the sky too, then of Barbe, and he even called softly: "Old girl!" For the weather brought tenderness and uneasiness. But there was no answer and there was a moment of stillness, then the walking began once more. Jacquou had an impulse to get up and go see. Far off in the fields, Honoré was shouting to his horse. The sky looked like a field of violets. Finally, a huge leaf appeared on the doorsill. It was dry. The wind had torn it from the forest and carried it off and had laid it in the grass. Since then, it had been pushing it gently toward the house. Jacquou stood up, leaned over, took the leaf, and looked at it all over. At first, he did not recognize it. It was dead, hard as a donkey's hide. After a time, he realized it was that solitary leaf that the old oaks enlarge at the tip of the last branch of the year. Jacquou threw the leaf into the fire. Barbe returned with her parsley, then Joséphine with the water and the children.

They were almost at the end of the year's ploughing. Honoré turned up the last bit of earth. He stopped the horse. He wiped the ploughshare with his hand. The clod was sticky and rich. He had ploughed less than the preceding years. The old man probably had some idea in his head. He had planned only two fields instead of four. In the wake of the plough the soil was steaming. Honoré looked out over the wide plateau. Far away toward Mouille-Jacques and La Jourdane, he also saw the light vapour from the ploughing.

In fact, everything was rather at an end. Here was winter coming on. The snipes were crying in the Ouvèze Valley. What misled one was that usually they finished later. The forest was still thick and the burning sky rested on the green foliage of evergreen oak and ash.

The horse was weary. He was sweating. He shivered and sneezed, making his harness rattle. It would be better to go home at once. We don't seem to notice, with our coats and trousers to protect us; but animals, all naked as they are, feel keenly if the cold weather is on the way, or if it has come. So much so that this horse had already coughed once. Honoré had had to get out the veterinary book and make a pail of herb brew.

In other years, when the work was finished, they didn't need the horse to tell them; they knew by themselves that it was cold. The mountain wind strikes one full in the face. Here the winter always begins with strong winds. Begins, I mean, far in advance. It is not yet official according to the calendar, but one is forced to warm one's self and one is glad to have the outdoor work done. This year it was still warm and, except for the sweat and weariness, even the horse might not have perceived the turn that things were taking up there among the stars.

The mists that Honoré had seen in the direction of La Jourdane were not the vapours of ploughing but really the steaming of the ground. Bobi was dragging the harrow. He had said to Jourdan: "You rest; I'll do it."

"You don't know how."

"Exactly," said Bobi, "you know how. It doesn't amuse you. It does amuse me. You just watch those clouds that are like mountains. Sit down. Imagine that you are climbing them to go up into that white forest to catch some little does."

Once, as there was no sound—he had stopped the harrow to watch the flight of some plovers—he heard a galloping in the forest. Aurore came from under the cover of the trees. She was still riding her dappled mare. She caught sight of Bobi, turned her bridle, and went back into the forest. He shook the rope reins and said: "Giddap, Coquet, let's get to work." And he began to walk again through the field beside the harrow. Once at the end, as he was turning, he caught a glimpse through the branches of the pale, motionless form of the mare. "Giddap, Coquet!" Again he began the slow climb toward the forest.

Thus he made the round trip two or three times. The white phantom of the mare was still motionless beneath the shelter of the branches like a great apple blossom. Finally the rider decided to come out of the woods. She advanced into the field. She stopped a few steps in front of Bobi.

"I forbid you," she said, "to look as if you know so much. Don't imagine anything beyond what I say to you. I despise you. Nobody can respect you. You are viler than a worm. You are not worthy of being loved. You will never understand what love is, or how defenceless a person is against it. You haven't even the right to think about it. When people like you, one wonders first if your heart is capable of it. It's the simplest kind of honesty. But you are not even honest, and the river has more heart than you. If I were sure of being able to make you unhappy, I'd curse you."

For some little time she had been striking her mare's belly with her heels, but at the same time she was pulling on the reins and the animal was dancing in the dusty earth. She loosed the reins.

He watched her fleeing. He tried to understand why this girl fled in such anger and why she had spoken.

The words and fields were silent. The sound of galloping grew faint in the soft lands toward Fra-Josépine. Bobi went back to the farm.

Jourdan was sitting on the doorsill, facing the setting sun.

"I'd never seen the autumn," he said.

"However, this isn't the first."

"I never had the time."

Bobi thought of Aurore, mounted on her mare, like the sky in May. All the time she had been talking, her eyes had avoided all earthly things and she looked into the distance where the mountains raised their dream lands above the mists.

"There are lots of things," said Jourdan, "that I had never noticed before. Details. And they are very important."

Bobi sat down beside him. Mechanically he filled his pipe. He kept it in his mouth without lighting it. He seemed to be having some difficulty with it. It is true that he had never been in love. That word was as tasteless as flour paste. He had felt for some time—to be exact, from that evening of the past summer when he had gone to help the harvesters—that his body had begun to burn in two or three definite places. He felt the burning and a dull pain, and physical, but all around his heart. He could still hear Aurore saying: "The river has more heart than you."

It was that very evening, among the scattered sheaves, that he had for the first time felt his aching body. He might say "his aching heart"; it was the same thing. There were only men in the field. It was in Jacquou's stubble. The harvest was meagre. The men had sung. They were still humming. Their arms shone and their faces were black as lead from exposure to the rage of the sun. All the wheat was on the ground. He remembered very well. It had been suddenly like an annunciation. Something awaited for a long time, perhaps always, had announced itself by the odours of dry straw, flour, and sun.

He straightened himself up. He looked at the field. The forest of sheaves was lying on the ground. He envied Honoré and Jourdan, and Jacquou, old as he was. He thought of Carle with Madame Carle, Randoulet with Honorine. Those sweet homes, those beds. He had a sudden need of a shelter for his body; thinking less of those homes and those beds than of a desire that had suddenly burned within him as he heard the cracking of the grains of the thin wheat: the desire to be sheltered beneath a hand that caresses your face.

Ah! The body is like the earth: it makes its own clouds and it groans beneath the storms that arise within it. Joy is difficult. There is a great difficulty.

"I see," said Jourdan, "that this season is like the time when there were bands of wolves around the villages."

The important thing was to know why Aurore had spoken, why she had spoken with that brutal and evil voice, why she had spoken without giving him time to think. There was a great mystery. Aurore! I must know why you live so fast. Why you put all your strength into living fast. This speed that has dried and hardened your cheeks, made your eyes wild; and from time to time you turn your head to take a deep breath like women at peace. Once. One single time. You must drink deeply then, as we do, the odour of the countryside and the season. The perfume, the colour, the form of things, must penetrate you, Aurore! Why, then, do you flee?

Or perhaps it is not flight, Aurore, and you are irresistibly borne toward something? Tell me. Do you know, Aurore, that one can never pass beyond the horizon? No matter how fast you fly, no matter how powerful you are, how resolved your head may be, and how swift your fair, supple body, warm, brown, and perfect, that I once or twice held in my hands— barely held: the time to touch you and let you go—however perfectly you may be built to penetrate the magic horizons, you will never go beyond them. Wherever you are, wherever you stay, wherever you stand motionless, the world is like the one you covet.

"There used to be bands of wolves around the villages," Jourdan was saying. "And, as I think of it, this season is an uneasy season, and in those days the weather at this time of the year used to be unsettled. You don't remember because you are younger. By the way, what part of the country are you from?"

"From the mountains."

"Then you must have known about it."

"No, but I've heard them talk about it."

"There used to be a slope," said Jourdan, "planted with ash, then pastures and a border of birches, the most beautiful ones I ever saw. Like all trees one sees in one's childhood; I was three years old. It was dark at four o'clock in the afternoon. My mother and I were alone. The door shut. The bolt, the double bar, the password. Without this word, even my father could not have got in.

"The wolves began to howl. My mother came and sat down. I knelt down in front of her. She spread her knees, I hid my head in her skirts. She closed her knees. I could hear nothing more."

"You could hear nothing more," said Bobi.

"Nothing more. She patted my hair."

The evening had become like lead.

Bobi could not forget Aurore's words. Every day he looked toward the edge of the woods. He saw only the coming of autumn. In vain he listened. He no longer heard the galloping of the dappled horse, or only far, far away toward the heath, out there where the earth resounds. It might be the mare or it might be something else.

Everyone was waiting for propitious weather for sowing. The seed had been prepared, but for the moment there was still too much wind, sometimes from one direction, sometimes from another. There is nothing worse. It heaps the seeds in one place. The grains fly out of your hand; it gives your field a sort of ugly wadding with tufts and bare patches. They had really decided to sow less. And precisely for that reason it had to be well done. It was pleasant to watch the weather and say, no, not today, and then to know there was no hurry and that the moments of life are good to live, even those during which one has nothing and one waits to have, even when one has something to do that is urgent. Why urgent?

The wind made the earth smoke in all the harrowed fields. It also swept great gusts of leaves stripped from the forest.

Randoulet appeared.

"Ah, friends," he said, "next week I'm going away."

"Where are you going?"

"You'll find out."

He had winked and licked his lips. Whenever he was pleased, he made everybody else pleased.

Bobi took several steps into the field to pick up a leaf. The wind had just poured more than a thousand over the clean harrowed field. Yes, they were whitebeam leaves.

"What are you looking at?"

"I'm looking at these leaves because usually at the base there is the stem of the fruit and sometimes the dried nut."

"Always the dried nut."

"The birds have eaten the rest."

"I think," said Bobi, "we ought to leave these leaves in the fields if we find any. And each time bury them a little. A press of the heel and it is quickly done."

They were at that moment opposite Jacquou's land.

"I think," said Bobi, "that with this dry kernel a tree can be made. This seems to be a mechanism that works all by itself. The birds eat the meat. The kernel remains. It doesn't weigh anything. The wind carries it off, the tree is sown. Here, we are between two forests. If trees began to grow a little here, it wouldn't be bad. What do you think?"

"I'd like to live to see that," said Jacquou.

Now that there had been two or three night dews as abundant as rain, the grass had begun to be soaked. They suddenly perceived that all of Randoulet's land, the great meadows of the Maple Tree Farm, the low swampland, and the willow grove had been left in the first regrowth.

"Have you made the second cutting?"

"No." He winked.

"You can smell it," said Jacquou. "The odour of grass is stronger than in former years."

"It must be ripe, thoroughly ripe."

"It *is* ripe, thoroughly ripe," said Randoulet, and again he winked.

And turning toward Randoulet's land when the wind blew from that direction, one got an odour of wet grass, stifling as the odour of a sheepfold.

Randoulet winked several times, looking from one to the other.

"If I only have three days of fine weather," he said, "next week I'm going away."

When a meadow is left like that, what happens? It grows thick. Everything that is too spindly disappears. From the head, let us say, all that is between the head and the roots is lost. But the head and roots remain. That makes a thick growth. It is a primitive method, but in a wild country, in the very high mountains, it is done, and at the very beginning of white spring, primitive man scratches the frost. Beneath the growth he finds new grass, fresh, green, sweet, tender—the kind that sheep are crazy about. Notice that at the same time, the grass grower of the plains who has made his usual cuttings couldn't find you a blade of grass in his field to save his life.

"I think that next week we can sow without any trouble," said Jacquou.

In fact, high up in the sky, there were very gay little clouds, white and round like flowers, that did not move. That meant that the calm was already up there and that gradually it would descend and still the wind.

He looked at the whitebeam leaves in the field.

"I can imagine," he said, "what it would be like here with two or three groves of trees. How long does it take?"

"A whitebeam takes five years," said Honoré, "but there is something that grows quicker."

He stooped down to look closely at the harrowed earth. "Look."

They crouched down beside him.

At certain places, in the folds of the earth—and those folds were a little dark with dampness and life—there was a little green moss. Looked at closely, when you took it in the tips of your fingers, it proved to be seeds. They were tiny seeds, some star-shaped, others shaped like moons. There were only these forms. All like the inhabitants of the heavens: stars with five, six, seven, or eight points; round or crescent moons, all with their green starlight.

They took some in the palm of their hands.

Jacquou, with his fingertip, tried to separate the species. "There were four or five different kinds."

"Cattle grass," said Randoulet. "This is sheep's fescue"—he pointed to a minute, star-shaped seed with five points—"and this is campion and that *vollaire*. Bouncing Bet. This, this one must come from the edge of the pond. This is surely wild oats, and that, madder, and this, bedstraw. That one, I don't know."

"The wind did not wait for next week, it sows all by itself."

"Yes, the wind sows."

"That comes from my place," said Randoulet. "Those are my plants. I can recommend them to you."

They all stood silent a moment in deep thought.

Jourdan and Bobi went back to La Jourdane through the autumn wind that was sowing trees and plants.

It was impossible to forget Aurore's words.

There were several days that were hard and milky, like marble. At last, one fine morning, the weather was calm.

The night before, an extraordinary thing happened to Bobi. He had a dream and he saw the river's heart. Usually, he never dreamed, or else just those little dreams that everybody has in which one runs with bent legs or falls into holes and then wakes up. But this time it was a real dream. This one must mean something. There was a river. Its banks were as sharp as a knife. The water at the edge was shallow and a blackish-blue like the blades of cheap knives. Bobi had instinctively drawn back his feet. In the middle of the river the water was rising and falling. This river resembled the Ouvèze and five or six other rivers that Bobi had seen, but chiefly the Ouvèze. It had the same voice and then that appearance of coolness and shade. At the place where the water was moving, down on the bottom, Bobi saw the heart: it was as big as an ox, heart-shaped, red, full of blood, pointed, and beating: plouf, plouf, plouf.

He woke up. He remembered Aurore's words: "The river has more heart than you." What upset him was those cutting edges and the evil look of the river. What did it mean?

He lay awake until morning. He could no longer sleep. He tried, but he kept thinking of the river with the powerful heart. Outside there was not a sound; no wind or animals. And day broke, still and solid as a mountain of glass.

"Where is the little rice bag?" asked Jourdan.

"Which one?"

"The one we emptied, the white one?"

"Behind the bread trough."

"It isn't there."

"It was there," said Marthe. "What do you want to do with it?"

"It is handier," said Jourdan; "I am going to sow."

"It doesn't hold so much."

Jourdan turned.

"It holds its peck and a half."

You can't explain to a woman the old instinct that makes a man want a clean bag for the seeds he sows.

"The weather is like iron," said Jourdan.

Jacquou had already started. He took great strides. Honoré followed him, then the hired man, pushing the wheelbarrow. The fine weather looked as if it would hold for a good while. Not the tiniest cloud was to be seen. They could not smell the wind. The blue of the sky was as pure and as deep as in summer. It was the slightest bit discoloured at the place where it touched the horizon, but it was so smooth and hard that even there, without a trace of haze or smoke, it held the copper reflections of the forests and fields. It was cool.

Carle had come outdoors.

"Are we sowing today?" asked the son.

"We're sowing today," said Carle.

They went back into the kitchen.

"We're sowing today," they said.

Madame Carle went up to the attic. The grain was beautiful. She took some of it in her hand.

The man at Fra-Josépine had been in the fields since dawn. He returned to the farm house. He reappeared. He was carrying a sack. He threw it on the ground at the end of his field. He went back to get another.

At that moment, there were eight men on the open plateau: Carle, his son, the man at Fra-Josépine, Jourdan, Bobi, Jacquou, Honoré, and the farm hand. They were far apart.

There was the plateau; then on one side the Ouvèze Valley and on the other side the Plain of Roume. The Ouvèze Valley, although strangled, shady, and eaten by thick adrances of evergreen oaks, also had fields. These fields were of irregular shape; here eaten by groves, there worn away by mule paths, there sunk into sandstone quarries, here torn away by the river. The land was sloping or raised by the upthrusts of the first hills. In the middle or at the edge of these fields there were stones gathered under the plough or the harrow. Piles as high as houses, all of smooth stones dazzlingly bright in the sun.

Men came there also. They came from poor little lonely farms in the hills. They walked, their wives carrying sacks, their children carrying sacks made to their size and age. From time to time, they rested under the biggest oaks. Groups could be seen reposing, others walking single file along the paths. Then those who had been sitting down stood up and set out again for their fields, and those who had been walking entered the shade. And they all gradually approached the waiting fields.

The Plain of Roume is broad and fair, stretching as far as eye can see beneath the sky. If the town is not visible, it is because it is far away, on the other side, where other hills begin, other mountains, other valleys, with shade, springs, green trees, and echoes. At this season of the year, the plain is the colour of gold: fields, orchards, and vineyards. There are great roads going in every direction. Here and there at a crossroad sings a grove of poplars. Over it, too, lies the wide, serene sky.

Men had left the town in little drays drawn by good trotting horses; boys on motor-bicycles, the seed bags fastened behind the saddle.

The marvellous fine weather could hardly be seen in the town, for there were the macaroni factories with their smoke; but one felt it. In the open country, all those who had left the town perceived that the sky was really as smooth as porcelain. Then the dust on the roads and bypaths began to rise in clouds. The men reached the fields. The wheat fields were at some distance from the town, in the plain, flat, slightly rough, weighed down by the great sun without a shadow or the hope of a shadow.

In some places, ten sowers arrived in a dray. Trucks followed with the sacks of wheat. There was an overseer. He would say: "You go there, you there, and you here." He would count the paces between each sower. He would say to them: "Let's see your arms." The sower displayed his arm. The overseer decided whether he would place the men one pace, two paces, or three paces apart, according to the length of their arms.

At other places there were five or three or twenty. And then the owner appeared. He waited alone at the edge of the field. He had his private automobile. He got out and slammed the door. He stood a moment, then he approached the trucks that had brought the wheat. He made them show the grain. The overseer took some in his hand. The owner bent over the hand. He did not touch it. He said: "Manitoba or Florence?"

At other points there were sowing machines, but only ten or twelve, because hand labour is very cheap in these rich plains, isolated in the middle of the vast uncultivated country. The mechanical sower is always a great expense. It is not always easy to pay for it. The weather controls everything; whereas, whenever you want the arm, it is there. When you don't want it, you let it alone, and in the mean-time it costs you nothing. It goes where it pleases with its owner, who takes care of it, who is responsible for it, as God has decreed.

You could count about one hundred and fifty sowers in the Ouvèze Valley and more than six hundred on the Plain of Roume. Here on the plateau, eight.

The grain was ready. Jacquou looked at the sky. He had the first handful of grain in his hand. He looked at the sky. Jourdan looked at the sky. Bobi did too, and Carle, the son, the farm hand, Honoré, the man at Fra-Josépine. It was instinct. There they were, far apart on the wide plateau, each one standing there with the first handful of grain in his hand.

Yes, everything looked right: the sky, the ground, the air, the seed, the hand, the head, the desire. Jacquou swung his arm and cast his first handful of grain. He took a step forward. Jourdan cast his handful. Bobi, Honoré, the farm hand, Carle, the son, the man at Fra-Josépine. The eight started forward on the plateau.

In the Ouvèze Valley, the hundred and fifty glanced at the sky, then one swung his arm, then two, then twenty, then a hundred, then the hundred and fifty, and all began to advance in the fields of the Ouvèze Valley.

In the Plain of Roume, the overseers shouted, the helpers ran to the trucks to bring the sacks of grain to the scene of action. The sowers were in their places. They also glanced at the sky. They were not sowing for themselves. One might even say that they were sowing against themselves, but they had the handful of grain in their hands and grain has an old electric force that penetrates the toughest skin and lights up the most savage hearts, and when one has a handful of golden grain to cast before one for the sowing, whether it be for you or the Pope, if a man is worthy of the name, he is forced to look at the sky.

They were, for the most part, dried and tanned mountaineers. In their houses the bread mouldered. The grain crackled in their hard hands. Their legs were ready, their arms, their heads, all of them. They had seen the sky. "Forward!" shouted the overseers; and the six hundred sowers started across the Plain of Roume.

Some went toward the north swinging their arms, others toward the east, others toward the south and the west. In all directions of the compass, men began to walk step by step, swinging their arms. The movement of the arm was in rhythm with the step. The right foot advanced, the hand entered the sack. The left foot advanced, the hand left the sack; the arm swung and the handful of grain scattered at the moment the left foot touched the ground. Thus, right foot, left foot, sweep of arm, roll of hips and shoulders; all together the men moved steadily along invisible and interlacing paths that were the paths of the sowing. The earth received the shower of naked grain. From time to time, the silhouettes of two men, who were in reality far apart in the empty fields, came together. It was only in appearance, and it happened because one of the sowers was going toward the east and the other toward the west. At first, they could be seen moving toward each other, steadily, with the noble deliberation of this grave, useful march; the body slightly bent by the weight of the sack, the head bowed to look to the ground. The step, the arm, the step, the arm—the two men approached. Who is it makes them advance? What is the slow and powerful force that urges them onward? Is it in their legs? (One can barely see the tiny black legs open and close.) Is it in that arm that is beating the air like a wing? Do they advance, borne forward by the air, and is that arm the oar, the fin, the wing? No, the force *does* come from the legs. That is apparent now. The cumbrous body, weighed down by the sack of grain, is dancing on the legs. The arm is the rhythm, the arm is the spirit, the arm casts the grain, the arm commands, the step obeys. The grain flies. Without haste they draw closer. One step, two, three; in a moment they are going to be as if facing in the dance under the lindens. Here there is no music save the light swish of the flying grain. It is soft and faint, but so many hands are sowing that gradually in the air swells the supple music for this heavy dance of labour. There! The two men are face to face. They lift an arm, they lift a leg, they advance. They approach each other. They close. The two arms are raised; they are going to strike each other. They are about to fight. They raise their arms. There is only one man now. Now there are two again. They have passed each other. They separate, without haste, always at the same pace, in the same cadence, the step, the arm, the step, the arm; one moves toward the east, the other toward the west. In reality they had not seen each other. They are sowing wheat. The weather is fair.

In less than no time, the whole Plain of Roume was covered with birds. They wheeled in great clouds five or six metres above the ground. They screamed. They were like black haloes above the sowers. They swirled in confused flight. They flew up in clouds and scattered in the sky. They alighted in the sown field. Again they rose into the air. They floated in the sky in great flocks like a gold-flecked scarf wafted in the breeze.

Before the steps of the sowers fled big blue-bellied grasshoppers, beetles in silken armour, iron-coloured earthworms, hordes of ants. When the men reached the end of the field, they all turned at once. Those who had faced toward the north looked toward the south. Those of the south went toward the north, those of the east, those of the west, turned and set off again, and in all the directions of the compass, in a "passepied," the paths began to weave in countermarch. The grasshoppers chirped, the ants rushed from the ground like foam on the water. The birds floated, screaming. The earth was charged with seeds.

In the men's wrists, the first pains were beginning to grip the muscles. The music was now the swish of the wheat, the cry of the birds, the crackling of the grasshoppers' wings, the rushing of the ants, the muffled tread of feet, the panting of the men, the chugging of the trucks bringing new sacks, the distant neighing of a horse. And the grain fell over the ground.

As the morning advanced, the weather grew even clearer and more settled. The sky was as motionless as a stone. The sun burned as in midsummer. The overseers began to run along-side the troops of sowers. "We've got to finish the whole thing today!" they cried. "The weather is too calm. It will not last."

There were acres of ground where the seed had not yet fallen. It was the middle of the morning, getting on toward noon. The sowers lengthened their stride. Then the overseers began to run once more.

"Keep your stride. Faster, but keep the length of your step."

At a certain moment, Jourdan and Bobi came to fill their sacks at the same time. They had not spoken to each other all morning, one being here, the other yonder.

"This weather gets on a person's nerves," said Jourdan.

They still had two plots of ground to sow. It was not too much work.

"A pipe?" said Bobi.

"Yes."

There was a whitebeam tree at the edge of the field that still gave a little shade. They went and sat down. They looked out over the plateau. They were absolutely alone in all this like castaways at sea. They listened. From the direction of the Plain of Roume came a dull and regular murmur like the sound of river waters. From the Ouvèze Valley came the tinkling of bells.

"Everyone is sowing."

"The others up here must have come out, too, only we can't see them."

The plateau seemed deserted. Finally, far off, rising from the land, they saw a black silhouette that for a long time seemed like a tree trunk. Then they saw that it moved. It was swinging its arm. It must be Jacquou; it was in his direction.

At the end of the morning, Marthe appeared. Bobi and Jourdan had begun to sow again. They saw her walking over the meadow toward them. She was bringing the soup.

"Well, men?"

They continued to swing their arms a moment longer, then they turned.

"Well, woman?"

She was already bending over in the shade unpacking the kettle. They could smell the bacon soup.

"It's a funny thing," said Jourdan, "whenever we sow, we always make bacon soup, and when we reap, too. Try to find the reason. It's a custom."

"Customs should always be kept," said Bobi.

"It's natural," said Marthe. "This morning, the bacon got into my fingers without my having anything to say about it."

"If it wasn't bacon soup," said Jourdan, "I wouldn't believe I'd been sowing. I'd go back to the field to see if it was true. But I smell bacon soup, so I know I've sown."

Marthe had brought three thick yellow earthenware plates, deep as bowls. She poured the soup into them from the lip of the pot. The white cabbage and the bacon made the broth spurt as it poured.

"Plates! That's luxury!" said Jourdan.

"Convenience is easy," said Marthe.

"That was heavy for you."

"It will be nicer to eat this way."

She sat beside them in the shade of the whitebeam tree.

The grain lying on the warm earth exhaled its good seed smell. An odour almost stronger than the odour of the soup, and the scent that came from Marthe was that of a healthy woman and of perspiration.

"I wonder," she said, "if you have sown under the good stars."

"Yes," said Bobi, "just now I saw them."

In the part of the sky where the sun had already passed, stretched a watery colour, slightly green, transparent and shimmering, and at times penetrated by a gleaming oiliness that was neither cloud nor haze, but simply the work of autumn in the sky. And deep in the sky, in spite of the clear noonday light, several stars were visible. They were exactly like grains of wheat.

"According to the occasion," said Bobi, "and the weather, those are the stars of the sowing season. They are called 'houses' because, for a long time, it is in them that has been lodged the hope or the despair of the tillers of the soil.

"You can see…" he said.

And he swallowed a spoonful of soup.

"…the house of the golden eagle, the house of the lamb, the house of the crown, the house of the harp, and the house of the silver lion."

"The ones we see," said Marthe, "there are five of them, if I count aright, and they are in the form of a triangle."

"Soup," said Bobi, "has a considerable value."

"I cut the cabbage on the grater," said Marthe.

"The ones we see today," said Bobi, "are the house of the harp. They are seven. Two have been hidden in the distance. Look, they are coming out."

Seven stars could now be seen above the Ruffin Mountains.

"Well?" said Jourdan.

"The harp," said Bobi, "was like the accordion in those days."

"Well?" said Jourdan.

He looked out over the plateau. The form of the distant sower had disappeared. They were alone, the three of them. They were alone, Marthe and he, and at their side this man who talked about the stars.

Bobi chewed a mouthful of bacon and bread.

"I'll tell you; that means joy and more joy."

"The others see them, too."

"Yes, if they are looking."

"You can be sure that they looked," said Marthe, "but perhaps they saw only five."

The Plain of Roume still roared dully like a river.

"It's the sign just the same," said Bobi.

Marthe listened to the sounds that came from below.

"They're hard at it," she said.

"We saw Jacquou," said Jourdan. "Oh, we could barely see him, way over there, like a fly."

"The weather is for everyone," said Marthe; "nobody could miss it or put off the sowing."

In the Plain of Roume, pain was sowing. Every time they grasped the grain in their hands, the pain entered the wrists like knife thrusts. It hurt, too, at the place where the shoulder is attached to the neck. The men had to sow faster and faster. It was four o'clock in the afternoon. Over the whole width of the plain, from being trodden, the pale crust of the earth had begun to fume beneath the steps. The sowers walked in a cloud of dust. They scarcely saw one another now, save as shadows. Their eyes were dry and sandy, their throats lined with dirt. They were men from the mountains, accustomed to pure, light air. They all ached at their wrists and shoulder blades. Every gesture was pain. In vain they warmed it with their efforts; it was a pain that did not ease with warmth, but remained crystallized, whatever you did. Every gesture was pain. It took three gestures for the grain to fly over the ground. They had to take two steps to have the time to make these three gestures. At the end of the two steps the three gestures were completed, the handful of grain was scattered over the ground. There were three pains, without counting the secondary ones: a pain in the wrist, one in the elbow, one at the shoulder blade—to say nothing of the pain which from time to time ran through the bone of the arm the whole length like water in a pipe. They still had about a hundred kilometres to do in stepping off the fields in all directions, taking all of them together. They made a little less than a step a metre, about twelve hundred steps for one kilometre. Two steps for three pains. It grew worse and worse. The dust-laden air was hard to breathe. It gave a bad taste to the mouth, the nose, the thoughts, hope, visions of the future. With three pains they threw a handful of grain on the ground. Three hundred seeds, two hundred wheat ears, twenty grains to each ear for the next harvest.

After lunch, the owner returned. He had gone to eat in town, in his dining room that looks out upon the quiet little Rue des Observantines. He had returned and seen the dust. He closed the windows in his car. He stayed inside waiting. Two or three times he tapped on the glass. Each time the overseer came up. The owner did not even speak. He held up his wrist watch. The overseer nodded "yes" with his head. He began to run along the ranks of the sowers.

"Faster, boys, faster!"

"Go to hell!" replied a huge blond fellow.

This wasn't the time to get mad at that. "After all," thought the overseer, "he is right." He ran after the other sowers.

"Faster, boys, faster! Five o'clock. We've got to finish."

He reflected that in the granaries there was still lots of grain from last year. Because it hadn't paid to sell low. The grain was mouldering. Well, let it rot!

"Faster, boys!"

They were mountain lads. They could no longer remember their home. It was scarcely three days since they had left their country. They had been hired to sow in the Plain of Roume. Now they were sowing in the Plain of Roume. It was five o'clock in the evening. They had forgotten the country they had left only three days ago. It seemed that they were years, and hellish years. There were the three pains: one in the wrist, one in the elbow, one in the shoulder blade. Three pains, two steps, a handful of grain. They were six hundred sowers; the earth fumed. More than a hundred kilometres to go in all directions. It is five o'clock. We've got to finish this evening.

"Faster, boys! Faster, you fellows! Faster, my lads! We've got to get this done this evening. Sing! Who knows how to sing?"

"I do," said the huge blond.

He was at the end of his endurance. The three pains had suddenly arisen, rigid in his flesh like the marble saints in church porticoes. He could bear it no longer. He was ready to do anything else, no matter what.

"Sing," said the overseer.

He began to sing.

"Sing," whispered the overseer, "but sing fast. In that way they will sow fast. They won't notice."

The big blond was resting his arms. He wasn't sowing any longer. In relief, he fell into step beside some other sowers. They were five comrades who were from his village. He sang fast.

He asked only one thing: to walk with his arms free. He would have done anything at all for that.

The evening was beautiful. Jourdan whistled. He had just cast the last handful of seeds. Bobi still had three handfuls before the ground was completely covered. He cast two, then this was the last. He stopped and turned around. He answered the whistle. It was finished. The evening was as sweet as willow sap. The two men met under the whitebeam. On the horizon the form of the distant sower was still visible—perhaps it was Jacquou—the size of a fly. He had stopped. He must have finished, too. The evening was peaceful and made for repose.

They saw the stag and all his herd coming. It had been a long time since anyone had seen them.

Bobi was shaking out the sacks.

"There they are," said Jourdan.

And Bobi understood at once that he was speaking of the stag, the does, and the fawns. It was a wild herd and seemed to have been created for the heart's solace and delight.

The stag called toward the two men but did not come any nearer. He stopped on the other side of the field. He stretched his neck, opened his mouth, and called a long sort of phrase in which were repeated three kinds of syllables and clickings of the tongue. That lasted a long time. With head lowered, he seemed to be explaining something. Behind him crowded the does and fawns. Only their trembling ears were visible.

The stag stopped speaking. He awaited the reply. Bobi whistled.

"Wait," said Jourdan, "I'll whistle, too."

He wanted to. He whistled.

The stag listened to the voices of the two men. For a moment he stood motionless, his head lifted. Then he began to walk in a circular path around the whitebeam tree. He had a noble, precise step that shook his neck. His antlers were broader and larger than before. They sprang from his forehead, thick and black like the roots of an oak. Behind him, in single file, came the does with tiny, light, rapid step. They were obliged to stop from time to time, so as not to pass the male. Then came the fawns. There were five. They were as red as foxes.

Thus they encircled the whitebeam tree at a distance of forty or fifty steps; then, always at the same pace, the stag broke the circle and moved out upon the plateau in the direction of the place where the distant sower was sometimes visible. Finally, the stag broke into a gallop. All his family followed. The fawns leaped in every direction, but they had good legs and did not allow themselves to be outdistanced. They were soon only a ball of dust, then nothing. The evening grew silent once more.

"Wait," said Jourdan, "let's sit down, there's no hurry."

"The weather is so soft," said Bobi, "it seems as if we are in the middle of summer and that we're swimming in warm water."

"I feel it," said Jourdan, "clear up to my armpits."

He raised his arm. He uncovered his hairy armpit, tufted like a nest. He rubbed it with the tips of his fingers. The light wind cooled it.

The fields were well garnished with seeds.

"Now, it will have to rain."

"It is going to rain. The Rhône is full. The horizon looks threatening."

Far off in the evening sky, from north to south, hung a formidable bar of black cloud.

Upon reaching the farm house, Jacquou felt thirsty. He had sowed all day long. His mouth was full of the taste of wheat and earth.

"I saw two little specks about as big as flies over there toward La Jourdane," he said. "They must have been Jourdan and Bobi."

He went to his cellar. This was a narrow silo hollowed out of a mound about twenty steps from the house. It was closed by a stone door. Inside, there was a room. He entered. It was cool and smelt of roots. His mouth was full of the taste of dirt and wheat. In the darkness, he knew where to find the dipper. It was a big bowl carved from a birch block. He held it under the spigot and filled it. He drank it at a gulp. The taste of wheat and dirt descended to his stomach. In his mouth was the taste of the wine. It was his wine. New wine, made a month ago with the grapes of twenty rows of poor vines. Although it was new, it was ripe. No longer sweet. All the sweetness of the grapes was changed into tartness on the tongue and into a warmth that suddenly flamed within him.

"Life is beautiful," he said.

He filled the dipper. The wine frothed black. The foam sparkled on his lips and tickled them.

"This wine," he said, and clicked his tongue.

"Do there any inns exist
Where from eve to morning mist
Maids can guard their innocence?..."

He wanted to sing. He wanted to say: *wheat, wheat, wheat,* in song, with accordions and fifes and dancing steps. He wanted to dance with a young woman who smelt of sweat, to press against her, to feel her soft contours. To dance!…

"Strike up the music! Seventy-five! Yes, sir! Nothing stale! We aren't city folk."

> "It's no great thing to do a crime
> With all the weapons handy…"

He drank another dipperful. The wine was cunning. He was suddenly entirely freed from his cares and his muscles relaxed like the ropes of the great wains when the hay has been emptied and they rattle against the sides. He came outside the door. The evening was still and blue. Jacquou had only the strength to sing:

> "It will never be known
> The number of victims,
> They say fifty-three,
> So the servant told me.
> Tremble, ye nation,
> For the crimes of this house!"

He cleared his throat.

"Come, drunk!" cried Barbe. "Come, lord of the earth, the soup is ready."

> "In the year 1833,
> On the second of October,
> Toward noon, in front of the jail,
> They played their final role.
> Thirty thousand witnesses saw
> The heads of the three brigands fall."

After supper, Bobi came and sat outside La Jourdane. Night had fallen; all the stars were out, except those hidden behind the mist that was rising from the Rhône. There was the house of the golden eagle, which signifies purity and courage. There was the house of the crown, which signifies that the reward is eternal. There was the house of the silver lion, which signifies that the goodness of the heart is visible. But the house of the harp, which signifies joy and music of joy, was no longer to be seen.

"To love, to love," said Bobi. "What did she mean? That word is as tasteless as bread soup."

The rain did not come right away. And Carle appeared.

"You must come and help me," he said.

He had already been to Jacquou and his man. But Randoulet had gone.

"With Le Noir, three days ago. But," said Carle, "you must come and help me cut my hay. It cannot wait."

What he did not say was that he had something to tell them. He was reserving it.

Carle's meadow was already bearing its third crop. The men all got in line: Carle, his son, Jacquou, Honoré, the farm hand, Jourdan, and Bobi.

"This makes several times now that we've worked together," said Jacquou.

First the doe-hunt, and today Carle had not hesitated. He thought: I have only to tell them and they'll come. They had not even remarked about it. They had all come with their scythes ready and got in line.

They walked together in the same direction through the grass. The scythes all went together and the grass fell. The steps were taken at the same time. There was a sort of mute music that drew them on. It was not a complicated kind of music as for dances, where there are the polka, the mazurka, and the waltz. It was like drum music. No need to think: the body fell in with it of its own accord. It was the sound of the seven steps together, of the seven swishing scythes, the harvesting scythes, of the falling grass; then seven steps, seven flying scythes, and so on. This was repeated without growing fainter, always in the same rhythm. They did not feel fatigue. They were surrounded by the yellow grass. The tops of the grass with their grains and plumes frothed lightly like foam on water, reflecting the sun. The grass did not weigh on the scythe. It bowed beneath the wind and rose again, then bowed beneath the scythe and rose no more. With great sweeps of the blade the scythes attacked the sombre green undergrass full of dampness and shadows, and of little echoes and long black corridors along which fled a procession of ants, moles, and snakes.

At noon, half the field lay on the ground. There were no trees around Carle's meadow. In order to find a little shade and shelter, the men went into the tall grass. Here they made a round nest. All seven lay down in a circle. They ate their bread and cheese. They were far from everywhere. The grass made a barrier.

"I have an idea," said Carle.

He raised his finger in the air: listen! He motioned to them to listen to the wind. Beyond the sound of the grass, at the other end of the earth, could be heard the neighing of horses.

"The mares are in heat," said Carle.

"It's had my black one for three days," said Jacquou.

"I hear that it's also got the two belonging to Madame Hélène," said Carle.

"It will get mine, too," said Jacquou. "I put my white one in the pasture so she'd calm down and not hear my black one too much. I have an idea that that doesn't help any."

"It is nature," said Jourdan. "It is the flush of autumn."

"Yes," said Carle, "the mares are in heat. And so," he said after a moment, "I have an idea: suppose I let my stallion loose? And you loosed your mares?"

"What?"

"I have the feeling . . . well, look here: this isn't the first time the stallion has known your females. And what sort of foals have we had? Outside the red one that you sold at Aubergat, what have we had?"

"Ah, no," said Jacquou. "I have the blue one too; the one we christened Satan; the one Honoré could hardly hold."

"You could hardly call that an animal."

"When you had the reins at the ends of your arms you would say so."

"No," said Carle.

The grass had grown still.

"I'm talking about a beautiful animal," said Carle, "a real horse."

"I think," said Bobi, "that that might produce something very fine."

"Listen," said Carle. "Once I saw some races. At Saint-Sigismond, in the mountains."

"I saw them once too," said Jacquou.

"The ones on the twenty-fourth of June?"

"Yes."

"In the linden lane?"

"Yes."

"At night?"

"Yes."

"Then, say so if it isn't true. There is a lane of linden trees there. Great big old ones. Not one of them is straight. They are all twisted by the mountain winds. Because it is in the mountains. They line the horses up under the lanterns, lanterns that make a great deal of smoke and red flames. The horses are little animals with long tails and manes that have never been cut. Then everybody begins to shout and the horses are off. I was near the start. I saw the lanterns, with, as I said, smoke and flames; and the horses, I tell you, little, strong-backed beasts, all covered with long hair. I heard the shouts and I saw the horses start. They ran the whole length of the lane of lindens. But that is not the race. This is what happens and what those who know see. There aren't any riders, did I tell you? No? Well, I tell you now. The horses go up into the mountain and gallop through meadows, over the torrent, through the forest, over the shale slope. They come to the high pastures, they enter the new grass, and that is the end. They stay there. If you are smart, you go and sit at the edge of the woods to see them galloping. The twenty-fourth of June is Saint John's Day. The moon was beautiful. You could see as plainly as in daytime. I have never seen anything more beautiful. And yet I was down below in a poor place."

They continued the mowing all the afternoon.

"Hey!" said Jacquou's hired man. "Those are things that can be done."

"What are you saying?" asked Jacquou.

The other lowered and raised his scythe twenty times before replying, and he took twenty steps, and beside him Jacquou took twenty steps cutting the hay.

"I'm just talking to myself," said the helper.

All the way home, Jacquou talked about the horses.

"*I* know that race."

"Was it before I was married?" asked Honoré.

"Sure," said Jacquou. "What has your marriage got to do with it?"

"I said that because you've never been away since then."

"That's a mistake I made," said Jacquou.

When he reached the house, he winked. He called the farm hand.

Honoré was moving toward the shed. Jacquou called him.

They came. He said to them: "Listen!"

He winked. He said: "Suppose we play a joke on him?"

"Who?"

"Carle."

"How?"

"I'll tell you," he said. "Let's eat our soup."

The whole house was asleep. Jacquou got up. He called his farm hand. This fellow, who was asleep in the stable, replied: "Here I am, master."

He was thinking: "If his fit is going to take him at night, life won't be worth living."

But in the candlelight, he did not see Jacquou's sad look, but Jacquou's gay look. The fold in the shaven old mouth was gently laughing. He opened the door of his son-in-law's room and called: "Honoré!"

The latter got up, too. Outside the window was the great, round, red, full moon. It lighted Joséphine, asleep and uncovered to her waist.

"Cover her up," said Jacquou.

"Leave her alone," said Honoré, "when women are sleeping the moon ripens them."

"The sort of ripening," said Jacquou, "that will be more bitter than sweet for you. I know her, she's my child."

"Let her alone," said Honoré. "I know her too; she's my wife."

They were in the hall. Jacquou was smiling; the farm hand was smiling. Honoré was rubbing his eyes.

They went down to the stable. In a pen were the sheep. The odour of urine was overpowering.

"Hold the candle," said Jacquou.

He made the sheep get up.

"They are lying in the dung," he said.

"That keeps them warm," said Honoré.

"I change their bed regularly," said the farm hand.

"I know," said Jacquou; "that isn't what I meant. They will always lie in dung, do what you will. Look at their eyes."

The candle light made the eyes of blue stone sparkle.

"Is that what you got us out of bed for?" said Honoré.

"You backwoodsman!" said Jacquou, turning on him with disdain.

He made a wry face and spat in the straw.

"Hold the candle up. They have eyes that look like their brains are shining through. This backwoodsman is more disgusting than an old pig. Wake up! Sleep? I'd like to know where sleep will get you!"

Behind his back the farm hand made a gesture as if to say: The old boy has been guzzling.

"In here," said Jacquou, "that's a different matter. There's something in sleeping."

The cobweb-hung ceiling sagged low like the roof of a cave. The odour of the animals forced one to breathe sparingly. At each breath the thick, fetid air choked one. Midges danced about the candle flame. A moonbeam illumined scythes, spades, ploughshares, horseshoes, harrows, and the steel of the tools reflected a phosphorescent light that penetrated to the farthest corners of the stable.

"It's as calm as the devil here," said Jacquou. "The smartest are fooled by it. Here everything happens from beginning to end"—with a slow sweep of his hand he designated the whole dark stable—"and all without exasperating anyone, without boasting, without being the prouder for it. Perhaps," he said, after a silence, "perhaps they *are* proud, perhaps they realize that we are poor fools. What do you think?"

Honoré was asleep on his feet.

"Hey!" said the farm hand.

"Hey, what?" said Jacquou.

"Would it be possible?"

"Would what be possible?"

"What you say?"

"Mind your own business," said Jacquou.

They all three went toward the back of the stable.

"Animals," said Jacquou again. "Sheep and pigs, and goats and horses."

They had come to the horses.

"Be quiet," he said. And he stopped speaking.

"Look," he whispered later.

Roughly he shook the sleeping Honoré.

"No noise," he said in a whisper, "but wake up, you damned backwoodsman."

There were three animals lying in a dark litter of straw. Two were sleeping peacefully without any sound other than their breathing. They were geldings. One was sleeping, but she was softly neighing between her lips and quivering. It was a mare.

"She's dreaming," said Jacquou.

She had pink nostrils.

"She's like a stream," said Jacquou, "she moves from one end to the other. She is asleep but emotion is stirring her. Go open the door."

The great door, when opened, revealed the night toward the east, that is, in the opposite direction to the moon. The sky was terribly black and without depth, but the air was heavy with the odour of decaying leaves. One star, all by itself, very green and low on the horizon, was blowing a cold little north wind.

"Blackie!" called Jacquou. "Oh, black mare, wake up!"

She twitched her ears but did not open her eyes. She stretched, straightening her hind legs.

"Come on, old girl!"

He touched her. She did not wake up at once. She knew that it was not time for work and there was no reason for waking her. She thought that it was in her dream. But she smelt the odour of autumn, and the cold from the star that came in at the open door. She woke up and stood up at the same time.

"Let her alone," said Jacquou. "Oh, Blackie!"

She shook her head to find out whether she was still tied. She was no longer tied. She did not even have her halter on. She stretched her neck toward the door. She began to neigh a piercing little complaint. The other horses awoke. The sheep were trampling their beds. The sow grunted. The mare walked to the door. Her legs creaked. She continued to neigh and shake her head. When she reached the doorsill she stopped an instant. She was on the threshold, half in the night, half in the stable.

The farm hand raised the candle. They could see a kind of force swelling within the mare. At last, she darted out, first at a trot. After a moment they could hear her galloping.

It was dawn when Carle was awakened by the uproar that was shaking his stable. He was on his feet in an instant. He said: "What is that?" He looked around for his trousers, with his eyes not yet open. It sounded as if someone were demolishing the house with a sledge hammer.

The stallion was struggling against his chains, his side racks, his bars, and his bonds. Sparks flew beneath his iron shoes, the planks cracked, a cloud of dry hay dust filled the stable.

Carle tried to calm him with his usual words but he was forced to shout them with all his might, and that did not have the same effect. Carle danced about the maddened animal. He tried to put himself in front of the stallion's eyes.

"If he sees me," he thought, "perhaps he'll stop."

But this did not help. Fortunately, there was still the great girth under the animal's belly. Carle's son had come down too.

"Pull from your side!" shouted the father.

They both pulled on the ropes. The girth raised the struggling horse and he lost his footing. Immediately he grew still. He let his legs and neck hang. He was separated from the earth.

"What a business!" said Carle, wiping his brow.

Madame Carle had come to the door in her nightcap.

"Get out," said Carle, "sometimes the odour of a woman is enough."

"It isn't my odour," she said. "There is a mare outside. She is dancing in the pasture."

Carle opened the peep-hole in the folding door. In the light of dawn, a black mare was dancing in the middle of the pasture.

"It's Jacquou's Blackie!"

Then he remembered what he had said while they were cutting the rowen and he began to smile and raised his finger.

"Go into the kitchen," he said to Madame Carle. "I know what it's all about. You make some coffee. We're coming. You stay here, son, you're going to see. Go along, Philomène."

Then he said: "Shut the door to the corridor now, and open the big door."

The son opened the big door wide. The autumn dawn lighted a clear sky where blue and white were beginning to show.

"Get a stick," said Carle, "and make that little hussy dance a little farther away. When she gets to the bottom of the pasture, you get out of the way."

He untied the stallion. He took everything off him. He took shelter behind the stall boards and eased the rope of the girth, first on one side, then on the other. The stallion touched ground once more. At the same time the girth fell off. For an instant the stallion stood motionless; then, head down, without looking where he was going, he bounded toward the open door.

Carle's son had taken refuge behind the fence. The black mare, driven to the far end of the pasture, was returning at a little trot. The stallion was galloping so hard toward her that he passed her. Then she wheeled about and followed him.

The nuptials of the horses lasted all day under a sky alive with a cavalcade of clouds and races of mingled shadow and sunshine. The stallion bit the mare's nape. She hollowed her loins as if to spread and then she bounded away toward Randoulet's verdure. They galloped side by side, their manes smoking. The stallion kept trying to bite that warm, tingling spot behind the ears. The mare felt on her nape the stallion's saliva that grew cold in the wind made by their galloping. She longed for shade, grass, and peace. She galloped toward shade, grass, and peace. The stallion would pass her, then return to her. Their breasts crashed. They reared against each other. They beat the air with their fore hoofs. They pressed their shod hoofs into their hair and the iron shoes slid in the sweat. They shook their heads, then fell to the ground and started off again at the same gallop. When they thus came to rear and clash, their male and female odours followed them a moment before dispersing in the cool wind.

Toward the middle of the morning they came to the great fields of grass that Randoulet had left standing. It was like an ocean of fresh hay, ripe beyond maturity, full of seeds, and on either side of the stem, two long tobacco-colored leaves that fell to dust at a touch. The field had no limit or end. Neither the stallion nor the mare knew grass growing wild. In spite of their great desire, they were both rooted by their four feet before this immense marvel. Their large eyes reflected the yellow of the grass. They could not eat because they had too great a longing for each other, but they sniffed in the odour for a long time. It was exactly what they both needed.

At an amble, they entered the thick grass. Gradually the hay rose to their breasts. The seed pods burst, the crushed dried leaves rose in blond dust.

At the end of Randoulet's pasture lay the pond, prostrate in its autumn sleep. It reflected the sky. It was like a hole in the earth through which the deep day could be seen. But before becoming empty and blue, with the reflection of birds and clouds, its shallow waters ran beneath the tall grasses mingled with rushes and reeds.

When the two animals reached it, they felt the coolness of the water rising up their legs. Their hoofs spread in the mud. They sniffed the odour of the pond. Their eyes were dazzled by the reflections in the water. They could hear the alarmed sharp snapping of the fins of big fishes. They began to dance up and down and the water splashed in long white arrows that sparkled in the sun as they shot above the grass. Then the coolness touched their bellies and their loins and their thighs, and it was already like the beginning of love. They felt the calming of the wildness of the passion which drew them toward each other. They rolled over in the water, crushing the grass and the edge of the pond and the mud. As the water bathed them they felt their wild passion change to tenderness, and when they rose again, a little stupefied, shivering, and covered with mud, they gently licked each other's nose, first around the mouth, then around the eyes.

Then, as they looked at the vast world about them, they perceived, far toward the north, the brown and green line of the forest. They circled the pond. After a long time they left the big pasture. They walked across country. They came to the forest. Almost all the trees had brown dead leaves. They sought the cool shade. An odour came from the east that told them that in that direction stood tall trees all green from root to tip.

They met a stag and some does and fawns. The stag fled at a bound; the does followed; the fawns bleated. The herd had left behind a strong odour of mating. The stallion put his head on the nape of the mare's neck. The mare stood still. The stallion did not bite. He began to walk on. The mare followed. He walked in front now, toward the green trees. At last he found them. They were almost at the edge of the forest. They were cedars. One in the middle was taller than the rest. It was very dark. It cast a black shadow. The stallion and the mare went toward the shadow that was shot with green rays. There they stopped. The stallion rested his heavy head on the mare's withers. She offered no resistance. The stallion remained a long time motionless, smelling the odour of female hair. Then, without raising his head, he gently approached the mare's great body that was trembling like a swarm of flies with quivers of desire. He licked her nape. He bent his head and gently nipped the mare's ears. She hollowed her back to open and stood waiting. Then he mounted her and made long and peaceful love.

Afterward they ate grass. They drank at the brook. They came out of the woods. The mare thought of the stable. She trotted quietly as if she were in harness. The stallion galloped beside her and around her. He would dance and go ten times as far as she in his gambollings. He cut off her path. She turned around him and continued to trot straight toward the stable. On the open plateau he succeeded in stopping her and making her submit once more for a long moment.

They were several hours wandering thus, then they came in sight of the stable. The roof rose above the earth. But they had made a wide detour toward the west and they came to the pastures where the white mare was. She bugled loudly and came and leaned against the fence. The stallion galloped toward her. The black mare took several steps in the direction of the stable, then resolutely stopped. She looked to see what the others were doing, then she began to eat.

The stallion tried to leap the fence; the white mare tried, too. At last, by pushing hard enough, they cracked the wood. Then the white mare rushed head on and split the fence. Carried onward by her momentum, she galloped over the fields. The stallion darted in pursuit. The black mare followed. Night was falling. All three horses disappeared at a gallop over the wide plateau. The stallion had already bitten the nape of the white mare's neck, and traces of blood were visible on the white hair. The mare was laughing with open lips as she tossed her head.

Mademoiselle Aurore had stopped at La Jourdane. From the woods she had watched Bobi's departure, then she approached at a walk. In front of the door, she sprang from the saddle and entered the house, after making sure that Marthe was alone.

Marthe was alone. Aurore loved the smell of this house. At one spot in the kitchen, on a nail, hung a corduroy coat. It had a strong odour. Aurore sat down beside it. Everything seemed different and bright as soon as she smelled this odour of corduroy. Marthe had little to say. She came and went about her business. It was a wonderfully peaceful moment.

Marthe told her about the horses' honeymoon. Jourdan had seen them. They were galloping, he had said, all three of them alike, as if they had been harnessed abreast to the same cart.

"You must watch out for your animal," said Marthe. "If you should meet them, she would be apt to throw you in order to follow them."

"She would not throw me," said Aurore.

"Then she would carry you with her," said Marthe.

Aurore breathed deep the odour of the corduroy coat.

But just the same, she went home rather early and put the mare in the stable.

Night came. Aurore and her mother were in the little sitting room that looked out on the terrace. They had left the big windows wide open. These were the last days it could still be done. But the warmth was nearly gone from the air.

The full moon rose opposite, rising a dull red, over the mountains. It illumined some clouds that resembled horses in flight. Crupper, back, mane, thigh, nose bone. Aurore strained her ears to catch the night sounds, but the night was silent. The frogs had gone to their winter sleep, the shrill grasshoppers were dead, the trees had hardly any leaves, there was no wind.

Aurore thought that the mare could carry her off. A cavalcade of lumbering red horses crossed the sky in front of the moon. The autumn night smelt of corduroy. Mounted on her mare! Carried away by the rushing stallion and the mares! All harnessed to the same cart! She shut her eyes. She saw the corduroy coat hanging in the kitchen at La Jourdane, that smelt so good, that kept the shape of the living shoulders and arms.

"I'm going to bed," she said.

"I'm going, too," said Madame Hélène. "Wait, I'll close the windows."

She closed the big windows and the odour of autumn disappeared. The sitting room smelt of varnished wood and slightly damp upholstery.

"It isn't warm any longer," said Madame Hélène, "and yet it is stifling here as soon as it is closed on this side."

In the middle of the night, Aurore heard a noise. Her room was on the side toward the fields. She got up and went to the window. The moon was now shining unobscured. There were three real horses playing in the meadow. Aurore recognized Carle's stallion. The other two must be mares, one black and one white. The two females were teasing the male and sometimes he had to leap high because they had buried their heads under his thighs. Then he began to gallop a little, and from the field he called softly toward the new stable.

Noiselessly, Aurore opened her door, crossed the landing, and went downstairs. She was in her nightgown and barefooted. Downstairs she lighted the storm lantern and entered the stable. The mare was troubled and restless, terribly nervous, and no longer aware of what she did. When Aurore approached her, she tried to kick, but she stayed her leg and let it fall again with a whinny.

"So that's what the matter is?" said Aurore.

The mare looked at her, trembling. Aurore and the animal loved each other dearly. Aurore put her hand on the damp pink nose. The mare nibbled the little hand and pulled at her tether. Aurore untied the halter and took out the bit. She walked toward the door. The mare followed her. Aurore walked slowly because of her bare feet. She opened the big door just wide enough to let the animal through. The smell of autumn came in once more: the odour of corduroy.

"Come," said Aurore. "Go on out, alone."

———

Autumn died three days later. It was packed with long bloody clouds and the sky was already cold. There was no wind. A dull tramping sound came up from far down in the Plain of Roume. It grew louder and louder. Jourdan, Marthe, and Bobi listened to it all morning, and by noon it had become so loud that they left their meal and came out to see what it was. A heavy dust was smoking over the trees of Grémone Forest. All three went forward a little, then they saw Randoulet's flock emerging. The shepherd Le Noir was walking at the head beside Zulma. No one knew how Zulma had sensed the arrival of the beasts. The fact is that she had gone to await them that day at the Croix-Chauve. Perhaps she had been waiting for them every day since the departure of her father and the shepherd. And now Zulma was walking first before the flock, beside the shepherd Le Noir, who now wore a look of great importance and swung his long staff as he walked, to keep even the alinement of the first sheep behind him. He looked neither to the right nor to the left. He did not even look straight before him to see where he was going, leading his flock. He looked straight ahead from habit. He was happy to be walking at the head of the flock wherever it might go! No matter how far! Just so he, Le Noir, shepherd of the plateau, shepherd ordinarily of fifty sheep, be now, by the whim of the master, the leader of these five hundred sheep.

Zulma had tied back her hair with two twisted rushes. The rams' bells tinkled. The dust rose in whirls. The weary sheep nodded their heads. The flock was coming out of the woods. It looked like a spring of muddy water, opening in the trees and beginning to flow, winding first over the plateau before coursing over the edges down into the valleys below. They passed behind the long row of delicate, spotted birches. Zulma was visible, then Le Noir, then the animals. At last they descended the first hummock of land that went toward the pond. Zulma and Le Noir disappeared. The last of the flock had not yet come from the woods. Nothing could be seen but sheep, no other humans. Only a black dog, who must have hurt his paw, was limping along the edge of the flock.

Jourdan, Marthe, and Bobi went back into the house. The soup was cold but they ate it. The noise continued.

"That's what Randoulet has been up to," said Jourdan.

"Winter is coming," said Bobi. "The fold is too little. He will have to let them stay outdoors."

"He got them in the mountains. He has let his big meadow go to grass. He didn't cut it again. The snow does not gather on dry grass."

"He might build a fold of logs," said Bobi. "We could all do it together to help him."

After a moment Jourdan said: "We might, yes; but now I don't think that is what he wants, or what we want, either.

The noise grew dimmer. In the evening, the voices of the distant mountains could be heard.

Jourdan fumbled in his pocket. He brought out a piece of oak branch, as thick and as long as his hand. He laid it beside his plate. He kept on eating.

"Pass the ham, Marthe. I went into the forest a while ago," he said, "and I picked up this piece of wood. On the way back I walked slow, and with my knife I scraped the piece of wood and took off its bark."

"You can't hear anything now," said Marthe.

They listened. They could hear only the sound of the iron sheep-bells.

"They've gone into the grass."

"I think that with us, too, someone's been and scratched our bark."

"I think," said Marthe, "that we understand many things better."

"Is it true," said Bobi, "that snow does not gather on dry grass?"

"It doesn't stay as long," said Jourdan. "In the Alpine pastures, at the end of September, the sheep eat grass covered with frost."

"But nobody knows how many of them die of it," said Bobi.

"Scarcely the weakest," said Jourdan. "It makes a strong breed and a trifle wild."

He was caressing the piece of wood from which he had scraped the bark.

"What is there still to eat, Marthe?" he said.

"I think there is some dried cheese," she said, "that was overlooked in the back of the cupboard."

"Give it to us."

It was goat cheese, rounded with the palm of the hand, encrusted with savoury and bergamot, but as hard as stone. Jourdan tried to break it but was forced to cut it by striking with his fist on the knife. The meat of the cheese was yellow, smooth, veined with white like the inside of a chestnut.

"I don't think building a fold with tree trunks is what Randoulet wants. He has started more than all the others with his great field where he has allowed the grass to remain. We want to become strong and wild again."

"The wood is prettier without the bark," said Marthe, who had been examining the piece of oak branch. "You can see like little shining streams, slender as white hairs."

"What you are saying, Marthe, is the opposite of what Jourdan said."

"On the plateau," said Jourdan, "it has always been our way to think about things for a long time. Because in our farm work there are not many of us. Every time we plough, or sow, or harvest, we do it for ourselves."

"What Marthe has just said, about the wood without the bark, is the opposite of what you said with your 'strong' and your 'wild.'"

"Perhaps not entirely the opposite," said Jourdan. "But it is certain that it will be hard to forget what we know.

"Listen. Let's see if we don't hear anything more," he said after a moment.

"Nothing more," said Marthe, "no more sheep-bells, nothing. They must be hidden deep in the grass or almost there."

"Open the door and see."

She opened the door.

"You can hear the mountains that the winter wind is bringing closer to us with all the rumbling valleys," she said.

Jourdan put some dry wood on the fire.

"Give us some brandy this evening, Marthe."

She poured some into their glasses. She poured some into her glass. They looked at the colour of the alcohol. It was a cold white, without any reflections, like ice under a grey sky. It smelt strongly of grape twigs and the vineyard.

"The last time we drank a health," said Jourdan, "it was spring, that morning Carle's son blew his trumpet on the plateau. You said it was the last time we'd drink together. We're drinking again today. You were wrong."

"I'm going to shut the door," said Marthe; "the wind is bringing clouds and you can't see the stars any longer."

As she came back to the table, she put her hand on Bobi's shoulder.

"We thank you," she said.

"The truth is," said Bobi, "that to be joyful for a long time is very difficult. I wonder if it is even possible? Everything we have done looks as though it hasn't helped very much."

"Perhaps," said Jourdan, "we have a big advantage over the others. We have let the ground go from under our feet. In reality, to be joyful is to be simple."

"I think," said Marthe, "that perhaps I've lost the skill of spinning wool easily as I used to see it done at Marie Farm."

"No," said Jourdan, "you don't do it like that. The thumb does not rub against the two fingers but only the index finger, like this. That makes the size. From time to time, your second finger comes and rubs, too. That makes the softness and the length of the thread. Look, I'll show you. Do you see? Try it."

"I am trying, but I don't know when my second finger should come and rub my thumb."

"The wool will teach you. You do it unconsciously."

"Because," said Marthe, "this evening there were brown sheep and white sheep, and by putting the two threads together that would make a pretty thread."

"The stallion has three mares now," said Jourdan.

Then he sat silent a long time, looking into the flame of the fire that was wildly shaking its hair in all directions, for the wind was coming down the chimney.

"You aren't saying anything more," said Marthe; "has the brandy put you to sleep?"

"I was thinking about all those whitebeam trees that the wind has sown in the furrows where we didn't sow wheat this year. What do *you* think of all that?" he asked Bobi.

"I no longer know," said Bobi.

15

That winter afternoon the men were gathered in Carle's barn, listening to Randoulet. He was telling how he had managed to get the sheep.

"I went to Roume. I took the Sisteron bus. We got to Sisteron at nightfall. Le Noir was with me. We put up at the Lion. There are big stables there but now they use them for automobiles. A lot of them pass through there. After supper, we smoked our pipes on the bench in front of the inn door. I counted more than forty cars in no time. I said to Le Noir: 'Come along, this makes me dizzy. Let's walk awhile.'

"We walked down the street. There is a superb hardware store, much bigger than the one in Roume. I had not been to Sisteron since 1903. It's changed. We went clear to the end of the street. It's better laid out than at Roume. The stores are all in a row. We went back to the Lion. I said to the innkeeper: 'We may come back this way with some sheep.' He said to me: 'Ah!' I said to him: 'Yes. Then we'll stop here.' He said to me: 'Stop here? How?' 'In those stables.' 'Don't count on that. We don't put sheep up any more. I need the whole place for automobiles.' I said to him: 'That's funny!' He said to me: 'Where are you from?' I said to him: 'Grémone Plateau.' 'Ah, that's the reason! Well,' he said to me, 'for more than fifteen years we haven't put up sheep at my place or any other.' I said to him: 'In 1903'...He said to me: 'In 1903 it was my father.'

"The next day we took the bus for Embrun. There they said: 'No smoke.' So, you see.

"From Embrun, my idea was to go to Valsainte, sleep at Valsainte, and the next day go up Paille Mountain, where I know the shepherds. But I thought it over. I said to myself: those shepherds; you haven't seen them for twenty years. Le Noir said to me: 'Maybe they're dead.' I said to him: 'Why do you think they're dead?' He said to me: 'Because everybody dies.' I said to him: 'That's possible. As a matter of fact, I hadn't thought of that.'

"I thought that over all along the way. When we got to Embrun I went to the Café du Clos. I said: 'Good day, ma'am; you don't happen to know if there are any shepherds at Valsainte?' She said: 'I don't know.' 'And on Paille Mountain?' 'I don't know.' 'Then give us a litre of wine.' I said to Le Noir: 'What'll we do?' He said to me: 'We've come too far to go back.' I said: 'At any rate, we'll go up tomorrow. We'll see. We are men!' 'Yes,' said Le Noir. Then he said: 'We did well to come together. Alone, a man might lose heart.'

"I looked for an inn. I remembered one where I had slept before. It was a hotel, not for us. We went back to the Café du Clos. There was a blacksmith in there, standing in front of the counter, drinking. It was pure luck. I looked at him. I said to him:

"'You aren't Barthélemy's son?'

"He said to me: 'Yes. Why?'

"I said to him: 'I recognized you by those big eyebrows of yours.'

~ 300 ~

"'Ah! My father had the same.'

"'Exactly.'

"'Did you know him?'

"'Yes. But that's at least twenty years ago.'

"'He's dead.'

"He wiped his hands on his leather apron.

"I said to him: 'Sit down with us.'

"He sat down.

"I said to him: 'So you have kept your father's trade?' He said to me: 'Yes, just about. It isn't the only thing I do.'

"From one thing to another, as we talked, after having said who I was, where I came from and where I was going, I spoke to him about the hotel and I told him that it was not for us and that we didn't know where to sleep.

"He said to me: 'If you aren't particular, perhaps I can put you up.'

"We said to him: 'You can bet your life we aren't particular.'

"Then he said to us: 'But it will be straw, it will be in the barn where I keep my farm machines. If you like, it's at our disposal, but that's all I have.'

"We said: 'You can be sure that there we shall agree. Let's drink on it.'

"And we drank.

"He took us to his barn. His wife had agreed with him on it. He had lighted his storm lantern.

"I said to him: 'What is all that?'

"'Farm machines.'

"'What?'

"'Reaper-binders, mowing machines, rakes, sowers.'

"Then I said to him: 'You have everything done by machines? Your arms must shrivel up.'

"He said to me: 'You like to joke. Didn't you know that there were machines like these?'

"'Yes.'

"'Where are you from?'

"'From an extraordinary place, don't worry.'

"'But where?'

"'The top of the world: Grémone Plateau.'"

They were all there together listening to him in the barn on Carle's farm. Outside was the winter afternoon. And they realized that this was the top of the high country and that it was of them that Randoulet had spoken in the low country.

"Then he said to us: 'Well, sleep with the machines and don't let them scare you.'

"He carried off the lantern and we lay down in the straw. This barn is just on the edge of Embrun, where the road turns. The door is all broken, with cracks in it as big as my arm. Every time an auto passes with its headlights shining ahead of it, the light comes in through the holes in the door and the whole barn is lighted up. Not a chance of getting any sleep.

"Ten pass, thirty pass, fifty, a hundred. Le Noir is here to tell you if it isn't so. Finally I called him: 'Le Noir!'

"'Yes.'

"'You asleep?'

"'No.'

"'Your eyes open?'

"'Yes.'

"'Do you see?'

"'Yes.'

"It was the machines I was talking about, the agricultural ones. I said to him: 'Look!'

"'Oh,' he said to me, 'that one; I saw that long ago.'

"It was one that had sort of wings shaped like a wheel."

"And," interrupted Le Noir, "I was lying lower down than the boss. The wings were right above me, on the level with the ground. Just next to me there was like a row of stars."

"You didn't tell me that!" marvelled Randoulet.

"And," continued Le Noir, "I put out my hand and touched them. They were cold and the edge cut like the edge of a knife."

"Those," said Bobi, "were the blades of the mowing machine."

"Yes," said Carle, "you harness a horse to it and the horse makes the whole thing go."

"The wings," said Bobi, "that was the big wooden paddle, and the rows of stars were the blades of the mowing machine."

"How does it work?" asked Jacquou.

"The horse draws it," said Bobi. "The wings turn. The wings push the grass against the blades, the blades cut, the grass falls."

They were silent a moment. Jourdan cleared his throat. The wind on the plateau gently shook the echoing barn.

"Then," continued Randoulet, "everything was dark. I heard Le Noir stirring in the straw."

"I was stirring," broke in Le Noir, "because I was under the wings and just against that row of knife blades. Every time it got dark, it seemed to me that the machine creaked softly as if it was about to move."

"A hell of a night!" said Jacquou.

"Oh, yes! A hell of a night!" continued Randoulet. "The little sleep I did get was full of nightmares. Ah! The whole time I had those iron teeth biting my leg or those forks sticking in my stomach, that wooden wing turning and knocking me on the head, and those wheels passing over me. It took the wind out of me. I drew back. I woke up. I called: 'Le Noir!'

"'Yes.'

"'You asleep?'

"'No.'

"'Ah, what a dream! Could you sleep?'

"'No.'

"Then, toward morning, there was a still longer time of darkness. And you could think you were alone. It was cooler, too. I slept. I dreamed of Grémone Forest. Blue.

"And then, fellows, day broke, full, little by little, while I was sleeping soundly. I was awakened. I woke Le Noir. We got out of there. Outside was the Hautes-Alpes country with its morning like gold, the grass shining, the poplars, the sound of streams. We hired two mules at the village of Les Conches. We set out. At first we crossed a few valleys. We crossed the Durance River. We crossed some more flat land, then we began to climb with fewer and fewer fields. And then I began to think about the sheep. And you?"

"Me, too," said Le Noir.

"And I began to sing."

"Me, too," said Le Noir.

"That must have been fine," said Jacquou.

"The sheep we bought," said Randoulet, "here's what they are, and anybody can know it. They're an Alpine breed. Pure, I can tell you, and not at all the first come. The fathers and the mothers were from Saint-Véran. They were born there, they lived there, they died there. Not dead like sheep, dead like men, and buried. That's the first thing. Then, here's what they have that the others don't have: hide on their bellies as thick as this" (Randoulet showed the thickness of his finger), "their heads are bevel-shaped, wool like iron. All that makes it so they can lie down in the snow like you can in your beds. Because of their heads they are like trees: you put them here, they stay here; you put them there, they stay there. They have no will of their own, like some of those sheep from the coast that you see on the roads. Easy to watch. And besides, marvellous eyes, peaceful, teachers of patience just to look at them. We bought them all at Remusat, on Paille Mountain, five hours from Valsainte.

"Listen," he went on, and he raised his finger in the air. He stood silent. The winter wind shook the barn. "Those are not ordinary markets now. They aren't the markets of our time any more. You'd say they were like the old times. I brought five hundred sheep all at once in the mountains, because of their breed, but also because of something else, because of me, because I reflected, because"—he leaned toward them—"listen."

They leaned forward.

"I'm cleaned out of my last sou. Five hundred sheep, that makes a sum. I said to Honorine: 'You can wash out the bureau drawer now.'

"I have never been as happy as I am today!"

16

Bobi scraped his pipe. It was better than ever and the dampness in the air improved it continually.

The first days of winter had been filled with great heavy rains. There could be no big frosts. Everything remained soft and wet. The water oozed through the deep humus of the forest. The very air was charged with the odour of water; and that is what gave Bobi's pipe such a good taste.

He was walking through the forest. The mares had returned to the stables a long time ago. The third day of the rain, the stallion had come and cried at Carle's door. Since then, he was quiet in his old bed. Only Aurore's mare still ran about a little. At first she had whinnied at a door that no one opened. But of all the mares on the plateau, she was the one who best knew the forest and freedom (for Aurore's thighs were energetic but not very strong), and she went back to the woods. Aurore was hidden behind the door, watching through the keyhole, saying to herself: "No, I don't want you any more; stay with your stallion."

One night Aurore heard the tiniest cracklings of frost. She went downstairs and opened the door. The mare came in. But it had been understood between Aurore and the animal that the door would remain open. Aurore thought: "I won't keep her in. She will understand that I am not keeping her. If she wants to go, let her go. If she stays, it must be from a real desire and not because of a door."

From time to time the mare went off, galloped away, stayed a day in the rain, and came back streaming with water as if she had come out of a river, with huge russet leaves clinging to her flanks.

Bobi heard the mare galloping. He did not know that the animal and Aurore were each left to her sorrowful liberty. What he knew was quite different, and only what had been seen by Madame Hélène's narrow vision. Madame Hélène had come to La Jourdane. She was more and more agreeably plump, all tenderness and languor. Her eyes were rimmed with blue flesh that shone like the sun. Two or three other places in Madame Hélène's flesh shone like suns: the corners of her mouth, the hollow of her elbow when she extended her bare arm, the place at her throat that rose from the top of her blouse. To look at that was almost unbearable. She had sat down. She had said:

"Aurore doesn't talk any more. Aurore glues her nose to the windowpane. Aurore watches the rain and doesn't stir. Aurore hardly eats a thing. I feel that the child is not sleeping."

She thought that the sole remedy was to catch the mare, tie her to the manger, and go on as before.

Since the rains had let up. Bobi went into the forest every day. The sky hung low and black. La Jourdane, like all the farms on the plateau except Fra-Josépine, had only narrow little windows, built to resist the wind. At this season of great clouds and cold, the house was really inhabited only by the huge fire on the hearth.

As soon as one went outside, the pipe had another taste: the taste of little trails and paths, the taste of dead leaves, of humus and natural dung hills that warmed the great roots in the forest; the taste of shining bare branches on which the shivering birds had died, one after another, and that were now trying to sing by themselves, without birds and without leaves, the song of naked branches in the winter wind. These branches had a strong, tepid, animal taste. Other magnificent tastes crowded about the pipe, mingled with the smoke, melted on the tongue; tastes full of men's most cherished dreams.

As he walked through the forest, Bobi drew on his pipe in short puffs. He did not touch it. He kept it in the corner of his mouth. He no longer felt its weight in his teeth. He was smoking grey tobacco reinforced by a little that was humid and browned in the stoneware pot. It was lightly packed, slow to kindle, and burned slowly from the inside.

"I'm buying myself a stag," he said, and he looked at his pipe.

Since the arrival of the stag on the plateau, he thus called those deep inward joys that he gave himself. Today, the stag was the taste of winter, bare forest, low clouds; walking in the mud, hearing the bushes scratching his corduroy jacket, having a cold nose, a warm mouth. He felt free and agreeably alone.

He heard the mare galloping in the woods. There was no other sound, save the light scraping of the clouds through the treetops.

He tried to explain why that animal no longer settled down in her old stable. She had taken a liking to her new life. He pictured Aurore leaning against the window, looking at the bare sycamore trees of Fra-Josépine and the terrace cluttered with dead leaves. Suddenly the galloping sounded exactly as on the day when Aurore had spoken so fiercely about love.

There was the same silence over the earth, the same crackling of the branches, the same galloping. It seemed that he could hear the voice saying: "You have less heart than the river."

He continued awhile longer straight ahead until he came to a little eglantine bush, bare and leafless, but with two big red berries still clinging. He looked at the two berries all alone in the dead branches. He turned back. He tried to see through the forest screen. The sound of galloping had begun again, a little fainter. The mare was running northward over the moss. Bobi left the forest path; he entered the woods directly and moved toward the sound. He walked as before, with no more haste. The mare was running over the moss. She must be enjoying herself, racing back and forth, and sometimes leaping high in the dim light, to fall back again on the thick moss. She was still far ahead. She made no more noise than a hare. It was easy for him to track the mare to the spot in the heart of the woods where she was playing. He walked through the little bushes, he scarcely troubled to go around the big ones. He passed through thin screens of branches, straight on, through puddles, over sandy slopes, sandstone, soft burdock. He went no faster than before, but his shoulders were squarer than during his stroll. He had taken his hands out of his pockets. His arms were stiff at his sides like the pillars of porticoes. His head and shoulders were thrust forward. His pipe had gone out. It was no longer a stroll.

The mare's bright little hoofs began to strike the porous rock in which the forest had hollowed caves. Bobi changed his direction. This way the sounds were louder. It was a cliff, above the slopes that dropped to the plain, that gave birth to the echoes of sky and caverns. The hammering sound of the gallop rose to the clouds, then fell again to the earth. This sound, multiplied, made one conscious of the solitude. There was nothing left in the whole world but Bobi pursuing the mare.

He crossed the fields of moss, then marshes of decayed mushrooms. Big drops of rain hung at the tips of the dead branches. The clouds brushed the treetops.

When the sun marked two o'clock, the mare had almost vanished from the world. She was no longer to be heard. There had been a long silence, with only the sound of Bobi's steps and the sound of his heart. Nevertheless, he had made a mighty effort. He had put all his strength into his steady stride, but, as soon as he approached, she would flee. She glided toward the coombs; she acted as if she were about to rush headlong down the slope to the Plain of Roume. He stepped out onto the shale and let himself go, carried downward by a torrent of stones. He caught himself against the oak stumps. Up above him he could hear the mare galloping through the birches, up there where there is space and one can make speed. The sound died away in the distance. He climbed back up. The birch wood was deserted. Nothing obstructed the view. There was nothing but the spotted trunks planted upright here and there with their lovely bark like the skin of a girl. Nothing else. Not a sound. Not a trace. The grey day lighted up the naked wood. Far beyond the birch grove could be seen the blackish edge of a section of the forest where firs and larches grew. Solitude. However, Bobi pressed forward. He kept the same stride. It had not occurred to him to walk faster or to run. He continued at his usual pace.

He tried to push away the solitude with his forehead, with his beam-like shoulders, with his chest, his man's mass, as one does in a storm against the wind and the rain. He felt he must catch up with this mare, seize her and take her prisoner in his grip. Then, the solitude would crumble like a mountain of clouds that hides the bright sky and the hundred thousand paths of the stars.

"For I *have* more heart than the river."

A little shining moisture softened his lips. Not a sound. Gradually the solitude, like a sandstorm, drowned the forest. No more trees, no more air, no more joy, nothing but the desire to reach the invisible animal.

The mare had stopped behind the line of firs. She was cropping the wild hay. Bobi reached a forked birch and from there he could see the mare. She was ten paces away. She did not move. That was why he had not been able to hear her. All the forest emerged from the solitude with its colours, its high-vaulted walls beneath the oaks, its stairs of rock, its carpet of moss, and the great sleeping wind that inhabited it like a serpent.

The mare scented the man. She approached the line of trees and put her head through the fir branches to see who was walking in the birch wood. She had large, calm eyes. She sniffed the odour. Bobi was wet with the rain that had clung to the bushes. He smelt strongly of corduroy. The mare remembered that odour.

One afternoon, before the horses' escapade, Aurore had entered La Jourdane. Nobody was there, save that corduroy coat hanging on the nail by the hearth and that retained the shape of the shoulders and the bend of the arms. She had taken that coat and carried it off. She had kept it close to her body, in front of her, lying across the saddle. She had gone deep into the woods. She had tried on the coat, putting her woman's arms into the sleeves that had held the man's, pressing her woman's breast against the breast of this invisible man. The mare remembered. And at night, they had returned to hang the coat on a nail in the shed.

With a little whinny, the mare tried to make the man understand all this. Bobi moved away from the tree against which he was leaning. He advanced. The mare withdrew her head from between the branches and fled.

He pursued her far to the south, and far to the north, to the east, and to the west, toward the sun that was setting behind the clouds. Two red rays had pierced the mud of the sky, and far off on the plateau two mounds of earth burst into flame.

The mare was no longer as before, detached from him, and he in pursuit unknown to her. Now she remained almost within reach of his hand. Always hidden but so near him that he could hear her when she slipped in the decaying mushrooms or when she whinnied softly with that little voice she had had when she recognized the odour of the corduroy coat. He knew very well that it was useless to run, but best to follow with his slow, sure step, for in those things, if one really would succeed, it is tenderness, love, that impels the desired one into your grasp. It is not a question of force. And if one is not to succeed, there is no help for it; the desired one escapes in spite of the deepest cunning. He went forward, at his pace, changing his direction, following the leapings, crushing the bushes, crossing open spaces, slowly sinking into the cracking branches of the cut wood. Finally the mare left the forest. Bobi left the forest. He stopped at the edge. All was over. A little daylight still remained. The mare was fleeing with all her might, far away across the frozen plateau. She disappeared, then there was no other sound.

At the same time, the world and everything had vanished. Bobi saw in his mind the face behind the windowpane, over at Fra-Josépine; the eyes that must now be watching the night, those cheeks, that brow, that hair, that were the very essence of speed. He would never be able to overtake Aurore.

He returned across the hardened fields to La Jourdane.

"Where have you been?" said Marthe.

"Out around."

"You are all wet."

"I've been walking in the woods."

"What's the matter?"

"Nothing."

"You look sad."

"No."

"Are you tired?"

"No," he said; "what I've been doing, I could do every day without ever growing tired."

He sat down. She went over to him. She touched him gently on the shoulder.

In the midst of the winter calm, the men rediscovered ancient joys in all the secret recesses of their bodies. Joys in their armpits, in their elbows, in their knees, and in that part of the shoulders that rises from the neck of one's shirt and that is more sensitive to cold than to heat. To all these joys could be given names of animals. There were dog joys in the spine: to stretch, to feel the heat rising along the loins like the growth of a plant with glowing branches and broad leaves of soft, caressing warmth that folded gently over the breast to shelter the heart and lungs like a silkworm cocoon. There were fox joys in the legs that walked over frozen paths and, in spite of the cold, were well lubricated. The suppleness of the thigh, the cold that seized the skin and a centimetre of flesh around the leg, while from deep inside the body flowed a burning blood that descended to the legs, and thigh, knee, calf, and foot began to live with an ardent force. That was no longer a part of man, but it was a part of the world, like mountains, torrents, clouds, or the great wind. One could walk all day long just for the pleasure of walking. There were bird joys in breathing the glacial air, and all the while the foliage of the blood wrapped the lungs with great velvet leaves burning like silk.

All the birds of the plateau had congregated above Randoulet's pasture—even the birds from the Ouvèze Valley, from the plain, and from the distant mountains. As the cold closed in, they came in greater numbers and among them strange varieties. There were some very rare species, almost unnatural; some of those breeds never seen by man. Some came from very far away, with plumage that bore the tints of lands sown with plants of the Far South; and even some whose feathers smelt of the sea. As soon as day broke, they would rise, singing, to the clouds.

Marthe had wanted to give them wheat again. She had swept the threshing floor, heaped upon it two kettlefuls of grain that she had kept out from the harvest expressly for that purpose. But the birds did not come.

"They aren't coming," she had said.

She had looked up into the empty sky. She was in despair.

"Randoulet gives them more than you," Bobi had replied.

"So for nothing but a little grass…?" she asked.

Her big pitiful eyes looked at the empty sky and her arms hung listlessly at her sides.

"Not 'nothing but a little grass,'" Jourdan had said, "but twenty big hectares of grass left standing with seeds, stems, leaves, and even tufts of late flowers."

"Here or there," said Bobi, "it doesn't matter. Whether it be you or Randoulet, that isn't important. The main thing is that the sky has stayed open. Look! Above our heads it will not close over all winter. Not only will we have all our birds alive but even those of other parts of the country. The sky is already closed over many regions. Above us it stays open."

"But," she said, still looking at the sky, "flight is possible all over the plateau, and I am sure that Madame Carle and Joséphine and Mademoiselle Aurore have swept their threshing floors and poured out bushels of grain. And now we are deprived of the birds."

"No," said Bobi, "we can hear them."

They listened. They could hear the cries of the birds.

"And we can stay outdoors; look, without being under a sky that frightens you with its emptiness, as we were last winter. Who knows but that maybe because all those different wings are flying yonder above the great pasture, we feel even here that something continues to keep us company?"

"Yes," said Jourdan.

"And maybe soon some of them will come to your wheat."

"Perhaps," said Marthe, "that is so. I am always in too great a hurry."

"What we have to realize," said Bobi, "is that nothing is actually for our use, but all the same, in the end, everything is for our use and reaches out toward us to benefit us. The birds do not belong to us. There, above the pasture, a whole nation of birds has gathered, and by that we are assured that the sky will not close in over us all winter. That is really something."

"That's a good deal," said Jourdan.

"For," said Bobi, "the sky closes in over country where all the birds are dead."

"Yes," said Marthe.

She knew that he was right, but she was thinking about the joy of feeding them. It was not her fault. It was her woman's desire. Reason cannot prevail against the desires of the body, and it is a mistaken idea to attempt it.

"Yes," said Marthe to herself, "but *my* pleasure is to watch the bird eating the seed that I give it and to watch it wallow in the heap, and do this and that with its feet, and that with its beak, and that with its feathers."

She was talking to herself, and she stopped suddenly, for she had just caught herself imitating the birds with tiny movements of her arms and shoulders.

"If they are looking at me," she thought, "they'll think I'm crazy."

They had not noticed her. They were looking out over the wide plateau. The gloomy solitude that they saw from the house stretched as far as eye could see. The fields adjoining the house had been planted in flowers. But now, beneath the low winter sky, they were only bare fields covered with a hard armour of frost. Beyond, the heath bore a few junipers. There was not a living thing in sight, save a blue shadow cast by the slowly rolling clouds, and that was creeping over the stones. The horizon was as black as night and shut in on all sides.

Marthe thought: "One of these days, I'm going to the birds' pasture."

She looked at this strange landscape, so sad and mute, all around her. She said to herself: "Yes, but there I don't have to be afraid. I'll not be alone. Zulma is guarding the sheep."

She could not remember who had told her that Zulma was keeping the sheep, but she was sure that someone had told her.

Zulma had become the queen of the sheep. The queen and everything. She was heat, cold, rain, sun, and wind to the sheep; the joy and the sorrow of the sheep.

They were wild sheep, with foreheads of marble and eyes full of harsh mystery. It had been necessary, after all, to watch them.

"It isn't just an idea," Le Noir had said, "but something I know. What do you think I can do, alone in all that big place? And especially since the sheep are going to roam in all directions without asking anybody's leave, but...."

He puffed a moment on his old pipe filled with moist tobacco.

"But," he went on, "man is something, just the same; you can't say he isn't."

He had set up a sort of encampment for himself in the middle of this vast field of old matted grass. He had refused to construct a shed.

"You must never build a cabin," he said.

He touched Randoulet's arm.

"Listen," he said, "do you trust me?"

"Yes," said Randoulet, chewing on his moustache.

"Then let me alone."

"You will freeze," said Randoulet; "we'll have to bring you back, stiff as a log."

"I'll build a fire," said Le Noir.

And then he went and untied the old bundle of sheepskins, tanned three years ago. He had scraped all the salt from them and had put them to soften for four or five nights. He began to cut from them mittens, hoods, shoes, chaps, leggings, capes. It was at that point that Zulma came to him. All this took place at the farm house.

"Are you going to the festival?" she asked.

Le Noir was very fond of Zulma. He understood her. He knew how far that still and shining gaze could see.

"No," he said.

Then he thought: "Why did she speak of a festival? Who has been talking to her about a festival? Where did she get that? There has never been a festival on the plateau."

"What festival?" he said.

"The festival," she said. And with a vague gesture she indicated the lonely country that lay flat beneath the grey sky.

When he had cut out his complete costume from the sheep-skins, he tried it on. Clad thus, he had doubled in volume. He had become a big man. He was obliged to make very slow gestures and take very deliberate steps. But he looked like someone. As Randoulet said to him: "You look like some-one."

"Who?"

"Nobody in particular. But I mean that, like that, you begin to be someone. And you think," continued Randoulet, "that a cabin wouldn't have been more convenient?"

"No," said Le Noir, "you have to live in the same air with those brutes."

This was also the opinion of the sheep.

"When you get an idea in your head," said Randoulet, "you don't have it in your feet, one might say."

But he was forced to accept it. His huge flock had begun to spread out in all directions over his vast wild pastures of more than twenty hectares, and wander off. He said to himself: "What do I care? They won't really get lost. I'll find them again. They won't leave my land."

But he would not have the joy of seeing his sheep. He could no longer count on the joy of seeing all that happened: the rams, the ewes, the lambs.

Le Noir went off to the middle of the pastures, to his chosen spot. He set up his camp. And on all sides, like little springs that have opened up, the sheep came single file, and first they crowded around the shepherd, then they spread out over a bigger space but without disappearing, no longer going straight ahead seeking the spaces of the sky and solitude, but sniffing in the direction of the shepherd, and sometimes, at the approach of those vast nights that announce themselves without stars, they breathed toward him from deep in their throats a great word that, said Le Noir, "gives you the same feeling as those words that little children cry when they call you."

Le Noir had been there about two hours when Zulma appeared. She must have walked directly in his footsteps.

"How did you manage to find us?" he said.

But he saw that it was serious. Zulma had arranged her hair in tight plaits like the weave of cloth. She had made herself a thick crown of rotting old spikes of sheep's fescue. She had made herself a necklace of green rushes and two bracelets with twists of green hay that she had pulled from beneath the grass. The sheep around them got up and looked at her.

"The heather isn't in bloom," she said, pointing to her ornaments of grey grass.

"That has been over a long time," said Le Noir.

"I didn't know," she said. "If I had known, I would have put some by."

"So," said Le Noir, "you haven't noticed that the Ouvèze hills were all purple two months ago?"

"Yes," she said, "that was the sky."

"No," said Le Noir, "it was the heather."

"When you need things," she said, "you never have them at hand."

She made a slight, housewifely gesture such as she had seen her mother make. She looked about her. She saw the sheep. She put her hands on the woolly heads.

As Le Noir told Randoulet later: "From that moment, I only argued on principle. It had been settled a long time ago."

"But," said Randoulet, "you are both idiots; what has that to do with the sheep?"

"Sometimes a man would think your head is like a pig trough," said Le Noir.

The discussion rose high. Randoulet had grown red and all the hair of his eight-day beard stood out on his cheeks. The perspiration ran down his forehead as from the edges of a pond, and he talked fast, he got mixed up, he ended by being able to say only: "But then, explain, explain, I say."

"What do you want me to explain?" said Le Noir. "You can't explain. Either you understand it or you don't; that's all."

He had turned very pale; he talked with a deep, strange voice; his hands were trembling, and he avoided looking at Randoulet, glancing sometimes to the right, sometimes to the left, but never straight at his master.

"Yes," Randoulet said at last, "and then?…"

He had swallowed a good mouthful of air and was calming down.

"Then?"

"Then," said Le Noir, "I said to her: 'Wait, I'll try the costume on you.' I had to take off her bracelets and her necklace, but she kept the crown. I gave her my chaps, and my cloak, and my leggings, and my hood, and my armlets and all, and my stick. I said to her: 'Mind you keep the fire burning.' She said to me: 'Oh! I know!' The dog stayed with her of his own accord. You've got to let her stay."

"I'll let her stay willingly," said Randoulet, "but then, won't she come back home any more? Is she going to turn into a sheep-woman? Is she going to stay up there all her life?"

"No," said Le Noir. "From time to time she will come back. Don't worry. All we have to do is to carry food to her regularly."

"I'm perfectly willing to let her stay," said Randoulet slowly, "if that pleases her."

"That pleases everybody," said Le Noir.

"Not me very much," said Randoulet. "She's my child, after all."

"She is happy," said Le Noir. "That is all a father can wish for his daughter. And then, I can tell you that it is necessary for the sheep."

Evening fell. They went toward the house, where Honorine was lighting the lamps.

"What did you mean by your 'pig trough'?" said Randoulet.

"Nothing," said Le Noir; "I meant a pig trough."

"What has that to do with my head?"

"Nothing," said Le Noir. "It's just because in a pig trough there are only the remains of soup and rotten potatoes. You get it," said Le Noir. "After all, when animals understand things right off, we ought to understand them too."

They struck their heavy boots against the step to rid the soles of the mud.

That evening Honorine said: "All this business is a mystery to me."

"Shut up," said Randoulet. "Women never understand anything. However, it is easy. Even the animals themselves understand it."

Zulma sat motionless a long time. She was listening. She had heard the birds. They were in the warmth beneath the weeds. They were calling. They were talking to one another in little voices. They must even be going about from nest to nest along little corridors hollowed out of the mat of the pasture. From time to time long frost-covered grasses nodded their heavy heads because the birds were jostling their roots.

The sun did not appear. But, suddenly, in the middle of the cupola of grey sky, a bright spot of oil swelled and rounded like a shaggy fruit. A stem of frozen grass cracked. After a moment its icy sheath slipped along the stem, uncovering a little flesh still green. Here and there grasses freed themselves of their coating and a blue-green watery light like the reflections of water began to quiver over the whole extent of the pasture. It was noon.

The birds began to fly about. Zulma watched them. They came out of the immense grey prairie. They burst the thin coat of hoar frost that clung to the grass. They shook off the icy dust and darted skyward. There were great hoopoes, like gold, that with three strokes of their wings touched the ceiling of clouds.

The girl's encampment was in a hollow about twenty metres in circumference, round as the inside of a bowl, that in the summertime was the site of a deep storehouse for grain. Here was the great sleeping fire. From time to time, enormous embers burst slowly and noiselessly, revealing snowy hearts deep inside their red flesh where pulsated the blood of the fire.

Zulma was dressed in the clothes that Le Noir had cut out of the skins for himself. But she was big. She had fine breasts, heavy and round, and hips that filled out the man's clothes. She was like a woolly giantess. From the collar, for which Le Noir had carefully chosen the shining, curly hair of a little merino lamb, emerged the placid face, with full, straight lips, still eyes, wide nostrils, straw-coloured hair plaited in a hundred tight plaits like threads of silk cloth and wearing the crown of spikes of sheep's fescue.

She was looking straight before her. She did not stir. She was listening. From time to time a noise welled up from the silence of the meadow, at first almost imperceptible, then like the lapping of water on the sand. Only a few peeps could be heard from the birds. There were no more birds in the sky save, high up, the flash of two hoopoes that were fighting against the hazy ball of the sun.

An unseen ram spoke to his ewes. Then the sheep appeared about the hollow of the encampment. The girl called to them. They came down to her. They were carrying birds hooked in their wool. They lay down in the hollow around Zulma, around the fire, on the slopes. They kept on coming. They came to the edge, they stood a moment, looking. They had little stunted horns, foreheads on which the wool foamed tumultuously, and eyes terribly cold and blue beneath their wool. They came down, forcing the sheep already lying down to get up, crowding about Zulma. Soon the whole hollow was full. The rest of the flock lay all about in the meadow above. An old black ram asked several slow grave questions of a ewe lying beside Zulma. The birds loosed their little claws from the wool and began to flit from one sheep to another. The ewe sneezed. A little griffon glided among the animals and came and sat near the fire.

The day was russet from the muddied reflections of the sun. Not a thing stirred. Only the birds hopped from sheep to sheep.

The winter revolutions of the heavens slowly swept the clouds toward the north. Glacial shadows walked on the earth. One of these blue shadows greeted Marthe at the edge of the pastures. She had made up her mind to come. She was now standing before the huge expanse of grass. No one could guess where the flock was. At first she walked at random. A mournful cooing, like that of doves, stopped her. Some sheep that had risen up behind her were talking to her. They came close enough to touch her. They sniffed her woollen skirt. Marthe had her hand in her apron pocket. She gave them a handful of the grain that she had brought for the birds.

The sheep began to walk. She followed. It was really a wild country and a frightening one. In this winter light, in this cold, in this weather where one breathes sharp air that hurts the throat, it was strange to see grasses whose spears were freely opened for the seeds and now hung at the tips of the stems like things unknown in the world.

The oats had grown thick at the base of the stem and had broad leaves like those of the acanthus. But especially the stems brought new strength to their bodies, which were three times as big as the body of the stems one usually sees. The seed that usually was enclosed between two long blond barbs had fallen on the ground for its natural sowing. Nothing remained but the light armour which had protected it and which, beneath the frost and the rains and the wind, had become like copper. All had changed in proportion. The grass was no longer the simple grass about which one knows, for example, that for bryony or oats the width of the leaf will not exceed the width of the finger, and the stem the size of a knitting needle. This grass was on the march toward a life superior to that of grasses. Here was freedom. Suddenly, all grew out of bounds, escaped the measure of Man, and was trying to regain its natural stature.

"Oh!" thought Marthe. "This is paradise on earth!"

It was sad: winter, solitude, the untamed world; the size and the force of the grass frightened her, but she sensed that this was an earthly paradise.

For more than two hours she walked behind the sheep. She continually thought of the earthly paradise. When she stumbled; when the grass knotted about her ankles and she was obliged to make an effort to free herself; when she struggled painfully to go forward; when the sheep turned their heads toward her and cooed mournfully like doves at noonday (they had beautiful, unfathomable expressions, and it was bitter not to be able to understand them); when the birds flew about her; when she saw that they were at home, lords of their land, masters of their grain, masters of their liberty; when she caught sight of two enormous blue ones, doubtless missel thrushes, that were asleep in the warmth of the great roots of the wild wheat; when she felt herself a stranger; when for the first time she breathed in the powerful odour of frozen hay; when she felt lost in the grass; when a great golden bird began to fly silently above her; when she began to see strange faces in the clouds, gentle smiles, wide as the sky itself; when she realized that it was too much for her, and she felt despair and hope vanish from her heart; when she suddenly thought of the kitchen at La Jourdane, that warm and glowing thing built by her and Jourdan and that was now sheltering Jourdan and Bobi, whom she had left only a short while ago, and when she saw the light of her house go out in her memory like the flash of a sou thrown into the water (a gust of wind forced her two cold hands to her breast), she called out:

"Mamma!"

The golden bird plunged into the grass. The sheep turned their heads and looked at her with eyes in which all was explained.

They were approaching the flock. Animals were stirring in the grass. A ram stood up, his head trembling beneath the weight of his horns. Marthe heard a woman's voice singing. It was as if all the lamps of the sun had illumined the harvests. She cried:

"Zulma! Zulma!"

Immediately the singing ceased. It was a dreary song. Marthe went forward. When she reached the edge of the hollow, she saw Zulma in the midst of the sheep. She recognized her by the crown of sheep's fescue. Marthe went and sat down beside the girl. The griffon had not barked. He had only stopped licking his wounded leg.

Zulma spoke first. "Fine weather," she said.

"Where do you see the fine weather?" said Marthe.

"Everywhere."

"I don't see it," said Marthe.

She was trying to get her breath. She was breathless from fear and sadness.

"I am the fine weather," said Zulma.

At that moment Marthe noticed that the girl had a monstrous body, enlarged by the voluminous sheepskin clothing.

"Let me rest a little," said Marthe.

She meant: Let me get used to it. I am beginning to see that you are beautiful, that perhaps everything is beautiful that the black sun has light, that you are perhaps really the fine weather....

She thought: "Now I am talking like her, without regard to what people say to me, but only what I want to say."

"Oh, as for rest," said Zulma, "first you have to know what rest you are talking about. What do you want to rest, your arms and your legs or your head?"

"Everything."

"With me," she said, "it is mostly my head. Doesn't yours bother you?"

"What?"

"Your head?"

"My child, why don't you talk like other people?"

The instant she said that, Marthe saw the birds. They were then all clinging in the sheep's wool. They were not stirring. They moved only their eyes. They were of every colour. Even in Zulma's wool, a greenfinch, recognizable by its copper wings, green head, and silver belly, was fast asleep.

"I don't know," said Zulma. "How do you talk, the rest of you?"

"Oh, my child, we talk as life makes us talk."

"I never know what you others mean."

"We mean that life is sad."

"I don't understand, Madame."

"Sad, do you know what that is?"

"No."

"Content; when you are content, do you know what that is?"

"No."

"When your father told you to come here?"

"No. How do you expect him to tell me to come, Madame? I tell you, I don't understand you when you talk."

"Suppose he had said to you: 'Zulma, go watch the sheep.'"

"But he can't say that. Nobody can say it. Look, Madame, there's one over there near the fire getting up to come to see me. Well, he wants me to scratch him behind the ears."

"Instead of saying 'Madame' to me, you might call me Marthe. You know very well where I live. You came there. You remember very well we all ate together. Anyway, you know very well that we've seen each other for twenty years. I have hushed you to sleep in my apron when you were a little thing."

"I don't know," said Zulma. "I listen to what you say when you talk. I say to myself: they say 'Madame' to each other, so I'll have to say 'Madame' to them, because when I talk the way I know how, you don't understand me. I remember your house very well. I went there for the stag. You dried my stomach. I know that they don't call you 'Madame,' but I have more courage when I say it to someone."

She gave Marthe a long look.

Marthe's thoughts were in a whirl. All that she smelled, heard, and saw did not touch her directly now, but first crashed against her heart. She felt moved to talk to Zulma and to herself. "I had never seen her eyes," she thought, "I don't think anyone has seen them. She always keeps them hidden. I see them now!"

They were calm and wide open, but shot through with green flashes.

"I haven't any courage," said Zulma. "And perhaps it is best so."

"Why should you want courage?" said Marthe.

"You have all done something for me. *You* dried my stomach. I had lain down at the water's edge to pick cress. My stomach got wet. You lifted my skirt. You rubbed me with a dry cloth, and then my stomach was warm. Ah, but you see," she said, shutting her eyes, "now I can't talk like you any more."

For a long time they sat silent.

"Madame," said Zulma, "since you are here, I'd like you to explain everything to me. I love to have you touch me with your hand because your hand is as white as flour."

"I don't know anything, my child."

"You ought to know. The women sing it."

"What do you mean?"

"My mother prepares new milk for the little lambs and she puts barley meal in it to thicken it and make it nourishing. Then she stirs it with a long stick and she sings:

"'I had a fine treasure all my own.
Who has stolen it away?
It is love, it is death.'"

"I know that song," said Marthe. "I used to sing it, too, when I was young. This is the way it begins:

"Marie, with her fair white feet,
Stood before her door.
But the shepherd passed by
Without a glance for her."

"That's the one, Madame."

"Certainly," said Marthe. "It is '*L'Amour, la Mort.*' All women have sung that song when they were young."

"*I* don't sing it," said Zulma.

"Well, what do you want me to explain?"

"Nothing," said Zulma, "let's sit awhile without talking. Since you came, you haven't done anything but talk, and I don't understand you. Rest, as you said."

The silence began. One could hear the grass, the cold, the birds' plumage, the sheep's wool, the sky.

Marthe returned to La Jourdane with the night. The men had set the table and built a great fire.

"We've taken charge of things for you," said Jourdan. "Look! We have done your work. Today we are going to wait on you. The one time that the mistress goes out! Well, how are you, my old Marthe? Not tired?"

"No."

"And did you see the birds?" asked Bobi.

"I saw them."

"You don't sound pleased."

"Listen," she said to Bobi, "now I think it is going to be difficult."

"What?"

"Well," she said, "I think now that you can't make joy last."

At once she noticed how Bobi's face clouded over.

"Who made you say that?" he asked.

He no longer questioned like one who had the answer ready; she sensed that perhaps he already knew.

"And," she said, "I even believe that we ought not to desire it."

Bobi did not reply.

Marthe gave an account of her afternoon with Zulma. The three of them had just finished their evening meal. The two men were filling their pipes.

"She always says what she means," she said. "She goes far to seek things where we others would not go."

The two men lighted their pipes. The tobacco was humid. They leaned several times toward the fire to light it.

"What she told me," said Marthe, "she told me twice."

Then she rose from her chair and went and put out the lamp. The three were now illumined only by the fire in the fireplace. Marthe drew her chair to one corner of the hearth. Her face was in the shadow.

"Here is what she said," said Marthe. "First she said to me: 'And for us, who is the shepherd?'"

Marthe ceased speaking. She wanted to show them the period of silence which in the midst of the vast prairie and the winter had followed the first words. The clocked ticked. The two men puffed gently on their pipes.

"Then she said to me: 'I am the shepherdess.' And about her all was peace and repose."

17

Spring leaped with a single bound upon the earth. The green jonquils stood above the grass. The eglantine trembled beneath big blooms. The air was bitter and pungent like the sap of the fig tree.

Jacquou went out every day. He strode across his fields, then over the heath which separated his fields from the others'. He kept licking his lips. Finally they became chapped.

"It's the weather," he said.

The inflammation spread all around his mouth. The rims of his eyes grew bloodshot.

"Keep still a little," said Barbe, "calm your blood."

"Ah," he said, "you have understood."

"What?" she said.

"Well, my dear," he said, "for the first time, I am not master of myself."

He had spoken with his boyhood voice, with calm and deliberation.

"You ought to take a purgative."

"I am taking the purgative I need," he said.

Nevertheless, Barbe made him a brew of agrimony. After several days he was cured. He looked as usual.

One evening as he was returning home, he went around by the stables. The days had grown longer. The air was soft. They had opened the doors and set up hurdles to keep the animals from getting out. The ewes, the lambs, the little donkey, the goats, the horse crowded against the bars. They sniffed the evening air. There was the smell of flowers in the direction of the fields. The black mare put her head out. Jacquou had the habit of giving her bread. He found a crust in his pocket. She crunched it between her big teeth.

"Well, girl," said Jacquou, "are you full? Yes or no?"

The next morning, Jacquou saddled the horse.

"I am going to La Jourdane."

He still lifted himself easily in the rope stirrups, and, once settled in the saddle, he heaved a sigh. He felt his strong loins, his heavy hips, his solid thighs. He went off at a walk. The horse flipped her tail at the little golden flies. The fields that surrounded the house had always been kept as meadow land. This time they were thicker. Jacquou had sown them twice without saying anything about it.

One night he got to thinking about all those humps of black earth raised up by the grass roots and that sleep in the under-growth of pastures. He had said to himself: "I'm going to give back some seed to all that." He had chosen from more than a hundred paper packets and he had especially selected the packets on which coloured labels of the most beautiful flowers were pasted. The method he knew better than anyone. A meadow is grass. The flower is good for nothing. What counts is what is between the flower and the root. The flower does nothing for the animal. "And who knows that?" he had thought. "What do the rest of you know about it?" ("The rest of you" meant the ancestors, the fathers and the grandfathers and all those who had created meadows and pastures before this spring.) "What do you know about animals? Suppose, by chance, this flower," he said to himself all alone in the middle of the night, "suppose this flower gave hair or eyes or teeth or horn or hoof or who knows what fine part of the beast? What do you know about it?" Thus, in the night, he argued a long time with the shades of his ancestors. The borderland of his sleep was all bright with oxen and cows the colour of flame, and sheep and horses and goats of extraordinary beauty.

Now, from his horse, he saw his broad foaming meadows. The little celandine, the big celandine, the daisy, gold grass, whitlow grass, and the little bitter cress displayed their flowers. He rode through the field and the smell of honey rose around him as the horse brushed the plants with his legs. Farther on was his bright wheat. Then two fields where he had sown not wheat but narcissi, as Jourdan had. It had become the favourite flower of the plateau. It grew easily. Suddenly he understood, thanks to it, that all the soil under the ground was full of water. Beyond was the heath lying under the blue haze. He thought that some day they would have to come to some agreement about this heath; all would get together, plough it up lightly, and strew it over with flower seeds. Plant trees, maples, elms, birches that he loved so well. Birches with bark as soft to the eye as the haunches of a doe.

He thought of a consoling world. He longed to know the new colt that must be in the belly of his mare. He imagined it with a skin of ochre spotted with white. He could see it with a transparent mane blowing in the wind and legs as thin as a young girl's wrists. He could see him galloping. Jacquou was going at a walk across country. He passed through Jourdan's narcissi and arrived at La Jourdane.

"Are you cured?" asked Marthe.

"I was only sick on the surface," he said, touching the skin on his face. "It was badness in the blood."

"That has healed up wonderfully," said Marthe. "And so, here you are out for a ride?"

"No," he said, "I came on purpose. Where is Jourdan?"

"Come in."

He tied his horse to the shed post.

"To tell you the truth," he said, "I have been very uneasy."

"What about?"

"About what I had on my face."

"It wasn't anything serious."

"No," he said, "but it wasn't pretty."

Jourdan was busy making a big set of shelves for packages of seeds.

"I am going to get it ready," he said, "so as to have it all handy when I need it. We have time now to do everything."

"See here," said Jacquou, "I came about something. We ought to let our animals run loose."

"You know," said Jourdan, "I don't have many. I just have my horse. And my sow."

"Where do you have her covered?"

"The boar at Fra-Josépine."

"Is she full?"

"She will farrow in about twenty days."

"Well," said Jacquou, "come down off your stepladder; come and sit down. I've got half an hour. Where is Bobi? I'd like to explain it to you."

"Bobi is in the forest. There's something new about the stag and the whole herd."

"What is there new?"

"Something good," said Jourdan.

"Well, come and sit down," said Jacquou. "I say that you must want everything or nothing."

"I say so, too," said Jourdan.

"I say," said Jacquou, "that all this winter I've been asking myself a hundred questions. Day and night."

"So have I," said Jourdan.

"I waited for spring."

"So did I."

"And spring is here."

"Yes."

"And I understand those things," said Jacquou tenderly.

"I understand them, too," said Jourdan. "But I haven't many animals to let loose. I've never been a stock farmer. I've been more of a crop farmer."

"As a matter of fact," said Jacquou, "you could keep on with the crops."

"That's what I'm doing," said Jourdan.

"I've become…" said Jacquou. "Here, I'll have to talk to you differently. I am happy. No, I haven't become happy like a fool. Before I saw the white bull…"

"What white bull?"

"One night I saw a white bull."

"Where?"

"Standing in front of me."

"In the meadows?"

"No, in a dream."

They were on the threshing floor. Before them the fields were sleeping under the pale morning and the mist. The larks were singing.

"A bull!" said Jacquou. "He was planted in front of me, face to face with me. From his hoofs to his shoulders his legs made an arc like the beam of that wheat crusher. His head had a nose as broad as my two hands. His horns opened straight out."

Jacquou stretched his two arms forward.

"Yes," said Jourdan, "that is indeed a dream bull."

"I had plenty of time to see him," said Jacquou. "He stood there. He did not budge. Neither did I. I looked him all over as if someone had said to me: 'Your life if you don't learn by heart all the places on his body where the moons, half-moons, and stars of his muscles shimmer.' On his skin, at times, there was a shiver as when a fly alights and it made a sparkling in his coat like a star. But it wasn't a fly. It was a little explosion of his strength in that spot. At other places, flat muscles turned, smoothing his coat and making it white all around. That is what I called moons, half-moons, and stars in my dreams. When the bull disappeared I woke up. It was my usual time for waking. When he came to me, it was my usual time for going to sleep. He stayed the whole time without either of us getting tired, he or I. All night long."

"When was that?"

"Around March."

"Had the cold gone?"

"It had just gone."

"Were we still having rain?"

"No. There had been three very sunny days. Then the fog had come up and we had days when you couldn't see anything but fog. It was one of those nights. What do you think of it?"

"Nothing."

"In the same way," said Jacquou, "I had the dream about the goat, about the horse, the dream about my mares with ten flame-coloured colts. The dream about the sow. I haven't any sow. Maybe I dreamed about yours. Anyway, a sow."

"She'll farrow," said Jourdan, "just at the time when the days get really bright."

"What do you say to it?"

"I don't say anything," said Jourdan. "I say that you have been dreaming about animals."

"Yes."

"*I* have been having dreams about plants."

"Ah!"

"Not regularly," said Jourdan, "but I have been dreaming green."

"Then you and I, both of us, have been dreaming about plants and animals. And when did that happen to you?"

"About the same time as to you. I remember the foggy days."

"Did you dream about a great many?"

"I think that I dreamed about them all. Only, they were mixed. It wasn't like with you with the bull or the sow, one animal for each dream. It was a green dream, all mingled."

"With me, yes," said Jacquou, "each time it was a single animal. It couldn't be any more. When I began to see it, I had only one wish: it was for the animal to stay there so I could see it clearly. And it would stay there."

"I saw strange things," said Jourdan. "One time it was a blue and white plant like fog, shiny, rather thick and damp, just like fog that comes after heavy rains. It didn't look as if it was planted in the ground. It rose very high and hung down like the foliage of a tree. I watched it falling slowly back from high up in the sky. Its leaves were divided like wormwood leaves. But I tell you, it was damp and ashy-coloured and shiny, and oily when you crushed the tips of its leaves in your fingers. And no matter how little you crushed of it, it gave off a powerful odour, a smell that you were crazy about right away. An odour that was a little like that of the dregs of grapes and the dregs of olives mixed."

"We haven't been dreaming about ordinary things," said Jacquou.

"No," said Jourdan.

"Why?" said Jacquou.

"I must say," said Jourdan, "that those dreams please me very much, and that since then, they have given me some ideas."

"I saw that," said Jacquou, "I saw it just now by your shelves and your packets."

"Next year," said Jourdan, "I am going to have some unusual seeds."

"Seeds of what?"

"Seeds of grasses, seeds of flowers, of…"

"I see," said Jacquou.

"Since I dreamed about plants," said Jourdan, "I've wanted to create some. And I shall create some."

"I've got to go," said Jacquou.

Jourdan accompanied him to his horse. As he had done back on his farm, Jacquou put his foot in the rope stirrup and slowly threw his leg over the animal.

"I'd like to have seen Bobi," he said, "but I think that we shall have the opportunity."

"The fact is," said Jourdan, "that the stag came back yesterday evening and brought us his two females."

"Did they come willingly?" asked Jacquou.

"Willingly. They grazed all around the house. The does came to me, and to Bobi and Marthe, as if they had always known us."

"As if they had always known us," repeated Jacquou.

He turned his horse toward the fields covered with flowers over which a warm little breeze was running.

"I should like to have," he said, "a fine bull and a fine cow, a fine ram, a fine ewe, a fine she-ass for my donkey who is already fine, and to have a beautiful stallion from the bellies of my mares. My hands itch to create fine animals. Good-bye."

"Good-bye!"

He went off at a walk.

This visit intrigued Jourdan enormously. He thought of the plants he had dreamed about. Now, at the same time, he was obliged to think of the animals of Jacquou's dreams.

"We want to create…" he thought. "It is curious how all that warms us."

He heard the sound of a step. He thought that Jacquou was coming back. There was nothing in the direction of the vast field that lay deserted beneath the fog. He looked toward the forest. It was Bobi returning. He was still far off, but in the silence the sound of solitary steps could be heard distinctly; especially since the fog made an echo. In this direction the fog lay across the sun and was pierced by the rays that opened deep bluish caverns in it.

Bobi was returning from the forest and was switching his leggings with a branch of beech. The hundred thousand little drops of water that weighed down the fog made a magnifying glass and Bobi was seen magnified: shadow limbs and body twenty times as big as his own limbs and body. At the centre there was only a blacker spot and that was his real body. But if he made a gesture with his arm, it was the gesture of an arm twenty metres long and as big as a barn door, and he cast the shadow far over the ground. If he moved his head, it was the movement of a whole hill. But when he took a step, it was only the step of a man. It was a giant dancing in one spot.

That morning Bobi had brought in a beech branch, with three buds, three green shoots bathed with dew. And when he unfolded them one after another, he saw them swollen with a resinous gold-coloured sap. Spring!

Madame Hélène had had the barouche brought out in the yard at Fra-Josépine. She had said to old Cornute: "Get a wad of hemp stems and a bucket and wash this carriage for me."

She came to see how the work was progressing. Old Cornute had already polished the wood and the springs.

"Madame," she said, "you ought to have it repainted."

"Nonsense," said Madame Hélène. "You always have such ideas, Cornute! For what I use it, riding over the fields!"

"Yes," said old Cornute, "you ought to have it repainted a sky-blue."

Thus far spring had remained mild. It now became savage. It crushed Randoulet's broad meadows under heat and wind. The birds all flew away. The last that remained in the nests hidden in the grass, listened to the sound of the big roots as they awoke, and the flow of the sap in the stems, and the hissing of the sap as it spread in the leaves, and the lapping of the sap which came out in bubbles from all the cracks in the buds. Gradually these birds began to be afraid. It was then that they noticed at the edge of their wings a little rust-coloured fringe that astonished them. At first they tried to pull it off with little pecks of their bills. But it was not dirt; they saw that they were feathers. Their eyes also grew bigger. They had need of immense reflections. They had to leave their nests to fly, screaming, through the sky.

But in the south and in the north of the sky, the battle was at its height. The wind was fighting against the clouds. The south was heavy with exhalations from the sea. The clouds piled up in mountains. The wind came from the north, still as cold as in mid-winter, but not so fierce. When the clouds were piled high, they slowly tumbled down before the wind. At first that astonished the wind. There was a moment's calm. The cloud pressed down with all its weight. A blue night covered the earth. Then the wind filled out its lungs, fought, shouted, hollowed long red tunnels in the rain. The sun streamed through all these cloud tubes like underground water through galleries that lead from cave to cave under the mountains. At the same time, the wind roared in the sky as in an organ.

Bobi ran toward the barn. He went in and closed the door. Then, leaning against the wall, he tried to catch his breath. An old longing was in him. He had forgotten all about it. He had not begun to think of it gradually; no, he wanted it all of a sudden. He shot the iron bolt. Here he was alone. The skylight was sometimes filled with shadow, sometimes filled with sunshine. Bobi looked for some empty sacks. He found four. He spread them on the floor. He lay down on the sacks. At that moment, he could hear outside all the sounds of the world. He tried the acrobatic stunts that he used to do. The one he called the man-frog, with thighs on shoulders; and the man-snake, with arms and legs knotted about him. He heard his knees crack. He was aware that his joints had grown stiff. He got up. And so his suppleness was lost! At that moment, the wind had torn apart an enormous cloud and was carrying off fragments of it, successively filling the barn with shadow and sunlight, then more shadow and sunlight. Bobi felt that a perfect somersault was inscribed in his loins. Perfect, round as a ball! When the third cloud shadow passed over, he leaped. He landed squarely on his feet. Then he had another desire to leap and he threw himself upward once, then again, without noticing that the barn floor was rumbling under him like the skin of a drum. At last he stood on his feet, intoxicated, emptied of strength, happy, under the skylight just at the moment when the wind had carried away all the pieces of cloud and the gentle blue sky was sweeping silently over the earth like the wing of a bird.

"Where are you?" called Jourdan.

Bobi hastened outdoors. Outside, he was dazzled by the light. In the viscous air, thickened by the vapours from the ground, the sun's rays seemed to come from everywhere.

"Look!" cried Jourdan.

He pointed toward the line of the horizon. Out there a horse was galloping. It was bare and riderless. It disappeared, raising the dust on the heath. Then they saw a flight of wild geese approaching. They were coming up against the wind.

"The narcissi," said Bobi, pointing to the fields.

But the wind did not allow them to talk like men. It began to blow with such force that it cut their words off at their teeth. The wild geese were flying with all their strength, but they were not moving from the spot. They seemed nailed in the sky like some new daytime constellation of great pure white stars.

"Orion!" shouted Jourdan. "Orion-Queen Anne's lace!"

Then the wind cut their loins and they ran before it to the house. Marthe had lifted the cloth curtains at all the windows so that the daylight might come in. It entered freely. You could see the kitchen distinctly on all sides. You could hear the wind rattling the walls. Marthe's eyes had more colour than usual. During the night the wind did not cease, and long sulphurous flashes of lightning flitted through the rolling clouds.

Every morning, Bobi went behind the shed. Usually at that hour the sky was nothing but a cavalcade of joyous clouds, bright and sparkling with sunshine. As soon as he was out of sight, Bobi made one, two, three somersaults, one after another. Sometimes four. Then, intoxicated, he came back to the house as if nothing had happened.

Something curious had happened that no one had ever noticed before, and that attracted the attention of Carle and his son. That particular day, they returned home as intoxicated as Bobi after his four somersaults. They were taking a walk, father and son. They were not talking. They had come to the end of the meadow where, for the first time, a year ago, the son had seen the stag. At the bottom of this meadow, there was, as in former times, an ancient noria, where the ground made a hump. They climbed up. As they went, Carle saw that a birch tree was beginning to grow of itself and was soon going to be tall enough to stand above the grass.

In flat country, a very small elevation is sufficient to permit one to take in a great distance. From the top of the mound, Carle and his son could see far around them. There was a high wind. The sky was flowing from the north toward the south. A pale dust, dust of ash blossoms, rose from the forest and flew toward the south. Carle and his son were both sad with a not disagreeable sadness. As when one sees other people going away, and the one left behind says to himself: "Who knows what awaits them? At any rate *my* house is fair." One thinks of them lying in thorny bushes on rainy nights. One thinks of the good bed at home. One desires at the same time the good bed and the thorny bush in the rain.

Carle and his son were contemplating all this vagabond world that was being swept southward. In running their glance over the fields they saw a curious thing that Carle called "spring" when he spoke about it to the others. No one knew exactly what he meant, nor did he, but he said it. From the top of the ancient noria he had seen all the roads of the plateau distinctly marked on the landscape. Never before had he or his son, who had climbed on the hillock more than a hundred times, realized that all that could be seen from there. It had to happen on that particular day teeming with departure and wind. This came from the fact that the new season had made the grass grow thicker everywhere and that amidst all this verdure the roads appeared more vigorous and fresh. There were cartroads with the two ruts clearly traced. There was the footpath, the bridle path, the highroad, the false road that those of the plateau were supposed to keep in repair, but which they never kept up except by the natural work of their passage and that was blue as the sky on that day because it was worn clear to the granite. All these roads met, crossed, and separated. They joined once more, they separated, went toward Grémone Forest, went toward the Ouvèze Valley, toward the mountains, to the south, to the north, to the east, to the west, regardless of time, darkness, or light. They were of a formidable force. One was a little sadder in looking at them. At the same time, the blood thumped dully like two or three deep drum beats in the ears.

"And," said Carle, when he was telling about it, "the roads join other roads. There are not any roads that just stop. The roads are endless." And he stretched his arms toward the four points of the compass. "Spring!" he repeated.

The others remained silent. They saw it all as clearly as if they were on the mound of the old noria.

That evening, for the second time, Carle let his stallion out. It was not a question of momentary flashes. It was a question of freedom. The animal went straight away at a gallop. Carle noticed that behind him a new path had opened whose grass kept the trace. That relieved his sadness. He did not care; it was not a painful sadness, but like a need of bitterness, as when the body needs purifying and one drinks a brew of agrimony.

The great battle in the sky continued. But on the plateau the riderless stallion appeared and disappeared in a cloud of dust. He had become a wonderful creature, capable of almost magic leaps, and often in the night he neighed in the whistling of the wind.

Madame Hélène could not sleep. She found a little peace only by laying her cold hands on her breast. Sometimes a flash of lightning lit up her room, then the dull crash of thunder shook the house as if it came from inside the earth. The wind had made the weathervanes sing. Now they were motionless in the current that blew steadily in one direction at night, and they only complained softly from time to time with a regular little moan. Madame Hélène had no peace save in touching her breasts with her cold hands. It made her sad to find them hard and burning. The moaning of the wind pierced her flesh and wailed against her heart. The window was loosely joined and its panes shook and rattled. The wind could pass down the chimney. It came and leaped on the counterpane. It was a warm wind. It pressed gently against Madame Hélène's body. It treated her like the foliage of a tree; it penetrated deep inside her; it brought its warm disturbance to the centre of her being, where she had always thought herself strongest. The wind moaned. Its moaning could be heard sweeping through the night and it woke the echoes in the mountains and in the vast halls of the forest. The house trembled. Not only the walls, which were hit squarely by the gusts and against which Madame Hélène sometimes heard the sandy scraping of the clouds that swept along in wild whirls on the level with the ground; but also in the heart of the house, the most secret doors came to life between their iron fastenings. Madame Hélène's sadness was mixed with peace and came from nothing human.

"I can't complain of anyone," she thought artlessly, "not even of myself. All in all, I am very well, at peace."

She repeated to herself: "At peace, at peace," with the blowing of the wind; and the moaning brought still more gentle sadness and warmth. And it was a very desirable sadness.

But the voice of the wind came as from a wooden throat with almost human sonorities, whereas the moanings of the weathervanes were creakings of iron. They did not enter the flesh, following the modulations of the nerves and blood vessels, flowing along the easiest paths, but they cut straight to the heart like a knife. The nerves ached, the arteries seemed suddenly to be drained by some breach inside the flesh. At those moments, Madame Hélène had only the help of her two cold hands. She thought of Jourdan. At first, she had quickly closed her eyes, but she saw more clearly with her eyes shut and now she kept them open. She looked at the window filled with night where the constellation of the ram was inscribed in lines of gold. She did not see the stars crushed by the wind and hairy-like oat seeds. She saw Jourdan's eyes. She did not see the night flattened against the panes. She saw Jourdan's dark body. She did not hear the moaning of the wind. She heard her own old moanings and, powerless to struggle, felt a shadow force press her thighs and spread them.

One night she heard a cry that was neither the wind nor the iron weathervanes. There was something animal and tender in it. It spoke more directly to the heart than the wailings of wind and metal. As soon as she was touched by this new voice, Madame Hélène felt her youth awakening in her body. She began to talk to it.

"Well, what do you want?" she said. She was whispering. She was trying to put off as long as possible that moment when she would no longer have the strength to resist. "What do you want? What is this that is happening to me? What have I done to the good Lord for this to return? What do you expect me to do with you now? I am alone, you know that very well. He has gone. There is no one beside me. What are you doing here? Let me alone!"

Suddenly, she thought that it was Aurore who was crying. She was relieved. She jumped out of bed. She lighted her candle. She opened the door to the hall. Aurore was in fact standing there in her nightgown.

"Was that you crying?" said Madame Hélène.

Aurore was at the great hall window and she was looking out.

"I am not crying," she said.

"Who made that noise?"

"A horse," said Aurore.

Then Madame Hélène knew that it was indeed the whinnying of a horse. She sighed.

"We must go back to bed, my child, and get quiet."

Madame Hélène returned to her bed. Now there was nothing but the wailing of the wind. A silent flash illumined the room. Madame Hélène closed her eyes. She no longer tried to struggle against the immense shadow, hot and heavy, that she saw very distinctly before her. Gradually she fell asleep, and as she laid her hands over her round breasts she pictured sails of boats, swelled by the wind and wafted away.

Spring continued to be violent. All the fields of narcissi were in bloom. Lightning flashes illumined the nights. The wind never ceased; on the contrary, it increased in violence. It smelt of stone and rain. It came from the high mountains where the snow was beginning to melt. Sometimes it had the raw odour of granite.

During the daytime the denseness of the clouds cast a shadow over the earth. On certain mornings, a moment of calm would give repose to the trees and the grass. A bird would sing. The trunks of the birches that had just been swaying unceasingly stood erect with a sigh. In the meadow could be heard the dripping of the dew. The pigeons came out of the dovecots. They made a circular flight in the air, then once more they took shelter.

Jourdan's sow had only eight teats. She had nine little pigs. The ninth was so transparent, in spite of fat, skin, and blood, that you could see daylight through him. As there was no place for him to suck, he had to be fed with a bottle. Jourdan went to Jacquou's for milk. Then Jacquou said: "I'll give you my goat as a boarder for a while; that will be easier. Come get her tomorrow."

The next day, Jourdan harnessed the cart and set off to get the goat. The weather was still the same, a trifle blacker.

Jourdan had planted Indian corn. It was growing. Around La Jourdane grew all that was necessary for life. The low-blowing spring wind was teasing the field of green wheat, just enough to strengthen the stem to support the full ear. There was enough wheat for four people for more than a year. In making his field of narcissi, Jourdan had discovered a spring. A tiny one, no bigger than a pipe stem. At first he took it for a worm. He thought he would gather it in a basin of earth mixed with clay. It lay there sleeping. It permitted him two or three new things: first a vegetable patch—the place was marked on the ground by a deep, almost blue, green—big cabbages, beets, beds of spinach, sorrel, onions, garlic, tomato plants at random. Then, the greatest innovation of all: a large patch of flax. For several reasons. The reason that Jourdan gave was: "I like the blue of those flowers." The other reason he did not tell. It was: "I see ahead. I see two or three years from now. We'll be glad to have all that here." He had also planted some hemp. He had begun to put some to ret in his basin. He had tried to beat a little bunch. From that came two or three new ideas: to seek in the forest a tree whose wood would not give: to fell it, bring it to La Jourdane, saw it on the long saw, make planks, set up a wooden instrument for beating hemp. That tree might perhaps be a small walnut, or a small oak, or even a small cedar. Cedar wood smells good. The sawdust of cedar wood is intoxicating when one breathes it, it smells so good. To have his instrument of cedar, a tool of cedar. First, it would be necessary to fell this tree. There was another instrument he needed. Right away. Marthe would be so pleased. A loom. Bobi had said that he knew how it was constructed. Jourdan remembered vaguely. Marthe recalled some motions, and from these motions she recalled the machine. Bobi had drawn two uprights on a piece of paper and Marthe had said: "You are wrong. Here it doesn't make that line, it goes like this. Because when you work the pedals, this thing rises and if it went like that you'd hit your knee. Yes, my man."

"That is so," Bobi had said, and he erased his line and drew another following Marthe's finger as she said to him: "Here, begin there and it will be right."

A loom. Of cedar. Jourdan was wild about this loom. He could see it. He could hear it. The sound that he heard brought back memories of his youth, his mountain country, his father, his mother, his old home, their old life, their old peace, their fine old peace. Life is beautiful! Life is beautiful, by God!

"And you, horse, have you gone to sleep? You lazybones! And when will we get to Jacquou's? And the little pig, when is he going to have his milk? Have you thought about that?"

He touched the horse with the tip of his whip.

"We'll make that loom, all right, believe me! I'll take a knife and at the top of the frame I'll carve a stag with big horns and then does on each side of him. All around, on the uprights, everywhere."

He saw the stag that he would create with his knife. His bone-handled knife that had a very sharp-pointed blade. He saw the stag's horns as wide as tree branches. Beneath them were sheltered the does, scraping their spines and feet as they passed beneath the low cedar boughs. All that would be designed on the cedar crossbar and uprights of Marthe's loom.

He heard a sound behind him on the heath. He stopped his cart. He listened. It was the rolling of a carriage.

"There she is again," he said to himself, "but what is she doing like that?"

For some time, whenever he went out or was alone in the fields, he heard and then saw Madame Hélène's barouche. She appeared, then she began to drive all around him in a circle without ever approaching. As far as he could tell, Madame Hélène was driving alone. She had harnessed two horses, she drove hard, at a long trot, sometimes a little gallop, often standing up, without any precaution, tearing across country with all her might.

He shouted: "Madame Hélène!"

He beckoned to her with his hand: "Come here!"

Instead of coming, she continued to circle around him. Then she went away.

He said to himself: "She didn't hear me."

But the next time, whether the wind carried in her direction or he called louder, he distinctly saw that the horses had heard. Therefore she had, too. He began to beckon to her again: "Come here!" She looked in his direction, but she did as before: she turned and disappeared.

"What's the matter with her? She saw me!"

When he returned home he asked Marthe:

"Have you seen Madame Hélène?"

"Not lately."

"She hasn't said anything to you?"

"No."

"She didn't seem angry?"

"No," said Marthe, "why?"

"It's funny," said Jourdan, "this makes two or three times that I've seen her in her barouche. She rides in a circle around me. I call to her. She looks at me, she hears me, but she doesn't come near."

"Maybe she has something else to do," said Marthe.

Jourdan, in his heart, was not satisfied with this explanation. He thought: "It's odd."

The heath was bare. The sky was all in a tumult, but silent, for the wind was passing high. Jourdan heard the barouche approaching. He was in a hollow. Madame Hélène could not see that he had stopped. He heard the horses' little bells, the sound of the springs, and even Madame Hélène's voice, a voice as sombre as the springtime and that cried: "Hari!" Then all was still.

He was about to call out, when he thought: "She has stopped because she did not see me come out of the hollow and she thinks I've stopped. So she doesn't want to meet me. I can't make it out. I wonder what is going on? What have I done to her? Why follow me and stop? Why prowl around me in a big circle?"

He thought: "The best thing to do is to go back, to meet her and say to her: 'Well, what's the matter?'" But immediately afterward he thought that, on the contrary, it would be better to go on his way without seeming to take any notice, without saying anything, without showing anything. For he was very fond of Madame Hélène. He loved her skin, the colour of her flesh, her manners, her eyes, the shape of her nose, the sound of her voice, her way of walking and moving her arms. It was to him that she came for refuge when her husband had gone mad.

"Jourdan," he said to himself, "don't cross her."

He touched his horse and started forward once more.

"Yes," he said, "a big loom, standing upright like the ones they have in the mountains."

He came to the place on the plateau called "Mouillure." It was a broad, damp depression with rushes and horsetail. It was enveloped in fog.

"There," said Jourdan to himself, "if only she forgets herself, it will be hard for her not to meet me."

In fact, one could not see ahead. One moved blindly. If one stopped, the peculiar noises of the fog deceived the ear. Everything was different.

He was just about in the middle when he heard someone calling him. He stopped his horse.

"Who's calling me?"

"I am," said the voice.

"Who are you?"

The voice came from the left.

"Madame Hélène."

"It's you," said Jourdan. "I didn't hear you coming."

"The ground is soft," she said.

"Where are you?"

"At the left, in the willows."

Deep in the fog he saw a darker shadow. They were the willows.

"Wait, I'm coming to you."

"No," said Madame Hélène, "don't move."

"I wonder what's the matter with you?" said Jourdan almost to himself, but she heard.

"There's nothing the matter," she said.

"You are following me."

"Yes."

He did not know what to say.

"Where are you going?" she asked.

"To Jacquou's, to get the goat. I have a little pig that cannot get his mother's milk."

"What's the matter with him?"

"The mother has eight teats and he is the ninth."

"That is the fate of all," said the voice.

Jourdan heard the axle of the barouche creak, then the branches of the willows rubbing against the leather hood.

Madame Hélène was turning the horses around. Then she struck them with the whistling whip. She was gone.

When Jourdan emerged from the bottom of Mouillure he looked to the right and left. All was deserted. There was not a sound. Madame Hélène had disappeared.

He whipped up his horse and he broke into a swift trot. He thought of nothing but jumping onto his seat, holding the reins tight, striking again with his whip. He reached Jacquou's, talked a few moments about the rain and fair weather, took the goat, turned face about, and went back to La Jourdane.

As suddenly as the wildness of spring had burst, there fell the calm of peaceful days. You felt it immediately, hard and solid as if made of cement and iron. The forest was covered with leaves. It was twice as big as before. Before, it was only a screen of black wood against the sky. Now it was fat and swollen. That corner of the sky was hidden. The tiniest tree, formerly a slender wiry pillar, black and glistening with rain, now covered and thick, had become an inhabitant of the world. It took up room. There was less emptiness in the sky. That was evident, but one felt it even more by shouting or making a loud noise. Before, the sound rang in the void; now, it sounded in a living throng.

The days were golden.

Jacquou had a craving for meat and blood. A living hallucination born of his desires surrounded him. He saw marvellous animals with transparent bodies passing before him like smoke. He now had one great ambition. He wanted to own the animals of his dreams, to raise them, make them walk on the earth, put them there on Grémone Plateau, where there was nothing else to do, where now there was something to create. He saw before him a long and beautiful task in which to employ his hands and his head. His body required a great deal of strength. He set up a flat stone on the threshing floor. It was an old wheat crusher. He went and got a kid. He tied its legs together and laid it on the stone. The creature stretched out its neck, its breathing stirred an ancient dust of wheat husks.

With the tip of his thumb, Jacquou felt the blade of his knife. He seized the kid by the ears. He drew its head backward. He cut its throat. The animal had uttered a cry. The inarticulate moan continued to issue from the hole of the wound. The blood quickly stopped flowing. It was all on the ground. The little feet stopped trembling. The kid opened its lips and began to laugh.

Jacquou skinned it. The animal did not yet have bones, but cartilage as white as snow, in flesh white with youth. He split the belly and emptied it of the stomach and entrails.

He called his farm hand.

"Dig me a hole," he said, "and bury this."

He pointed to the place.

"Over there," he said.

He intended to plant a rose bush in that spot.

He put to one side on the stone the liver and the heart and lungs. A faint vapour steamed from these shreds of flesh.

After these days the weather was heavy and still. The men and women were filled with longings, but none dared yet to make their great dreams come true.

Springtime sadness was upon them.

18

The Shepherd's star lighted the nights.

"They also call it Venus," said Bobi.

The nightingales sang.

Jourdan and Bobi went into the forest carrying their axes. Marthe hitched the horse to the light cart and went to Randoulet's for wool.

Jourdan said: "First we must have two cedar uprights two metres thirty in height."

They looked for young cedars. They found some at the edge of Grémone, at the place where the more thinly planted part of the forest received the full lash of the cold mountain wind.

The first tree, when it was felled, seemed small. However it measured three metres. The tip was too young to make strong wood; there remained just about the required length. It was about forty centimetres thick, fifteen centimetres square utilizable the whole length.

Jourdan said: "That will do."

The two men filled their pipes and smoked meditatively.

"We must leave the upper part of the roots," said Bobi. "That will make the foot."

"A good idea."

He picked up one of the chips that had flown off when they began the ax strokes.

"The fibre looks workable," said Jourdan.

He took out his knife and tried to cut out a design in the wood.

After a moment Bobi asked: "What are you doing?"

"I'm trying something," said Jourdan.

He had traced and cut out a five-pointed star.

"Orion!" he said. "I intend to carve all that on the lintel. Orion, the stag, the does, the trees."

They cut down another small cedar in about the same section. They fastened it with ropes. They dragged it over to the other. After that, it had been agreed that Jourdan should go to meet Marthe to bring her here with the cart, so they could get the wood home that day. In the meantime, Bobi would lop off the branches, then he would cut up three or four old cedar branches into pieces eight centimetres thick and a hundred long.

"Cut four, or maybe five. We can always use them."

Jourdan went off.

Bobi had an ax that cut well. The cedar that he was stripping of its branches defended itself by its odour. The resin wept from every part of it. It was a powerful aroma that clung even to the steel of the ax. Every time Bobi raised the tool he wafted the odour. Soon the entire little clearing where he was working was perfumed. The air was warm, the sky dazzling like flame.

Toward noon Bobi had finished making a litter of the blue branches from the two trees. He sat down on the bleeding trunks and ate his cheese. The world droned softly. Through the drooping foliage of the cold, black old cedar that sheltered him, Bobi saw the wide expanse of the plateau. The earth was silently alive.

About this same time, Mademoiselle Aurore went down to the stable and saddled the mare. She was accustomed to fasten the girth at the fifth hole. She pulled. The buckle barely came to the third.

"Don't bloat yourself," she said to the animal.

It was the first time that year that she had come to the mare to make friends and say that all was forgotten. For Mademoiselle Aurore wanted to see Bobi. To speak to him. To see him. To hear him. To touch him. To say to him: "Let's be friends as on the day you caught me running because of my heart. Because my heart was too weak for me to run fast and far; because my heart is made for something else. Let's be friends as on the day I dried your hair with my apron." Make up with the mare, saddle her, mount her, gallop through the springtime to La Jourdane and see Bobi, just be a woman, once and for all. Say to him: "Here, forgive me. Forgive everything I said to you.

"The truth is that…there *was* truth in what I said to you, for if I said it to you it was because…"—if she could only touch his corduroy jacket.

"Don't puff yourself out, be good; I am friendly, you see."

She patted the mare's nose. She tried to pull tighter. The buckle scarcely came to the third hole. Aurore checked the saddle blanket. It might have been folded and be making an extra thickness. No. She said to herself: "Is it the leather? Did it freeze this winter and shrink? Leather does not shrink when it freezes." But she had one great and swift desire. She fastened the girth at the third hole, thinking: "If the saddle is loose or if it threatens to turn, I'll know it all right." She mounted like a man, gripping the mare with her legs.

Once outside, she rode straight ahead. The mare was sulky and tossed her head and shivered. She went unwillingly. Aurore made her turn her nostrils toward the forest, forcing her to see before her the green of the trees and to breathe the odour of sap that came from there.

"Are you angry?" asked Aurore gently. "Can't you forgive? Did I begin it? Wasn't it you who ran after the horse without paying any attention to me? Do you think that was nice? Aren't we going to be friends any more?"

She gave her a friendly squeeze with her knees. The shape of the animal's belly had something strange about it. Before, at the place where Aurore's calf touched the mare's flank, it was soft and barely warm. Now it was hard and burning.

Aurore sang:

"We're going to see the man. He will talk to us. He will look at us. He will take us to the forest."

When he had finished eating, Bobi stretched. He yawned. He lay down on the litter of blue branches. Immediately he felt sleep coming. With dreamy motions, he heaped up a little pillow of leaves under his head. At first he had a dream in which he was beside a man who was beating on a copper drum. The drum did not make any sound, but at each blow, Bobi's whole head was cool inside like lungs that breathe in mountain air. He half awoke. He rubbed his nose. That came from the strong odour of the cedar boughs. It was the odour that was ringing in his head. The copper drum was his closed eyelids coloured by the sun. He half opened his eyes. Between his lashes, he saw the wide stretch of the plateau all copper in the sun. He shut his eyes and fell asleep again. He had a second dream. This one came slowly. He dreamed that he was lying on a bed of cedar boughs and that he was half asleep. He heard someone walking in the forest. He said to himself: "That isn't Jourdan." Someone lay down beside him. There the dream lingered a long time. Nothing stirred. The weight that pressed down the leafy bed was still there at his right side. The dream began again. A hand touched his hair. He said: "Why do you bother about me, dry me, say to me: 'You'll take cold'? For, afterwards, you don't care about my head any more, and all the winter rains have soaked me so that they've sunk a good centimetre in my hide.

"It doesn't take long to get used to having your head dried in girls' warm aprons," he said, "and afterwards you miss it.

"Yes, Miss," he said, "that's a fact."

It was very difficult to talk to a hand and to a warmth along his whole right side as if someone were lying close to him. He did not want to stir, or move a thing, not even the tip of his little finger, because his dream said to him: "Don't move, if you want it to last."

"Well," he said, "is there anything else? Touch under my chin, it's rather plump there. I love to have someone touch me under the chin."

He thought: "How would I dare say that to Aurore? How can I talk to Aurore, Miss, to my heart's content? All the same, it's true that I love to have someone touch me under the chin. I'd love to have her touch me. Why not simply say what I have to say? Especially as she is here beside me?" For there was no reply to all the words he was saying, save only the warm response of that form at his side.

The hand touched his breast.

Then he woke with a start. He even half got up. The woman, too, moved away from him ever so slightly. But she was still warmly near. He did not recognize Joséphine at once.

"Who are you?" he said.

"As if you didn't know me," she said.

"That is so," he said. "Have you been here long?"

"A good while."

"Is it you who were here just now?"

"Who did you think it was?"

"That's so," he said. "And what was I doing?"

"You were sleeping peacefully, without stirring, without breathing, without a sound. And I had to put my ear to your mouth to hear your breathing and to reassure myself."

"I didn't talk?"

"No," she said. "Why should you have talked, since you were alone?"

"Were you smoothing my hair?" he said.

"I haven't touched your hair," she said. "I only put my ear to your mouth."

He looked at her ear. It was fleshy and pearly, like a wild lily flower.

"It sometimes happens," he said, "that people talk in their sleep."

"This time," she said, "you were sleeping but you were not talking."

"That surprises me," he said.

"You seem to be saying that I am a liar," she said.

"No. But I had the feeling I was talking."

She raised her head. She looked at him with half-closed eyes, the cunning eye shining through the lashes.

"When one does that," she said, "it is because one is thinking of a loved one."

"Just so," he said.

"If I had listened harder," she said, "I would have found out who she is."

"I was thinking of you," he said.

"Liar!"

He noticed that she was still stretched out beside him, nearer than a moment ago. From her ankle to her hip, she was close against him. He wanted to move away. She seized his hand.

"Stay," she said.

She was breathing fast.

"Say your lie again."

"I was thinking about you."

"About what, my mouth?"

She suddenly thrust her face toward him. Her lips were swollen with blood.

"Yes."

"Waiting so long!" she said.

She pressed her mouth on Bobi's mouth.

"Why?"

She spoke in her caress.

"Why?"

The word made her lips tremble. He tried to answer but he could only hear himself groan and sigh. He heard her sigh also. He held her in his arms. He laid her in the leaves. The mouth with the blood-swollen lips was hot and powerful. The moaning flowed out of it like juice from fruit.

He made a movement.

"Wait," she said.

But it was a "wait" during which she held him still closer. He felt her slipping her hand between them to untie the string of her skirt.

"Come, come," she said.

She drew away her hand.

"Come" she said.

He heard his temples beating. He felt himself freed. He was reluctant to open his eyes, so happy were his closed eyelids.

Joséphine's burning face was still crushed against his. The big soft lips were silently trembling. The mouth was all wet with saliva.

He called softly:

"Beautiful!"

"I am so happy," she sighed.

She caressed his hair.

"And you?"

Yes, he was happy! Yes, he was happy! Now he knew what happiness was. He was in a place that spread wide about him like a desert. All the sweetness in the world was in that soft mouth crushed against his cheek and whose salty taste still lingered on his tongue. He put his hand on Joséphine's chin. He touched its curve. Then Joséphine's warm, sensitive neck. Then, the breast beneath the blouse. The breasts. Joséphine sighed suddenly. The hips. And then there was no more clothing: the thighs were bare.

No, he had never known what happiness was!

"What shall we do?" she said. "I can't live without seeing you. I can't wait any longer."

Then he heard the world returning around them: the cedar, the trees, the forest, the fields, the mountains, the torrent, the roads, the men who walk over the land, the great farms, the five families, the houses, the lamps, the fires, the faces, Marthe, Jourdan, Honoré, Jacquou, Barbe, Randoulet, Zulma, Honorine, Madame Hélène.

Joy?

There is no joy.

Aurore had entered the forest but not far and without ever leaving the light of the border. As soon as she perceived the buildings of La Jourdane, she came out into the open fields.

"That's where we are going, over there," she sang. "We are going to see the man. It is he who is the shade. It is he who is the water and the sun. Get along, old girl."

But at La Jourdane, everything was shut. In the shed there was no cart. Aurore listened. Even the stable was silent. She called. She heard the echo from the well. She wondered where they had all gone. As she stood there, motionless and the more sensitive because grief was slowly rising in her throat, she felt something stir in the belly of the mare.

She leaped to the ground. She looked at that belly. It was moving with a life that had nothing to do with the life of the animal.

Aurore put out her hand and touched the coat. It was the place which, just a while ago as she was riding, seemed burning. It had stopped. There was nothing but the slow movement of respiration. Aurore felt all over the belly. Underneath, instead of being soft, it was heavy and tight, as if it contained a bundle. Suddenly there was a sharp jerk. Then three. And at each point that it struck, the sun made the coat shine, then it designed with its lights and shadows the nebulous shape of a creature that inhabited the belly. The mare did not move. She seemed happy.

Aurore took two steps backward. Her forehead was divided by a forked frown. She looked around her. She picked up a stick used to hold the cart brake. She struck the mare on the nose. She struck her on the eyes, on the neck, on the shoulders, on the haunches. With all her might. Without a word. Her teeth were clenched. She avoided striking the belly. Finally she struck that too. And she dropped the stick. The mare had only moved aside and Aurore had run after her, striking her. Now the mare continued trying to avoid imaginary blows. Aurore leaped for the bridle and jerked the bit.

She put her foot in the stirrup, rose to the saddle, pressed with her legs, harshly; with knee and wrist made the mare obey her; went straight toward Fra-Josépine, urging the mare at a gallop, But at the edge of the rise, the animal stopped and began to tremble.

After a moment, the mare painfully climbed the slope and cut across the fields with a weary little step.

19

Jourdan and Bobi had set up the loom. There it stood in the kitchen of La Jourdane. In order to fix it solidly, it had been necessary to tear up the tiles in the floor, dig down in the dirt, and plant the roots of the two cedar uprights. As if anyone had ever heard of planting trees in the house! Only, they had afterwards sealed up the holes with mortar. Thus the two uprights were firm and the loom was a part of the house. It could neither be moved nor carried away.

"Nor sold," Bobi had said.

It had its roots and its foundation in the soil of the plateau.

"What do you think?" Jourdan had said. "Would anyone buy it from me?"

"Sure," Bobi had said.

It was an upright loom, for they had had difficulties in trying to make the real plan of the horizontal loom. Marthe could not remember the position of the transverse bar or the pulley, or how one managed to move the blades. She sat there imitating, with hands and feet, a person weaving at an imaginary loom, and she got all mixed up. Finally the two men were so bewildered by all the confused motions that they themselves no longer knew how it could be done.

"Yes," said Jourdan, "as long as it was on paper, you thought you knew it all. Now that it really has to be made, come down off your high horse."

Then they started all over again with the first principle. They said:

"No, Marthe, don't go away. Wait. What do you do first? Let's see the motion. What are you pulling? Where are the threads hung?"

"Here," she said, "they are hung there, like this."

"Good. So you need your transverse bar here, the 'yoke' as we call it where I come from. There, we've found one place. And then?"

Thus, from one part to the next, and always ruled by the requirements of that imaginary cloth that Marthe wove from memory, they were led to plant the two cedar posts and to weld in one piece the upright loom, the house, and the earth.

"For," said Jourdan, as if struck by a light, "that will all hold together: the earth, the uprights that are wood from the forest, the house that is of stone from our land. You can say what you like," he said, "but that will be the best thing of all."

And he went and opened the bread trough. In it he had hidden the lintel of the loom, the heavy roof piece. He brought it out. He presented it to them, saying:

"Come over to the window. You see," he said to them, "here I have made a stag with his branches. And then here, a doe; there, two does; there, three does; there, four. I have put in more than there really are. It is better. There, this criss-cross is the net that we used to catch them in. Here, this thing that looks like a snake is the road that goes from our house to the mountains, and there is the mountain, and over all is the sky. But, I'll come back to the sky presently. Look. There I have put the stag again, and this house is La Jourdane. It is when the stag comes to La Jourdane. There, I've put him in again, but in the forest. There, it is spring. I have made buds on the trees. You see? Everything is plain. Here, I wanted to make a narcissus flower. That wasn't a great success. There is the stag again. There is a horse. Here is another. You see, Marthe, there, on both sides I have made a long straight line. That means that we are all alone here on the plateau. And then that is the sky. Look. This is the best of all. See: here is Orion, there is the chariot, there are some stars like a fork, here are others like I don't know what, scattered around, here are some more that look like a scorpion. And so, there is the world. I made it."

"Well!" said Marthe.

"Ah!" said Jourdan. "You think I don't know how to do anything?"

"Now it is my turn," said Marthe.

And she went and brought the wool. There were five basketfuls. She brought them out one after another. And each time she said: "Look, look, look!"

The wool was lying in the baskets, all ready, in soft skeins; washed, combed, fluffy, and white like a baby lamb.

Jourdan whistled.

"Oh, Marthe!" he said.

For he was touched by the care and thoroughness and the amount of work.

"Who would have thought that you had spun as much as that, and that you spun so well!"

He bent over the baskets.

"How did you do it?"

He touched the wool.

"It is so soft and even."

"It came back to me little by little," said Marthe, "and I even think that at one place I made it up."

"Yes," said Jourdan, who was feeling the wool threads, "you can feel that it is springy inside."

"Hey, Bobi," he called, "come on, I'm getting impatient. Come; we are going to set up this beam where I've carved everything. Come, because I'm anxious to see Marthe at her shuttle."

Bobi had finished setting up the cedar uprights. He had smoothed the mortar with his hands. The trace of his fingers was visible.

They raised the heavy piece of wood to place it in its sockets. They hoisted it above their heads. They laid it on top of the two posts. Then they took two steps backward to look.

They were deeply moved by what they saw. The past could no longer vanish; it was all inscribed up there. The two men took each other by the arm and stood shoulder to shoulder.

"Have you thought of the shuttle?" asked Bobi.

"I am thinking about it."

"I *have* thought about it," said Bobi.

He dropped Jourdan's arm and went to rummage in his hiding place which was that little heart of shadow between two olive jars. He returned with a completed shuttle in his hand. It, too, was of cedar.

"A cedar knot!"

Carved slowly with a knife.

"All against the grain!"

Without a roughness or hump; smooth all over, like a woman's cheek.

"Run your hand over it, you'll see!"

"What conceit!" said Jourdan with a smile.

For Bobi swallowed half his words as he talked, fast, fast, to tell all about the beauty of the shuttle, which was evident anyway.

"Who? Conceit?"

"You."

"Yes," said Bobi, "that's so. Unfortunately, that doesn't last."

He weighed the shuttle in his hands. He was stirred with a deep uneasiness. It seemed to him that everything in the world was wounded and about to die.

It was a splendid shuttle of cedar wood. That evening the loom was completed. It took up the whole back of the kitchen. They had to drag the bread trough into the hall, change the position of the hanging wooden rack where Marthe was accustomed to hang her pots and ladles, push the table aside, carry into the back bedroom the heavy armchair that nobody sat in. The new occupant was robust and sweet-smelling. It was all ready to begin to work. Jourdan, Marthe, and Bobi gazed at it in silence. Then Marthe swept up the remains of the plaster. Now they could sit down awhile to spend the first evening in the presence of the fine guest. But, as soon as they tried to speak, they perceived that all the familiar echoes had been disturbed. The voice no longer sounded as it had sounded before in this room. This tall thing of cedar wood that they had created intended to hold its rank firmly. They covered the fire and went to bed.

The next morning, when Bobi woke up he wondered: "What is that?"

It was a noise.

It was barely light, but it was day.

He jumped out of bed. He opened the door. At that moment Jourdan's door opened too.

"Listen!" said Jourdan.

The sound came from downstairs.

"She's working!" Jourdan almost shouted.

And they dressed like mad.

They descended very softly. They went more slowly as they crossed the hall. The sound was regular: hit, slide, strike. It made one walk steadily, in time. It said: "You just wait and see."

Marthe was working. She was standing, facing the great cedar frame. Above her, dawn had lighted the pediment carved with the stag and the chronicle of the past.

The handles of the warp rods clicked. The shuttle hissed as it left the right hand, struck the left hand; hissed upon leaving it, struck the right hand; hissed, struck, with a very noble, very slow rhythm of force and care. Each time Marthe's arms spread like wings, her hands opened, closed, cast, seized, cast. She advanced and withdrew her body in cadence. She was like a great bird dancing on one spot and fanning its breast. The comb bar struck heavily against the growing woollen cloth. The beam creaked from time to time as it turned. And all those sounds were repeated, one after the other, each in its place, without ever failing, for each one did a definite work, but very slowly, for Marthe's two hands controlled everything. There was another sound: Marthe's skirts that swished like foam amidst all those slow movements.

The cloth, when they examined it, was extremely coarse, but without a flaw. It was heavy. If you laid a piece of it on your shoulders it weighed like a coat. The folds that it assumed with the movements of the arm were simple and lovely, quickly created, effaced and created again with the movements themselves. Folds they were not accustomed to see in the materials they had used until now. It was white as snow.

One day that week they saw Barbe coming to the house.

"Well," she said, as she sat down. "Let me get my breath. Everything is all right. There's nothing wrong. Don't be uneasy."

She got her breath.

"I set out," she said, "to get a look at the wide world once more."

She explained that she had set out on a final tour; saying that she was coming to spend a day at La Jourdane. From there, she intended to go to Randoulet's, then to Carle's. Then she would return to the farm.

"I thought," she said, "that, with age, time gradually gets short and I said: 'While you are still whole, you'd better make the rounds once more.'"

Jourdan told her that that was a good idea, and that she must sleep at La Jourdane that night. She accepted at once, since that had been her intention. He told her that the next day he would hitch up the cart and take her wherever she wanted to go. But she refused because she wanted to go the whole way on foot, slowly, since there was no hurry, and the weather was fine.

"For I have a great deal to see," she said, "almost every-where on this wide earth."

It was a three-day journey for her old legs. While she drank her coffee, she looked all about her with her little iron-grey eyes.

"Ha!" she said. "*There's* a piece of furniture!"

"That's a loom," said Marthe.

"What?" said Barbe.

"Yes," said Marthe, "like the old ones."

"And where did it come from?"

"They made it."

Barbe stood up.

"I can scarcely see anything any more," she said. "Let me look."

She approached the loom.

"Why," she exclaimed sniffing, "that's fine wood! Your men have good noses. That smell is a wonderful pleasure."

She stood without speaking, but she examined everything minutely, putting her wrinkled old face close to each part. She touched the uprights, the warp rods, the hanging warp. She weighed the shuttle in her hand. She unwound a little of the thread, listening to the wooden wheel inside. She felt the weight that held the beam. She pulled on the thread of the woof. She selected a warp thread, and pulled on it. She said: "Good!"

She pushed Marthe aside. She took the shuttle in her right hand. She pulled the warp bar and cast the shuttle. Once. She caught it in her left hand. She stood thus a full moment thinking, remembering. Then she sighed and all of a sudden she began to work in earnest.

The sound was swift and clear. Barbe made scarcely any gestures. The very smallest, shortest gestures. The warp bar she barely touched with her finger. And the bar obeyed. The shuttle flew of itself, without any effort. It rested on one side in the right palm. The hand did not shut and the shuttle flew all alone toward the left palm, like a bird that alights and then darts away again.

All three had come close to watch her work. They saw the cloth being built under the comb and increasing from moment to moment, like water rising in a pool.

Then Barbe began to sing. They could not hear all the words. They heard: "Love joy, love joy," then the clacking sound of the rods of the shuttle, of the bar, the dull trembling of the uprights, then:

"Love joy, love joy!"

"What is that you are singing?" shouted Marthe.

"What?" cried Barbe.

"That song."

"Yes," cried Barbe.

But she kept on singing and working as before.

Bobi and Jourdan stepped back. They were fascinated, like larks, by the sight of this shrivelled old woman who vibrated ceaselessly in a myriad of tiny little motions, and by that word, joy, joy, joy, that rang regularly through the weaving as if it were a part of it. They tried to go outdoors, but they came back again. They tried to busy themselves with putting a new handle on one of the axes. They could not succeed in calming their thoughts. They were entranced. They could both have been caught under a hat. Marthe had not tried to resist. She watched and listened. She gently swayed with Barbe's gestures, as when the wind strikes on one side of Randoulet's pond and on the opposite side the waters ripple.

At last Barbe uttered a wild cry and stopped.

"This takes me back to when I was a girl."

"You are a wonder!"

"I did that until I was twenty-four years old. There were six of us: Adolphie, Louise, Marie, Berthe, and Angelina. In my old home. In the mountains. Three in the house under the chestnuts, three in my house by the torrent. When three of us finished, we would call to tell the others. And then, and not before, all six of us came out, and immediately the fellows at Antoine's came out with the accordion. There was one, my dear, with a little moustache!…If Jacquou had come along a year later, I shouldn't be here, believe me!"

"And the song?"

"Ah! That's the song we sang: 'Love joy!' That's all I remember."

"Ha," she said all at once, looking at the three of them, "where is my stick? I must be going."

"But you are sleeping here," said Jourdan.

"Not now. I'm leaving now."

"Why?"

"The loom," she said. "And all the same," she added, "perhaps I can accept something. If you still want to take me in the cart as far as Carle's?"

"Yes, but you haven't even seen your little goat."

"I'll go see her while you harness."

She followed Jourdan to the stable. She saw the goat. She patted her, but she was thinking of something else. She did not speak to the creature. It was certainly not necessary, for the goat was cared for like a lady here; that was evident; but just the same, one little word would not have done any harm. Only, when one has an idea…

However, she did think of the little pig.

"And your ninth," she said, "well, how is he doing?"

"The truth is," said Jourdan, "that he is twice as husky as the others."

"It is often like that," she said, "for those who haven't room at the breast. That makes them stubborn against fate."

All day long, Bobi and Marthe were alone. They scarcely spoke. Once, Bobi went out to the shed and he could be heard finishing his ax handle. Marthe made certain that he was really out there, then she approached the loom. She unrolled the beam and she compared the cloth she had woven with that Barbe had woven. At another time, Marthe went to the well. The chain could be heard screeching. Bobi approached the loom and looked it over from top to bottom with a severe air. When the chain stopped squeaking, Bobi softly went out the back door.

Toward evening, Jourdan came back from Carle's.

"Soon," he said, "they will all be here. She doesn't do anything but talk about the loom. And when she talks about it, everybody listens."

"Did she talk about it at Carle's?"

"Right off. You'll see. It's going to be like it was with the stag."

"It *is* a kind of stag," said Bobi.

That evening, they did not set the table, but they cut a goat's cheese in three parts and they sat out on the doorstep, the cheese in one hand, the bread in the other.

Night fell, peaceful, filled with warmth and leaves and stars.

Marthe said: "The loom is set in the soil of my own house."

The men ate in silence.

"And the mistress of the loom," said Marthe, "is not me, but Barbe."

"What kind of cheese is this?" asked Bobi.

"The goat has more milk than is needed. I have used the rest."

"Jacquou's goat?" said Bobi.

They sat silent a long time.

"I wonder," said Bobi, "how that happened about the wool at Randoulet's?"

"He said to me: 'Why, yes.' He sheared four or five sheep. He said to me: 'Will this be enough?'"

"And then?"

"Then he left me there and he began to run toward the pond, stirring up a great flock of wild ducks."

"Has he any land in wheat?" asked Bobi.

"No," said Jourdan.

"And for his bread?"

"When he brought back his sheep, he bought some flour down in the plain."

"Did you buy the wool?"

"No," said Marthe, "I tell you that he wasn't worrying about that."

"And when he hasn't any more flour?"

"I'll give him some," said Jourdan.

Night was now lying over all the horizons. In the sky shone the familiar constellations.

"All for each other," said Bobi.

CHAPTER

~

20

One thing disturbed Bobi. Joséphine was coming to La Jourdane. The others had one reason; she had two reasons for coming. And there would also be Mademoiselle Aurore. He thought of the year before, when Joséphine sat opposite him and Aurore by his side. Now all that was changed.

She came, in fact, with Jacquou and Barbe. She had arranged things so that Honoré did not come. Barbe had a hundred things to say. Jacquou listened and examined everything gravely. He was in a deep and conscious peace. Joséphine dragged Bobi off to the stable, saying:

"Let's go see the goat."

Just then Marthe was saying: "Come in."

And the others went in slowly, sensing that this was going to be very important. The sound of carts was heard to right and left along the roads coming from Carle's, from Randoulet's, and from Madame Hélène's.

"Me," said Joséphine.

And with a cooing sound, she hungrily kissed Bobi's mouth with her burning wet lips.

Bobi was thinking that this was the time for serene and solemn construction and, despite that, here he was in the act of killing all joy. But gradually he responded to the fiery mouth and he caressed the breasts that were crushed against his breast.

Randoulet appeared, round, pink, and joyful. His eyes, which for two months had been contemplating the extraordinary growth of his great meadows of grass, were full of dreams and sunlight. He brought with him Honorine, Le Noir, and Zulma like a statue of marble and straw. Carle came with Madame Carle and his son. Madame Carle was very formal. She had not yet grown accustomed to these gatherings. But she said softly as she pointed to her husband and her son:

"Oh! They told me. They have talked to me about it all winter."

Bobi was uneasy about Aurore, and when he entered the house, he looked at once to see if she were there. Neither she nor Madame Hélène. A little later, Madame Hélène arrived, but alone. Then Joséphine entered, with a wisp of oats in her teeth, looking as if there were nothing unusual.

"Here is what I have to say," said Bobi. "First, who has any wheat?"

"What?" said Jacquou. And then: "I have some."

They all said:

"We all have some. Who has wheat? Why, sure, we all have some. Why?"

"Wait, and you'll see," said Bobi. "Have *you* any?"

He had turned to Randoulet.

"I have," said Randoulet.

"He's a liar," said Le Noir, "like a tooth-puller."

"Mind your own business," said Randoulet.

"If I did," said Le Noir, "you'd be in a fine way!"

The master-shepherd's eyes were shining and his mouth bright red as if his words were burning.

Randoulet went: "Bo, bo!" and shrugged his shoulders.

"A hard head, a little pitcher, a saltlick, a mountain of manure, a hazel nut, an animal forehead, and a headache—that's what you are," said Le Noir.

"You ought to talk to your master more respectfully," said Honorine.

"For," said Randoulet, "if ever you talk rough to me, I'll start you out on the long roads, some day or other. Look out for your tongue!"

"Look," said Le Noir, "he hasn't any wheat. This fellow is dying with his mouth open."

"No!" shouted Randoulet.

"We are all right," said Honorine.

"But," said Bobi, "your wheat? On what part of your land have you sown it?"

"I beg your pardon?" said Randoulet.

"Where is your wheat field?"

"You know very well I haven't any."

"Then it is wheat that grows in the air?"

"It is wheat that grows with sous," said Le Noir, "and I can see the time coming when that man is going to say to me: 'Let's go down to the plains with the sheep.' For he will be forced to sell some, maybe to sell all of them, to make sous and to buy flour. For that fellow you see there, who is my boss and who hasn't any fields, that fellow, my fine people, harvests without need of sun or scythe. But do you know what he is harvesting and what he makes his bread of? He makes his bread of his happiness. He has never been so happy as he has been since he got his big flock up in his big meadow. But you'll see that maybe tomorrow, or the day after tomorrow, or next week, he'll say to me: 'Come along, Le Noir, we're going down to the plains.' And he will go and sell everything. Because I have seen what is left in the flour barrel. I know. I am not talking just words. I am not talking to say: 'I have wheat.' *I* am not a liar, I'm not."

Randoulet shrugged his shoulders, but he hung his head.

"You, you have a habit of talking to yourself when you are alone in the fields with your sheep," he said. "Up there, what you say is not important. But there are people here. It isn't necessary to say things that hurt."

"I didn't mean to hurt you."

"Marthe," said Bobi, "just show what you have done with Randoulet's wool."

Marthe said: "Move a little."

Jacquou stepped aside. Marthe lifted the lid of the flour trough. She took out of it the woollen cloth.

"I put it in there," she said, "to dry it a little. But not to bleach it. The wool was as white as snow."

She shook it out. Flour dust filled the four big rays of sunshine that fell from the window.

"Look," said Marthe. "Feel."

The women crowded around her.

"Don't lower the comb," said Barbe, "but strike it a sharp blow on the woof and then, instead of making the 'wheat grain' weave, it will make you the 'rice grain' weave. It is firmer," she added.

"What do you think of it?" said Bobi. "Suppose we were dressed like that?"

"That white," said Jacquou, "isn't practical for going about the land or the stables."

"There is a blackish wool," said Randoulet.

"Yes," said Bobi, "and just the colour of the earth."

"There is the sap of the eglantine," said Jourdan, "if you let it drop into a pot and boil it, it gives a green colour to dye the wool."

"As for that," said Barbe, "you also have the husk of corn that makes a yellow, and ever so many other things."

"We'll find out about them all," said Jourdan.

"But," said Marthe, "you haven't seen yet how this looks on a person. Come here a moment, Zulma."

The piece of cloth was three metres long and two wide.

"Take off your straw crown," said Randoulet.

"Leave it on her," said Honorine.

Marthe covered Zulma's shoulders with the woollen cloth as with a mantle. She draped her figure in the great piece that fell.

"See the shepherdess," she said.

The girl appeared in all her beauty. They could see that she had plump little hands and a round, firm neck. When Marthe dropped the material with her right hand, long folds like trunks of young birches hung down Zulma's figure to the ground. And they saw that she was tall, well formed, broad of hip, healthy, assured, and of striking beauty. She did not move. She dropped her eyes. For the first time, they could see that her cheeks had the pure line of egg shells.

"I cannot…" said Madame Hélène.

"What's the matter?"

"I do not know," she said, "I have just seen. I am old. It came like a flash."

Her eyes filled with tears, her lashes were wet.

"That doesn't look like an ordinary woman," said Jacquou softly.

"Let her rest," said Madame Carle.

"She isn't tired," said Honorine.

"Yes, maybe," said Madame Carle, "perhaps that is true."

"What we need," said Bobi, "is to live leisurely. Let us give wheat to Randoulet. He won't have to go down to the plains to exchange his sheep for flour."

"Nobody has ever fed me," said Randoulet.

"You will give us wool," said Bobi.

"Well," said Barbe, "come and see how we work to dress a beautiful girl."

She stood in front of the loom and began to move her arms with that light, precise motion that testified to her long habit of weaving. The cedar uprights moaned, the cloth vibrated dully under the first shocks of the comb, the shuttle hissed, clacked. They had all gathered around, the women close about Barbe so as almost to hinder her, and all eyes went from right to left, and back again, following the shuttle, and all the eyelids blinked each time the comb struck the cloth.

Suddenly they were simply one common body. There were no longer Bobi or Jacquou or Madame Hélène or anyone. There was no longer the lung of one, the heart of another, the leg, the loin, the eye, or the mouth; but all eyes together followed the shuttle, and in all the breasts at the same moment range the dull blow of the comb as it struck the cloth. The cadence of the warp rods forced their breathing in time with it. Then gradually these beats fused and there was only one beat, and all the lungs breathed together. All eyes were fixed on the shuttle; Bobi's blue eyes, Joséphine's green ones, Marthe's brown, the reddish brown, the grey, another blue, a beautiful deep violet that belonged to Jacquou, a keen, cold one that belonged to Carle's son. And the shuttle carried them along together, right, left, right, left, as if they, at the same time, wove with all those glances, to unite them in one solid body. They were all attached to the shuttle at the same point, at that spot in the cedar shuttle where the polished wood reflected the sun. At one end they were attached there. At the other end the glances were attached to the eyes of Bobi, Jourdan, Marthe, Joséphine, Madame Hélène, Madame Carle, Carle, his son, Honoré, Randoulet, Le Noir.

All eyes moved in unison from right to left, right, left. The muscles that moved the eyes were making the same effort together in all the heads. The particular thoughts in each head were cut at the same time by this regular motion, this regular effort, like straw under the chopper. On this side of the chopper was the handful of straw with all the stems separated from one another, but on the other side of the chopper there was only a confused heap of straw hashed in tiny pieces.

In like manner, on one side of the warp, on the upper side that went from the warp rods to the bar above, on which the stag and the stars were carved, were all the wool threads, each one separate, each with its strength, its colour that at times changed the colour of the thread next to it by some almost imperceptible thing which is the special character of the thread. On the other side of the warp, the under side that went from the warp rod to the beam, was the cloth. It was no longer thread, it was cloth—all the threads gathered and united, and the union of all the subtleties of shades of each thread shimmered in the cloth like the lights of mother-of-pearl in seashells.

Each time the comb struck it was like the thump of a drum. There were reverberations to the very foundations of the house and into the soil of the plateau. Each time Barbe tightened the woof thread, this happened. The ear listened for it. It came, it struck the ear, the blood carried it through the body. But at the same time, it struck in that hollow, in the keel of the ribs beneath the breast, where Joséphine was so sensitive, where Madame Hélène was so sensitive, where Madame Carle suddenly put her hand, saying to herself: "What's the matter with me?" With each blow, she felt at that place a delightful and intoxicating pain, as when one is in a cart and suddenly the horse jerks into a gallop. That spot where Jacquou, Jourdan, Carle, Randoulet, and Le Noir felt as if seized in a grip, where a good many memories awoke in Bobi, where it had only to touch to give Carle's son a desire to turn his head swiftly to look at Zulma, still dressed in the wool cloth, standing apart from the group, alone, in the four rays of the sun that fell from the window.

Barbe wove at the cedar loom that seemed like a living thing.

"Why," said Bobi, "should we each have our little field of wheat? Suppose we had one big field of wheat for everyone, that we'd all sow together and cut together, and that would produce wheat for everybody without our having to say '*my* wheat' or '*your* field,' and without one of us, the one who gives us the wool, being offended when we give him wheat, since he would have ploughed and sown and reaped and winnowed and threshed and ground and kneaded and baked the wheat of all with us all together as his own wheat?"

"What's that you are saying? What did you say about wheat?" whispered the men.

"Come here."

They gathered around him.

Barbe was tightening the cloth with the shuttle and the rods, and the loom squeaked and groaned.

"Suppose next year," said Bobi, "we made one big field of the best land, whether it belongs to you or to another? First, maybe we could arrange it so that this field will be partly on your land, or on yours, but that isn't definite. The most logical thing is to choose the best land, whether it belongs to you or to you—what difference does that make, since we'd all be working together? And the wheat would belong to us all, and the important thing is that it must be fine."

Through his speech range the blows of Barbe's comb as it tightened the weave of the cloth, the beautiful woollen cloth, in rice weave, thick and heavy and pure as the snow. The thumps of the dull drum beat on their ears. The blood swept them along with the sound of Bobi's words. The blows struck the warmest and most sensitive places in their breasts where they had hidden their secret hopes and cares.

Jacquou began to speak. He looked at his wife at the loom, his old wife. He would never have believed that she was still so strong, so strong to weave, so powerful in all that she commanded in her earthy old peasant heart. For he remembered the time when he had gone to get her in her village, high up in the blue mountains where the storms are born. They are blue only when you see them from a distance. When you are up there, the earth is the earth, grey as everywhere else, like all earth. Who can tell what makes people come together and go through life together side by side? You can't live alone. There is already the proof if you will only take the trouble to look at it. What had they done? What could they do, Barbe? He cleared his throat from time to time and spoke low, in spite of all his coughings, with a little voice that was drowned by the noise of the loom. Good days, bad days, but surely nothing solid, that is certain, and always the fear that everything would crumble when things go fairly well. But what is certain is that there is nothing solid, and there is always the struggle against fate.

Jourdan and Carle began to talk without waiting for Jacquou to finish. It was a question, in short, of the heart and no longer necessarily a question of mere food, if one might put it thus. The wheat...

"What are you saying?" asked Joséphine.

"We are talking about the wheat."

"I heard you say 'heart.'" For some time she had been want-ing to talk, too. She had one great desire: to talk so Bobi would hear her.

"The wheat," one said, "they always say that it is the main thing. No, it isn't the main thing. Ah, no, indeed! That is just the point. Of course it is necessary. Of course it is exactly like the air you breathe. If you stop breathing, you can't keep it up a long time or you'll die. If you have nothing more to breathe, you die; we know that. We know the beautiful, great, power-ful value of wheat. Who says any different? Nobody. We least of all, because we are the ones who know it best. But it must be exactly like the air we breathe. We ought to use wheat as we use air. We ought to use it without thinking about it, mechan-ically, involuntarily, like something without value. That is just the way to put it. Exactly that, like something without value, like air. Like something inexhaustible that you take and swal-low and there it is, with no value, absolutely like air. Because you would not need to devote so much time to this food that you swallowed, and that was an end to it. I don't say it is not agreeable; certainly I know it is pleasant to eat. It is a joy. That is what makes blood. That counts. But what I mean is that it doesn't count for everything.

"I mean that when one has only one single joy, it is like when one has only one lamp or an only child. Suddenly all might go out, or even, I mean, that a single lamp, although it is lit, sometimes isn't enough if it is all alone in a big room. For the fact is we have many needs and not only the need of wheat. If you consider, look how many things we want which seem important to us, and if someone said to us: 'Give up eating to get them,' we would willingly give up eating. But it is as necessary for us as it is to breathe. And so, let's make it so it doesn't weigh us down, so it isn't hard for us, but very easy, and then we'll have time for all our other needs. When all is said and done, things are simple if you go about them with a good will."

"Yes," said Carle.

There was great approval in Carle. He spoke, he said his say. He agreed. And, at his side, the son nodded, yes, with his head, and even Randoulet, who was listening with a frown, but who was all stirred in the hollow of his breast by the dull blows of the comb that was tightening the weave. He approved too. He heard Jacquou on his other side going on to talk about his dreams, about his marvellous animals, his bulls almost too fine for this world, his cows with their cream-coloured udders, that even talked at times, until one wondered how Jacquou could have imagined them. Their eyes were as big as the bottoms of bottles, and so calm that he could stand in front of them to shave. He talked of them as if it were all true, as if these animals were already there. And yet they were still in his dreams.

But Randoulet understood because he knew what it was to be linked to beasts as with iron bolts and nails. And it was useless to tell him that sometimes one went without eating so as not to do without some other nourishment that one considers at the moment much more necessary. For what was he doing with his sheep, if not that very thing?

"Joy and peace," thought Bobi. "Joy must be tranquil. Joy must be a habit and quite peaceful and calm, and not belligerent and passionate. For I do not say that joy is when one laughs or sings, or even when our pleasure is more than bodily. I say that one is joyful when all the habitual gestures are gestures of joy; when it is a joy to work for one's food; when one is in an atmosphere that one appreciates and loves; when each day, at every moment, at each instant, all is easy and peaceful. When everything that one desires is there." And unfortunately, there was Joséphine; and the sound of the loom and all the voices could be a roar fit to burst one's ears like the roar of the torrent, yet what he heard plainest was the sound of Joséphine's breathing. And the dull blows of the loom could be repeated by the echoes beneath the earth and the foundations of the house, and make the soles of his feet vibrate; what really made him shudder from head to foot was that warm little shock of Joséphine's breath as it struck against his right cheek. And he knew that she was beside him, that she was looking at him with her green eyes. He knew that her mouth was full and hot. He knew that her breasts were just the size of his hollowed hands, that for him she was full of joy, which, when he felt it, was more than a bodily joy. He was aware that henceforth for him joy would not be peaceful. And he stood there fighting and struggling because joy is nothing and is not worth the trouble if it is not abiding.

"We might first…" said Bobi.

"Listen."

"Be quiet, Barbe."

"What?" shouted Barbe.

"Stop a minute, we can't hear ourselves talk."

Barbe stopped working.

"This is what we might do," said Bobi. "This year, since it is too late, we will start, if you like, by having a common harvest. We'll cut each field, but we'll tread all the wheat on one threshing floor, on the floor of all and every one of us together. We'll put the grain in a single barn. It will belong neither to one nor to another; like the stag. It will belong to all. As much to Randoulet as to us. And next year we'll choose a field where we'll all sow our wheat together. We'll have a little more time," he said with a grey little smile, "to spend on what we want to do."

At the moment when everybody was getting ready to leave, Bobi went up to Madame Hélène.

"I think," he said, "that it will be more difficult for you because you have a farmer. I don't know if he'll want to become a part of our association."

"I don't know," said Madame Hélène; "however, I can always put into the common fund what comes to me as my share."

"Yes," said Bobi, "but ask him just the same."

What would the man decide to do?

Madame Hélène had probably said to him: "This is what we are going to do. What do you think of it?"

"I have not seen Madame Hélène again," said Jourdan, "not once. Not since the day we set up the loom. That day, I noticed that she looked at me as if she had something to tell me. But she did not say anything."

Nothing more had been seen of Mademoiselle Aurore. Summer was approaching. The wheat was blue-green.

"I'd like to go to her house and ask her," said Bobi.

"Ask her," said Jourdan; "although," he added, "it seems to me a sure thing."

"What?"

"That she will give her wheat."

"I think so," said Bobi, "but I'd like to know if her farmer will give his too."

"What is he like?" asked Jourdan. "For, after all, you know him better than I do. What does he look like?"

"I think," said Bobi, "that if he gave his wheat, it would be very important."

He felt the need of believing in joy. Joséphine had destroyed order and peace. She appeared often. It seemed that for her the plateau had no distance and that it was her very life to come. At the slightest disturbance in the air, Bobi would say to himself: "She is there." He would go behind the shed. She was there.

She would say to him: "Come."

They would go to the forest. In order not to be seen, she would slip behind the bank of narcissi. She said: "You are my life. I cannot live without you."

"If I should die?" he said.

"I'd die."

"If I hadn't come?"

"Ah, then…"

He thought of his past life, red and black, like glowing coals.

"I might not have come," he said. "There were seven chances out of ten. What would you have done then?"

"Nothing."

"Joséphine, I'd like to have the time as before."

"The time for what?"

"The time, that's all. I mean that now there is you."

"Don't you want me any more?"

"Yes!"

"Don't you love me any more?"

"Yes, I love you, but what we must realize, Joséphine, is that around us, in spite of everything, is the whole world."

He said all this to her very gently and he looked at her with his clear eyes. He told her sincerely what he thought. He was unhappy at seeing her despoiled of everything. He could not understand that perhaps she was richer than all the world. He did not know that the gravity of that face was much more joyous than laughter.

"I'd like you to benefit from everything."

"You are everything," she said, "and you alone are all I want."

Since the nights had become as warm as the days, the high mountains could be heard singing. The melting of the snows made them stream with water. The ice that hung against the valley walls had crashed with the roar of thunder. The larch forests, having resumed their foliage, had clothed the slopes; the grass of the pastures had softened the harshness of the rigid sky against the glaciers. And all the echoes were awakened. Streams and torrents everywhere were bounding like sheep in flight or cavalcades of great white mares. High up in the mountains, where the dells were gently hollowed like the palm of the hand, and where the wall of eternal ice came to rest, the neighing of the glaciers could sometimes be heard. They remained another moment in suspense, then suddenly they reared with the cracking of their iron muscles and the freed avalanches galloped headlong toward the abysses. Then, along the veins and arteries of the wide land in the midst of which was Grémone Plateau, with the streams, the torrents, the rivers, the underground springs, flowed the awakened strength of the waters.

The sounds of the mountain came down the wind, and when the wind changed its direction, it brought the creakings of the broad plains covered with a wheat already crackling like an insect carapace.

One afternoon, Bobi felt that he must absolutely know at once what the man had decided. It no longer helped to be carried along by Grémone Plateau in the resounding of the wild songs of the mountains. He felt more and more withdrawn from the world by the black work of passion.

"I'm going to see Madame Hélène," said Bobi.

"It would be better to go straight to the man," said Jourdan, "and explain everything to him."

"This isn't the moment yet," said Bobi.

The sycamores of Fra-Josépine were in full leaf and the murmur of the branches built a great silence around the manor. Bobi mounted the terrace steps. He looked through the French window: the sitting room was red and deserted. The panes reflected a leaden sky.

"What do you want?"

The door at one side was open; Mademoiselle Aurore was there.

"I'd like to see Madame Hélène."

"Come in."

The sitting room smelt of ancient furniture rubbed with wax.

"Sit down."

She indicated a chair near the window. She went to the back of the room where there was a little reddish shadow and sat down in an armchair. The tall clock ticked slowly. Outside, the sky was growing darker. Bobi heard a manly and peaceful voice singing. There was only that sound outside. The heaviness of the air had weighted down the trees. The branches hung motionless. "That is the first one I've heard singing of his own accord," thought Bobi.

"Is Madame Hélène here?" he asked aloud.

"She is not here," said Aurore.

"I thought that she was coming."

"She is coming, but later. I had you come in to wait for her."

"Isn't she in the house?"

"No."

"Will she be long?"

"Yes."

"I don't know if I can wait."

"Just as you like."

"I wanted to ask her something important."

"Ask me; maybe I know better than she."

"That man," said Bobi, "does he often sing as he is doing?"

"Often."

"Always so calm?"

"Always."

"We have decided to put all our wheat together, and I had told Madame Hélène to ask him if he wanted to be with us."

"It is I who did that commission."

"What did he say?"

"He said: 'If he doesn't know in advance, it is because he understands nothing.'"

"He goes all the way in whatever he does."

"He didn't say it in a mean way; on the contrary, he began to laugh."

"He ought not to have laughed. It's a very serious thing."

"But, indeed, he seemed to think that it was very serious."

"I don't think that you like me, Mademoiselle," said Bobi.

"I do not like you, certainly," said Mademoiselle Aurore. Then she added: "What do you mean exactly?"

"I mean that you have no friendship for me."

"Friendship is something else," she said. "Why should I not have friendship?"

"Once you spoke to me violently and in terrible anger. I could not make a gesture to answer you. I was as though turned to stone."

"I did not say a quarter of what I wanted to say to you."

"However, Mademoiselle, another time you dried my head with your apron."

"That was before," she said.

"That was before," he said, "and I never knew why all of a sudden I had lost all merit."

She was silent a moment, then she said in a low tone:

"You have lost none of your merit. Stay where you are," she added, for she had just heard the chair creak. "From here where I am, I can see you. The light is behind you and it seems to be coming from you."

He leaned toward her.

"I can't see you," he said. "You have put yourself in the shadow. Listen to me. I am only a poor fellow who used to perform acrobatic tricks in the villages. That's what I am. But gradually I have discovered that my heart could understand everything. And I think that is the greatest misfortune that can befall a living creature. I barely know the man who is singing outside beneath the sycamores. He told me that I was a poet. You have just spoken as I speak."

Mademoiselle Aurore's voice was the very voice of a shadow.

"Don't worry," she said, "you do not know the greatest misfortune on earth."

"I don't know if it's the greatest, but I know one, and it isn't a small one. When you are on the summit of a hill and dawn has not yet come, and your path goes on before you. You can think that it is all flat in front of you because the darkness is ahead where anything can be imagined. But gradually day dawns and, behold, now you see before you at first a little valley that grows deeper, and behind this land other valleys, then mountains, peak after peak, far into the distance. I do not lack courage. Men do not lack courage. I think that I will go down into the valley, mount the slope on the opposite side, and gradually, with my courage and my strength and my hope, I'll climb up the path over the highest mountains. But now the light grows brighter, and deeper and deeper sinks the valley before me. The first valley, the one that is quite close to me, that just now was full of night and in which the road seemed to lie as straight as a rod. There it drops deeper and deeper. What I thought a while ago to be the bottom was only a sheet of mist; the bottom is far below. And now in the brighter light I see bushes and undergrowth on the sides of that slope, and forests and thorns, and the tracks of wild beasts, and ravines and walls of rock. And the light grows brighter, and something tells me that it will continue to grow brighter from moment to moment to all eternity, revealing more and more thorns and walls, and obstacles, and lurking dangers, and crossings, and impediments.

"And so one gives up the hope of scaling those peaks where, however, the light is sparkling like the leaping of a wild goat. And so one gives up thinking that one's strength and courage and hope will permit one to descend even into the first little valley that deepens from one moment to the next. But now, in despair, one cries within one's self: 'Let me take only one step forward. That is all that my strength will permit!' And the light keeps growing brighter!"

He had spoken rapidly, as if transported, but without a gesture. He stopped to get his breath.

She remained silent.

"And the light keeps growing brighter!"

"Don't worry," said the shadow voice. "You will never know the greatest misfortune on earth."

"Why?"

"Because you are a man."

"You make them out to be stronger than they are."

Outside could be heard the singing of the man; it was calm and slightly sad.

"I'll find out if you are lying," said the shadow voice. "You cry within yourself: 'God help me to take one step!' But the light that increasingly illumines the world takes away all your hope. And this is what you thought immediately after your despairing cry: 'I'll go straight up there with wings!' Up there are the summits where you said the light leaps like a wild goat, didn't you?"

"That is so," he said; "one never entirely loses hope."

"And that is a mystery to me," she said.

"That is life."

"I cannot tell," she said.

"You are unhappy?"

"Yes."

"Of that great unhappiness of which you speak?"

"Yes."

"Explain it to me," said Bobi; "perhaps there are ways of making wings grow in your body."

"Ah, no," she said, "it is such a humble unhappiness. It is a thing of common bodies," she added after a moment.

"Go away!" she cried, starting up. "I lied to you. I am not unhappy!"

22

The heat was everywhere; in the sky, on the ground, down inside the earth, and even in the waters. Summer had come. It warmed the plains much more than the plateau, and often during the day the high lands were silently assailed on three sides at once by puffs of torrid air that tasted of dust and grain.

The world felt an ever-increasing need of life. The little birds left their nests where it was too hot. They perched on branches for the first time in their lives. They tried to sleep, but as soon as they closed their eyes, they would lose their balance, and fall, wildly beating their wings, and then a little coolness caressed their breasts beneath the down. Then, all of a sudden, they learned how wonderful flying was, for their bodies and for the very joy of it, and they went from one tree to another, and even into great treeless spaces. The delicious sensation of the cool air stirred by their wings made them grow bold. They darted straight up into the sky until, stunned with fear and dizziness when they saw beneath them the receding earth with its green fields, shrieking, they tumbled like a rain of stones.

The bees and the red-, yellow-, and blue-bellied flies were in adoration around the larches, whose trunks and branches were all sticky with the new sap of the year. The thick throng, blond as a ray of vibrating sunshine, at first danced with a droning sound before the tree. It was a noble and panting flight, almost motionless, trembling with worship before the divinity of saps and living forces; then, darting like arrows, the bees and the flies entered the foliage, drank a drop of sweet blood, and rebounded into their dance of joy. The tree purred.

More and more, the paths of animals interlaced by day and by night, through heath and forest. The foliage of the windless bushes never ceased trembling, brushed by the fox, the weasel, the marten, the rat, or the fuzzy wings of the owl. The bats had come out from the caves. By day they slept in the shadow of the cedars, which were now blacker than the shadows in the deepest hollows, and as soon as evening came, they scoured the air in awkward and stubborn flight. The colour of the evening, or sometimes the moon, illumined their little white breasts. All the varieties of grasshoppers had emerged. All the varieties of ants were alive. All the varieties of butterflies lived their lives, and all the flies and beetles. The lizards all came out of their holes, stretched out in the sun, woke up with a start, breathed foam, grew quiet, fell asleep, went off heavily into their holes, their fat bellies waddling between their short legs. All the snakes had finished their courtship and, uncoiling, went on their solitary ways; the males toward their battles with field mice, rats, birds, and small fishes; the females toward the warm dust of the heath to lay their eggs and to hiss softly while waiting for them to hatch.

The hares had not yet had their little ones, but already they had reached the solitary cantons of the forest, for the moment was near. It was a place in the heart of the woods, near three enormous rocks piled in such a fashion as to resemble a table.

This little eminence did not project from the woods; the height of the trees levelled everything. On this knoll, all the hares had their little ones together. This was the most fiery period of the courtship of foxes and all the carnivores. There was nothing to fear from that direction; they ate almost nothing, they only called their calls all day long, night, morning, and evening, without a pause, and they galloped along endless paths, panting, foaming, thin, with a wild and terrible eye, sometimes scraping their empty, hollow flanks against the hard heather of the moors as if to free themselves of a knife or fork of iron. During this time, the hares could have their young in peace. They did so. There were so many that at times the grass of the slope could no longer hold them, and they all rolled, squeaking, down the hill.

The courtship of the carnivorous beasts suddenly came to an end. The males sniffed toward the open heath; their eyes stopped trembling, and they licked their lips with tongues as red as fire. The females hung their heads and began to reflect. New paths of animals crossed beneath the bushes. The leverets now streamed from the slope, no longer dragged by the inert weight of their bellies full of milk, but they tried the powerful spring of their hind legs.

In all the empty places left on the earth by the death of an animal, there were three or four newly born.

In the heat of the day the otters slept under the willows. At the edge of Grémone Forest all the squirrels were gathered. No one knew why. They were all there. They were not gambolling. They were all singing together a grave, almost imperceptible little song, but in which they used so much force that their whole bodies trembled.

The pond, alone among the rushes, sometimes began to seethe. Great swellings and foam arose and little parallel waves ran over the mud of the bank to submerge myriads of willow fleas that were swarming in the damp sand. Huge carp that had spent the whole winter in the black depths rose again to the surface and leaped out of the water, dazzling, heavy, and noisy with their splashings.

At the edge of the pond there was a wide border of thinly sown rushes, washed by a shallow overflow; a sort of half-swamp. At the place where the rush sprang from the water, it wore a little reddish-brown ring. It was the image of the water, it was like an aureole, it was all colours; it trembled and mixed the colours; it was like a fine dust. This was the soft spawn of whitebait. There were thousands upon thousands of rushes, and they all sprang from a little ring of spawn, and when the light wind gently swayed the marsh—and that wind was only the breath of the wheat ripening in the hot plains—the docilely kneaded spawn prepared within itself the bodies and the white hearts of the future fish.

The old stag had come to bathe in the pond. He had suddenly remembered it one evening when, after rubbing a long while against his doe, he had found her coat too soft. Then he went and rubbed against the trunk of a beech. That was more satisfactory. But suddenly he thought of the coolness of water and he remembered the pond. He set out at once in spite of the night. He took ten long strides, stopped, then called to the doe. Sneezing and tossing his head, he explained to her at length the joy of the water yonder. At first the doe listened, then she rolled in the leaves without answering, all in her own joy, whinnying to herself, more widely separated from her stag than if she had been a doe from the moon. Then he set out slowly, putting a great deal of nobility and solemnity into his gait and muttering to himself.

He reached the water's edge just when the moon was at its zenith in the night. He walked through the swamp. Nestfuls of ducks started up and fell back again. He entered the water, and when the cold touched his belly he roared with pleasure. Then, deep in the woods, the doe answered. He swam toward the middle of the pond where the moon was crushed and splashing jets of light. The cold water beat against his lips and eyes. His long legs buffeted the water. From the tips of his hoofs rose clusters of bubbles, sparkling like stars and incessantly renewed. The great carp were sleeping just beneath the surface. All together they would leap into the air, making more noise and spray than another swimming stag and they began to flee before the creature. It did not occur to them to dive, but they swam on the surface with their backs out of the water. The moonlight illumined their scales and the little waves extinguished the light beneath the blue foam.

Then the deer felt beneath his body all the depth of the pond, a profundity that made weight and solidity under him and that swayed as if the whole world were swaying beneath him. He saw long fishes that seemed green, then white, leaped up red and fell back black, with large mouths opened over dazzling saw-like teeth. He saw great immersed vines, fierce and supple as snakes, and as if made of dream wood, so powerful that they had risen to within two fingers' breadth of the surface, yet seemed rooted in the deepest reaches of the pond. Their leaves were broad and light.

He saw crayfish floating. He saw tiny silver fishes. He saw brown eels. He saw a long water spider, thin as a cobweb, diving with folded legs, and dragging after it a chaplet of bubbles. In each bubble was enclosed a tiny newborn spider. He saw the gnawed body of a rat. A little fish was tugging at it to unwind an end of the entrails. He saw the silver of the foam that sparkled in his lips. He saw the great globe of fish, plants, rats, trees, does, and stags.

Then he bellowed.

The foxes stopped on every path, listened, replied, and began to run. The badgers growled. The otters began to miaow and sharpen their claws against the willow trunks. The tawny owls called to one another. The squirrels screamed in the branches, the rats ran like mad into the swamp, jostling the reeds; the ducks flew up again and then settled back. The weasels, the field mice, the grasshoppers, the lizards, the beetles, and the great moths were aroused. The silent snakes darted their lighted tongues above their eggs, and the doe called a long, long call with a great warm voice full of love.

Then the stag came ashore on the opposite side, the world grew calm, and gradually silence reigned. He listened. He shivered. The water dripped from his coat, splashed onto the stones of the shore. More than twenty times he crossed and recrossed the pond, and finally all the fishes went and buried themselves in the deepest holes and he was all alone in the water with the reflection of the moon. At each crossing he bellowed, and each time the vast world replied. Finally, overcome by fatigue and so burning with joy that he smoked like a brazier, he lay down in the grass. Day was breaking. He saw the doe approaching. He could not move. He no longer desired to move. He whined to her. She came and licked his muzzle gently, carefully, all over, as if he were the trunk of a maple streaming with sweet sap. The light of day rose and established itself. The doe entered the water and swam along the edge. When she was quite wet, she came back and lay down beside the stag. She pushed her head near the great panting head, with its joyous eyes. She lay, her lip against his to breathe the air he breathed out, and thus they fell asleep.

One afternoon, the squirrels that had been sitting motionless in the branches at the edge of Grémone Forest uttered a cry and decided all at the same time. They leaped down from the trees. They came out onto the plateau. They stopped to listen. They heard the fox bark. They looked at one another in fright. They perceived in one direction the trees of the forest where they could go to take shelter among the branches, and there was still time. They looked in the other direction at the emptiness of the flat lands where there was no shelter but where their longing drew them. And then they had a formidable burst of courage: What good does it do always to guard one's life carefully like a soft little hazel nut? Can one not, in one good fling, cast it wholly in the direction of one's longing? It seemed to them that a great phantom squirrel was saying this to them; a gigantic squirrel, bigger than twenty mountains, and that in listening to its mad voice they would become as big as he. It was only summer speaking to them, and life. They became as big as the phantom squirrel and they went out onto the plateau. The fox of the coombs caught up with them near Mouillure. Toward evening, all that were left took refuge in a willow. That tree had no beech nuts. Here and there they scratched the bark with their claws. Out of it came a little flour and a drop of sap. It was a magic food. They had never been so happy. The sky was of an extraordinary depth. They remembered the battle with the fox. The sky and the fox were fused in the squirrels' hearts with blood and stars. The branches of the willow lulled the dreams of the little creatures. They had set out toward the fruits. At the first stage they had not found any, but they knew that the world would soon be covered with them. Already the air smelt of sugar and fermentation.

Everywhere the heat was swelling the fruits. Until then, they had only been tiny green globes or the soft cases of a milky flour. Now they were ripening. The whole world was troubled by the swelling of the fruits. There was not a parcel of ground that was not scoured by animals in this great game of desire and waiting. The ants sought the strong brown stems of datura; they climbed in long columns to the withered flower; they entered the corolla; they went in to explore with their tiny feet the green ball of the pistil. A few more days of heat were still necessary for it to be perfectly ripe. They descended once more. No sooner in the grass than they crossed the little trodden path over which a rat had just passed. It could be heard farther along sniffing toward the oats. If the beard of the grain was green and beaded it meant that the grain was not yet ripe. To be ripe, it must have a brittle yellow beard. At that moment it smelt of sour milk. But the rat was still thinking of many things. He thought of the poppy capsules. He loved the black seeds. With a rapid thrust of a red tongue, he licked the tip of his nose.

When the animals had lain down to rest, they heard scratching underneath the ground. It was the moles hollowing out little corridors in the direction of certain fruiting roots. Deep in the earth the pale fruits of the roots were rounding out. In the grass, the fruits of the grass; in the water, the fruits of the water; in the trees, the fruits of the trees. Not a stem, not a tube of the fibre, not a trunk, not a branch, that did not abound in fruit. No kind of sap that did not come to rest and dream in the little round alembics of fruit.

Moss, oats, firs, cedars, poplars. The tallest tree here rises twenty metres; the deepest root bearing tubers goes to a depth of five metres. Twenty metres above the ground to five metres below, there are more than fifty layers of fruits of all kinds, all nourishing, all gradually enlarged by the patient heat of summer. There are fruits for all teeth and for all tastes.

The Plain of Roume was covered with round fruit like a blanket over the earth: watermelons, muskmelons, squash. A layer at a metre and a half from the ground of peaches, apricots, green apples, green plums. The orchards groaned under their weight. The little trees were thick with leaves and fruit. The shade beneath them was dark and cool. Here the grass was lush. The days were unbearably hot. The women came out under the trees, buried themselves in the depths of the orchards. They spread covers on the ground. They brought all the town's young children, from three months to two years old. They were half naked, with round little buttocks divided by a bluish cleft. They crawled about in the grass.

The plateau, higher up in the sky, produced scarcely any round fruits, but spiked grain, beech nuts, clusters of woody seeds. It was also richer in tubers. At certain places the earth cracked, exposing deep in its chasms abscesses of bluish roots toward which hastened a procession of beetles and ants. Sometimes little rodents enlarged the hole with their paws, plunged in their heads, and scraped the clotted flour with the tips of their little pointed muzzles. Flocks of birds wheeled whole days above the whitebeam trees, the wild plums, the mulberry bushes. As soon as night came, they alighted. With the morning they flew off again like the smoke of a brazier that the breath of dawn causes to flare up once more.

The sun rolled smoothly from one edge of the empty sky to the other. The husks opened with a crackling sound, the seeds flowed onto the ground, the spike of the oats cast its seeds, the burdocks shed seeds, with a single explosion the mosses expelled little golden grains that were wafted away by the slightest breeze. The datura heads split open, freeing from their shells of white satin the three nuts the colour of night. Cabbages full of moisture and penetrated by the heat gave off a strong odour. Beets, onions, turnips, big carrots rose from the powdered soil, pushed out by their swelling flesh. In all the sun-bathed places in the mountains, wild apricot trees dripped sap and juice. Only some marmots came to lick their syrup.

The wheat was ripe.

Beyond the orchards in the Plain of Roume it stretched as far as eye could see like the flooding of an immense river charged with silt. It had levelled the slight undulations of the soil. There was nothing but it alone. It warmed like the sun. It was like a copper mirror, and stifling rays sprang from the fields of serried spikes. The height of the straw concealed roads and paths.

When the big owners came out from the town to see their fields, they were hidden with their automobiles between two walls of riches. They could no longer see either the low sky or the expanse of the fields about them, or the arrangement of the solidity of the earth in the high mountains on the horizon; they could see nothing but wheat, wheat, wheat, wheat; walls of wheat without a gap, without a break, without a fissure; millions upon millions of stalks of wheat that passed swiftly before their eyes; walls of stalks of wheat that brushed past on each side of their heads, stunning all reflections, shocking them with a sickening void, as if they were about to penetrate into the very flesh of gold.

They set up recruiting tables beneath the plane trees in the market place. They had written to the mayors of the little mountain communes: "Tell your people that we are recruiting men for cutting the wheat." They got together in groups in the Café des Sports to say among themselves: "We'll pay so much a day, no more, not one sou more." The wheat of the boundless fields blew its hot breath through the streets.

Immense flocks of rooks and birds of all kinds alighted in the wheat fields.

The men came down from their mountains. On their shoulders they carried scythes, blade separated from handle, in two places. Two came along this path, one along that one, four on another, ten on another, twenty from there. They met at the crossroads. They entered the town by the north gate. The shopkeepers had taken in their stalls, for the street was crowded with men from the mountains carrying on their shoulders the demounted scythes; men of ample step, shoulders, and gesture, who jostled the stalls without intention. They went from one table to another. They called out to each other in their incomprehensible dialect. They discussed the daily wage. They said it was too little. They gave their names. They were inscribed on the lists. They were given a paper on which was written the name of the place where they were to sleep. Sometimes, even, a quartermaster sergeant accompanied them to the barns. They put down their tools. They lay down. They began to sing in unison.

Then the whole town was still. Gestures were arrested. Everyone listened.

The men of the mountains sang great poetic choruses of love for women and of the battle against the demons of life. Through the secret flesh of the townspeople passed a terrible wind scented with the bitter odour of almond blossoms. The whole inner order of the city trembled. The windows of the houses were wide open because of the heat. The voices of the men of the mountains were more charged with stars than the night. But the vast wheat fields blew dry and hot. Once more strength returned to continue habitual motions: to plump the pillow, bolt the door. The voices of the mountaineers grew quiet. The hours of the night now rang far apart in the silence.

On the plateau, the harvest began with a feverish little haste. Suddenly they all remembered that they did not have to hurry. They were frightened at seeing their fields so small. A little sadly they said:

"We did not need to do this work all together. One single person would have been enough."

"We are working in *our* field," said Bobi.

They were at the moment in Jacquou's field. Randoulet was there with the others. It was he who bound the sheaves.

Randoulet said:

"I am going to show you how they cut in my country."

"What country?"

"A country," he said, "where straw has value."

He wiped the palms of his hands on his pants, he seized the scythe, he winked.

"For," he said, "straw is used there instead of tile, and the longer it is, the better."

He gave a sweep of the scythe just above the ground.

"And," he added, "entire and unbroken."

He had borrowed Honoré's scythe.

"You son of a bitch!" said Honoré. "To get an extra centimetre of straw, you are going to break my scythe for me on the stones. Give it to me, you son of a bitch!"

But Randoulet displayed his skill.

If you have ever seen a swallow, in a swift plunge, brush his breast over the water, and fly up and swoop and rise, without ever wetting the tip of a wing…

"That is how he mows," said Honoré.

"Come and see."

They approached. It was really something beautiful. The fields were not of sifted soil like those in the plain. Here it had gained little by little on the heath and was consequently full of stones. It seemed as if Randoulet sensed them in advance. His scythe wavered, never twice in the same rhythm. It was a work of taking one stalk at a time, slow and precise. Randoulet's muscles were all constantly in full play with waiting or action. He swung the scythe, held it back, made it pass flat over the stones, plunged the tip of the point, raised it, swung it once more. Each cutting required new gestures. Each time the necessary gestures came exact and perfectly timed for the scythe to be safeguarded and for the wheat to be cut off at the ground. It was a joy to watch. Everybody watched. They had all gathered, men and women. They took a step when Randoulet took a step. There was a single mower.

Jacquou stooped and picked up a stalk of wheat. It was cut level with the ground. It was whole, as if untouched, mowed as if by a divine mower. Jacquou kept the stalk of wheat in his fingers. It was too beautiful. A work not done any more. "It takes time to do that," he said to himself. "One must have time to waste," he thought, "to mow like that."

He followed the mower, holding the stalk of wheat in his fingers like a candle.

"Or one must be very poor, need everything. Or one must be very rich and do it for pleasure, for joy, for the sake of doing it well. And so in those things, rich or poor, it is all one, and poverty is wealth."

Randoulet reached the end of the field.

"There," he said.

He had mowed a row. They were not unhappy after all.

Yes, but the fields seemed little. The eye was accustomed to ricks of a certain size, these were smaller than in other years. Usually there were sixty big ones; this time there were twenty-four.

"Middling-sized ones," said Jacquou.

And at night they were not tired.

And, without fatigue, the body was lonely in the long pearl-coloured evenings. For they were used to being deadtired when the weather was like that. By owning the wheat fields, they became wheat fields with their dimensions, their burden of sheaves and of ricks, the lustrous evening lying over the stubble. All had changed save the evening. They suffered from not being tired. The mind could not adjust itself to it.

They had decided to camp near the fields. The nights were miracles of coolness and perfume. They had lighted a small fire, not for the heat but for the light. They were lying all around it on beds of straw. Before going to sleep, they all half raised themselves on their elbows. But in vain were they gathered together; they felt alone. They could move their arms and legs without pain. They were not tired. The first who fell back on her litter of straw was Mademoiselle Aurore, then Madame Hélène.

"Come," said Madame Hélène; "good night."

They could be heard settling themselves in the straw to sleep. The last to lie down was Joséphine. She still called a couple of times: "Say! You over there! Are you asleep?"

Jacquou was snoring. Nobody answered.

"I am going to put a little more wood on the fire," said Joséphine, talking aloud to herself.

She got up. She came over to Bobi. She stooped down to pick up some dry little twigs. Her hand sought the hand of the man, found it, remained there, burning and heavy.

Joséphine sighed. She returned to her place and lay down.

The silence and the night enveloped half the earth in the curve of their wings. The stars made so much light that one could see the black outline of the mountains.

At the end of two days, Jacquou's field was mowed, in sheaves, in ricks. The cropped stubble made everything more lonely than ever.

"Now let's go to my place," said Carle.

His field was not near his house. It was at the other end of the plateau and at the edge, just at the beginning of Grémone Forest. It overlooked the plain at a place where the ravine dropped in a steep slope. It was a field that he had inherited from his father-in-law, one of the pioneers of the plateau. Originally, on Carle's field, there had been a birch wood. The father-in-law had cut down the trees, pulled up the stumps, burned the undergrowth, spread the ashes, and made a field that was by far the best of them all for wheat.

Since the two days of camping, eating, sleeping all together in the fields, they had forgotten the houses. The sky was so solid all around!

"What we could do," said Carle, "is to take the carts and go over there in a caravan."

It was ten o'clock in the morning.

"We'll still get there early. We'll make camp near the woods. We'll have time to make the soup and to sleep. We'll start tomorrow morning early. In two days that too ought to be finished. From there, we are quite near Jourdan's field. What do you think?"

They thought "Yes."

Carle had suddenly thought of the time they had set out in their carts for the doe hunt and he longed to feel once more that happiness created within him by a new excursion, by the swaying and the creaking of the side rails.

"The moment one has the time."

The time was not lacking, either for talking or for hitching the carts, or for planning all there was to be done in the new camp at the edge of the forest. In spite of the loneliness of the wheat fields there was now a sort of a solemn joy in feeling poorer in grain but so rich in time!

Jacquou had three great blue wains. But his two mares were full.

Mademoiselle Aurore hung her head.

"Full," said Jacquou, "like cows." (He had a broad smile in his old box-wood head.) "You might say they have never been so big."

"Someone will have to walk to La Jourdane," said Jourdan, "and bring back the horse from there."

Two carts would be enough. By packing in closely they would do. Jourdan gave the key of the stable to Carle's son, who had good legs.

About four o'clock in the afternoon, the two blue carts were hitched and a little later they started off slowly, at a walk, across the fields. Marthe and Madame Carle began to sing. Madame Hélène hummed softly. The swaying of the cart jostled them. Joséphine looked straight ahead of her with sorrowful eyes that saw nothing. The women all had the same look. Mademoiselle Aurore was seated in the middle of the cart.

After an hour's distance, they met a stranger. From the direction in which he was walking, he seemed to be crossing the plateau diagonally, coming from the mountains, going toward the plains. They called to him. He came up to them. He looked like a man from the mountains. On his shoulder he carried a demounted scythe and in his hand his few effects tied up in a red cotton handkerchief.

"And where are you going?"

"I'm going down to the plains."

"What an idea to come this way!"

"A queer idea," he said. "Do you know that there are deer on your plateau?"

"Yes, we know."

"Ah! Then, there is only one?"

"No, there are several."

"I saw one," he said. "I was following the natural route."

He meant the regular traffic road that crossed the Ouvèze below at the left by the stone bridge, wound around the plateau, and, after a wide detour, entered the Plain of Roume.

"It seemed to me that there was one in the bushes."

He was silent for a moment, looking from one to another with his wild, shining eyes.

"For," he then continued, "my home is in the deer country. I've been gone twelve days. My wife is red-haired Catherine, and I have two little girls. I said to myself: 'It isn't possible or else it's one that has followed you.' But I wanted to set my mind at rest. I went into the woods and from one thing and another, by evening I was too high up to think of descending again. I said to myself: 'Keep on up, cross Grémone. Now that you are here, it is shorter.'"

"What are you going to do in the plains?"

"I'm going to hire myself out for the haying."

"Ah," they exclaimed all together, "that's right!"

"If you weren't in a hurry," said Jacquou, "we'd ask you to come along with us! We'd take you a little way. But it isn't exactly your direction."

"Yes," said the stranger, "but I am in a hurry. The deer has made me lose a good day. Everybody has already begun down there. Good luck."

"Good luck."

He went on his way.

They reached Carle's field at seven o'clock in the evening. They approached the edge of the plateau, from where they saw the whole plain. Yes, everybody had already begun down below.

Day was coming to an end. The slanting rays entered the plain by the mouth of the valley and brought out in relief against the distant background all the ranks of mowers, the upright wheat, the fallen wheat, and the ricks. The workers looked like black ants. They were everywhere. They could be seen in unceasing motion. The entire plain, from one side to the other, was filled with wheat and mowers. They were too high up to hear the sounds. All was silence save a buzzing noise. In the distance, the light, broken up by the thick wheat dust and earth dust, fused in colourless rays that had the dazzling whiteness of snow. The stranger they had met was on his way down there. He would unwrap his scythe and add his work and his strength to the work of all. It was late and down there there was no halting.

They made camp on the edge of the plateau in order to have the spectacle before their eyes. They had tied the horses to the trees and lit a fire to warm the soup. At last, night filled the valleys, advanced along the plain, pushed out the light. The dust fell back. They saw that on the other side of the broad plain there were other hills, other mountains, for the light touched them, made them stand out in the indistinctness of the distances, gave them form for a fleeting instant before letting them be covered by the night.

The sun lingered a moment on those up here who were higher than all; the fire, the blue carts, the horses; it was a little circle of solitary light on the border of the night. Silence had come. Down below, a tiny red fire was burning. It was like a speck. It blinked. It was an earth star. It must be a lamp. It moved. It was hidden behind a black mass that seemed to be a curtain of cypresses. It reappeared. It grew steady.

They watched it for a long time to see if it moved any more. Then, looking out over the whole plain, they saw that numerous red lanterns were lighted. They were the lanterns at the threshing floors.

The next day they mowed the whole of Carle's field. Without talking, without wasting a moment, with all their strength, lost in a yellow and stifling work that normally would have lasted two days.

Mademoiselle Aurore wore a flowered skirt. It ballooned over her hips; it revealed her bare legs. She had round, plump knees like babies' heads. She walked behind the mowers, twisting a sheaf string. At every seventh step, every seventh swish of the scythe, she stooped down, gathered the fallen spikes in her arms, held them against her, tied them with her string. She threw on the ground a sheaf that now resembled a woman with her waist, her body in a pleated skirt, and her hair of barbed spikes.

She found herself behind Bobi. He was moving like a person who has got back into the swing of it. He was going ahead madly. He went too fast not to get out of breath. He stopped.

"You are bleeding, Mademoiselle," he said to her.

At that moment his eye was clear and dark, like the sky when the rainbow appears.

She had scratched the calves of her legs on the thistles and the tubes of the stubble. At one place it had bled in a stripe of black blood with a tiny point of red still oozing.

Bobi came to her and knelt down. Mademoiselle Aurore was in bitter need of tenderness and gentleness. She saw the blood; she saw the clear, dark eye. She was powerless to move.

Bobi washed the little wound with his handkerchief and saliva.

During the daytime, everything was bearable. As soon as evening came, Mademoiselle Aurore's body began to suffer acutely. Her heart ached. A pain at the tip of her heart increased with each beat, becoming at last so strong that it seemed to spread through her body to her very fingertips. Neither the velvet of the leaves nor the peace of the evening brought her relief. In vain she dreamed farther on in her life; she saw no hope. She lay curled up, waiting for sleep. The fields of wheat smelt strong. The magnificent evenings calmed everyone but herself. She alone remained alight in the darkness.

She was lying at the very edge of the plateau. She had only to turn her head to be able to see, beside her, the wide gulf of the plain covered with night in which flamed the red lanterns of the threshing floors. Except for the colour of the tiny twinkling lights, produced by the burning of nut oil in the old charred wicks, one might have taken them for stars. There were no barriers between the night of the sky and the night of the earth. The great constellation of the Scorpion, stretched along the horizon, was prolonged, enlarged by two or three tiny red fires. It was very difficult to distinguish the horny tail of the beast of the heavens from the fires of the most distant threshing floors on the plain. The whole night was empty; where the lights were there was work or preparation for work. Mademoiselle Aurore's pain was so intense that she saw it bursting like the golden branch of lightning that springs from the clouds. Down below, under each of those flickering lamps, they were rolling the threshing floor with great lead rollers.

Toward the middle of the night, Jourdan got up. He was to leave before the others for La Jourdane, to prepare the communal threshing floor, to sweep away the old dust, set up the pole. He made his bundle and left without waking anyone. Mademoiselle Aurore heard him go off. He crossed the point of woods. After his passage, a fox began to bark and two phosphorescent eyes gleamed and went out.

Madame Hélène sat up. Mademoiselle Aurore wondered what she was going to do. She went off softly in the direction Jourdan had taken. Mademoiselle Aurore, her head on her arm, pretended to be asleep. She had closed her eyes. She saw nothing but her flashing pains. She heard her mother walking in the woods, then stop. She listened a long time to her blood roaring in her ear that was pressed against her arm. She opened her eyes. The fire was going out. Her mother had not come back to lie down. Aurore got up in her turn. Softly she went around Marthe's prostrate body. She entered the woods. There was not a sound.

There *was* a tiny sound that she recognized at once. Madame Hélène was sitting in the grass and she was weeping. Mademoiselle Aurore sat down beside her without a word. Madame Hélène took her daughter by the shoulders and drew her close.

"We are alone, alone," she said. "Alone!"

And she continued to weep.

They set out in the morning. They rode through the woods in the two carts. The women were singing; even Madame Hélène and Mademoiselle Aurore. At La Jourdane they found Jourdan, who had swept the threshing floor, set up the pole, brought out the flails, arranged the harness of the crusher. They began to mow Jourdan's field.

It was to this field that Bobi had first come. It was from here that he had said: "Orion-Queen Anne's lace."

They were near the farm house and no longer camped. They came in and ate at the table. They cooked in the fireplace. The women shared the bedrooms. The men slept in the straw. They had had to gather in the wheat scattered in the three fields and heap the sheaves about the threshing floor. They began to thresh.

There was naturally a rotation of work for the horses and men, especially during the night.

One evening, Jourdan was on duty. He was turning his horse. It was midnight. Everybody was asleep. He looked toward the house. The window of his room was lighted. Marthe and Madame Hélène were sleeping there, both in the same bed, and Mademoiselle Aurore in the little iron bed. He said to himself:

"Perhaps someone is ill."

It had been very sultry during the day and they had drunk more water than usual.

He drew near the window. He was about to call out when he saw Mademoiselle Aurore. The candle was on the chest of drawers. Mademoiselle Aurore had opened the top drawer. She was softly fumbling inside.

"What is she doing?" wondered Jourdan. "Perhaps she is looking for a handkerchief. It is more than ten years since I've put anything in that drawer!"

Then Mademoiselle Aurore appeared to have found what she was looking for and she blew out the candle.

The next day it was still hotter. The threshing floor was like a sun. It burned. It was four o'clock in the afternoon. A gunshot was heard in the forest. It was quite close. The horse stopped turning. Carle's son, Randoulet, Le Noir, who were pitching the wheat, stopped. The people who were untying the sheaves stopped. They looked at one another. Silence.

"Get up!" said Jacquou.

He urged the horse on. The others began to pitch and to untie once more. The horse made three turns, four, five, six. The iron pivot creaked. Jourdan threw down his fork. He went into the house. He went through the kitchen.

"What do you want?" said Marthe.

She was busy peeling potatoes. He did not reply. He went up to the bedroom. He opened the top drawer of the chest. He came downstairs again. He went out. He returned to the threshing floor. He looked at all the women. He went up to Madame Hélène. He touched her on the arm.

"Madame Hélène!"

She stopped untying the sheaves.

"And where is Mademoiselle Aurore?"

"She was here."

"When?"

"Just now."

"A long time ago?"

"No, I don't know," said Madame Hélène. "Why?"

"Nothing."

She called: "Aurore!"

Her voice rolled like the cooing of a pigeon. The horse stopped turning.

"She was here," said Joséphine.

"Yes, but where is she now?"

"I saw her go off in that direction," said Honorine.

It was toward the stable.

Jourdan went toward the stable. Madame Hélène followed him. Then Honorine followed, then Joséphine.

"Whoa!" said Jacquou. And he stopped the horse, which was about to start off once more.

"What's the matter?" asked Bobi.

"The little lady."

"But she was here a moment ago."

"Yes."

"She quietly went in that direction," said Le Noir. "I saw her."

"What?" said Randoulet.

"The little lady."

"What's the matter?" asked Carle.

"The little lady."

"What?"

"No one knows where she is."

"Good heavens!" said Madame Carle.

They looked at her. The others had not returned.

"I'm going to see," said Jacquou.

They followed him.

"No," Jourdan said to them, "she is not here. She came here but she went away again. Here she has trampled the straw. Look."

Madame Hélène called: "Aurore!"

Jourdan quietly signalled to Bobi: "Come."

He made a sign to Jacquou and to Carle.

"Where are you going?" cried Madame Hélène.

"Stay here," said Jourdan. "We are going to look over there. It is nothing. She had the habit of wandering off. Perhaps she has gone to the forest."

They all stopped talking.

"No," said Jacquou, pushing Madame Hélène back, "you stay here."

She wailed: "No, let me go. I want my daughter. I have only my daughter. Jourdan!"

Jourdan turned in his steps.

"Why, no," he said, "you know very well, we're going to find her. It is nothing. Don't get upset."

He said to the women in a low tone: "Keep her."

But she heard him, and as Joséphine put her arm about her waist she struggled. She moaned: "My child!"

"Why, no, why, no," said Jourdan as he moved away. "Come," he said to the men.

Marthe had come out of the house and drew near.

"What's the matter?" she asked as she passed the men.

"Nothing," said Jourdan. "Keep Madame Hélène."

They turned the corner of the house. They began to run.

"It's over there," said Jourdan.

He pointed to a grove of birches that stood out in a point.

Twenty paces from the grove they stopped. They saw her lying in the grass, barefoot.

Bobi called: "Aurore!"

A magpie sang.

Slowly they approached.

Aurore had fallen over backward. She had fired a shot into her mouth. She was no longer a woman. Splashes of brain and blood radiated around her and illumined the grass and the world like a terrible sun.

They heard Madame Hélène crying again. She had escaped. She was coming. Jourdan ran to meet her. He had to chase her to the right and to the left before seizing her in his arms.

"My daughter, my baby! Give her to me, Jourdan."

"You must not look at her," said Jourdan.

Then she stopped crying out and silently allowed herself to be led away by the women.

Outside, a starless night and heat that was suffocating. Aurore was lying on the bed; they had hidden her head in a sack.

"You are wrong, Madame," said Barbe. "Drink this poppy tea and get some sleep."

"I'll not sleep."

"That doesn't help."

"I want to keep my eyes open, yes, open on the vile world."

"You are upsetting yourself," said Barbe, "and you are keeping her from the peace that she deserves now."

Joséphine went out of the room. On the stairs she met Jourdan, who was coming up.

"Where is the brandy?" she said.

"Who for?"

"For me. I can't hold in any longer. It has turned my stomach. I am going to vomit. It is too much for me."

"What!" said Jourdan. "Has she already begun to smell?"

"No. It is from having seen the blood. They have washed her hands, but she still has blood in all the folds of her skin."

"The cupboard on the right. The middle shelf."

Downstairs, Joséphine looked for a glass and found none. There was only a little candle of no size at all; she could scarcely see anything with it. She drank from the bottle.

She thought: "Where are you, my darling?"

She looked outside. The men were in the shed beside a lantern. They could be heard sawing and nailing boards. Bobi must be with them. Upstairs, Jourdan was smoothing Madame Hélène's hair. She let him do it. From time to time she shivered.

"Are you cold?"

"Yes."

The window was open. Because of the body they had to leave it open. The night had never been so sultry and so hot.

"That is fever," he said; "drink the tea."

"No, they want me to drink poppy so I'll sleep."

"Drink the poppy and sleep; at least it will be time gained."

"Lost," she said. "My child is going away. And you want me to sleep. Why so much evil? I haven't done anything to you. Haven't I had enough?"

"You have had too much. We are doing what we can to keep you from all this sorrow."

"That doesn't keep it away," she said. "Oh, then, now . . . "

Marthe and Barbe were making signs to Jourdan: "Let her alone, don't talk to her." He saw the gestures. He left her. He went over to the bed.

He could not remember ever having seen a night so hot and sultry. The window was open, but it seemed sealed tight with black cement, without a crack. He thought at once of a storm and that it made things spoil more quickly.

Mademoiselle Aurore's hand was lying peacefully on the shroud.

Marthe and Barbe softly approached. They two alone had thought to take off their shoes and to put on felt slippers. Barbe had put on Jourdan's cord-soled slippers. Madame Carle was seated in the shadow, in a corner where the light of the candles did not penetrate. She could not stop crying. She saw that she was the only one; Madame Hélène was not weeping. But she could not keep her heart and her eyes from shedding tears. Her heart ached, her eyes were wide open; she felt them open much wider than for seeing; and the tears flowed. Her eyes opened so wide that in spite of the heat she felt cold in her head. She thought: "I ought to take off my shoes, my feet bother me. I ought to ask Marthe if she has an old pair of slippers."

"What do you think?" asked Marthe in a whisper.

"What about?" said Jourdan.

"This child," said Marthe, "do you think we can wait until tomorrow to put her in the box?"

"I think so."

"That makes eight hours," said Barbe.

"Eight hours already?"

"Yes, it is midnight."

"The time goes fast," he said.

"Because," whispered Marthe, "come and look."

She half turned to Madame Hélène.

"But the mother must not see."

She lifted a little bit of the sack that hid the upper part of Mademoiselle Aurore's body.

"Light of my eyes! Wine of my heart! The most beautiful! My daughter! The joy of everyone! Miracle of days and nights!" sang the deep, low voice of Madame Hélène.

"Look," whispered Marthe.

"No, cover her, cover her," said Jourdan, pushing Marthe's hand.

"No need to see," he said.

He was frightened by the odour.

"So soon!" he exclaimed.

"There's a storm in the air," said Barbe.

"I am going to tell them to finish the box as fast as they can," said Jourdan in a low voice.

He bent toward the two women.

"You must not fail to make her drink the poppy tea," he murmured, with a nod of his head to indicate Madame Hélène.

"At the first sign of morning," said Barbe.

"She will get tired out," said Marthe, "and then she will drink it."

"She must," said Jourdan. "What good is it to suffer?"

Barbe sighed.

"More than you'd think," she said. "Sometimes it takes the place of bread."

But they stopped talking. Madame Hélène had raised her head. She was looking at them uneasily. She must have smelt the odour.

Jourdan tiptoed from the room.

"Rest, Madame," he had said; "put your head on your arm, here on the back of the chair, and close your eyes a moment."

He went down the stairs holding fast to the banister. The world was falling to pieces.

Joséphine was still downstairs in the kitchen. Standing there, struggling with herself in a great silent battle. Without the will to take one step to right or left, forward or backward. "Do you feel better?" asked Jourdan.

"Yes. I had a drink. Do you know where Bobi is?"

"No," he said.

"Isn't he out there in the shed?"

"No."

The night was so black, so thick, that it no longer had either depth or bounds. You took one step, twenty steps, a hundred, and you were still in the same spot. There was nothing: no sound, no form, no odour.

The night eased all pain because it had abolished the world. It had abolished the strongest griefs, because it was infinite; without limits, or bounds, or beginning, or end. It imparted the peacefulness of a cloud, a cloud that is a part of the sky and yet moves in the sky.

"It has come back! It is impossible! I must go away!" said Bobi.

He went off toward the south, instinctively, because in the north were most of the farms and all that they had done there.

After a moment, he was swallowed up in the night where there was no longer south or north.

He drew a deep breath: "Humph!"

He had suddenly had the radiant vision of his mother.

"More than ten years! What does that mean? Come on, get along with you!"

And then, his whole life! He saw himself in the process of being built by time. He heard the sound that time had made in building this man called Bobi.

Joys, griefs, sorrows, enthusiasms, loves, deaths: deaths: my mother is dead, Aurore is dead; the trowel of time, the cement and stone, the mortar, the plaster, the beams, the sound that time had made in building this man.

"Everything has failed," he said.

In the midst of the darkness he heard the almost imperceptible stir of immense trees that were slowly living their lives.

It was Fra-Josépine. Bobi could see nothing. He approached. He touched a moss-covered wall. It was the terrace wall. He thought of Aurore. He had seen her, a short while ago, only a moment ago, not long before, lying on the bed, her head in the sack, her white hand on the sheet. He thought of her as he touched the wall. As he walked along, he felt that above him rose the house and that he was nearing the place where the windows must open into the little red sitting room, now black like all the rest. He passed the place. He came to the steps. He passed the steps. He found the wall once more. He kept on walking. He came to the left side of the house. He saw the light in the farmer's house. A single light. It must be the open door. He went toward it. He touched a field of wheat still standing. He circled it. Now this light gave form to the night. All of a sudden he felt the extraordinary heat, the stillness of the night.

"What is going to happen?" he said.

He tried to look about him. He could see only in the direction of the lamp. There only did the night have depth.

He drew near.

"May I come in?" he said.

"You may come in," said the man.

He did not seem surprised. He was seated at his table as for the visit of the year before. He was reading a book as before, but at the same time he was eating bread and cheese.

"I didn't expect you this evening," he said; "neither this evening nor others. In short, not for some time at least. What has happened?"

"Look here, it's all over," said Bobi.

The man turned down his page at the corner and shut the book.

"How did it happen?"

"Mademoiselle Aurore has killed herself. She took some cartridges from the bureau drawer and the gun that was hanging under my coat. She shot herself through the mouth."

The man had risen.

"And Madame?"

"She's back there with the women."

The man came away from the chair and table.

"I'll go," he said. "We must…That little thing! No, they don't need women. They don't need those men. They need a little reason."

He looked at Bobi.

"It is not easy," he said, "to play with the stars."

"No," said Bobi, "that is not the difficult thing; the difficult thing is to do the impossible."

The man was lighting the storm lantern.

"It is to desire," he said, "to desire the impossible."

"I am to blame," said Bobi.

"No," said the man, "not as much as you think."

"What time is it?"

"Half-past two."

"Day ought to be breaking."

"Day will not break today," said the man.

He closed his knife with a click and put it into his pocket.

"Haven't you noticed the weather?" he said.

"No."

"A hurricane has been moving up from the south ever since the sun set last night. That is what I was waiting for."

Bobi looked out the door. There was no sign of dawn. Bobi touched the man's arm.

"This ought to teach us a lesson," he said. "We must not try anything more."

The man set his lantern down.

"We must try reason."

"We are not capable of understanding it."

The man went into the shadow and got his heavy sheepskin jacket.

"I'm in a hurry," he said. "I can't answer you." Coming back with his sheeplined coat, "Perhaps," he added, "looking at this, you are thinking: 'With this heat no one needs fur.'"

He threw the jacket over his shoulders.

"It isn't for me," he said, "it is for her, the lady. I am going to wrap her in it, to bring her back. Sorrow makes one feel the cold. Don't worry, perhaps I'll be able to manage with reason."

He took the lantern and walked toward the door.

Bobi went out. There was still no sign of dawn. The lantern lighted a few metres of ground and a half hundred spears of the wheat that was still standing.

The man closed the door.

"So," said Bobi, "you don't believe in the mysterious?"

"No."

"However, there are things that are beyond your comprehension?"

"For the moment."

The man doubled up his fist and put it square in the middle of the lantern light.

"The struggle," he said, "never ceases. That is why one must know. Mystery is convenient as a relaxation. It is a mystery; there is nothing to be done about it. Rest? No! Never rest. A battle clear to the end of the world. And even," he added, in a slightly dreamy tone, "never an end to the world, since the battle is everlasting."

"I had come to tell you something," said Bobi. "You will see. Back there are all the women except Zulma. She is watching the sheep. I had come—how can I express it?—to light your way. I had thought that, since I was leaving . . . "

"You are leaving?"

"Yes . . . . It would be you who would seek the joy for all of them, and with your means which are not the ones I like. Then, I wish to light your path and show you the mountain that bars your escape. You shall be warned. You shall have no excuses."

"Do it quickly," said the man, "I am in a hurry. There is one out there who is cold because of sorrow and who is waiting for this fur-lined jacket."

"Do you know what the oldest occupation in the world is?"

"Yes."

"It is that of the shepherd."

"Yes."

"And it is always the same."

"Yes."

"For thousands upon thousands of years sheep have always been tended in the same way, and the dog runs as he ran in those ancient times and the shepherd has the same repose on his staff."

"That's agreed, everybody knows that. There remains to be known what you have to say."

"I mean that no one has yet invented a machine for guarding sheep and that it will never be invented."

"Who's talking to you about machines?"

"No one."

"Then," said the man, "you must know the secret cause of my troubles!"

He realized that Bobi was no longer beside him.

"Hello!" he cried.

He could hear steps going off toward the south.

"Hey!" he shouted. "Where are you going? Don't go toward the south!"

There was no answer.

24

The first glimmering of dawn appeared. All the land to the south for fifty kilometres lay enveloped in the storm. On this part of the plateau there were no trees. The only vegetation consisted of a sort of alfa grass, scintillating like quartz, that stretched as far as eye could see. This morning the only light came from that grass; the sky was unillumined.

For the inhabitants of the plateau this region had no name. They never spoke of it. When they had to speak of it, they said: "Out there," pointing to the shining waves of the wilderness.

To go from the boundary of Fra-Josépine to Randoulet's pond, or even to the northern edge of the plateau, to the extreme limits of the pastureland, to the place from which the Ouvèze River could be seen curving and entering peacefully into the mist-covered Plain of Roume, required scarcely a day, by walking leisurely at a man's pace. But toward the south the plateau stretched out for more than seven days' march, all in this double light of which the most dazzling part came from the grass and vibrated like a white flame.

If a person were able to make this seven days' journey, he would reach the southern edge of the plateau. This was an abrupt cliff more than sixty metres in height, all of sandstone, and without a trace of moss, dominating the big village of Saint-Julien-le-Forestier. Saint-Julien-le-Forestier was in an enormous oak forest. From the top of the cliff, one should be able to see the round and smoking village with its carapace of tiles, like a great rain-beaten brazier on which a crust of ashes has hardened but whose crevices still breathe smoke. One ought also to be able to see the great woolly forest. To the people of Saint-Julien those lands up there, spread out in the sky, were the wilderness. They never climbed up. There was no path. The cliff was full of birds. When on fine days the sun struck it squarely upon its whole surface, one could see it was soiled by long blackish streaks. These were the outcroppings of subterranean streams or the oozing of century-old nesting places. The echo of the forest made the whole face of the cliff sing.

To light what it was lighting, the dawn would have done better to have stayed where it was. The first gleams had revealed the movement of the clouds. There had been a rent in the east, just at the sharp line of the high mountain peaks, and a very pure little green light had come through. It penetrated far into the southern horizon, lying just above the earth like water. The sky was reflected in it. The clouds were low, but as far as could be seen, they did not touch the earth like storms that close in the horizon. On the contrary, they were hollowed like the roof of a cave. In the few moments that the light of the dawn remained pure, it reached out a great distance without encountering anything but grass, grass, grass. At last it touched the ledge that overlooks Saint-Julien-le-Forestier and it illumined the heart of the storm. This was an immense door of cloud. Beyond, a night as solid as stone, as when a miner's lamp lights the end of the gallery and he sees the wall of coal. But the light of the dawn was quickly clouded, then it stopped flowing. There remained only a sort of grey gleam that issued evenly from the whole grassy expanse.

At that moment Bobi was skirting Silve's abandoned fields. He had not yet entered the real South that began beyond the farm house. He saw the house about a hundred metres ahead. Dawn struck it squarely and, in contrast to the black sky, it was as white as a house of snow. Silve's fields were covered with sturdy brambles.

"So, vagabond," Bobi said to himself, "here you are once more on your way?…"

He looked at the sky.

"Well, let's go."

He walked along the field toward the house of snow. He was still full of visions that flowed into one another like shuffled cards. He no longer had the sensation of being in the world. The sight of Aurore, dead, had taken the place of his heart. From her came the blood that coursed through his body; blood thick and black, slow to flow like that congealed in Aurore's hair.

He could no longer visualize his own body, or feel it, as one usually does. To say: here are my arms, my head, my body. He had a different perception of himself. He was a sheaf of images. He saw lands flat as playing cards, with trees, farms, fields, and the winding roads drawn flat on the cardboard. On all these cards was the figure of a man or a woman. There was his mother; there was the drummer who had followed him once on his tour of the country; the man with a red beard who lived in the forest farm in Clans Col and at whose house he had slept the winter of 1903 when it had been so cold; again his mother; a woman named Fanette; his mother once more; Aurore without a face and with hair stiffened with blood; a woman called Sonia who performed on the flying trapeze in village squares, in the evening, by the light of a carbide lamp;

again his mother, always milk-white; the man called Fabre, who had the travelling theatre of the Lauzon Valley and who acted astronomic plays on the boards with his wife called Milky Way and his children called Orion, Uranus, Sirius, and Centaur.

"And now," Fabre would say, "here is Orion surrounded by animals and rivers!"

"Oh, yes!" thought Bobi. "We are the food of the beasts in the sky."

Then the light grew dimmer and there was only the grey light that came from the grass. But now it was day.

"And what of it?" he thought.

"Well," he replied, "here you are again on the highways."

"Yes, with my baggage!"

"Yes, with your baggage, and then? . . . Are you big enough to carry it?"

"I have carried baggage before; it isn't that, but this time I am to blame."

"To blame for what?"

"For everything."

"The one who is responsible for everything does not exist on the earth. On earth, one is to blame for nothing. I assure you."

"You think you're smart."

He passed Silve's house. It was dead and still. He thought: "It is just two years since Silve hanged himself. That was while I had gone for the stag. One, two, three dead: Silve, Aurore, the house."

The sharp-edged roof seemed soft; the skeleton of beams was rotting beneath the tiles. Strips of fallen plaster had revealed the muscles of stone, which was rotting too. Moss was eating the walls. A shutter hung from its broken hinge; the window was open. It was a hole. The roots of a big vine had

destroyed its frame and they were already loosening the stones
and splitting the wooden shutter. The fountain beside the
house had ceased flowing but its basin was still full of water. It
was choked with broad, dark green plants. It smelt of dogs and
manure. The door of the house was no longer visible, hidden
by tall grass, lilac bushes, eglantines that rose to the second
story.

"House fallen to decay!"

"You have never seen such beautiful plantains. They have
grown straight. They are going to live like wild trees."

"A house that can no longer be used!"

"For all that you can see, you wonder if it can be of any use.
Use to whom? You? Certainly not; it can no longer be used as
a house, but are you sure it isn't good for something else? You
are always talking about it."

"Silve is dead and buried and Aurore is dead. They are
going to bury her today."

"You are to blame."

"Yes, to blame, I've already told you that. I'm to blame."

"What do you think you are?"

"More than you think."

"Nothing."

"However, I came along, I said: 'Orion-Queen Anne's lace.'
It was something that was in my head, so I said it. They heard
it and it passed into their heads. So . . . "

"So what?"

"So I am something!"

"The devil you are! Well, yes, you are something, idiot, like
all the rest, like everything that is in the world, nothing more."

"More."

"Nothing more. You and the others: Silve and Aurore and
the house. Aurore is like the house, no more than the house. In
the world."

"On the earth…"

"I didn't say 'on the earth,' I said 'in the world.' Shut your mouth, won't you? You are still there parading your Orion-Queen Anne's lace. If you are to blame, as you say, then you are the vilest of creatures."

"Yes, I am the vilest of creatures."

"Look before you leave it, for you will never see it again. See how the house has become a grove of trees. Next year it will be hidden by the lilacs. It will become a mountain of lilacs, and when it is all in bloom, the people who pass by along the hill paths, on the roads of the Ouvèze Valley, on the mountainside, will catch in the wind the odour of lilacs. Come, old fellow, get going, you old son-of-a-gun. Don't believe too much in death."

"Let death alone."

He had passed Silve's house. Before him now stretched the South with its luminous grass. No light in the sky. No reflections. Clouds. No horizons. A dense, pearl-coloured vapour hid everything to the ground.

"Let death alone," said Bobi. "Don't talk about it."

He walked on for some time. He looked behind him. The house was still visible. As he walked he listened to the sound of his steps. The soil was of round gravel. The tufts of dry grass crackled. He had got into his stride for long walks. He made hardly any effort. His legs moved mechanically. He had not grown any fatter. He was as thin as on that winter night when he had stood at the edge of Jourdan's field, listening to the scraping of the plough in the night and the puffing of the horse. His hair was still stiff and fell in two wings on each side of his temples. He turned his head to look at the house once more. It had vanished. Not even the form of the trees was visible. In that direction as in front of him, as at the right and the left, the sky pressed upon the earth with all its weight.

He had entered the real South.

"A fine solitude," he thought.

"Well, you've always been asking for it."

"Shut up!"

"What are you planning to do?"

"I don't know. Walk."

"Walk where?"

"Out there."

"Don't be a fool. Where are you going?"

The storm looked as if it was going to be a big one.

"First, what time is it?"

"You've no need to know the time. You know that you can walk all day and all night if you like."

"I know, but where does this go?"

"There! That was something to have asked yourself before coming out here."

"I could always go back."

"No. You know perfectly well that you can never go back."

"What did you think I said? Do you think that I meant something else?"

"Yes, you meant that and something else besides. I know you. No, now you can never go back, to find the road or for anything else. You are a man?"

"Yes."

"Well, man is man. Go straight ahead. In this direction, it must go toward Saint-Julien-le-Forestier. That is too far. What you must do is turn left in an hour or two. You will be just about above Val d'Arène in the Ouvèze Valley. Above it. That village with the plaster factory. Good. Four hours and you will be at the edge of the plateau. You will go down through the larch woods, straight ahead. You cross the Ouvèze. In Val you go into the inn called the Hunters' Rendezvous. There a bacon omelet. A little wine. You haven't a sou. You see that sous *are* good for something. Yes, I know. Shut your mouth. Walk and don't talk. I am the one who is right. Shut it with your poetry. So, this is what you do. You say: 'I'll stay here. Give me a room.' They give you a room. You know that you pay every three days. Yes, that's the mountain, those are mountain customs, don't let it upset you. Tomorrow you will see about that. You can go and help in the plaster quarry...."

"Or," said Bobi to himself, "here's what I can do; what I did once in the high valley of La Méouge, at Buis, at Verdier, and at Bar. I said to them: I will tell you some stories, and I told them stories. Those like Fabre's about the stars, or legends, or stories that I make up."

"If you like, or rather, if *they* like. If they are unhappy wretches, then, yes."

Into the breach of the cloud in the east glided a ray of the former green light of dawn, and the door rising far in the south was illumined on a slant. It still opened upon coalblack depths.

"You see that it is good for something, my Queen Anne's lace."

"For what? I'd just like to know for what?"

"When they are unhappy wretches, as you say."

"Don't get stuck up. Don't get stuck up because you think you are the remedy for misery. Idiot! There isn't any remedy. If you have to be told that again you are crazy. . . . Do you want to know what you are? Exactly? The poppy brew that Marthe made for Madame Hélène; that's what you are. You put people to sleep."

"Why are they all eager for sleep?"

"Because they haven't the courage to live in the boundless sadness and solitude of life."

"And so I give them companions and joy?"

"Yes, as in dreams."

"That is not what I wanted to do."

"That's why I'm telling you."

"I wanted to give them real companions and real joy."

"And especially yourself."

"Yes, myself, too."

"I said 'especially.'"

"I heard you."

"Then listen: man is alone in this world. There aren't any companions."

The door of clouds was illumined, as if a miner were advancing beneath it with his lamp.

Then all went out. A rumbling shook earth and sky. Down underneath, in the darkness, echoes hollowed valleys and dells. Silence returned. There was only the cat-like tread of the clouds. The whole sky was advancing at enormous speed, heavy and unfaltering. But the high door of coal had not yet begun to move. It remained remote, aloof, with its heavy hinges and its black cornice that the day could not pierce. Dawn, however, was ended. But still there was no increase of light. It was even growing darker. The reflections of the grass could no longer rise to the sky. They stayed flickering over the ground, from tuft to tuft. The stillness levelled everything. It was no longer possible to imagine valleys, forest, depths, and sounding corridors along which walked the wind. There was no sound, and from moment to moment the silence grew deeper. There was nothing left but this flat earth.

It was hot. Bobi took off his shirt. He rolled it tightly, as small as possible. He stuffed it into the big pocket of his corduroy trousers. With the palm of his hand he wiped the sweat from his body. He looked at his shoulder. It was round and brown. The flesh, thickset and muscular, clasped the bone of the shoulder like a blacksmith's mighty hand. Beyond that, the black sky overhead. He examined the other shoulder; it was similar. He moved on once more. Even his step made no sound. The silence clung to his heels. The air wrapped him as in warm wool. At the left, the clouds were slightly blood-coloured. At the right, blue; ahead, black, formless, widespread, almost motionless. Over their face rolled shapes: a horse, a serpent, a bird.

"Nor joy."

"What did you say?"

"I am continuing what I was saying a moment ago."

Bobi shut his eyes and threw himself to the ground. His nose was filled with the odour of sulphur, and there was an acid and sickening taste on his tongue. Bobi grasped a tuft of grass in his hand as if to hold on. The shrill whistle that had pierced his ears hissed deeply then was still. He listened to the echoing thunder as it rolled away in the distance.

"That one did not strike far away!"

He stood up again. He remembered the tree of fire that had suddenly sprung up at his left. He walked toward it. Ten steps. He found the grass burned a metre's width. The echo continued to dig deep into the valleys and to widen the plains below. Vast world! In the sky, the bird and the serpent were fused.

There was no need to run. No, keep on walking at the same pace. It was the storm. He had seen, in his solitary wanderings, more than a hundred storms. The echo on the far horizon was meeting mountains, forests, valleys, and plains as resonant as sheet iron.

All that sound surged back again.

"In seven hours I shall be at Val d'Arène, in seven hours. Seven hours, seven hours."

He walked on. He rubbed the hair on his chest where a little dirt had clung. He touched his pocket. The shirt was protected.

"At Val d'Arène, in seven hours. A village, an oil lamp. It will be dark early. A bed. I am hungry. Seven hours. Seven hours."

"You are walking very fast."

"I am walking at my usual speed."

"It's funny how you like to lie! Why tell me that you are walking at your usual speed when I know that your pace is one-two, one-two, broad, solid, one-two. You are rather proud of it; you have said enough times that you have a broad, solid step. And not *one*-two, *one*-two, as you are doing now. If I tell you that, it is because you are going to tire yourself out."

"I am strong."

"Then you are afraid."

"Afraid of what?"

"There! That's right. That's your real pace. With that you can go far. So wasn't it simpler to do it right away when I spoke to you about it?"

"What do you think I am afraid of?"

"I said that for your pride. *I* don't know. Afraid of the lightning."

"What do I risk?"

"Getting killed."

"Yes, but at a single flash. So much the better."

"Very well, all right. We're agreed."

He felt himself bitten on the shoulder by a cold drop. He looked. It was so big that it ran. Another drop struck his forehead, another his chest, then his head, his shoulders, his back, his ears, his eyes. The rain was hurrying over the whole expanse, puffing as in a forest. Now the blood rose to his skin. The rain was not cold. On the contrary, it was hot. He pushed back his eyebrows with the tip of his finger. His eyes were somewhat sheltered. It was a stiff rain, but steady.

"How, agreed?"

"There isn't any joy."

"I did not say so."

"But death sets one free?"

"Yes."

"From joy? Answer me!"

"Let me alone. I've got to get to Val d'Arène. I'm tired. I haven't slept. I've been walking for ten hours since yesterday evening. I'm hungry. Let me alone. Aurore is dead. I can't see her any more. Ah, let me alone. What good is strength? What are eyes good for? They saw her! If it is to see, to what end? I want to see her again. I want to hear her voice now."

"Keep on walking, you are too near."

"What did you say?"

"I say that you are still too near her to see her again and to hear her with the voice she had when she talked to you in the fields. And the world kept silence."

"I must go away from her in order to find her? Someone is cheating there!"

"No, that is the game. There is no joy."

Since long before dawn, a storm without thunder, but terribly hot, had been crushing the oak forest twenty kilometres to the south of Saint-Julien-le-Forestier. At first it had weighted down the trees with a long rain of hail. At that period of the summer, the foliage of the oaks was as hard as leather. The hailstones might be as big as chaffinches' eggs, yet they could not tear the leaves. But they remained in the forks of the branches. They heaped up in little white pyramids. The trees cracked beneath their ox-loads. The heat surged as from the throat of a furnace. But the hail did not melt. All the grains fused into a single block of ice. It seemed to be coated with blue phosphorus. It was black, with impenetrable shadows. But all the blocks of ice were lit like lamps. The rays of the hailstorm also gleamed. This luminosity lit neither leaves nor trees. It stayed there on the ice like the spirit of phosphorus. All the birds were gone. The forest was alone. The hail fell unceasingly. The branches began to break under the weight. They all broke slowly, tearing the trunk, and pulling off long strips of bark before crashing beneath their weight of ice. Then the phosphorescent glow climbed up the trunks, licking the sap. It sparkled like a diamond on each drop of sap, its thread trembled along the oozings and when it reached the source of the wound, the seething of the sap gave it a cold joy that made it almost dance like a flame. All the trees wailed in the fire. But there was no light. There was the shining wraith and the night. At last, all these gleams were rolled into one ball. Slowly they flew off into the sky. Still without lighting a thing. As they passed above the forest roof they vanished.

Suddenly the night was illumined over a vast arena revealing, between the mountains of clouds, valleys through which silently spread an immense river of gold with a thousand tributaries. Then all was dark. The hail ceased falling. Day came. The trees were bled white. They could neither move nor moan.

By the time it reached the plateau, the storm had already been for some time in the Ouvèze Valley and the Plain of Roume.

It was composed of an enormous chain of mountainous clouds that rose in the sky to formidable heights in endless stages of peaks and plateaux, bearing secondary chains ever higher in the heavens. The base of this mountain of clouds broadened into valleys that appeared to be filled with strange phantom-like trees, whose foliage was on one side sombre as the night and on the other bright as snow. All this world was in travail. The valleys hollowed before one's eyes, so deeply that all of a sudden the two edges rolled up like woollen cloth, swelled into hills and rose slowly toward the mountain peaks. Avalanches rushed down and flattened out. From the edge of the oak forest of Saint-Julien-le-Forestier as far as the village to which the men of the plateau had gone to hunt the does, high up in the northern mountains, this outline of the storm with its geography of mountains, valleys, plains, torrents, snows, and black sands, was invisible because the whole country was covered with shadow and rain beneath the clouds. But the shepherds who at that time of the year watched their flocks in the highest summer pastures of the Alps could see it in all its architecture reared on the distant horizon.

At first it advanced simultaneously through the Ouvèze Valley and in the Plain of Roume. It seemed to be looking for something. The incessant revolutions of its aerial landscapes resembled the process of respiration. So far it made no sound, but in its panting, little whitish vapours, swirling like the whirlpools of an angry river, freed the restless force that had been concentrated like gas in a mine.

With a single stroke it lifted all the water of the Ouvèze. This occurred in the high valley of the torrent, well above Val d'Arène. The storm suddenly darted a black nebulosity, pointed at the end like a serpent's head. The water began to boil. The cloud plunged its head into the torrent and began to dabble and to drink like an animal. The bed of the Ouvèze was dried up white as a bone for twenty metres, while all was sucked up in the cloud. Then the serpent raised itself, and striking to the right and left with a hiss, it lifted itself to its full height to fall again on the plateau, where it burst with a roar of thunder and a sheaf of fire.

It was at that moment that the rain began to fall, thick and heavy, but without anger. There was not yet an unleashing, but that green and glacial water of the Ouvèze had irrigated the troubled heart of the mountain of storm and already the force taken from the forest trees was germinating in roots of fire. From time to time little balls of lightning burst in the foam of the clouds.

In the Plain of Roume the storm had found someone awaiting it. The stubble, freed from the wheat, had ripened beneath the sun. Already, for several days, the last reapers could hear the earth crack. They said to each other: "What is it getting ready to do?" They hastened their reaping, casting uneasy glances to right and left. The earth did not feel solid under their feet. Not that it had a tendency to move. Everyone knows very well that fields do not start to capsize like planks of a cart, but it sweated a vapour that thickened the air like syrup. "It is going to play a trick on us," they said. "This thing can't keep up. You'll see that she's going to start something."

The earth cracked. There was no wind, but at times whirls of dust rose in the nudity of the fields and began to move like natural beings without being impelled by any visible force. Beneath the earth's crust could be heard a nibbling like the rising tide of an ocean of ants.

Before it had even touched the plain, the storm had been anticipated. Friendly warnings came to it from that direction. No one had left the town, where from moment to moment the darkness in the streets grew denser.

The storm had softly touched the plateau on three sides, and "yes" had said the heath, "yes" had said the grass that was hissing like horse-tails in the wind. The birds had been the first to scent the odour of that essence of phosphorus that had glowed in the forest. They have beneath their tongues a little membrane like onion skin and it had vibrated as soon as the first branch was torn off more than fifty kilometres away. The sleeping birds had awakened at once. Then, in bands, they had flown to the north, in spite of the night.

The hairy beasts had gone hunting. The insects had taken shelter deep in the earth by building covers and shields with saliva and mud.

The storm was advancing into the wilderness.

"Forward!" said Bobi to himself.

His body was already streaming with the rain. He was glad he had put his shirt into the shelter of his pocket.

In the Plain of Roume all proceeded calmly. A great black cloud was lying upon it, its belly touching the stubble, and it was slowly filling itself with the magnetic force of the earth.

All of a sudden, in the mountain of the storm, flowed twenty torrents of fire. The plateau, struck everywhere by the lightning, rang like a bell.

"It isn't true. If there were no joy, there would be no world. It isn't true that there is no joy. When you say there is no joy, you lose hope. You must not lose hope. You must remember that hope itself is joy. The hope that it will happen soon, that it will happen tomorrow, that it is going to happen, that it is here, that it is touching you, that it awaits you, that it is swelling, that suddenly it is going to burst, that it is going to flow into your mouth, that it is going to make you drink, that you will no longer be thirsty, that you will have no more pain, that you will love."

"This isn't the moment for joking. See what's falling."

"Let me alone. I must talk to myself."

"Ah! I was under the impression that you were talking about love. I thought that you wanted to joke to impress people. To make them think that you don't care a rap about all this. But this is jolly well the end of the world, old fellow. This is serious, you son-of-a-gun. You mustn't make fun of it."

"Yes, I was talking of love."

"*You,* I know what you're thinking about. You are thinking about Fanette?"

"Yes, of Fanette and Sonia."

"That's odd, old man. I think I know you, but you are always surprising me. As if this were the time!"

"This *is* the time. I don't want to die."

"Then, stir your stumps and move on, that is more to the point. Only, I am going to take this opportunity to surprise you a little. Just notice how well you see them, those two who are far away from you."

"That's so! Is it possible that you are right sometimes?"

"I am always right."

"Are you sure that I'll be able to see Aurore quite clearly in my mind?"

"Yes, when you have lost her more completely."

"Couldn't it be arranged so she would be here, now, at once?"

"No, because there is no joy."

"But the two others give me almost no comfort."

"That is the law."

"I am afraid."

"Tremble."

"She would save me."

"There can be no exception. Not even for a single person. And what difference can it make to the world whether you are saved or lost?"

"Fanette! I see her as she used to be. With her mountaineer's cloak, and I hear her speaking as they still speak in the orchards at home."

"Yes. What of it? It is Aurore you love."

"That is true!"

"Come, don't give yourself airs. Believe me when I tell you: nothing can be added to you. You are alone from birth. You were born for that. If joy existed, my poor old fellow, if it could enter your body to add to it, you would be so big that the world would explode in dust. To desire. That is all that you are capable of. It is a way that was given you for consuming yourself. Nothing is permanent. No matter how slightly a thing is arrested, it dies and is buried at a stroke in the place where it became immobile, like a red-hot iron in the snow. There is no joy."

"That is not true."

"What proves it to you?"

"Nothing."

"There is no joy."

"Yes, there is."

"There is no joy."

"That must not be true."

"There is no joy."

"Shut up!"

"There is no joy."

"Yes! I see it!"

"It is yourself you see."

His body was drenched with the rain. His muscles glistened. He walked without haste. The wind hampered his legs but he did not feel tired. There was no longer any daylight. The light came from the rain. And from the flashes of lightning. For them there was now neither barrier nor anything. They leaped from one rim to the other. The whole sky belonged to them. And the earth. There was now no difference between earth and sky. There was now no line of separation. More than the spray, the steam, the oily forces that traversed the rain, casting a shadow like the passage of a bird; even the magic of the lightning could not separate the earth from the water. The hundred forms of lightning: the wheel, the nail, the tree! The tree that is planted in the earth, cast by the heavens, and which nothing can resist; which makes all tremble with its roots and foliage; the bird of fire, the stone, the bell, the bursting of the world! And all is rent, all is seen at a flash, the far reaches of heaven and earth. Millions of torrents, rivers, streams of gold; millions of valleys, gulfs, abysses, caverns of darkness, in the flash of an eye, then all is extinguished. The serpent, the arrow, the rope, the whip, the laugh, the teeth, the bite, the wound, the streaming of blood; all the forms of lightning!

Bobi pushed on.

The sky roared without ceasing. The noise was so violent that one could touch it. It was hot as the wind from Africa. It floated. It beat with its wings. It drove the rain. It laid the spray. It rang in the hollows and only because of it could one be aware of the existence of plains and mountains, of valleys and walls of rock, and perceive the fantastic entablature of the storm rising to its dizzy heights in the sky. Each roar swept along with it echoes of all the forms in the world.

"You are uneasy, I can feel it. You'd be glad to have me tell you why it is always yourself you see. That was answered squarely just now, wasn't it? I was waiting for you at that point. I've been watching you ever since we began to talk. I knew that at a given moment you were going to say to me: 'I see it!' At the end of your arguments, precisely when you no longer see anything at all. Is that so? Good. I have no merit. I am a million times older than you. Who am I? Why, you, you idiot! Exactly as for joy. The 'un-joy,' as Fabre would say. It on one side, I on the other, you in the middle. The trinity. Do I exist? Why, no, I don't exist either. Why so much the better? Your sorrow and your joy, that is yourself. What did you say? Talk louder. What are you muttering so low? Ma! You're calling your mother? What of it? Do you want to have me play cards with your memories? I have won the deal. Look at this hand. I haven't Aurore's card yet. It would be in my hand sooner than in yours. What kind of difficulty can you make?

Your trumps help me. You were calling: 'Ma!' All the village children call: 'Ma!' That doesn't affect me; men who call their mothers. I find that rather ridiculous. Yes, I know, it is dramatic. Here, I play the Fabre card. Don't take it, it is an ace. That one was dramatic, you remember: Orion, Uranus, Sirius, Phœbus, the Centaur, and the mother, Milky Way. Do you remember: he caught Orion by the arm, and in reality the little fellow's name was Charles. That doesn't matter; my ace is good. And he would throw him into the wings, shouting: 'Orion exploded in the gulfs of the universe!' You could hear Orion crying: 'Mamma!' and see Madame Fabre-Milky Way advancing majestically toward the stage, her hands on her heart! It is fine, the theatre! Come, listen to me. Ma is a word. The word for your mother. When you called it she used to come. Now you call it and she comes no longer. You might be laid out with a blow, she would not budge any more than a mountain. So I play the card of your mother. What have you left in trumps?"

"No, listen. I'll beat you with Fanette also. With Sonia, and even with Aurore, even with Joséphine. Here, you haven't thought very much about that one since this started. You haven't a sound trump. Let's not play any more."

"Why, no, you are no more crushed than the others. It is the feeling of your solitude that makes you say that. You try to be proud of it. No, old man. All men are lodged at the same sign: 'Hotel of Solitude and the Three Worlds.' No one wins from me. They can play all their cards. It is always the same."

"The devil!"

"That one hit close! It seems to be getting exciting, all around. Turn to the left. To the left, I tell you. Who am I? I am your desire to live, in spite of and against everything."

"Beastly rain. You can't see a metre ahead. Keep on walking. Do you think that this is left? I am anxious to get there."

The storm dragged over the plateau. The flashes sprang from the ground.

"Lie down. Let them strike. That's over. Get up. Walk. There, to the right. Lie down!"

The bars of lightning hissed like forge iron. They did not die at once. They ran along the ground more than a hundred paces, burning the rain before them.

"That's over. Is this really left? Val d'Arène. The forest down there. No, that is only shadow. Walk along! Val d'Arène; the Hunters' Rendezvous! Everything's against you! Orion surrounded by animals and rivers!"

The flashes sprang from everywhere like the force of a forest.

"Run, run, run!"

"Don't run any more!" cried Bobi. And he stopped running.

"No," he said, "now I know. I have always been a child; but I am right."

The sweat steamed from his naked body.

Suddenly, he was warned like a bird by a sparkling under his tongue.

"Ma!" he cried.

The lightning planted a golden tree between his shoulders.

25

Jacquou had said that he would be back at five o'clock. He had gone to his farm to get the second horse. He had taken Barbe with him.

"I'll leave you there and you'll make the soup for this evening."

"If that is too much for you," Marthe had said, "eat here again this evening."

"We've got to begin again," Barbe had replied.

Carle and Madame Carle and the son had gone. They had offered three places to Randoulet, Honorine, and Le Noir.

"We'll let you off at Mouillure; you'll have only nine kilometres from there."

Jourdan had moved over to the trap and had put his hand on the side rail.

"Wait," he said, "all this wheat, what'll we do with it?"

"Let's go home first," said Carle. "Tomorrow we'll see. We'll divide it according to each one's due."

"It is not all threshed."

"We'll take it away."

"Well, good-bye," said Jourdan.

"Good-bye," said Carle, and he touched the horse.

The three Randoulets were seated behind and they nodded their heads without saying anything.

Madame Hélène had already left for home the evening before. Her farmer had accompanied her. She no longer had that chill that had made her teeth chatter when they buried Mademoiselle Aurore.

"No, thank you," she had said, "I don't need your coat any more."

She had shaken hands with them all, but without speaking. She got into her buggy. She did not turn her head.

This time, they had made an exception, and Mademoiselle Aurore was not buried at the edge of Grémone Forest, beside her father, beside Silve, in the little two-grave plot beneath the hedge of eglantine. They had dug the grave in the field of narcissi. The storm had prevented them from carrying the body far from the house.

While waiting for Jacquou, Marthe and Joséphine sat in the doorway of La Jourdane. Jourdan had gone all alone to the middle of the threshing floor; he stood amid all the wheat, thinking.

Evening came. It was after seven o'clock. The sky was all violet, without a cloud. The grass was extraordinarily new. In the clear air the forest could be heard murmuring.

"Look," said Marthe, "I saw them pass this morning."

She raised her head; she was watching a flock of crows.

"They were going down to the south. Now here they are flying back toward the north."

"The storm must have killed some animals."

"Especially in the South," said Marthe.

"So," said Joséphine, "that man said that he has gone away."

"He says he saw him come in the night and leave in the night."

"He will come back," said Joséphine.

"Once," said Marthe, "he went away, and then he came back. We went to wait for him, Jourdan and I, at the Croix-Chauve. And he came back with the stag!"

Jacquou appeared with his big blue cart. He had brought the two children.

"Back home," he said, "they do nothing but run around Barbe and she has things to do. Here, you, look after your children a little."

He went over to Jourdan.

"Well?" he said.

"Well," said Jourdan, "do as you like."

"I'll load the cart with what isn't threshed. That will make about six hundred kilos with the straw. And then I'll take nine sacks of grain. That's about my due."

"Come, then," said Jourdan, "I'll help you."

There was a little boy and a little girl. The little boy looked like Joséphine and the little girl like Honoré. She had green eyes and very long lashes, shining new like that grass that the storm had washed. Her cheeks were her father's cheeks but very tender. Her mouth was delightful. The boy had his mother's brow.

"The best age!" said Marthe.

"Yes," said Joséphine, "we should always stay like that."

That evening she felt no grief. She had never received so much from the world. It seemed to her that everything helped her. She drew strength from all; from the evening, the air, the colours, the fragrance and the murmuring of the forest. It seemed to her that Bobi now had a hundred ways of being with her. There was an assurance that she had never felt before.

She said to herself: "Soon I'll get on the cartload of wheat and we shall go into the night. Slowly. That will last a long time. The sky is already filled with stars. I'll put the boy to sleep on this side of me and the girl on this side."

She felt as though she were already lying down, borne away by the slow cart.

"He will come back," she said to herself, "I know he will."

Over and over she repeated to herself: "I know it, I know it, I know it."

Her lips moved but they made no sound.